Elihu Hotchkiss Shepard

The Autobiography of Elihu H. Shepard

Formerly Professor of Languages in St. Louis College

Elihu Hotchkiss Shepard

The Autobiography of Elihu H. Shepard
Formerly Professor of Languages in St. Louis College

ISBN/EAN: 9783337123376

Printed in Europe, USA, Canada, Australia, Japan

Cover: Foto ©Raphael Reischuk / pixelio.de

More available books at **www.hansebooks.com**

THE

AUTOBIOGRAPHY

OF

ELIHU H. SHEPARD,

FORMERLY

PROFESSOR OF LANGUAGES

ST. LOUIS COLLEGE

———————•◆•———————

ST. LOUIS:

GEORGE KNAPP & CO., BOOK AND JOB PRINTERS AND BINDERS.

1869.

PREFACE.

The exhibition of an autobiography to a reader naturally suggests the object of the author in writing and publishing it, and an explanation is generally gratifying, if satisfactory. The author of this commenced it at the earnest request of his daughter, several years since, in a blank book that she had provided for that purpose, that she might preserve an accurate genealogy of her ancestry as far as possible, and the chief incidents connected with their history, particularly that of her father and mother. That history was written out with his own hand, without the intention of publishing it in his lifetime, to 1866. Many interesting events have subsequently transpired, and he has traveled and observed much, which, together with the expressed wish of a very large number of his former pupils and friends to possess a history of the incidents of his eventful life, seem to furnish a reasonable excuse for him to essay their gratification.

In accomplishing this in his own peculiar style, he has taken the original copy, written for his daughter, and added thereto such notes as he has preserved of his travels and observations since.

The indulgent reader therefore, it is hoped, will pardon any apparent egotism, as most of the manuscript was prepared for the eye of his daughter only, and has been used without alterations.

THE AUTHOR.

CONTENTS.

AUTOBIOGRAPHY OF ELIHU H. SHEPARD.

CHAPTER I.

BIRTH AND PARENTAGE OF THE AUTHOR.

ELIHU HOTCHKISS SHEPARD, the writer of this record, was born on the 15th of October, 1795, at Halifax, Windham county, State of Vermont, in the presidency of George Washington. His father, Abel Shepard, was a merchant and trader in the East Indies in the early part of his life, and a farmer in Jefferson county, State of New York, during the last seven years of his life. He was born at Plainfield, Connecticut, August 29th, 1766, and died at Henderson, Jefferson county, New York, November 23d, 1815. He had been educated entirely by his mother, of whom I will write hereafter, and was a fine scholar, and spared no pains or expense to make his children such, four of whom became eminent teachers after his death.

He left his family a great estate, the most valuable part of which was a farm of three hundred acres on the shore of Lake Ontario, on which is the Shepard family graveyard, in which he, his wife, four daughters, three sons, one daughter-in-law, and one granddaughter, are buried, and appropriate stones set at their graves. In May, 1857, the eldest of his sons returned, after a long absence in the State of Missouri, and built a most substantial stone wall about the yard, and otherwise improved the site, so that it is probable it will remain for a long period.

2

The maiden name of the writer's mother was Sarah Dalrymple. She was born at Petersham, State of Massachusetts, September 1st, 1775, and died at Crystal Lake, in McHenry county, State of Illinois. She lived a long, useful, varied, and somewhat mournful life, as she bore eleven fine, healthy children, and lived long enough to follow seven of them, a granddaughter, and two husbands, to their graves. She was a small, healthy, active, and industrious woman, and took great pleasure in keeping her children clean and tidy, and advancing them in the world. Her education was that of a common school of New England in the days of the Revolution, while she was the eighth in a family of twelve children, who all lived to have families of their own. She died in the 77th year of her age.

I come now to write of my grandparents, all four of whom I recollect well.

Jonas Shepard, my paternal grandfather, in whose house I was born, was the great grandson of Thomas Shepard, a Welchmen of Caernarvon, a trooper of the British army in 1642, who, with two others, carried the petition of the army to Charles I.'s Parliament for redress of grievances, which was the first step towards Charles' dethronement, and to his own promotion under Oliver Cromwell, and to finally being compelled to quit his country and seek safety in the forests of Connecticut, in the town of Plainfield, where my grandfather, Jonas Shepard, was born in 1727. He was an industrious man, a good farmer, but a poor economist. He could not stand it with a young, growing family in the State of Connecticut, and in 1767 sold his patrimony, which had descended to him through his father, Caleb Shepard, born 1685, and his grandfather, Haziel Shepard, born 1663, and his great grandfather, Thomas Shepard, born in 1620, and the first of his family in America, and removed to Halifax, Vermont. There he purchased a farm of one hundred acres, and, with the assistance of one of the best women of this world, reared his large family of nine children : three by his first wife, and six by his last. Six were sons, and three daughters, who all outlived him, and took honorable and comfortable positions in society. While residing in this town, he witnessed the struggle of the Revolution, in which his two eldest sons were actively engaged, one as a captain of an armed ship of the State of Connecticut, and the other as an officer of the Massachusetts line of regulars—or Continentals, as they were then called—and was afterwards commissioned to suppress Shay's rebellion by the then Governor of Massachusetts, which he did by dispersing them at Springfield, and driving a large number into Vermont. These men sought his assistance to obtain an interview with his son, Gen. Shepard, which he refused, but allowed the eldest by the second wife to accompany a young man who carried an open letter to the general, asking the terms on which they might return home. They met him on the march northward, with 500 men, near Hatfield. He was much pleased to meet his young brother and to hear that the rebels were out of Massachusetts, and at or about his father's house, desiring to return to their allegiance, but would not look at the letter or have any communication with the bearer. He said, however, to his brother, very pleasantly, on parting: "You may go home and tell those gentlemen what you have seen, and assure them that if they leave their arms in Vermont and return to their families, who need their assistance this winter, they will not be disturbed while they stay at home and mind their business."

It was satisfactory. They left their arms with the old gentleman, where they remained until distributed to the neighbors, to be used at the obsequies of General Washington, and returned quietly to their homes, where they were never after molested, except, perhaps, by the jests of their friends for their participation in that affair.

After having resided in Halifax more than thirty years, and seen his children select their partners and occupation for life, he sold his property and went to reside with Samuel Hill, a farmer, who had married his youngest daughter, Esther, and a very pious man, belonging to the Methodist Church, in the town of Brookfield, Madison county, and State of New York, where four of his youngest children resided. He there, with his wife and his four children, joined the Methodist Church, and lived until 1809, when he died, without any apparent sickness, in the night in bed with his wife, being eighty-two years of age. He was a small, spare, black-eyed man, five feet six inches high, and had never had occasion to call the assistance of a surgeon or physician in his long, regular, but active life.

Of his first wife, I only know what his second wife said of her, that "she was a most efficient and accomplished lady, and the greatest fear she had on entering his family was that she would be subjected to the criticisms of her neighbors"—a fearful thing still among the New Englanders.

His second wife, my father's mother, was Esther Reed, born in Plainfield, Connecticut, in 1730, and died at Brookfield, Madison county, New York, in 1818. She was the daughter and only child of Stephen Reed, an Oxford graduate and civil engineer, who was sent by the British government to the province of Connecticut to settle the western boundary of it, and part of the eastern boundary of New York. It was a long and troublesome job, and is a crooked line yet.

After finishing the boundary, he opened a boarding school in Plainfield, Connecticut, where his wife died when his child was but one year old. He continued his school, raised and educated his daughter (who assisted him in teaching), died, and left her his house and other property, where she continued the school until her marriage, when she was about thirty years of age. On her arrival at her husband's house, she set apart one room and furnished it with her apparatus and library for the education of his children, who had attended no other school but hers. The two eldest were boys. She qualified them well for business, taught them mathematics, surveying, and navigation, and the use of the instruments pertaining thereto. When the youngest was fourteen years of age, their father engaged them good situations on merchant ships—the popular place to seek fortunes at that day. At their parting with her she gave the eldest her maps, charts and navigator's instruments, and to the youngest the chain, compass and books on surveying. Her labors were not thrown away on either of them. The eldest became a cruiser against the British during the Revolutionary War, and brought home and deposited with his father $60,000 in specie, and $200,000 in Continental money, which he kept until the close of the war, and then purchased a fine estate with a part of it on Hoosick river, and died on it at an advanced age, leaving it to his children.

The youngest served his country faithfully, as related, and died in Northampton, Massachusetts, where some of his numerous family now reside and manufacture silk.

After the departure of the boys, she continued to teach their sister and her own children until they were all educated in her own house, and qualified for the active duties of life. Keziah Shepard, the only daughter of the first wife, was married to Oren Smith, an attorney. and raised a large family in Colerain, Franklin county, Massachusetts, where she died, and where some of her descendants still live.

At the close of the Revolutionary War, my father and his brother Jonas were taken to Massachusetts by their father, and the eldest put as a clerk in a store in Boston, and Jonas, the younger, to a manufacturer of agricultural implements in Hatfield, because he had such a zest for fun and play that he was unfitted for the trusty situation of clerk in a store, and preferred the other less responsible, but more laborious business.

In these situations each distinguished himself. The first found himself, at the end of his apprenticeship, his master's confidential clerk at Canton, in China ; the latter, a foreman in the factory where he had learned his trade. He raised a large family in Madison county, New York.

Soon after the boys last mentioned left home, their sister, older than either of them, was married to Jonathan Angel and went to reside at Exeter, Otsego, New York, where they raised a large family on one of the best cultivated farms I have ever seen.

The two youngest sons, Elisha and William, remained at home and continued their studies, and cultivated the farm until their sister Esther, youngest of the family, was married to Samuel Hill, and went to reside at Brookfield. William accompanied them, became a Methodist preacher, a circuit rider, married and raised a large family in the western part of the State of New York.

Elisha Shepard was never married. He came, when about forty years of age, to my father's old mansion, before the family had left it, sick with consumption, and said to my mother, "I have come to die with my brother's family, and to be buried in the yard with *him*." He lived but a few days and was buried, as he desired, in the yard with his brother. He was a very plain, friendly, sober and honest man.

I have been thus prolix that I might leave some memoranda

where this branch of the descendants of Thomas Shepard may be found.

My maternal grandfather, Andrew Dalrymple, was the son of Scotch parents, his father being a Scotch officer of the British army, sent into Ireland to assist in keeping that country in subjection, and where my grandfather was born, at Belfast, in 1723, and brought by his father the next year to Boston, Massachusetts, where his regiment had been ordered to watch the French movements in America.

Andrew's father died while he was at school in Worcester, Massachusetts, and he immediately joined the British army, and continued connected with it until 1775, when he assisted his son David in raising and victualing a company to assist in driving the British Gen. Gage out of Boston. He had been receiving the half-pay of a British captain from the close of the French war, which, being stopped, he purchased a farm in Petersham, Massachusetts, where my mother and four others of his youngest children, of his large family of six sons and six daughters, were born. Thinking agricultural pursuits to be the most happy and independent mode of life, he wished none of his children to become mechanics. He purchased a large tract in Colerain, Franklin county, Massachusetts, and collected his children there in 1788, where he died in 1803, and was buried in what is called the New Graveyard, where a large monumental stone, near the road, marks his grave, and states that he was the first person buried in that yard.

His wife, my maternal grandmother, was Anna Winslow, daughter of Knelm Winslow, a farmer, of Worcester, Massachusetts. He was the fifth in descent from a passenger on the Mayflower, who landed at Plymouth Rock, Massachusetts, in 1620. She was born in 1728, and was educated in the schools of that town, which has long been celebrated for the literary taste of its inhabitants. Being married young to a British officer, who delighted in good farming when not engaged in the field, and having good public schools and libraries for her children, she devoted very little time to their literary culture. But no lady took more pains to fill her house with plenty and comfort, or with better success, and none ever qualified her children better for the active duties of domestic life. She raised twelve children, who, like herself and husband, were all above the common stature, except my mother, and, like their parents, were all blue-eyed, well-formed, vigorous, healthy and athletic, and all lived to raise families of their own. She died at Colerain, Massachusetts, in 1820, being ninety-two years of age, and was buried by the side of her husband.

Having mentioned these four grand-parents, and being acquainted with most of their numerous descendants, I think it proper to mention also some facts concerning them, which may be interesting.

Of all this large connection there has not been a marriage where there was the least consanguinity of the parties, nor one without the full consent of parents. Nor has there been a deformed child or an idiot born among them. No one has been so unfortunate as not to be able to obtain all the comforts of life in the circle of his own connection; nor has any of them ever been publicly convicted of a crime, although the piety and even loyalty of some have not been very brilliant.

CHAPTER II.

REMINISCENCES OF CHILDHOOD AND OBSEQUIES OF GENERAL WASHINGTON.

It is said by some that man is the creature of circumstances, and all the distinctions among men arise from memory and education. If this is so, the earlier the memory is cultivated the better, if not over-tasked. In my education and employment of life, I have had great exercise for memory, and few, probably, began it younger. Yet I have no recollection of learning the alphabet, or a time when I could not read.

I recollect three occurrences very distinctly that took place the summer before I was four years of age, as I have been informed by my parents. I will relate them, and from their nature it is probable most people will believe I would recollect them, if I could recollect anything.

The first was my sitting on my father's knee and having a double tooth extracted by Dr. Bemis, a Baptist preacher and beloved friend of our family. His tall figure, the blood, and my own reasoning about the pain, which I supposed had been increased by his great size, are all vivid in my recollection to this day.

The second was being pushed by another little child down a flight of new cut-stone steps, and striking my forehead on the sharp edge, cutting such a gash that it became necessary in dressing to take seven stitches to prevent the danger of a permanent scar.

The third was my baptism in the Presbyterian church, by Rev. Jesse Edson, in the presence of a full congregation, and being led by my sister Esther, an older child. Nearly sixty-five years have since elapsed, yet I cannot perceive that the recollection of any of the circumstances has become in the least obliterated during the last fifty years. All is still fresh in my memory as the events of yesterday.

The first event in history that attracted my attention and fixed itself in my memory, was the death of Gen. Washington, which occurred on the 14th of December, 1799, when I had but just entered my fifth year. As it was the most prominent event of the eighteenth century that I distinctly recollect, I will mention what passed in sight of and about me, from the receipt of the melancholy news to the close of the ceremonies.

Early on the morning after the receipt of the sad intelligence, minute-guns began to be fired, and were continued during the day, in sight of my father's house, which stood on an eminence near the village. This drew together almost every man of this patriotic town, for it was winter and good sleighing, and one-half of them had been in the Revolutionary army, as it was but sixteen years after the war, and Halifax never had a Tory in it, and had put forth its whole strength in the struggle. There was but one feeling—all were mourners, and, as one man, set themselves to preparing for the obsequies in the most appropriate manner. Col. Bullock and Captains Gates and Farnsworth, old officers of the army of the Revolution and our next neighbors, were most prominent. As arms then were scarce and all wished to participate in the ceremonies, my father brought home a large party of men, and distributed among them the arms that had been left with his father by Shay's men many years before. They must have taken more than one musket each, as they carried them off, not as soldiers do their muskets, but as men do a shoulder-load of poles.

On a subsequent day the ceremonies of the obsequies were performed. It was a fine, clear day, although winter, and at an early hour my uncle, John Clarke, came with his wife (my mother's sister) in a sleigh and took my mother, her nurse, and all the children to the church where the oration was to be delivered.

My aunt had brought a foot-stove well filled to keep us warm. It was the first time I had seen one used, and I have never seen one used since without recalling the scenes of that day. Before that time there had not been a cast-iron stove in a church in Vermont.

At length we began to hear the muffled drums; the galleries of the large church were filled to their utmost capacity, when a large number of old gray-headed men entered the church and slowly seated themselves about the pulpit. The orator, Rev. Jesse Edson, took his stand; the Revolutionary veterans, with reversed arms, filled the centre of the church, and the younger military the isles and border seats. My mother and family occupied a seat in front in the gallery at the left of the pulpit.

All being silent, the ceremonies commenced. The orator was a fine speaker, of much pathos, and his subject well suited to the occasion, which deserved his best efforts. I was no judge then of such a performance, but it was said he acquitted himself well. I presume it was so from a circumstance I will relate.

While gazing about on the audience, I observed many persons in tears, and among the veterans who stood leaning on their reversed muskets, Philip Crosier, my father's hired man, a large, healthy, robust man, about forty years of age, appeared also bathed in tears. I was astonished at that, as I then supposed men never wept, and immediately called my mother's attention to it. She said, "Philip's General, who was like a father to him, is dead." I understood what she said, and expected I should soon see him buried in the snow in the grave-yard near by, where I had seen others buried before. In this, however, I was somewhat disappointed, for as soon as the crowd withdrew my uncle took us to a house in the village, where, from the windows, we saw the procession march by. We then returned and saw the smoke of the minute-guns from our own windows during the remainder of the day.

The recollection of these scenes, at such a distance of time, fills my mind with gloom, which is heightened by the sad reflection, that all that great concourse of people are now wasted away, and those who then loved and cherished me are dead and in their silent graves, while I am old and must soon follow them there.

ᵗ CHAPTER III.

EARLY ATTENDANCE AT SCHOOL — CHANGE OF FASHIONS — FOURTH PRESIDENTIAL ELECTION.

When I had just entered my fifth year, William Starke, a good friend of our family, taught the public school near my father's house. He promised to see me safely home each night if they would send me to the school. I was, accordingly, promptly and regularly sent.

I was very fond of my teacher and he was very kind to me, and often carried me home on his back. I presume he was very kind to all his pupils, as I saw no one punished in his school. I was not required to study my lessons, yet I learned many things which I have never forgotten—some grave, some useful, and some amusing. The grave ones were learned from repeatedly hearing the recitation of the catechism contained in the New England Primer. The useful were from his lectures on the calendar or almanac. He taught its use to his pupils—the true length of a year, the manner of ascertaining when it is leap-year, and the difference between old style and new style, and that the Presidential election took place always in leap-year. The amusing was that the extended rights of women were not to be recognized this year (1800), as there was no 29th day of February in which to exercise their right. He said, however, this would not occur again in the next hundred years. These facts, and a few of the simple outlines of geography and astronomy, I learned at that tender age from that most kind and accomplished teacher.

The summer schools in New England were then generally taught by ladies. Consequently, my next teacher was a lady—a fine scholar, handsome, very accomplished, and the morning star of fashion. Nothing attracts an infant's attention earlier than a change of costume, and no person could have made a more complete change in it than did my teacher, between the close of her school at the end of the first week, and its opening on the morning of the second, and yet kept within the bounds of fashion. She had caused her long hair to be trimmed short like a young girl's, laid aside the fashionable dress of 1798, and assumed one that would be thought quite comely at this day. In this new array she had entered the school-rooms before us, and seated herself a little out of view from the door of the ante-room, and where we left our hats, so that I was in her immediate presence before I saw her. At first sight I had no doubt of her being a stranger, and having been taught to avoid staring at strangers, I gave her a broad berth on the way to my seat, at a little distance from her side, and began to take furtive glances at her and her attire. I soon recognized my teacher, "but, oh! what a change."

I was so young then, and am so old now, the occurrence would have been forgotten long since, had not all other fashionable ladies of that vicinity adopted the same fashion within a very short time after. It seems to have been a time of general change of fashion. Gentlemen of taste laid aside their sharp-toed shoes and boots, their knee and shoe buckles, their long stockings and short breeches, their long vests and ruffled shirts, their single-breasted coats and broad-brimmed cocked hats, and used those of the fashions of the present age.

These changes gave latitude to great garrulity among the loquacious, some uneasiness among close-fisted fathers and penurious mothers, but great zest and pleasure to the young, gay and fashionable, whose faces would now appear quite changed if viewed at the present day.

As the summer of 1800 advanced, the two great political parties, the Federalists and the Republicans, began to array themselves against each other and prepare for the Presidential election. Political parties then went to as great extremes as they have ever done since. There was no conservative party to allay or check either faction ; every man seemed to select his party and manifest a disposition to make his preference known.

I was not capable then of understanding the principles of either party, but a trifling circumstance taught me to distinguish the members of each party by inspection, and I often put my knowledge into practice. The fashions having been recently changed, the hats worn were mostly new, and the Federalists adopted a distinguishing badge and wore it attached to the side of their hats. It consisted of a small, black silk rosette, about the size of a silver dollar, surmounted with a gilt eagle. The badge at once attracted my attention, and perceiving that my father, who was rather a fashionable gentleman, wore none, I asked the cause. He explained to me its design, and tried to make me understand the difference between "Jefferson and liberty," and "John Adams and gag-law," which I heard so much about at that time.

Thus I had my first lesson in politics. After the Presidential vote was cast the badge disappeared, but the clamor continued through this remarkable and garrulous year. The result of that election may be found in our national history ; it does not belong to this record.

The reader may, perhaps, have begun to fear that I had quite forgotten my beautiful teacher, or that she had been lost in the maze or blaze of fashion. Not so, I can never forget one who taught me so many useful lessons. On the morning of our surprise, she waited till the usual hour for opening school, turned the hour-glass (the school time-keeper of that day), and gave the signal for business. It was soon very apparent she had not, like Sampson, suffered the loss of her ability by being shorn of her hair. She seized this opportunity to introduce a new branch of study into her school.

From the landing of the Pilgrims, in 1620, to about the close of the eighteenth century, the people of New England followed the peculiar pronunciation, it is said, which they used at Plymouth Rock. In the latter part of the last century, Noah Webster had published his American spelling-book. It was an excellent and popular work and had a great circulation. My teacher adopted it in her school, and had, on the previous week, discovered among her pupils a great deficiency in their knowledge of orthoëpy, and determined to remedy it by using that book and lecturing on its rules. The success she met with was astonishing. She required of such as could read that they should memorize the rules. This they cheerfully did, and several who could not read learned them from those who could; so that this lady's school was the best instructed I ever saw, except my own, in orthoëpy; and I learned how to teach it of her. The name of this excellent teacher, Miss Jane Smith, merits a place in this history.

CHAPTER IV.

CLOSE OF THE EIGTEENTH CENTURY AND COMMENCEMENT OF THE NINETEENTH.

In November, 1800, I had just entered my sixth year, and was sent with my sister, a little older than myself, to the public school on the first day of the winter term, when the New England public schools are usually taught by gentlemen. We expected, and were prepared, therefore, to meet a strange gentleman for our teacher, but, having had no hint of his appearance or size, we were quite astonished, on entering his presence, at his stupendous size. He was the largest young man we had ever seen, being well formed, having a well-defined Roman nose, and of a sober countenance. In fact, he was a giant in size, and also, as we found afterwards, in intellect and knowledge. He wrote a swift and beautiful hand, and was a profound mathematician. But he lacked some of the most important requisites for a successful teacher—a fondness and friendship for little children, and a familiar and easy way of communicating knowledge to others. He delighted more in exhibiting his erudition than in communicating it to his pupils. Yet his taciturnity did not militate much against me, for his scholastic pride prompted him to point out and show, and even do things that were a lasting treasure in my memory in after-life. So I cannot let the name of Thomas Miller, or his labor, pass without particular notice.

Having announced to us on one occasion that on a suitable moonlight night he would show us something pleasing in the movement of the heavenly bodies, we waited with impatience the promised exhibition. In the meantime he procured two long, well-dressed spruce spars, like flag-staffs, and caused them to be erected perpendicularly on a line with the west end of the school-house, about one hundred and fifty feet from it, and the same distance from each other, and waited for a clear night when the moon had about completed her first quarter. The wished-for time at length came, and all the scholars had notice to be present in time.

We were punctual in our attendance, and I passed one of the most interesting evenings of my life there, viewing the stars as they passed the poles, and hearing their names or the name of the constellation to which they belonged, from him. He taught us the difference between a fixed star and a planet, and showed that the planets were nearest to us—Mars, Jupiter, or Venus, being then in sight and eclipsing a fixed star beyond it.

Mr. Miller being a man of very few words, all he said was listened to and remembered. He said he was of the opinion that the Pyramids, in Egypt, were built for a scientific and not for a monumental purpose; that the line of one of their sides was exactly parallel with the poles of the earth, and that their use in science was now lost, as also the means of transporting the building materials to the site of the Pyramids. He continued to teach, at suitable times, the names of the different constellations, and had engaged my attention so much that I was unhappy when cloudy nights interfered with the coveted lecture on astronomy.

The century was drawing near its close, and many persons

made their remarks about it, so that children were given to know and understand what was meant by a century. But what made the children of our neighborhood notice the period more particularly was, that old Doctor Rice, who had been a surgeon in the British army, and was at the taking of Quebec with Gen. Wolf, and was 103 years old, lived in Halifax and was visited on the last day of the century by a large number of his acquaintances, who congratulated him on being in good health after living through the whole century. Almost all gave him some substantial token of their desire to see him enter on the nineteenth century in plenty. I think I shall be able to recollect him if I live as long as he did, which was 107 years, and I may, possibly ; and if I do, I shall have lived through this whole century, and witnessed the most wonderful improvements and transactions of any man then likely to be living.

On the first day of January, 1801, Rev. Jesse Edson preached a sermon in the Presbyterian church, which was near the school-house, when we attended and noticed that the greatest attention was paid to old Doctor Rice. Some one conveyed him and his wife, who was forty years younger than himself, in a sleigh to his residence, half a mile distant. The crowd detained the sleigh as soon as he was seated in it, so that all might take him by the hand and wish him a happy new year before he left them. He was a tall, spare-built man, without teeth, his lips much fallen in, his head well covered with hair, which was as white as snow, and, as my father said, a most thoroughbred scholar and gentleman.

Our teacher kept us bright in all our previous studies except the catechism, which he would not teach, or give a reason why he did not. He used all the means in his power to teach writing and arithmetic, saying that other studies were useless without them.

CHAPTER V.

THE ELECTION OF PRESIDENT JEFFERSON AND HIS INAUGURA-TION—THE PURCHASE OF LOUISIANA, THE GREATEST BARGAIN EVER MADE BY MEN.

The electoral college had failed in 1800 to elect a President of the United States, and, according to the Constitution, the election devolved on the House of Representatives. This produced a period of painful suspense to all the politicians of each party, for all knew the chances for success were about equal to each.

The day for the election at length came and the balloting commenced, when a most exciting scene followed. The balloting continued through the day, and to a late hour in the night, when Thomas Jefferson was duly elected President, and Aaron Burr as Vice President, to the great joy of most of the voters of Halifax, which was a democratic town at that time. A day of congratulation was determined on by the leaders, who fixed on the day of the inauguration for the ceremonies, which consisted of patriotic speeches and resolutions, made in the streets near our school-house, where we heard the plaudits and cheers of the rejoicing auditors for some time, and were then permitted to go out of doors and see the crowd, who were cheering and swinging their hats aloft, to our great amusement and pleasure.

The public mind soon became quiet, and politicians found subjects to engage their attention and conversation in speculating on the great events which were then transpiring in Europe, Asia and Africa. My teacher took great interest in what was passing in those countries, and formed what was called the "news class." It consisted of such as were able to read tolerably well, and who brought the latest newspapers. These were carefully read, and all obscurity explained. It was an excellent and useful plan, and should be followed in all the public schools, if the papers stated facts only, as they usually did in those days, in relation to foreign affairs.

Thus the time passed on, and I became familiar with the history of what was passing in the world, and had begun to realize that the town of Halifax composed but a small part of the globe, when the news came that President Jefferson had purchased the whole of Louisiana from France. That roused the Democrats to the highest point of enthusiasm and admiration of their favorite President. A day of congratulation was appointed, and ample preparations made to rejoice together. The school was suspended and opportunity afforded to all who desired to witness the proceedings.

The preliminary arrangements having been made, Jedediah Stark, an eminent attorney, addressed the audience, and was greatly applauded for his fine performance. He began by stating the object of the meeting, which, he said, was to rejoice at the consummation of the greatest pacific act that was ever performed by Democrats, *living* Democrats, whom they had assisted to elevate to office. He then stated that the act was the purchase of the whole of Louisiana. He next defined its boundaries, its extent north and south, east and west; its latitude, rivers, climate, soil and productions, as far as was then known. He then spoke of the advantage its possession would be to the United States, both present and prospective, and closed by saying there was good land enough in the territory, if divided, to give every man, woman and child in the United States a better farm than any one man owned in the State of Vermont.

I noticed his statements and on the first convenient opportunity asked my father to procure me a farm there. He suggested the propriety of my waiting a little until I became large enough to chop the trees and help fight the Indians and bears off it, and kill some of the mosquitoes. I asked if there were such creatures there, for Mr. Stark had not mentioned them. He said there were plenty of them there. That announcement abated my ardor for farming in the new territory.

But forty years afterwards I travelled across the territory from St. Louis to Santa Fé, when both those gentlemen were dead, and passing through the present State of Kansas, then a wilderness, I saw and realized that all which both those gentlemen had said was strictly true. My desire for farming revived, and I now probably possess what at that time would have been considered by Mr. Stark about my share of the purchased territory.

3

CHAPTER VI.

THE PLEASANT DAYS OF CHILDHOOD, ETC.

When I had entered my eighth year, my mother desired my father to provide her a more retired residence, as she had six small children who would be more comfortable in a situation where she could devote more of her time and attention to them, and enjoy more of their society and the quietude of domestic life. My father, therefore, purchased a small, well-cultivated farm of ninety acres, in the township of Shelbourne, Franklin county, Massachusetts, and removed his family to it in the spring of 1803. It was a township of good rolling land, situated on Deerfield river, well watered, productive, and well cultivated, in farms of about one hundred acres, by those who owned them. The inhabitants were very industrious, moral, well informed, and public spirited, and no town was better provided with good public school-houses and teachers. There existed a more perfect equality among the inhabitants of that town than any other I was ever acquainted with, and I think the most general happiness and contentment.

As my parents had resided many years but a few miles from there, they seemed acquainted with every one, and we were all welcomed as one of themselves. Their children came to get acquainted and play with us, and we entered at once into the full enjoyment of our new home and were happy.

When my father had established his family in their new residence he left for the field of his labor in the East, and our mother prepared my eldest sister and myself to attend the summer school. On the day set for opening the school the scholars were there betimes, and were amusing themselves in a grove of trees in front of the school-house, when one of the trustees came to us and said he came to open the school-house and introduce our instructor. We followed him and our teacher in, and he introduced her as Miss Fellows, of Amherst, and hoped we would obey her. I had already resolved on doing that, as I saw at first sight she was a friend to children—the indispensable requisite for a good teacher. The whole school seemed to have formed the same judgment and resolution, and adhered to them, and were a happy school. She required all to occupy the same seats they did at the close of the last quarter, which they did. This left my sister Esther, who was a little over nine years of age, standing with myself on the floor, with satchels full of books in our hands. Our teacher perceiving we were strangers, as well as herself, asked my sister our names and several other questions, and to show our books, which we did. After seeing what we had, she asked, " Who have been your teachers ?" My sister answered, " Our grandmother Shepard, our father's mother, and other teachers." She then gave us writing-desks and seats together, and left us to ourselves. This was as enviable a position as our ambition soared to, and confirmed our affection for our teacher at once.

The exercises of the school then commenced, and we watched attentively the performance of each individual, much the largest number of whom were ladies, some nearly as old as our teacher, and all well advanced. Our turn at length came, after we had heard all the rest and had overcome the nervous sensation of a first performance. My sister read first, with her usual confidence, and was attentively listened to ; she had read well, and I followed ; and, if I had not read well, when I turned to take my seat, I had pleased myself and had the pleasure of seeing my sister's black eyes turned on me with a smile of approbation. Those were moments of pleasure which can never be forgotten or ever repeated.

For several days our lessons seemed to be a kind of examination or review, until one of the older scholars suggested to our teacher that it had been customary here to be classed and have a head and foot of class, and to be ranked according to performance, as first, second, etc. Our teacher remarked that she wished all her scholars to be at the head and no one at the foot, and all number one ; and said she would try to make us such, and hoped we would assist her, which we promised to do. Any delinquent caught afterwards was reminded of the promise, and sometimes brought on the floor to renew it, and be informed that honor, veracity and interest were now all at stake. This was all the punishment that this child-loving teacher ever inflicted upon any one of us. She taught an excellent school, and quit in autumn with the applause and approbation of all her employers, and the lasting remembrance of her pupils.

Our capacity and scholarship in the meantime had become known to all our schoolmates as well as theirs to us, and we had formed such acquaintances and friendships as suited our taste and condition in school. Among our new friends who contributed most to our improvement and added zest to all our school-day enjoyment, was Miss Melinda Long, a child of the same age as my sister, and a fine, industrious scholar, possessing all the attractions that nature bestows on children, and emulous of attaining the highest point of literary excellence.

Classed with these two studious girls only, I commenced the study of the English grammar in the next winter session, when I was eight years of age. We made good improvement although our teacher seemed to pay very little attention to us. This we observed and it prompted us to assist each other, and developed all our capacity and knowledge.

Soon after the close of the session my sister died, which dissolved our class, as our next teacher—consulting her ease rather than her pupils' improvement, and saying to us that we were too young to study English grammar—separated us and taught no grammar class during the session. We both have since ranked as first-class teachers, but have found no children too young to study the English grammar who could read well.

As the time drew near for the winter school to open, I felt great anxiety to know what kind of a teacher we were going to have, and, hearing that he was at a neighbor's house, I went to view him, not thinking of a formal introduction, as I was so young. On my entering the house, Mrs. Riddle, the mother of several of my schoolmates, introduced me in the most flattering manner. I felt an overflowing of gratitude to her for it, and so expressed myself to her, and told Mr. Stuart, to whom I had been introduced, I feared I should not be able to make good what had been said of me. He assured me that from what he had heard and seen of me, we should enjoy ourselves well together.

The winter session of 1804-'5 soon opened without any formality or regard to class or attainment, and we arranged ourselves according to taste or circumstances, as best we could. Some older scholars who had known my sister Esther, but had not attended the summer school, represented to our teacher the position she occupied in this school and who her classmates were. He immediately came to us as we sat together, and, sympathising with us, promised to restore our class and enlarge it by such as we chose. I was not prepared for such a crisis, and deferred it to my surviving classmate, who said, "Plenty will join us of their own choice, if you think it advisable." Two young men and five young ladies were then assigned us as classmates. The Rev. Phinney Fisk, who died many years since in the Holy Land, a Protestant missionary and fine scholar, was one of them, and as his life and labors are made a part of the church history of our country, I refer to it. The others I have lost sight of in the interesting scenes through which I have since passed, but will try to give some record of Adam Stuart, the prince of teachers, and his labors of one session, when I had just entered my tenth year.

His whole conduct and actions are worthy of imitation by all who desire to make teaching their profession, or win the affections of others. He had nothing about him to attract attention, except good sense and a desire to make all easy and happy around him. Yet these qualities shown so conspicuously that an infant would not pass him without recognition as a friend. Not having sufficient time in the short days of winter to accomplish what he desired in the way of improving his pupils, he opened a volunteer night school, in which he taught elocution, modern history, and theatricals. France was just formed into an Empire and other great changes being made in Europe, which gave him a fine opportunity to be useful, instructive and entertaining. This success—the gratitude and affection of his pupils—seemed to be the only reward he desired, and he had them in their fullest measure.

The parting scene of this most excellent school was a kind of theatrical exhibition of our attainments, held in the grove in front of our school-house, on a pleasant afternoon in April, 1805. My teacher showed his kindness to me by selecting a declamation suited to my age and capacity, and, having trained me well, placed me, to my great delight and gratification, to open the exercises of the day, which he closed by one of the most eloquent and cheering addresses to his pupils that man could utter.

This performance added *éclat* to his already finished task, and he left us amid the tears and good wishes of all his pupils. After the exercises I was accompanied a part of the way home by my favorite classmate, Melinda, who said she was very glad Mr. Stuart had given me such a fine opportunity of exhibiting my improvement; that I had represented our class well and distinguished it, and that she meant to remain in it as long as possible and assist in sustaining its reputation.

I was much gratified at what she had said, as I believed it, and we remained in the same class two years longer, and were then as good scholars (in our own estimation) as could have been found in Massachusetts, of the same age. She became a good teacher, and died in the twenty-first year of her age, and I called my only child Melinda, after her, to which her mother prefixed her own name, Mary, and thus her full name is Mary Melinda.

CHAPTER VII.

THE BATTLE OF TRAFALGAR AND ITS EFFECTS.

In the autumn of 1805, the English fleet, under Lord Nelson, engaged the French and Spanish combined fleets, and nearly annihilated them.

My father saw at once what the effect of this battle would be, namely, that the English would be the rulers of the sea for a long time, and he prepared to quit it and retire to a farm with what he had left, after suffering immense losses by both French and English depredations at sea. He sold all his interest in ships, or merchandise in India, and was relieved of all care and responsibility, and could begin the world anew. He therefore selected a beautiful piece of uncultivated land on the shore of Lake Ontario, in Jefferson county, New York, in 1806, and on it saw the great total eclipse of the sun that year, while I and the remainder of the family saw it in Massachusetts at the same time. A total eclipse of the sun is such a rare occurrence at any particular place on the earth's surface, that the inhabitants within the space covered by total darkness generally pay great attention to it, and recollect the appearance of all natural objects in view for a long time, and even make the event an epoch. Such was the effect of this great eclipse at the school which I attended at that time.

The obscuration began to appear at about half-past nine o'clock A. M., and the total darkness occurred before twelve M., when, the sky being clear, all the stars then above the horizon appeared as brilliantly as if it were midnight. The birds had ascended their perches, the gloom of night seemed to pervade all nature, the thermometer had fallen, and breathless stillness everywhere prevailed, as if all feared this state of things was in danger of being made perpetual. The total darkness lasted about two minutes, and when the sun began to appear, hope, joy and happiness seemed to beam in every countenance, as if confidence was again restored from a lost state.

Early in the spring of 1807, my father began to improve his farm and to build a house, and so constructed it that he could have one room exclusively for the education of his children, which he proposed to do himself, as his mother had done before him, in her own house. Having finished his house, he removed his family to it in October of that year, and entered it on my birth-day, when I was twelve years of age. There were then no public schools in New York, nor were there any until 1811, when they were opened throughout the State.

As soon as my father and his family settled in their new house, he opened his family school and continued it four years, during which time his children improved to his apparently entire satisfaction, and no man, probably, ever took more real pleasure than he did in teaching his own children. His pleasing and satisfied countenance when looking down on his little children and seeing their first efforts to read, is fresh in my memory to this late day. Five sons and two daughters attended his family school, and no one else, for, although solicited to take other scholars, he always refused, saying his school exactly suited him, and he did not wish to increase or diminish it.

In 1811, the public school was opened and Mr. Gordon Hawkins employed as teacher. He was a most amiable and candid

gentleman and a very good English scholar. On opening our
public school, he viewed the books of several of the pupils,
and looked at mine and said : "These books require a more
learned person than I ever expect to be to teach them," and
dissuaded me from spending any more time on the classics,
and advised me to go at once to the study of a profession. I
informed my father of Mr. Hawkins' views, and expected to
follow his directions; but my father declined to give either
directions or advice, and said he had studied the law as a
profession when he was a young man, and yet had never practiced it a day; that he saw our country on the very threshhold
of war, and it was doubtful what occupation would suit me
best. He, however, purchased a law library from a retired
lawyer and brought it home, and I commenced the study of
law under the directions of Judge Silas Stowe, of Lowville,
Lewis county, New York, and continued it at intervals for
eight years at home and abroad, and until I left that State for
St. Louis, Missouri, in 1819, having resided in the State of New
York twelve years and more. During this time I had passed
from childhood to manhood, and had watched closely what
was passing in the world, and had an excellent opportunity
of doing it, as I had access to all the best means of obtaining
information, and was constantly with literary men, who kept
the subject always fresh before me. I was well, busy, and
active, and attended to business every day; and when I left
the State of New York, in my twenty-fourth year, I thought
myself well qualified to enter on the practice of law.

Besides studying industriously during those twelve years,
when not closely engaged, I had served in the army of my
country during the war of 1812, and taught in public schools
and academies three years. I had also taken all the degrees
in the Order of Ancient Free and Accepted Masonry, and
learned the lectures. I was therefore regarded as a profound
scholar, experienced soldier, and an accomplished Free Mason.

This condition in life differed widely from the picture drawn
to my childish eyes in 1805, before the great battle of Trafalgar (when I was expecting soon to accompany my father to the
East Indies, see the wonders of the world, and acquire the
riches of the East), and was produced by the result of that
conflict between foreigners whom I never saw. I therefore

have closely observed the effects of that victory on the British nation, and believe it was of greater benefit to them than any other they have achieved in this century. They acquired thereby a great augmentation of their military and naval strength, while they reduced their only dangerous rivals to a state of imbecility, from which they have not yet recovered. Our own country suffered greatly by it, for to man their ships they stripped our neutral merchant ships by impressment of their men, and even took some from our men-of-war in time of peace. It enabled them the next year to wrest the Cape of Good Hope (then the gate to the Indies) from the Dutch (and they hold it to this day), and to commit such depredation on American commerce that our Congress laid an embargo, in 1807, on all our shipping, and thus brought ruin upon thousands. It produced the non-intercourse act of a later date, and the war of 1812. Its effects have been felt by almost every nation of the earth, and by no family more than my own to this time.

The war of 1812 was declared on the 18th of June, 1812, by Congress, and on the 19th of July following, at dawn of day, a British fleet of four sail, under Admiral Yoe, appeared in front of my father's house, distant about two miles, going directly toward Sackett's Harbor, distant five miles, where the United States brig Oneida, of eighteen guns, lay guarded by her crew and one company of militia, with one long thirty-two pounder mounted on a platform, and without any protection by rifle-pits or earthworks of any kind. An alarm was given, and all the neighborhood rushed at once to the defence of the place, with every kind of weapon and with the greatest alacrity, but before any effort was made to form a line of battle, the British fleet, mounting sixty guns, had been beaten off by that single long thirty-two pounder, under the direction of Captain Woolsey and his crew of the brig Oneida, without the loss of a man on the part of the United States.

The cheers and joy of the assembling multitude surpassed description. Every one was a patriot, filled with the greatest enthusiasm and desire for battle. Beardless boys to grey-headed veterans of the Revolution were there, ready and willing to defend their country, or to follow the insolent Britons to Canada and punish them for their audacity. It was on Sunday, and the thunders of the sixty pieces of cannon had been heard over the whole country, and nearly all the men had assembled to defend the place. The eighteen guns were immediately taken from the brig Oneida and placed in a hastily constructed fort, called Fort Tompkins, which overlooked the bay and harbor.

This rendered the place safe from a naval force, but not from an attack by land. It was therefore ordered that a party of one hundred men should be sent to Cape Vincent, at the outlet of Lake Ontario, to watch the movements of the British and give notice of any movement toward the Harbor by a land force. Sixty men of our company of infantry volunteered to go, and forty riflemen of a company of Regulars joined us under Captain McNitt, our company commander being a neighbor. We left Sackett's Harbor on the 22d of July, 1812, in three boats propelled by oars, as it was feared sails might be seen by the British, and our boats captured. We arrived at dawn on the morning of the 23d, and found the place entirely deserted, and no one in the vicinity. We therefore occupied the houses for our quarters, and hid two of our largest boats, sending the third to the long island that lies at the upper end of the St. Lawrence, (and which is about seven miles long) with a squad of sixteen men to observe the British movements from the further end of the island. When the party arrived at the point assigned them, they saw a British boat leaving, with about the same number of men they had themselves, and they hailed them and asked the news.

The British said that they had just received the news that Napoleon with his grand army of four hundred and fifty thousand had left France to invade Russia. This we found in a few days to be the truth.

The citizens of the United States had been leaving Canada rapidly for several days with their goods and families, in compliance with the proclamation of the Governor, when three citizens came into our camp and stated that they and fourteen other citizens of the United States came to the town of Gananaqua, in Canada, thirty miles below Kingston, within the time limited by the proclamation, and reported themselves to a captain in command at that place as aliens, desirous of crossing the St. Lawrence into the United States. The captain said he would send them, and all others who should arrive, over the river on the next day, being the last day given in the proclamation. They waited at the ferry during the next day, and at sunset went to his quarters to get him to fulfill his promise, but found him too drunk to listen to them, and he only said, "Come to-morrow."

Early the next morning the whole seventeen went again to his quarters to get him to still perform his promise. As soon as he saw them he ordered them all to be arrested and placed in the county jail, and while on the way to jail, these three who came to our camp ran away and got a Frenchman to put them over the river, who also told them there were United States soldiers at Cape Vincent, and they had come to inform us of what had transpired. They had scarcely finished the relation of this outrage before it was determined to release the prisoners and punish the captain or burn the town. All were clamorous to begin immediate preparations, so that instead of ordering, our captain had only to consent to have everything in readiness. All the boats were examined, and all the hooks, poles, scoops, oars, and rigging put in place, and the oars muffled. Then came our captain's most perplexing duty. All wished to go and but sixty could be spared from the post, and one of the three boats must also stay and good boatmen to man it. It was, therefore, agreed between our officers that Lieut. Riddle, of the Rifles, should stay at the post with twenty of his best boatmen, and as many of the infantry who were not boatmen. This settled the question that all of us who lived near the lake could go, and also all who rowed well while coming down the lake. There was a well-timed proposition then made, that a draft for the twenty to stay should be drawn by the landsmen as they called themselves. This was accepted and done, and all were satisfied. Lieutenant Riddle, of the Rifles, did the same with the same effect. Those, then, who were to stay, offered us the choice of arms, filled our haversacks with the best they had, and our canteens with good whiskey, for whiskey was a part of a soldier's rations in those days, and none were afraid we would abuse ourselves with it.

We waited impatiently until darkness hid us from the opposite shore, then embarked and glided down stream with the stillness of fish, until we came within about one mile of the town, where we landed, leaving the boats in charge of a corporal and five men, and moved rapidly from the river to the road, about forty rods distant, where we were halted and formed in line, with the riflemen on the right and the three citizens who were to act as guides on our left, and, as I was the smallest man present, a corporal and myself stood next to them, and I feared I would be kept in the rear and not see much of the affair. But it ended quite otherwise, for I saw more than one hundred British soldiers run out of their barracks, and some of them nearly ran over me in their haste to escape, so completely were they surprised and frightened by us.

We did not attempt to stop one or take a prisoner, but fired on them as they ran down the street to a bridge over a stream that divides the town, most of them without clothes, except their pantaloons, and many without their arms. Capt. McNitt, with the riflemen and about twenty infantry, guarded the bridge, while the remainder of our men opened the jail, released all the prisoners, and destroyed the British arms in their barracks.

We killed six of their men in the streets, and wounded about a dozen, and we had one man killed by the sentinel, by the first shot that was fired, and one badly wounded in the foot. We were then ready to return, but knew the enemy had twice the men we had and that they could give us trouble if we let them have possession of the bridge before we were all embarked in the boats. Our captain, therefore, sent a flag of truce (of which I had the honor of being the bearer) to the commandant of the post, stating that none of his party had entered a private house and that he did not wish to do so, and, if he would assure him that no military force should pass to the west side of the stream for one hour, he would leave the town within that time and do no further damage; but if he did not give the assurance at once, he would burn that part of the town he was in possession of, and leave when he got ready.

On passing the bridge I was conducted into a store where the commandant was, who took and read the letter, and immediately commenced writing a reply and asking me questions, which I answered and in turn asked others. In answer to my question as to the invasion of Russia, he said that Napoleon had an army of four hundred and eighty thousand men with him on the march to Russia. Having prepared his reply, he gave it to me, and directed an officer to escort me to the bridge and wait until he saw me pass it, and then report to him. I at once accompanied the officer to the bridge, bade him "good morning," passed the bridge and delivered the reply. Our captain said, "All is well," and ordered his lieutenant to let no one pass the bridge for thirty minutes, and then to march the twenty men he had at the northwest corner immediately to the boats, but if any armed men appeared on the west of or on the bridge, to fire upon them and march by quickstep immediately to the boats. He then marched the riflemen back to the British barracks, where the United States prisoners, fourteen in number and twelve others, had armed themselves with what the British soldiers left in their sudden flight, and where our men who released the prisoners had procured two one-horse carts and drivers, to carry our dead and wounded to the boats. All these marched with the captain to the boats with all speed, and such as were not soldiers, together with the dead and wounded, were embarked with twenty soldiers and landed on the United States shore to secure them from the possibility of a disaster.

The thirty minutes having elapsed, our lieutenant formed us in a platoon in open order and marched us out of town, then by files to our waiting boat. On our arrival at the boat, we were immediately embarked and crossed to the United States shore, where our comrades had already landed. Here a general congratulation and feast of joy followed. The delivered and the deliverers were there, and none else. It was such a scene as is seldom enacted by men, and can never be forgotten by those who were present and actors in it.

Our next duty was a sad one, that of burying our dead comrade, who was a stranger to all of us at the time he joined the company, but a few days before. His name was Orvice, a young man from Vermont, and he was the first man I ever saw killed. He was shot about two yards ahead of me, as he was pushing down a rail-fence near the British barracks to let us through. We buried him in the woods with the honors of war, wrapped in his blanket (as is the fashion among soldiers where coffins are not at hand), and then made a rude tomb of poles over his grave.

Our party being too large to ride in the boats up stream, we were divided into three reliefs, each one of which was to navigate the boats and walk on shore in turn, boating two hours and walking four. We left the burying-place at ten o'clock in the morning, going up stream near our own shore and observing the movements on the Canadian shore, as that was well settled, while our shore was without inhabitants, and arrived at Cape Vincent before sunset on the next day, being less than forty-eight hours from the time we left.

On our arrival, our friends in camp were much elated by our success, and examined with interest the twenty new muskets we had brought with us, besides many sets of accoutrements, and all the knapsacks, clothes, and blankets the barracks contained. Our surgeon, Dr. Noah Tubbs, had also brought off the British captain's coat, commission, sash, sword and belt. These, with the twenty-six living witnesses released from prison, formed quite an imposing collection for examination and discussion among a hundred raw, inquisitive and idle Yankee soldiers.

Our thirty days' term of service having expired, our company of infantry returned to Sackett's Harbor, and were discharged.

CHAPTER VIII.

REMINISCENEES OF THE WAR OF 1812.

I had made my first essay in war, and was pleased with the excitement of battle and active service, but I had no taste for garrison duty, and therefore would not enroll myself in General Dodge's brigade of six months men then at Sackett's Harbor, as I knew he had been ordered there for that purpose, and returned home and resumed my studies.

The British fleet appeared almost daily in sight, and other causes of excitement retarded my progress so much that it was thought best for me to go from home to study, and as one of our neighbors was going to Genesee river for a load of fruit with a keel boat, I took passage with him, intending to go to Rochester. On our arrival at the mouth of the Genesee river, a United States quartermaster pressed the boat for the use of the Government, and told James White, the master of the boat, he would pay him three dollars a day for himself, and seven dollars per day for his ten-ton boat, and pay for the boat if he lost it, besides feeding all his people as long as they stayed about the boat, and also pay them their wages. This he accepted, which left me without any conveyance, with a heavy trunk, which his two men (all he had) helped me to carry to a farmer's house near the river, where I waited until the next day for a conveyance toward Rochester. Finding none toward noon, I walked back to the boat and found the men cooking dinner. They bid me stay to dine, and said White would soon be back, as he was going up the lake that evening. I therefore waited until he came, as I was desirous of knowing what use would be made of his small boat. On his return, he told me the quartermaster had pressed all the small boats in Genesee river and sent them up the lake to carry the army under General Van Rensselear into Canada and he would sail immediately. I had no time for deliberation, and walked on board at once, determined to see the embarkation of the army and view the Falls of Niagara before my return.

We were soon under way, with a light south wind, while our course was nearly west. Our boat had a good sail, but being flat-bottomed, and having no freight, we seemed soon in a very fair way of landing in Canada before General Van Rensselear, notwithstanding our men exerted themselves at the oars to the best of their ability during the whole afternoon to prevent our making lee-way. At sundown they struck the sail and we took our supper, experiencing meanwhile great anxiety for our safety, as the boatmen estimated that we had sailed fifty miles, and were then twenty miles from our true course.

After supper and while the men were discussing the manner in which the night could be most profitably spent, it was discovered that the wind had changed and was now fair. No time was lost in making sail, and, although the wind was very light, it relieved me of great anxiety and restored my hopes. The waves being nearly parallel with our course, the boat

rolled and tossed me into a most disagreeable fit of sea-sickness, which compelled me to sit up during the night, although
the agitation lasted but a short time after the wind became
settled in our favor.

As the day dawned we saw our own shore but a few miles
distant, and soon came within hailing distance of another of
the quartermaster's boats which had left the Genesee river six
hours before us. This cheered our people very much, and they
were still more pleased when told we were only twenty miles
from the mouth of the Niagara river, our destination. We
soon after saw it, and arrived there before twelve o'clock, where
we all landed and found the people very busily engaged in
conveying boats by land to Lewistown. As I had no interest
in the enterprise, nor any business to detain me, and having
no baggage, and knowing that a few miles' walk would remove
all the unpleasant sensations of my recent fit of sea-sickness,
I bid adieu to my friend White, and left for town on foot to
" see the show."

The walk, however, proved to be much longer than I anticipated and I was unable to reach Lewistown that night, and
spent the night three miles from town. It being cloudy in the
morning and fearing rain, I started early, so that I was near
the picket-line of the army at sun-rise. After breakfast I
walked down to the river to begin my examination of the
place and its surroundings, and to my astonishment saw the
boat in which I had come up the lake, and others I had seen the
evening before ; I also soon saw my friend White, who told me
that soon after I left him the previous day, the wind rose, and
being still fair, all the boats not on wheels started and passed
Fort George unnoticed in the almost total darkness of the
night; and that as soon as it was light enough for his men to
see the British cannon staring them in the face yonder, they
ran off and left him to watch his boat alone, and he wished I
would stay with him until he could get some assistance.

I told him I would stay with pleasure, as it would afford me
an excellent opportunity of viewing the opposite shore through
his fine telescope. He immediately handed it to me, and I
examined every spot within the reach of my vision as well as I
could have done had I stood upon the same ground, and even
better, for, being at a distance, I could at the same time view

its relative position with respect to all other places. Had it been incumbent upon myself to direct an attack on the place, I could not have been more careful in my observations, and I felt satisfied that I knew how every house and fence in the village of Queenstown was situated at that time.

After noon, two officers came and inspected the boats and tackle, and directed them to be numbered as they lay at the landing, beginning with the one highest up stream. This being done, the one I was in was designated "No. 5," and Capt. White was told to examine the opposite shore and determine how and where he could best land. A certain cedar tree was pointed out as the highest point at which a landing was expected to be made, and directions were given to steer for that point. Soon after several men came and said they had been detailed to aid in navigating the boats, and they wished to know to which boat each man was to be attached; that there was to be one boatman to each ton the boat carried, and some came on board and began to put the boat in order.

Seeing the boat had plenty of hands, I left, telling the captain I would be back to see him start. I then went up on the lights above Lewistown, and viewed the lunette battery above the village of Queenstown, and Gen. Van Rensselaer's camps about Lewistown, and was back at the boat about sundown. There I was introduced to Lieut. Gansevoort, of the New York militia, by Captain White, who also gave the lieutenant quite an overdrawn account of me, saying that I was at the battle of Sackett's Harbor, and helped surprise the British garrison of Gananaqua and released the American prisoners, and could assist him if I would, as I knew the opposite shore as well as the Canadians themselves. This statement rendered the lieutenant's importunity for me to join him quite irresistible, and I consented to join the company, went with him to his quarters, was enrolled, weighed, measured, and described, as is usual in armies.

This was on the evening of the 12th of October, 1812. I then measured five feet and five inches, and weighed one hundred and twelve pounds. I was an entire stranger to every man in the company, and was therefore formally introduced to it at roll-call by the lieutenant, who made some remarks, to the effect that he was responsible for my doing my duty. I then

4

found the cause of his prominence was, that the captain had
gone home sick and was not expected to return, and that he
commanded the company. All had volunteered to invade
Canada, and were ready to embark at the shortest notice in
Captain White's boat, "No. 5," and all had their arms loaded,
their cartridge-boxes filled, and forty cartridges each in their
pockets.

We were then informed that, unless it rained at three o'clock
next morning, we would be formed silently as we then stood,
and be marched by the left flank to the boats, and that no one
was to leave the ranks while on march.

We were then dismissed, and I went to the lieutenant's
quarters to receive my arms and a blanket. After receiving
my outfit, we took supper and strolled about camp to learn the
views of our friends concerning the coming invasion, and what
orders had been given. All seemed anxious to participate,
and desirous of being in the first embarkation, yet we met
but few who knew what boat they were to go in, or at what
time they would embark. In short, there were 2,500 men in
readiness to cross, and only eleven boats at the place of embarkation, and these capable of carrying but 600 men at one trip.
All, however, appeared to have been ordered to be paraded at
the same time, and all were in readiness.

At the usual hour we went to rest. I slept well, and arose at
the appointed hour and took my place in the ranks without
any incumbrance except my arms and ammunition. While
waiting in silence here a few moments for the order to move,
I called to mind home and all my friends there, my beloved
class-mate Melinda and others. A minute seemed like an
hour. I asked myself if I could be doing right. In an instant
the thoughts of the effects of the battle of Trafalgar rushed
into my mind and prepared me for the work I was soon to
engage in, and that same train of thought has often since urged
me to the performance of acts that I would not otherwise have
dared to attempt.

It was now the 13th of October, 1812, when the desired order
to march and embark came, and we obeyed it with alacrity.
Being the smallest member of the company, and marching by
the left flank, put me in the starboard bow of the boat, and,
as we were obliged to land and disembark from that part of

the boat, I was one of the first who landed. Our boat was well manned and well navigated, and meeting with no accident or opposition from the enemy, was one of the first moored to the shore, and landed highest up the river. The fleet of boats all started at the same time, and as the transactions of the day are fully and truly related in history, I will only state that part of them in which I personally acted, or saw acted by others.

On landing, we were all instantly formed, and told that our business and duty was to ascend these hights and spike the cannons, or as many of them as possible; that in doing so we must obey orders, and give orders if necessary to accomplish it; that all were to consider themselves as officers until it was done; that they had spikes to do it with in their pockets, and courage and ability in their persons to accomplish their task, and that we should strive constantly to pass the man we saw highest up or above us.

It was yet dark, about the first of the dawn of day, and the battle progressing at the ferry landing, when we began to ascend the steep ascent covered with low scrubby cedar brush. The cannon balls from the lunette battery were then passing over our heads toward the place of our embarkation and other points. We were about twenty minutes in groping our way and pulling ourselves up the steep acclivity by catching hold of the cedar brush through which we forced our way. About ten had already arrived before me, and were examining the condition of affairs, but none had as yet discharged a gun or created alarm, but were peering through the embrasures and crouching under the battlement. My proper place being at the extreme left, I ran a little further around to the west of the lunette and looked into it, as at every discharge it was as light as noonday. I thought I saw about one hundred and fifty men at the guns and in the rear of the battery, most of them matrosses with sabres. The flashes were very frequent and we had a much better opportunity of seeing them than they had of seeing us, as they were at their pieces and we a little distance from them. When about one hundred had assembled around the southern or front part of the lunette, an officer, whom I had not observed at any time before, gave the word "charge!" With shouts and yells we instantly rushed into the lunette, some over the battlement, some through the embrasures, and others around the eastern end of the lunette, firing at will, and attacking with bayonets and swords all opposers; so that in the space of five minutes every gun was in our possession and being spiked. We then quickly, without regard to our company organization, and without orders, formed in line just in rear of the spiked guns, gave three cheers, then loaded and shouldered arms. The British in the meantime had run down into the village, where the firing was still brisk, at and near the ferry landing, and where our assistance might be wanted to counteract theirs. Several more men had arrived up the hights and all were formed in line of battle and marched to the upper houses of the village, which was all on one street parallel with the river. The British had left about a dozen wounded in the stone house on the north of the street, and ours were placed in a wooden house opposite.

It was now light and we could see the enemy retreating in good order from the ferry landing to an orchard half a mile off, and followed by our people to the first field, where they halted; we then cheered, and our officers separated us into our respective companies, our company being formed on the right of the line north of the street or road.

The captain next on our left then congratulated us on our exploit and victory, to which we responded by three rousing cheers for the captain. Our lieutenant then ran out in front of the company, and slapping his hands together, yelled out, "My men, I am proud of you!" We instantly replied as loudly, "Three cheers for Lieutenant Gansevoort!" and gave them with a will, being joined by the whole line. Soon after some of the troops who landed at the ferry landing marched up to us, and the wild excitement abated so that we could look about and see what had been done.

Several had been killed and more wounded, myself among them; yet I was active, resolute and courageous as ever. I had received a severe cut across the outside of my right leg from a sabre in the hand of a matross while on the battlement, and a stab with the same weapon in the inside of the left thigh when within the lunette; and had a bayonet thrust between my wrist and musket, by one of my comrades in attempting to assist me while engaged with the British matross.

This state of quiescence was of very short duration, for the

British were being reinforced rapidly, and soon began to manœuvre as if on drill or to make a display; and finally, being formed in front of us in the shape of the letter E, with the bar of the letter in front, with music playing the British tune called "Shoveherup," they advanced at quickstep about half way to us and halted at the distance of about two hundred yards, where we had a good view of them and their arms.

I had torn my cravat in two pieces, and cutting a hole for my thumb through one piece, a comrade dressed my wrist, so that I participated in all the fighting of that day, until Lieutenant-Colonel Winfield Scott, of the artillery, late venerable Lieutenant-General Scott, assumed the command and drove the British from the field, ordering all the wounded soldiers to be conveyed across the river and the boats to return for the remainder of his command.

We had scarcely arrived at the boats when the battle was renewed, and no boat returned after we landed. I walked a little way up the river to see the battle rage and learn how it was progressing, and there saw several of our men rush headlong down the steep precipice on the opposite side as if running from their pursuers. They had come to a place so steep that they could not stop when they saw their danger, and were killed instantly.

This battle was soon ended and I took a view of the British examining their spiked guns and replacing their colors and sentinels, then shouldered my musket and walked toward camp. My arms, dress, and sad plight, soon attracted notice, and I was followed by several persons questioning me about the battle and what part of it I had been in. This provoked me, and I stopped and asked why they had not gone over and seen what part of the battle I had been in. I walked on then a few yards without being followed, when a man stepped out of a small shoe-shop, and, looking at me, said hurriedly, "Here, come into my house; I see you are bloody and have been in the battle and been hurt, and we will take care of you." This seemed friendly and reasonable, and I went in with him. In this humble cobbler's house I was treated with the kindness of a mother and the liberality of a prince. He assisted me to wash, and furnished me with his Sunday suit, while his wife washed, dried, and mended mine where they had been cut with a sabre. He also washed my boots, which were soaked with blood, and dried, stretched and polished them until they appeared quite new; had my wounds and hat dressed, and gave me such a recuperation, that on my birthday, two days after, I was enabled to bid adieu to my generous and humane benefactors, Peter Mason and his kind and tidy wife, with my usual gaiety, to their great joy and gratification.

With a clean dress and my military trappings well adjusted, I shouldered my musket, walked slowly toward the lieutenant's former quarters, and enquired for him or some other member of his company, as everything seemed changed. I was told by a soldier standing by that Lieutenant Gansevoort and all his company were either killed, wounded or taken prisoners, and that he helped carry all their property to the quartermaster's store on the day after the battle, and would go with me to it, which he did, and I there saw it being inventoried.

While looking on, an officer asked me what I wanted. I told him I could not say that I wanted any thing; but that as the property once belonged to my comrades, I wished to know it was safe. He then asked where I was on the day of battle. I told him on the company's left flank, until I was ordered to quit the field and cross the river. He said, "Come with me," and took my musket and conducted me to General Stephen Van Rensselaer's quarters, asking me my name and place of residence. There he introduced me to him and several other officers. The general asked me to state what I had seen and knew of the battle. I stated in substance what I have written in this book. He then remarked that I was the first he had seen that had assaulted the battery, and fought through the forenoon, that could give a clear account of what transpired; that the principal actors had been made prisoners, and the rest were so badly wounded, or in such a hurry to get home, that nothing satisfactory could be gotten out of them. He asked me how I, being so young, got into the army. I answered that I was not quite sure that I was in; that I had been enrolled but not mustered. I then related what had been done in the matter, and why. He remarked, "The sport is now all over; stay a day or two with us, and we will provide you a conveyance on to Rochester or back to the Genesee river." I said I would accept either with pleasure and gratitude, and would go and return my arms to the armory. An officer said he would do it; so I cast loose my belt and laid aside my scabbard and cartridge-box, and they examined the contents to find the number of rounds I had fired. It appeared, on inspection, I had used forty-seven rounds in the three several and distinct encounters of that day in which our company was engaged, and the dirty condition of my musket assisted to corroborate it.

It was now my birth-day. I was seventeen years of age, but I had only the appearance of a lad of fifteen years. I was a stranger to all about me, and they occupied elevated positions, yet they treated me as their equal, and bid me to come and be at home in their quarters. As I knew I was under no hallucination then, I asked myself what it was that these persons saw in me that induced them to treat me with so much attention. I came to the conclusion then—which I have ever since entertained, and have often seen exhibited—that it was the indescribable polish which education gives to the countenance, words, actions, and even dress, of the persons who possess it. Having mentioned dress, I should, perhaps, describe it, as it was fashionable at that time. It consisted of a high bell-crowned and narrow-brimmed beaver hat, a brown or snuff-colored broadcloth straight-bodied coat, a striped swansdown vest, grey satinet pants fitting closely below the knee, fine tasseled top-boots, a ruffled shirt, and a white cravat.

A captain of infantry, whose quarters were near the general's, asked me to accompany him to his quarters. I accepted his invitation, and spent four days with him. We visited Niagara Falls and Black Rock together, so that I left Lewistown at the end of the week very well satisfied with what the five senses had enabled me to enjoy during the time, and I left very confident I should not soon forget it or the kind friends I had left there. As promised, a passage was provided for me to Genesee river in one of the boats, which had been returned by the quartermaster to its owner. After expressing my gratitude to General Van Rensselaer for his kindness, and bidding adieu to him and friends, I was accompanied to the boat by Captain Stanfort, with whom I had been staying, and who, on parting, presented me with a blanket and his best wishes.

We then embarked, and under cover of darkness passed silently out of the reach of British cannon into the lake, where we felt safe. The wind being tolerably fair, we made good speed and arrived in the Genesee in the afternoon, where we found an armed United States schooner, commanded by a young naval officer in search of men to man the fleet then fitting out at Sackett's Harbor. He was a second-lieutenant, named Osborn, and on our landing came to us with his proposition. Our people seemed shy of him; he then addressed himself to me, asking what business the boat was in. I told him what it had been in of late, and that neither the boat or hands could do much more until spring, and that if he would suggest that to them after they had eaten, he might get some of them to enlist, as they were idle. While he waited, I tried to get a conveyance to Rochester, but found none for that day, so I returned to the boat for my blanket, and then started in the direction the boatmen had gone, and soon met them returning to it. Wishing well to the young man, I turned back, and from the crew of our boat, and another lying alongside, I assisted him to ship nine good hands that evening. I had passed through so much excitement within the last few days that I felt no disposition to study, and therefore accepted the lieutenant's invitation to accompany him back to Sackett's Harbor; so getting my trunk on board, we sailed the next morning, and arrived at Sackett's Harbor on the 23d of October, when I returned home and during the remainder of the year resumed my studies.

General Dodge's brigade garrisoned Sackett's Harbor until February, 1813, when their six months' term of service expired. They had suffered much from sickness; and when they were discharged nearly every man returned to his home, being mostly Federalists and opposed to the war, as the Federalists all were at that time.

The whole American navy of Lake Ontario was then at Sackett's Harbor, and it was of the greatest importance it should be preserved. The militia were therefore called upon to serve until other troops could be collected. Their private interests brought forward a good army and caused it to be disciplined, so that all the men of the country were prepared for battle. This induced the officers of the regular army to confide in them, and was undoubtedly the cause of a battle being gained there the next year by their assistance. The ice on Lake Ontario was thicker that winter than ever before known, and remained firm until April. There was also plenty of snow, and the largest cannons, cables, anchors, and gun carriages, to equip the fleet, were conveyed on sleighs from Albany to Sackett's Harbor. Vast quantities of arms, ammunition, provisions, and other warlike stores, were collected there, both for the army and navy.

Early in March the regular troops began to assemble, under the command of General Dearborn, and every preparation was made to invade Canada. I observed the progress and desired to participate, but I saw no suitable opportunity until the expedition was ready to sail. I then consoled myself by reflecting that there had been two expeditions fitted out and both were failures, and that if this should be like them, it would be all for the best.

The fleet was waiting for a favorable wind, and I was waiting for the opening of the mail, when a rifleman accosted me, asking how I was, and what I had been doing since we parted at Cape St. Vincent. I told him I had been up the lake to Queenstown, where I had seen something more flush than at Gananaqua. He said he had seen an account of it, and how basely some of the militia had acted, and asked me if I was taken prisoner. I answered him, "No. They gave me a blow or two, and let me off." He said I ought to go and return it now; that I would never have a better opportunity; that there were no militia going, and his captain would suit me. I therefore determined to see his captain and hear what he had to say. Having obtained the papers, we went to Captain Forsyth's quarters, where I was introduced and the object of my visit made known, which was to learn on what terms volunteers would be received in his company for the campaign. He said he would receive them as recruits or volunteer soldiers; that all such would be at liberty to leave the service at any time when not under orders or arrest, and receive pay and rations according to rank, and clothing as needed. I accepted his proposition and enrolled, promising to be at his own quarters at ten o'clock the next morning. I was punctual in my attendance and procured my outfit.

On moving about among the company, I found all the riflemen who were with us at Cape St. Vincent, who appeared glad to see me with them; so I felt quite at home. At 2 o'clock P. M. the order was given to embark with three days' cooked rations, which was received with shouts of gladness, and cheerfully obeyed; so that we were all on board the fleet before dark and ready to sail, the weather being very calm.

We spent the night in port, and on the next morning, April 25th, sailed with a light, fair wind, not knowing our destination, but supposing we were to attack Kingstown, Upper Canada. The fleet, however, bore west during the day and night, and about midday of the 26th came in sight of Toronto, or Little York as it was then called, and, passing the town, came to anchor about three miles from it and one from the shore.

On the following morning, it being calm, the boats were filled with infantry and riflemen and rowed toward the shore, with the infantry in line on the right and the riflemen on the left. When about five hundred yards from shore, the line was halted and the infantry ordered to advance, which they attempted, but were ordered to halt at sight of strong lines of infantry in front on the bank a short distance from shore. The riflemen were then ordered to land and attack their lines in flank. This was promptly done. Captain Forsythe, on landing, said, "Men, follow me!" and ordered the buglers to sound the charge; then, running up the bank and directly out from the lake until we were all on the bank, he ordered, "Halt at will—right face—Fire!" This gave every man a chance to dodge behind any cover, and also to shoot when he thought best. But, as all will perceive, the company was fighting from its rear, and its right had become its left in the movement. At our first fire the infantry landed, and the British retired to a position near their magazine, where a stand for a short time was made by them; and when they were forced from it, they put a slow match to their magazine, which contained fifty thousand pounds of powder, and exploded it, killing General Pike and many others, and wounding still more, myself among the rest.

I have no recollection of hearing the explosion, and was probably knocked down, as on the return of consciousness I was leaning on a stump and my rifle lying on the ground several feet from me. My first impression was that I had just awakened in some strange place, and could not conceive how

I came there, and began to look about, when I saw my rifle on the ground at a little distance, and, on taking it up, a man took hold of my arm and said, "Let us go to the shore." I went with him, and saw men crawling on the ground on their hands and knees; others dead, dying, and moaning; while some were carrying men off toward the shore. At a short distance from us we saw six men carrying one in a blanket, two of whom were field officers. Knowing they carried an officer higher than themselves, we followed them to the shore, where an officer brought the British colors to them and said, "General Pike, the British have surrendered the town, and here is their flag." He replied, "Put it under my head." It was done, and he immediately expired, while we stood round him.

I was then taken, with many others, to the surgeon on one of the vessels, where our wounds were dressed. My right shoulder was broken, and I had a severe cut in my forehead above the left eye. The surgeon dressed my forehead carefully, so that but a small scar appears; yet he so far neglected my shoulder that it is sunk one inch lower than the left, which caused me to wear a coat padded inside over the right shoulder to conceal the deformity of my person in after-life.

The riflemen had been extended so far to the left in the battle that they suffered but little by the explosion. The loss fell mostly on Colonel King's regiment and other infantry, so that I found only infantry for companions among the wounded. The vessel was quite small for hospital purposes, and we fared but moderately and suffered much.

After we had been on board about a week, and nearly half of our original number had died, our heartless surgeon returned about half of the remainder fit for duty, and sent us on shore to our respective companies.

Fort George had been taken, and our companies had been sent out to the village of Newark, so that when we were landed we found ourselves without a home for the night. Although perfectly safe, with new clothes, and well armed, I was as helpless as an infant, for I had a knapsack and rifle, a lame shoulder, and but one hand to do anything. All the others seemed better off, and, as there was a large body of infantry near, they took their baggage and went to them. I laid my rifle and accoutrements on my knapsack and walked off for assistance toward some people I saw on the shore at work setting up a fishing windlass. Soon after a man came with the fishing sein to them and said he was going back to Newark with his wagon. I asked him if he would carry me there. He said he would, and be glad to do so in order to have company home; and went with me and helped put my property in his wagon. At the first tavern he stopped and invited me in. I went in and he wanted me to drink with him, and on my declining, he said, "Very well; then you have to stay with me to-night." I answered promptly, as he had done, "Very well; I take all such punishments." I spent the night with him, and left my knapsack with him until after our return from the shameful surprise of General Winder, when both he and General Chandler were taken prisoners, and many of their men butchered by the Indians. This man, John Saddler, had been twenty years in the employment of a British fur company, and appeared to have a better knowledge of all British America and the northern part of the Louisiana purchase than any other man I have ever met with. His description of the Western prairies gave me the first real knowledge of their vast extent and fertility I had received. He said: "Look at the great lakes when frozen over in winter and covered with snow, and you see exactly how a prairie appears in winter when the grass has been burnt off in autumn and then covered with snow in winter. Then suppose the lake to be as fertile earth as you have ever seen on a large farm, well covered with good nutritious grass as high as your waist, and interspersed with flowers of every size, shape and hue, on stalks and stems from six inches to six feet high, and you will have some idea of the appearance of a prairie in summer." He had retired from business, purchased a fine suburban residence, fished, hunted and took pastime with his neighbors, and seemed to pass an easy and happy life. It was on one of these excursions he met and brought me to his house, where he treated me with the kindness of a father, as also, at sundry times, many others of our army; yet he was permitted to enjoy his property but a little longer, as I will relate hereafter.

After partaking of an early breakfast—leaving my rifle, knapsack and blanket—I hastened forward to the place where

I had been directed to meet our company, and found the ground vacated. On inquiry, I learned quite a large part of the army was in motion, going west, and our company among the foremost; I therefore pressed forward to overtake it.

About ten o'clock, we began to hear rapid firing, and soon afterwards, for a short time, volleys, as if by platoons retreating in good order. We quickened our step, but soon perceived that the firing was receding as fast as we advanced. I was with the Sixteenth Regiment Infantry, about two hundred of whom broke ranks and ran toward the front. I joined in the race to see what was doing, and soon passed British knapsacks, blankets and overcoats; and, a little further on, muskets, accoutrements and coats; and finally, British soldiers, tired out, and sitting on the ground, prisoners. We spent no time with them, but pushed for the front, which we came up with about twelve o'clock M., where our men were forming a line in a field, and where the British were attempting to make a stand, and showing about five or six hundred men, militia and regulars. While this line was being formed, General Chandler and staff came into the field and assisted us, there being very few officers present. Before the line was formed, the British began to retreat, and the pursuit was resumed without much order but with great spirit, and continued until four o'clock, when another feint of the same kind was made by the British on the apex of a hill in front. Here General Chandler and staff assisted to form the line again, and cautioned the men against pursuing in such hot haste and disorder, and bid us wait for orders. The line being formed, many officers came up and took their places; and at length General Winder came, and, superseding General Chandler, took command of us, elated as we were, as if just from a great victory.

The British were retreating in view through the valley ahead of us, and were being met by a reinforcement, also in plain sight. Here we were detained, viewing them and making our observations, until five o'clock, when we were ordered to march back to the stream we had passed, and encamp for the night, as there was no water where we were. Here our murmurs and misfortunes began. Many of the men said, " Yonder is water nearer, where the British are, and we are the lads who will get it for you, if you will let us." But back to the stream—that slaughter-yard for hundreds, and field of disgrace—we were doomed to go. An account of the affair is given in history; but I shall not have done what my daughter has desired of me, if I only say I was there and then refer to the history, without stating in my own language all I saw within twenty-four hours after I left the hospitable mansion of Mr. Saddler.

We started back in ill-humor, murmuring and saying, "If Winder had only stayed away, General Chandler would that day have taken every man we had now seen of the British, or driven them all into Burlington Bay." As we passed down the road, we saw a one-story house that had been used for a school-house and meeting-house, now being used as the generals' headquarters, and an ambulance near by, loaded with three demijohns, several wine-baskets, a keg, and sundry boxes. This explained the cause of our unnecessary halt; and some of the men peeped in at the door and saw the generals drinking, or said they did; and it was the last we heard of them in that army, or for a long time after.

Half a mile further down, we came to the stream, a little off the road, where it was about fifty yards wide and apparently eighteen inches deep, with yellow sandy bottom. Here on its woody bank we were to encamp, without tents or camp equipage of any kind, and the ground quite damp.

I had kept in company during the day with a good-sized young man of the Sixteenth Infantry, who had all that a soldier should have on the day of battle, while I was without a rifle, blanket or provisions; yet now I was the most independent of any, for I had my tomahawk and a rifleman's long heavy knife, and all wanted them to cut brush to avoid lying on the wet ground, and I accommodated as many as I could by lending both. They soon prepared long brush beds, built fires, ate from their haversacks of cooked rations, and discussed the conduct and folly of our generals very freely.

When the sentinels were set, we noticed none were stationed along the stream, and we went and examined it, fearing the Indians might attack us from that quarter. On examination, it was asked why we had not crossed the bridge and encamped on the dry bank opposite. Some answered, "Because we are left to protect the generals' demijohns."

At roll-call, we were directed to sleep upon our arms, and in case of an alarm to form instantly on the same ground we then occupied, and wait for orders. Our beds of brush were all in rear of this line, between it and the creek, and this line was the one the regiment was to form on, in any emergency. Another regiment was encamped in the same manner on the side of the road opposite, and the British prisoners—about two hundred in number—occupied a space between them on the road at the end of the bridge, in rear of the camp guard off post. The generals' headquarters I have described as up the road, distant half a mile. This was the state of the camp when my new friends spread some of their blankets on the brush for beds, retaining others to cover us with, and, with the kindness of brothers, invited me to lie down, while some covered us.

I took an outside berth, with my boots on, and, being tired, was soon asleep. I awoke after all the fires had died out, and rose and contemplated the stillness and profound darkness of the forest; then lay down and slept till about two o'clock, when I was awakened by a noise like cattle running. I instantly roused the man next to me, and said, "I think there is an alarm." He sat up in bed and listened. I put my hand on his shoulder. He said, "I think you have heard a stack of arms fall down." I felt him lying down, and then saw the first flash of a sentinel's gun, quickly followed by the sentinel running in among us, screaming "Indians! Indians!" and followed by them with yells that pen can fully never describe nor white men imitate.

A few sentinels fired while on their posts, and then ran in; but most of them ran from their posts into camp without firing, the British pursuing them quite into camp with their bayonets along the whole front line, and shouting and firing as they met opposition. This roused the sleepers in a moment. Some seized their weapons and called loudly "To arms!"— some tried to form in line—the British firing after the sentinels, and our own men firing among the crowd in their confusion of mind, affording all the light we had. The British shouting, Indians yelling, arms clashing, men screaming, begging, groaning, dying, swearing and fighting, created a state of affairs that satisfied me no line could be formed; and I waded across the stream with great difficulty, the bottom being quick-sandy. On rising the bank, I placed myself behind a tree, and looked back on one of the most frightful scenes that it is possible for the same number of men to make, and the most noisy. The light from the firing enabled me to discern our men and the British commingled; some holding each other, fighting, stabbing and cutting; others, with clubbed muskets, thrashing the enemy down with the buts; others running, or trying to run, across the stream, and all making the most hideous and indescribable noise imaginable.

This continued but a very short time, and the noise changed, so that the screams, implorations, cries and groans of our soldiers being murdered by the Indians, was all that could be heard, and that was fast passing away in death; when I began to seek a place of greater safety by groping my way up the ascending bank, and away from the stream, as I knew that removed me from the enemy.

In the mean time, I heard occasional discharges of artillery, at the distance of about two miles, between me and the lake on my left; but, not knowing they were signal-guns to show their position, I bore more to the right toward the road we had gone out on, and soon came near it, and halted to learn who were there, as I heard voices and footsteps. I soon satisfied myself they were two of our own men who had escaped; I therefore hailed them and told them who I was, and that I was alone. One said, "Let us be silent, and leave as fast as possible;" which we did until daylight, when we overtook a lieutenant and about twenty men, nearly all wet, mostly unarmed, and some wounded.

A hewed-log-house was soon seen on the road, surrounded by about twenty acres of cleared land. We soon arrived at it, and were ordered to halt, which all did, though some manifested some reluctance, but which was altogether useless with such a man as the lieutenant, as he had three dry soldiers who had been guards at the bridge and were driven from it after all fighting had ceased elsewhere. He said he was going to stay at that house until he had collected all who could hear a musket from the house, and ordered one fired then and at intervals of three minutes, and also immediately after each discharge of the cannon. Loopholes were made in the house by knocking out the chinking, the doors filled with rails about breast-high, and other preparations made for defence. In the meantime others arrived, so that at sunrise our party numbered over one hundred, all in about the same plight.

All that had been wounded, and all who had lost their muskets, were ordered to leave their ammunition and hasten back to the wagon-train and report themselves to the first officers they met. Having no baggage or arms, we traveled as might be expected of men who knew their proximity to the most relentless enemies; and, as the news of our disaster had already out-traveled us, we met no one until we were within five miles of Newark. Here we made a short halt, to examine the ground held by our enemies the day before, when they were attacked by our troops. It was difficult to realize the change that had taken place between the two armies in the short space of twenty hours after that point of time; and yet I could see but one cause to which to ascribe the change and sad disaster, and that was the bad behavior of General Winder.

After viewing the ground and making our reflections, we moved forward and soon met many officers, to whom we attempted to report ourselves; but all seemed so desirous of hearing the story of each individual, that we dispersed as if by general consent, and walked into the camp of a regiment of infantry lying in tents about one mile from Newark, where we spent the night resting ourselves.

I rose early in the morning, intending to go to Newark for breakfast; but, meeting with an officer I had seen the fall before, I was willingly persuaded to stay with him during the intense excitement that prevailed in the camp, and ascertain where my own company was. After breakfast, we went to the adjutant's office—the place of news in all armies—and heard about the same statement that now appears in our history of that sad affair, and that the remainder of our army was on its return. I therefore went, with another soldier, to get my rifle and knapsack left with Mr. Saddler.

We found him at home, and he appeared glad to see us, and insisted on our dining with him, which we did, and I stated to him what I had seen after I left him. He said he was very sorry for it; that he knew how the Indians acted on such occasions; that he once saw a war party butcher more than two hundred defenceless women and children of another nation he

5

was trading with, but he dared not betray the least compassion for them. They did not molest him because he was a trader. On our parting with him, he bid us come again and visit with him.

I have mentioned on another page that I would relate how this man was deprived of his happy home. It was in this wise: Our army spent the summer of 1813 in idleness, in the vicinity of Newark, and in September left to make the disgraceful campaign of General Wilkinson down the St. Lawrence to French Mills, and on leaving Newark wantonly set fire to the whole town and reduced it to ashes, Mr. Saddler's splendid mansion among the rest.

Accompanied by my martial friend, who carried my rifle and knapsack, we returned to camp, and soon after saw the remainder of General Chandler's shattered brigade pass by in a truly deplorable plight, one-half without shoes or caps, and many without arms. Having all my property together, I began to get it put in order, and had no difficulty or delay in doing so, as all seemed to regard me as a pet boy astray, and willingly helped me to clean my arms, clothes and boots.

Two days after, my own company, and that part of the army which had not been with General Chandler on the night of the disaster, came into the vicinity of Newark, and spent the summer in drilling and idleness. I immediately repaired to the camp and reported myself, and where I had been in search of the company since I was landed. The whole company appeared glad to see me, and expressed sorrow at my misfortune. But that could not relieve me, and I was discharged, under a surgeon's certificate, on the 24th of May, 1813, with one month's pay, and sent to Sackett's Harbor, on the small, swift schooner called "Lady of the Lake," arriving there on the second night afterwards.

I had been at home in quiet but one day, when the British fleet appeared in view, creating great alarm in the neighborhood. All the able-bodied men in the vicinity ran to the defence of Sackett's Harbor, except a few of the inhabitants along the shore where my father resided, who could see all the manœuvres of the British, and that, although the wind was fair for them to sail into the harbor, they were landing men on the western peninsula.

But we soon learned the cause of the men being landed there. A regiment of United States troops, in fourteen boats, were coasting along the peninsula, going to Sackett's Harbor, and the British placed some troops and Indians there to prevent the boats from landing, that they might capture them. The United States soldiers, seeing this, knew at once the fleet they saw was not ours, but belonged to the enemy, and ran their boats forthwith on shore, and made their escape as best they could through the enemy, passing round the bay and by my father's house that day to Sackett's Harbor, where they assisted in fighting them the next morning.

The British spent three hours in this manœuvre, while there was a good fair wind to carry them to Sackett's Harbor, and then directed their course thitherward; but the wind was falling fast, and soon ceased to blow, so that when their fleet was six miles from the town the lake became as still as a pan of milk.

Some superstitious persons present attributed this state of things to a special interposition of Providence to prevent the effusion of blood, but some others regarded it as a common yet very fortunate circumstance, as it gave us more time to prepare for their reception in a proper manner. It was very gratifying to our family, who all happened to be at home, as it afforded them a view of one of the grandest naval exhibitions ever presented to mortal eyes on this continent. A whole British fleet prepared for battle, becalmed in the bosom of one of the prettiest bays of the globe, with every sail spread, yet all hanging as loosely as a lady's apron, was a sight worth risking life to see, and will never be forgotten by any of us.

The British fleet remained in front of my father's house from five o'clock P. M. until dark, distant between two and three miles, while thousands viewed it from the shore on all sides, and wished our fleet that was gone up the lake would return and find these fellows here, thinking it would improve the scene.

There was no unnecessary alarm, as we all could see the full extent of the danger, and knew the necessity of the most prompt and energetic action, and all seemed willing to do whatever appeared necessary for the public safety. Before the sun set, all the women and children were removed from the vicinity of the lake, and all the men able to fight were in ranks on their way to the points designated for defence. My father had command of the picket-boat guard, and I proposed to go on duty with him, but he refused because I was able to row with but one hand. I therefore placed myself once more under command of Captain McNitt, whom I had been with at Gananaqua, and who then commanded his own company, posted to protect the left flank of the line of battle near the shore. This line of battle was formed by the late Major-General Jacob Brown, then a brigadier-general of the New York State militia, and was composed of such men as had been called out without formality on the same day, and others, old and young, who had come voluntarily to the defence of the place and put themselves into the ranks, without the hope of fee or reward, and in full view of the enemy prepared for battle. Their hearts were patriotic and true, but they lacked discipline and confidence in each other and in themselves, as not one in twenty ever saw a battle. The only shelter or defence they had was an irregular ridge or bank of sand and gravel, which the waves of the lake had thrown up on its shore, from one to three feet high. Behind this bank, 1,200 of this kind of troops, lying on their bellies, were to receive the attack and shock of 2,000 British troops, landing from forty barges and supported by the whole British fleet of Lake Ontario. The result was as might have been expected. The whole line gave an irregular and premature fire, and fled without order or halt to the woods in their rear. Captain McNitt had about one hundred men in his company, and over thirty of us had seen service; the result was, he received a more complimentary notice in the general's report than any other officer, and we shared the honor with him, for not one of us left him, but took fourteen prisoners, which showed we were not idle spectators of the scene. He has since been partially rewarded by being appointed keeper of the light-house erected near where the British landed, which office he has held since the establishment of the light, and although now above eighty years of age, takes pleasure in walking over the ground and showing visitors and strangers the different positions we occupied on the morning of the 29th of May, 1813, while fighting and defeating the British and killing their commander, General Grey, at the battle of Sackett's Harbor.

The particulars of the battle may be found in history of the war, and an account of the burning of the navy barracks and all the spoils taken at York.

Immediately after their defeat, the British hurried on board their fleet and sailed for Kingston, while we buried their dead. On the following day, which was Sunday, we buried our own dead, and returned home, having no further trouble with the British that summer, which was passed in making preparations for the fall campaign by the army in our vicinity and on the Niagara frontier.

In the following autumn, General Wilkinson began his ill-fated campaign down the St. Lawrence river, and concentrated his army in the vicinity of Sackett's Harbor, which roused the ambition of the war-loving youths of our neighborhood, and many volunteered for the campaign, myself among the rest.

I had become acquainted with an officer of the first regiment United States dragoons, who was recruiting at the village of Brownsville during the summer and wished to have me with him, and said his servant should groom my horse for me if I would enlist with him for the campaign, which I did most willingly. Three days after, we were ordered to rendezvous at Sackett's Harbor, and, on our arrival, were mustered in, it being the 30th of September, and left the next morning, without any drilling, for the active duties of the field.

The first thing learned in my new situation was to groom my own horse to avoid riding a poor one, and next to let no one ride it but myself. By attending to these two duties strictly, only transient and light duties were assigned to me, and heavy ones were avoided. My officers soon discovered I had a lame shoulder and how I came by it, and never called me forward to drill, but appeared to favor me as much as possible. I can never forget their kindness.

The autumn of 1813 was the most wet and rainy of any within my recollection. It commenced raining on the 20th of September where I was, and rained more or less every day, but one, for six full weeks. No soldier of General Wilkinson's army on that expedition will ever forget that rainy season while he recollects anything.

Grenadier Island, near the lower end of Lake Ontario, was the rendezvous of all the troops traveling in boats, and here the army was detained three weeks by a continuous rain; and it was said among the privates, in their tents, that our chief officers were as well soaked in brandy as we were in water while it lasted.

At length, when energy, patience and patriotism seemed quite exhausted, the order was given to advance down the river, the cavalry along the river by the road nearest the bank, the boats near our own shore to avoid any detention by the British, as they were moving down the river opposite us with a good army, and a lot of small armed boats to annoy our rear and pick up stragglers.

As the boats proceeded, their insolence would become unbearable, and a detachment of boats would have to be sent to drive them off, when they would shout, laugh and run back, or run to their friends on shore and offer battle, and when the detachment left them they would at once follow and renew their mischief. Thus we passed on to the vicinity of Ogdensburgh, opposite Prescott. Here the British had a good garrison, and we expected trouble in passing it, but for once our generals succeeded beyond their most sanguine expectation in passing it without the loss of a boat or a man in the profound darkness of the night and rain.

Ogdensburgh stands opposite Prescott, and the river Oswegatchie runs through the town and is crossed by a broad bridge. I was under command of Major Walback that night, and his command was in the rear of the column while passing through the town, and had just reached the bridge, when the British opened fire on the boats and on the town, but it was too late to injure us or the boats. We had passed them.

We had moved but a few miles further down the river before it became necessary to land and try the strength of the enemy in the field on their own territory. That part of the army in boats landed without seeing the enemy, and the scows that had brought the artillery came back and carried the cavalry over. After landing and being formed, we were immediately dispatched in search of the enemy. They were not hard to be found, and offered us business at once.

Not being of ourselves their equals, our officers reported

their position and appearance at headquarters, and we were sent in an opposite direction on a similar errand and with a similar result. It was found we were between two armies; we had seen them both, and a battle was inevitable.

We were in the township of Cornwall, on the farm of one Chrystler, a wealthy citizen, whose lands were divided by a considerable stream, then impassable except by bridges, of which there were two about two miles apart, one on the river road, the other farther north. Our army had landed below this stream, and prepared to stop the British above it on the west or right bank; but Chrystler had a stone house standing on an eminence near the river road, which, if held by either party, would command the passage of the bridge, and British infantry occupied it, apparently without support. This induced our generals to attempt to dislodge them. A battery of artillery was ordered over the bridge, and a column of infantry to support them, and our squadron of horse (held in readiness to follow any fugitives from the house) was immediately in rear of the infantry.

All being formed and in readiness, the march began at quickstep in the rain, and in less than twenty minutes the artillery had taken its position and began to unlimber, when a heavy column of British infantry appeared from behind the house and at once attacked the artillery before the infantry could be deployed to protect it, took several prisoners, and forced the whole column back in the greatest disorder.

This changed the movements of the day from attack to defence, and we were immediately sent to the upper bridge to stop the British crossing there and attacking us in flank, arriving just in time to save it from the possession of the enemy, who attacked us while we were tearing up the planks on it and drove us back, until a regiment came to our assistance from General Covington's brigade, who, hearing in that direction a brisk fire, came himself to learn what was the cause, and while he sat on his horse looking at us demolishing the bridge, he was mortally wounded and carried to his boat, where he died the next night. We were kept a short time in the same place, and then sent eastward to see what was being done there, and found that General Bissel had met the enemy coming up from Montreal and driven them back seven miles;

but that General Wilkinson had ordered the army to embark in their boats and cross to the other side of the St. Lawrence, and that it was being done rapidly.

There was no time to be lost. We galloped back to report, and found all the general officers had gone, and that Colonel Winfield Scott (the late veteran Lieutenant-General Scott) was commanding the twenty-fifth regiment of infantry which had been left to cover the retreat of the whole army.

He soon rode up to Major Walbach, and after a few minutes' private conversation we were marched slowly to the river, dismounted, and ordered to detach our swords from our persons and carry them in the scabbards in our hands. A few words of encouragement and caution were addressed to us, and then the order was given to mount and follow in open order by twos. We were already wet, and had often washed and swam our horses before; so we had nothing new to encounter but the intense coldness of the water and the greater weight on our horses than they had been accustomed to in swimming, which sank us lower in the water. There was no effort made to swim in a straight line to a particular point on the opposite shore, but to swim straight across the current; consequently we were nearly two miles lower down the river at landing than at our starting point. The infantry, having landed from their boats, saw us coming, and ran to assist us in rising from the water to the bank, which was of very difficult ascent at that place. On landing, the whole army was concentrated at French Mills, having accomplished nothing, and worse than nothing, for all the boats of the whole expedition were in a position that rendered them entirely useless, and the army in a worse condition, as it was at a great distance from its supplies, and in a wild and nearly uninhabited country, the St. Regis tribe of Indians being the chief inhabitants for many miles.

The whole army at once began to prepare rude winter quarters, except the dragoons, who were ordered to return to Sackett's Harbor to spend the winter. There, and in the vicinity, we were employed on patrols, scouts, and express lines, as there were no telegraphs, railroads, steam engines or balloons used by the army of 1813 in conveying intelligence. While engaged on one of the express lines, I assisted in conveying to the army the news of the burning of the Niagara frontier in retaliation for our burning the town of Newark.

In February, 1814, the army was removed from French Mills to the Niagara frontier, and that became the seat of war for the summer, while the strife at the east end of the lake was in ship building, some monuments of which remain to this day in the frames of two ships-of-the-line on their stocks, one at Dexter and the other at Sackett's Harbor, both on the same bay. The guarding of these two ship-yards formed the chief business of our army in that vicinity until about the 10th of June, when we were greatly relieved in the following unlooked for manner:

The British, having the superiority on the lake, blockaded Sackett's Harbor with their whole naval force, the American fleet lying within, waiting for the armament of the frigate Mohawk, which was in a fleet of boats coming by way of Oswego on Lake Ontario. The commander of the fleet of boats, fearing trouble on the lake, hired a band of Oneida Indians to escort the boats along the shore, and had proceeded to within twenty miles of Sackett's Harbor, opposite the mouth of Sandy Creek, when he discovered the whole British fleet at anchor but six miles ahead of him in his only passage. He therefore ran the whole of the boats into and up the creek about two miles, and placed the Oneida Indians in ambush along the west bank, within thirty yards of the deep narrow channel, and sent for assistance to the fleet and army. This was immediately dispatched. It consisted of two light pieces of artillery and our squadron of horse.

We arrived at the boats about two o'clock in the morning, and soon found there was to be no effort made to defend the boats, but to capture the enemy's, which consisted of one gunboat and six barges, manned with four hundred sailors and marines from the British fleet. They had waited during the night very silently, watching the mouth of the creek and searching the shore for a pilot, and had taken a very tall, thin, old gentleman and his three sons, by the name of Whittier, from their beds, to pilot them. But the Whittiers had just removed from Connecticut to that vicinity, and knew no more of Sandy Creek than of the river Senegal; and so the gunboat, followed closely by the barges, came into the deep, narrow creek, studded thickly on each side with alder—in which skulked the Indians, near the lake, on one side, and the neighboring militia, the dismounted dragoons, and artillerymen, crouched near the boats, on the other—just as the sun was rising, firing a large pivot-gun, charged with grape, canister and round shot, at random in all directions until they got near the boat landing, when the word "fire!" was given, and all immediately fired. The effect was terrible—one-fourth of the British had been killed or wounded.

Among the killed was the commander, who, when the gunboat first entered the creek, placed old Mr. Whittier in front of him, and at the firing, a musket-ball passed through the waistband of the old gentleman's pantaloons into the commander's abdomen, which killed him and threw him backwards into the hold, while he had so fast a grasp on the old shadow of a man (Mr. Whittier) as to pull him after and on him into the bottom of the boat, quite out of harm's way, and without injury to the old gentleman. The English immediately struck their colors, and screamed out, "Quarter!" "Murder!" and "Shame!" while the miserable Indians continued to fire until some of our officers ran up to the ford and actually knocked three of them down before they could be made to desist.

One hundred and thirty Britons were found to be killed or wounded, and two hundred and seventy were marched that day to Sackett's Harbor as prisoners. This loss of men reduced the strength of the enemy so much that Admiral Yoe withdrew his fleet to Kingston the next day, and we enjoyed quite a respite from the alarms of war in that vicinity up to the close of hostilities.

As soon as it was ascertained that the whole British squadron had withdrawn to Kingston, I was sent to General Brown's headquarters to inform him of what had transpired, and to return with his answer. I arrived at the general's headquarters on the 10th day of July, and delivered the message to him in person, he being an intimate friend of my father, and well acquainted with me. After reading the dispatches, he informed me that I would be kept at headquarters until the condition of our army should become changed, and act as guide, as I was well acquainted with the roads and country in that vicinity.

Two weeks followed before any change was attempted in our position, and I was each day on duty with the scouts, to learn the position of the enemy, and afford aids-de-camp Worth, Austin and Spencer opportunity to view and map the roads and farms in the vicinity, and on the direct road from Chippewa through Lundy's Lane to Queenstown, General Drummond's headquarters at that time.

Early on the morning of the 25th of July, two aids-de-camp called on General Brown and received orders to approach as near the camp of the British as they should think prudent, estimate their numbers, and report what they might discover of their movements, positions or intentions. They were soon in their saddles, and, accompanied by four dragoons and myself, proceeded down the road about two miles, when, emerging from a narrow strip of woodland, the British army appeared in line of battle, slowly advancing in the most perfect order and beauty before us, with their left wing reaching to and protected by the Niagara river, and their right extending into the woods northwardly. Lieutenant Spencer and one dragoon immediately returned to report at headquarters, while Lieutenant Worth proceeded to the front of the enemy's right wing, then in the woods, to learn their intentions. We soon met their scouts, who drove us back, but not before we had seen their pioneers cutting a new road by which to advance their artillery.

It was then evident the enemy had chosen this spot for their battle-ground, and that there would be no time lost on our part to begin the fight. The tremendous roar of the mighty Niagara, the din of preparation for battle, the rough voices of officers marshaling their battalions, the cracking of the whips of drivers and prancing of steeds, kept from the mind all contemplation of the impending dangers that threatened, and qualified all for the bloody struggle that followed. There appeared no disposition in either army to hurry or delay until all appeared in readiness. The weather was fine and clear, the ground dry and nearly level, and, all things considered, the strength of the two armies about equal. At about two o'clock P. M., our skirmish line in the woods on the British right wing commenced a brisk fire on a party who were protecting the enemy's pioneers while cutting a new road, and drove them all behind their flank, who returned the fire, and continued to fight until the action became general.

My duty was to act as guide, as I was well acquainted with the woodlands as well as farms in that vicinity, and while the sun was above the horizon I was kept very active in guiding different officers to and from that part of the field to General Brown's headquarters. On one of these trips, Lieutenant Spencer was mortally wounded, and fell from his horse, between mine and his own, holding to the bridles of both—one of the most painful sights I had ever seen, as he was a young and most amiable man, and one of my dearest friends. After his fall, I was under the immediate orders of Lieutenant Worth during the battle, and witnessed some of its most exciting episodes—that is, as much as a person could see on a field where ten thousand men were fighting ten hours with each other on one square mile of ground, in a perfect calm of the atmosphere, while a dense cloud of smoke hung over us, hiding both sun and moon (which was nearly full) from our view.

It is difficult to bring the imagination to realize the tremendous roar of the Falls of Niagara, the thunders of the artillery, the crash of musketry, and the shouts of battle, and yet consider the actors sane who could voluntarily participate in it with pleasure. Yet such was the case on that day. No one was ever charged with dereliction of duty on that memorable occasion, or with failing to exert his whole ability to achieve a victory.

The line of battle had been formed by General Scott's brigade, composed of the ninth, eleventh and twenty-second regiments of infantry, and Captain Towson's battery of artillery, with the twenty-fifth infantry to support it, near the river, at right angles with Lundy's Lane, or Queenstown road. When the battle had raged with the utmost fury for more than two hours, without any visible effect other than the loss of near one-fourth of those engaged, General Brown interposed the second brigade between the first and the enemy, and, bringing forward the whole corps of Major Hindman's artillery, the greatest exertions were made to break the British line, until it began to be too dark to write an order, when Lieutenant Worth (afterwards the celebrated General Worth), being wounded, sent me around the British right wing to ascertain if their artillery—then posted on a little hill before our left—were receiving reinforcements.

Being in the woods near our extreme left, I took an old timber road, and soon passed round their artillery and down a ravine in rear of their line of battle, beyond its centre, where I halted a moment to view the grandeur of the scene, which was sublime beyond description, the shot from Towson's artillery passing over my head, the earth trembling under my feet by the falling of the waters of Niagara and the thunders of the battle. As I mounted my horse to proceed, I saw a group of men between me and the British line, and as I gazed one of them turned round in such a position that by the light of the flashes I saw a star on the breast of his coat, and other badges of distinction about his person. Immediately after, I rode toward the river, and soon found myself among a detachment of our troops under Captain Ketchum, who had passed round the British left wing; and on my informing him what I had seen, he took me back to the group, with his party, as a guide. On our approaching them, I pointed out the man, and he called out to us, "What the devil are you falling back here for?" Captain Ketchum sprang on him, saying, "Hush! you are a prisoner!" Others seized five more of the group, and, throwing all six on their horses, forced them as fast as possible through and behind our line, when one of the British asked why we had not brought the "old man;" and, upon our inquiring who he meant by "old man," he said he meant Lieutenant-General Drummond, who was in the group, and we had only brought off Major-General Rial and one of his aids, and one of General Drummond's aids, and their grooms, and let the largest game escape—which was true. But it was useless to murmur, and no time was spent in that way.

It was then near nine o'clock, and every man present that could be expected. Two vigorous efforts had been made without effect to gain possession of the enemy's artillery. Col. James Miller then placed his command directly in front of it, and by a steady, quick, unfaultering movement swept over the hill, capturing every piece of it, and giving the most deafening shout I ever heard. It was instantly taken up and repeated by our entire line and the whole reserve.

Total darkness and silence for an instant followed, for a thick cloud of smoke hid the full moon. Soon, however, Towson (as General Brown said) "illuminated the heavens with the constant blaze of his artillery," and the battle continued another hour with great slaughter on both sides.

The British seemed to think they could not fight without their artillery, and returned and made two desperate efforts to retake it, but failed. They had taken off with them the horses, limbers, rammers and matches, and thus kept us from using them against themselves that night.

During this last exciting hour I had been on several trips for Lieutenant Worth (who was wounded) to and from General Brown to General Scott on the left, and General Ripley still farther to the left in the woods on our extreme left wing, and in every place I heard sad complaints of thirst, but not a word of fatigue or hunger.

Each army had now in turn had possession of the little hill that the strife had been for, and each had been twice foiled in attacking it; each had lost about one thousand of their best men for it, and now neither of them desired it. The British had come first on the ground, and they left it first, but in good order, carrying off their dead and wounded; and, on their leaving, our army did the same, leaving all their cannon except two small pieces, in good order, and retired to our former camp through a narrow strip of woods that was immediately behind our line of battle and had afforded shelter to our wounded from the commencement of the action.

About two hours after the firing ceased, I accompanied General Brown's aid-de-camp, Austin, over the field by moonlight. The dead and wounded had been removed from that bloodstained field, which had so lately been the scene of such frightful conflict and slaughter, and naught was heard but the roar of Niagara and the tread of our horses. The ground was nearly covered with the débris of battle, dead horses, torn clothes, broken arms, cartridge wrappers and torn-off ends of cartridges, for about three quarters of a mile, which was the whole distance on the road where so many brave men fell. We lingered about the neighborhood until after daylight, expecting General Ripley to return with our army, but were disappointed; he did not return.

After daylight, a party of British horse appeared in sight, and we retired unseen into the woods to observe their movements. They examined their artillery, and about sunrise the limbers and artillery horses arrived, when all the guns but two were hurried off, and a little later two ox teams hauled off those still without horses, and the dragoons followed them.

No signs of our army appearing, about nine o'clock Captain Austin returned to camp, and found Generals Brown and Scott had both gone to Buffalo, wounded. Thus terminated the battle of Bridgewater, or Lundy's Lane.

It may be a gratification to some of the survivors of that army to know that one of their number has since served three campaigns in the war with Mexico, and is yet in as good health as when he participated in that sanguinary struggle, and has written this account of it, in 1867, in his own autobiography.

This sanguinary battle having been fought without any very apparent advantage to either army, all due honors were paid the dead without the least molestation. All who had escaped wounds appeared thankful, and those who had received any seemed equally thankful that they were no worse.

Several days passed quietly, but a strict watch was kept on the enemy to learn their designs. This gave me a pleasant duty—to ride about the neighborhood and guide the scouts—until our army fell back to Fort Erie, when I was sent back again to Sackett's Harbor with a full report of the battle of Lundy's Lane, and spent the remainder of the campaign in bearing orders and messages from one officer to another at different places.

About the close of the campaign of 1814, the New England States began to elect the delegates to the celebrated Hartford Convention, and it was soon whispered that our regiment was to be concentrated at Greenbush to observe their traitorous movements, and disperse them when necessary.

In the hight of our anticipation of such a trip, the news of peace, the adjournment of the Hartford Convention, and the victory of New Orleans, arrived about the same time. The news of peace was received without any great demonstration of joy; and the victory at New Orleans was so very unexpected and complete that it appeared fabulous at that juncture, and we waited for a confirmation of its truth until it would have been in bad taste to rejoice, as the battle was fought three weeks after the treaty of Ghent had been signed. At the sound of peace, the delegates to the Hartford Convention skulked so quickly out of sight, and shrank from public notice, that it has ever since been considered quite a feat to find one of them and compel him to acknowledge it.

Thus ended the war of 1812, and all of us who had enlisted for the war were discharged, and I returned home to prosecute the arts of peace.

CHAPTER IX.

THE LAST DAYS OF MY YOUTH AND THE DEATH OF MY FATHER.

During the war of 1812, there existed in the United States two great political parties. The first and largest had declared the war and prosecuted successfully their declaration, and was denominated the Democratic party. The second and smaller, but still a large party, opposed the declaration of war, and was called the Federal party, and between the two parties a hostility existed little short of civil war. To such length was this spirit carried, that every person was presumed to belong to one party or the other, and to conceal his predilection was to incur the contempt of both and endanger his own popularity. My father belonged to the former, and was well known; while I, being yet in nonage, and having served in the army through the war, was regarded as an active partisan waiting to enter the arena on the same side, and possessing some influence with young men.

I had not laid aside my uniform clothing when my father advised me to review my classic studies before I prosecuted the study of a profession any further. I therefore made application to the faculty of Hamilton College, Oneida county, New York, to enter the junior class, then nearly half through that year's studies. I was informed I would be required to undergo an examination, and if my education was *quantum sufficit*, and I deposited the tuition fee for the whole junior year, I would be admitted. I at once assented, and deposited the required thirty dollars.

The next morning at nine o'clock was appointed for my examination by the President, who began a very studied inquiry into my father's pecuniary circumstances and his political views, which, in the frankness of my heart, I honestly and truly answered. He seemed pleased with the favorable account I gave of his condition in life, and suggested that "a part of it could now be used to great advantage for his son's advancement," and gave other hints that I could have understood at a later period in life, but did not then, as I did not dream that ten eagles would have more weight with that son of Minerva than ten months of assiduous study in advancing a student's position, and therefore left without leaving him a bribe, and retired to my hotel, where I anxiously waited for the appointed hour. I was punctual in my attendance, but after long delay learned that the Doctor had gone sleigh-riding, leaving no message for me. I was much disappointed, and at great loss to account for this strange conduct in the President of a college, and so expressed myself to Mr. Strong, Professor of Languages, there present, who then asked me to read and translate a page in Homer's Iliad, which I did (as he said) satisfactorily, and left. An hour later the President entered, and said, "Your studies are spread through all the field of science. I advise you at the next commencement to take the degree of Master of Arts, and not class." Having no knowledge of the real definition of these words, I made no reply, but warmed my feet at the fire. The Doctor then asked for my certificate of studies and character. I told him my father had been my teacher, and that he would be there the next week. This ended my education at this institution, as I was informed that my father's certificate would not be recognized as proof of the character or qualifications of his own son. I therefore withdrew and reviewed my studies alone, and am indebted to no college for a certificate that I am a scholar or a graduate of it.

My father and mother arrived the next week, on their way to visit my paternal grandmother, then eighty-five years of age,

6

at Brookfield, New York. I accompanied them, and spent about ten days with this most learned of my ancestors, who alone had educated my father, and could at that advanced age read and translate both Greek and Latin like any professor of those languages. Her mind and memory were yet brilliant, and she expressed the pleasure and satisfaction she felt on hearing me read Latin and Greek, saying I was the only one of her grandchildren she ever expected to hear translate the ancient languages. At that late period of her life, she related to me most of the brief history of her family found in this book.

After my return home, I prosecuted my studies with great diligence, until September, 1815, when I went to Lowville, Lewis county, New York, to study law with Ela Collins, Esq., a counsellor of great learning and merit. I had been but a few weeks there, when my father sent a messenger, with a horse, and a request that I would return home and take charge of his business. I had observed before I left home that my father's health seemed on the decline; but I could not believe that so great a change in his appearance, as I saw on my return, could have been effected in so short a space of time, though he was each day walking about his house and garden. I expressed to him the alarm I felt at his feeble appearance and frightful cough. He replied, "The doctor has taken me through a regular salivation, which is the cause of my apparent prostration. I hope to be more free of the cough in a few days, and regain my strength. Lest, however, I should be disappointed and leave my business in confusion, I wish you to settle with every one. Pay all balances I may owe, and take notes for what is due me."

I did as he directed, while he was gradually sinking each day, having received his directions how to act after his death. One evening, shortly after this, as I was holding him up in my arms in his bed, he said, "Lay me down, my son." As I did so, I saw he was expiring, and immediately called our family and friends from adjoining rooms, as I had been left alone with him a few moments while his watchers took a little refreshment, it being eleven o'clock at night, November 23d, 1815. He died apparently free from pain, and without a struggle or groan, in the forty-ninth year of his age, leaving a widow and eight children, of whom I was the eldest, having but just entered on the twenty-first year of my age. This was a sad affliction, and was deeply felt by every member of the family; yet as we were left with plenty of good productive property, we had it still in our power to select our own occupation in life.

I had already elected to become a scholar, and was well advanced. My eldest brother, Samuel, then in his nineteenth year, determined to become a farmer, and was well qualified for the occupation. We have both since distinguished ourselves in our respective occupations, and are in affluence; but we did not, at that trying season, forsake our mother or our brothers and sisters in their affliction, but remained at home and cultivated the farm one season, and then procured one of our cousins to take charge of it. We then divided an unproductive piece of land, detached from the old estate, as our shares, and left the family in plenty and entirely free of debt or any embarrassment. My brother cultivated his land as a farm, while I sold mine for funds to prosecute my studies.

During the twenty-first year of my life, I was very much exercised on religious doctrines, and I gave the subjects then presented to my mind a full and careful examination, the result of which was that I became as firmly established in my religious belief as I ever can be; and so, on the 9th of March, 1816, was baptised by immersion, and united with the Baptist church of the town of Henderson, Jefferson county, New York. I continued a member of that church more than three years, when they gave me a letter of dismission, which I still retain, with the fellowship of all Baptists.

CHAPTER X.

FIRST DAYS IN MANHOOD AND LAST DAYS IN NEW YORK.

When I arrived at the age of twenty-one years, on the 15th of October, 1816, I had taken a survey of the world and formed a plan of life, which had been greatly deranged by the death of my father, and the loss of a year from my studies in arranging his estate so that no part of it would be liable to waste. I had also felt the crushing weight of disappointment by the death of my beloved classmate, and my arrangements were of necessity to be formed anew. Still I was not discouraged. I had now to rely solely on my own exertions. I therefore resolved to use the means yet left in my power to acquire that knowledge which places its possessor in the front ranks of society and usefulness.

In my intercourse with men of all ranks and conditions of life, I had observed with what silence and tenacity Free Masons adhered to, aided and assisted each other and their families in all the ramifications of life and business; and I determined to become one, and learn what this great secret was that so many persons desired to know. Accordingly, on the day of my arrival at majority, I presented my petition where I was best known, to Lodge No. 356, in the town of Henderson, Jefferson county, New York. I was accepted, and initiated November 16th, 1816. I found the Order what I supposed it was, and the brethren found in me what they supposed I was, so far as I ever learned, since I spared no expense or pains to make myself acquainted with all the different degrees in their order, and the lectures appertaining to each, as fast as the rules of the Order permitted, and have always communicated that knowledge to others entitled to it without fee or reward.

I was the first Free Mason who taught the lectures on the degrees of Royal Arch and Knight Templars on the west side of the Mississippi river. I taught them first to the late George H. C. Melody, while I was the High Priest of Missouri Royal Arch Chapter, in the year 1823. I was again High Priest of that chapter in 1846; and in whatever position I was called to act, I was always sustained by the whole weight of my brethren Companions or Sir Knights; so that a brother's widow's tear or his orphans' cries were never heard or seen by my wife, who was always near me (with an open hand, like a Quakeress, as she was) to alleviate the wants and distresses of the poor. And now, since she has "gone to that bourne from whence no traveler returns," I trust that, in like manner, my only child may escape that pain; but if, in the course of human events, she should not escape so painful a scene, she may take the same pleasure in performing her duties as her parent has done before her in the same Order of which she now has the honor of being a member.

About the 20th of November, 1816, I returned to study with Mr. Collins, whose father-in-law—the Rev. Isaac Clinton, of the Presbyterian Church of Lowville, a most profound scholar—was at that time the preceptor of the academy at that place, a Mason, and a most influential literary gentleman, and had in his private residence one of the very best libraries I ever visited. It was always open to me, because my father and he were scholars and very good friends, and, my father being dead, I fell as a son under his advice and direction—although I was a Mason much in advance of him—and enjoyed the advantage of his life-long experience and acquaintance, as well as that of his literary friends and men of that taste who visited his house and the institution.

This introduced me as a teacher into the town of Martinburgh, about three miles distant, at a good liberal salary. I had been in ten battle-fields, but never had felt such trepidation or want of nerve as when I was introduced into that school and walked forward to address it. There were about sixty scholars present, of all ages from seven to seventeen, in their best attire and most pleasing countenances, a good majority of whom were ladies. The opening of the school was by prayer, and with profound decorum, which was always observed, and no Sunday school preserved better order than did my day school for four months, at the end of which term I closed it with an exhibition, and, on parting, received many tokens of kindly regard from my pupils and their parents.

This school established my character as a teacher, and I

afterwards taught two years in Lowville academy, Lewis
county, New York, with Stephen W. Taylor as principal, and
studied law at the same time. After a while I relinquished
that situation for a much larger salary in Adams, Jefferson
county, where I was untrammeled, as I was near my own
home, in the vicinity of which I was well known. In this
school I taught Ezekiel W. Robbins, afterwards a Senator in
the State of Illinois, and his two brothers, both of whom
subsequently distinguished themselves in their profession, as
well as several others, who taught in St. Louis, and in Alton,
Illinois, with great credit to themselves.

In the spring of 1819, I had all the arrangements made
to leave for Missouri, to spend my life in the West; but while
I was waiting for a passage on some vessel going to Niagara,
I was invited to deliver a course of Masonic lectures to
the Masonic Brethren and Companions of the forty-ninth
regiment of British infantry at Kingston, Upper Canada.
The invitation was accepted, and I accompanied the committee of invitation on their return, and was by them introduced to the assembled Brethren and Companions, and heard
their report read, accepted, and the committee discharged.
An adjournment was then had for dinner, and as I was
invited to dine with so many I was for a moment perplexed
for an answer as to whom I should accompany, but soon
rallied, and taking the arm of him I thought the eldest, I
told the brethren I would accept all their invitations in the
order of the age of those giving them. This seemed satisfactory to all, and I remained with them four months, until the
1st of October, 1819, lecturing every day on the several
Masonic degrees, from the lowest to the highest.

In the meantime, a military school was in session in the
building adjoining, four days in each week, for the instruction of young officers and officers' sons, and I was invited
to attend and enjoy all the advantages the school afforded,
which invitation I accepted, and there studied the British
rules of war under Masonic brethren.

Having determined to visit the cities of New York and
Washington on my way to the West, I left Canada and
arrived in New York about the 10th of October, 1819, and
began to explore the city. I visited a Masonic Lodge on the

evening of my arrival, and formed several new acquaintances there, among them two who were assisting in fitting out a ship for the Columbian Republic. They informed me that an agent of that republic was in the city, and would, they thought, be pleased to form my acquaintance; and one of them insisted on my going home with him and being introduced to the agent that night. Being idle, I was easily persuaded; so I went and was introduced to him, was sworn to secrecy in the whole transaction, and had the entire scheme explained to me, which 'was to fit out three ships in New York for the republic, and with them and a few landsmen seize Texas, make it a State of that republic, and a naval depot—cruise about Cuba and take all the Spanish ships possible and run them into the State, and so draw a great population of North Americans thither—destroy the Spanish commerce and assist in compelling Spain to acknowledge the independence of all her American possessions, and then make a peace and commercial treaties with them. War with Spain and the United States seemed inevitable at that time, and their coöperation was expected in the enterprise. The inducements presented to me to enter into it were so great that I abandoned my journey to Missouri and accepted the appointment of purser in the Columbian navy, and entered at once on the discharge of the duties of the office for the three ships then fitting out in New York.

I was quite ignorant of the duties of the office, but having procured an experienced clerk, who had been in the United States navy six years, I was enabled to give good satisfaction to those above me, and we had the three ships nearly ready for sea, when, on the 28th day of December, we learned that Don Mateo de la Serna, Chargé d' Affaires, had complained to our government that we were fitting out three ships in New York to cruise against Spain, which he represented at Washington and demanded our arrest. With the demand he assured our Secretary of State that Spain would ratify the treaty made by the Spanish Minister, Don Onis, ceding Florida to the United States and receiving Texas in exchange. This ruined our enterprise, as the United States marshal of New York had orders to stop and search the ships and arrest all concerned in fitting them for sea.

I was notified of my danger by a Knight Templar, and retired to another part of the city, sent a Masonic brother to the marshal's office to procure a list of the names of those to be arrested, notified all the officers of the state of our affairs, and appointed a place in the upper part of the city for a general consultation to be held there to determine on future action. I had in my possession seventy-one Columbian bonds of one thousand dollars each, seventy of which I made a special deposit of in bank, where they remained more than sixteen years. One I kept with me all that length of time, and sold it with the rest in May, 1836, for sixty-eight cents on the dollar and interest for seventeen years at seven per centum per annum, which amounted to nearly seventy-three thousand dollars, with which I paid every dime due for fitting, arming and victualing those ships.

Having procured a suitable room for our purpose, about sixty assembled, all of whom had been studying the Spanish language and drilling with muskets preparatory for the Columbian service, or who had advanced funds to fit out the expedition. I had procured a full list of the names of those to be arrested, numbering forty-three, of which number my name was placed the fifth. On the meeting being called to order, one of the eight captains present stated the object of the assemblage to be to make known to each individual our true condition, and to adopt a course of future action, either jointly or severally. A committee was then appointed to state in a preamble our true condition and present resolutions for our future course. I was named second on the committee, and saw at a glance I was expected to extricate the whole party from this difficulty, and that I could not avoid the task. Being in possession of all the facts and all the funds, I thought they constituted sufficient force, if well managed by me, to accomplish it, and therefore made no excuse, but set myself about it.

I paced the committee room and dictated the preamble and resolutions, while another wrote them out in full. The preamble set forth our true condition, and the necessity for speedy action 'and united effort to relieve ourselves from it. The resolutions were, that we would as one man abandon the expedition and accept of forty per centum in full for all we had advanced for fitting out the expedition; that we would never separate until we had thrown into the East river all our arms, consisting of a battery of eight pieces of field artillery, thirty pieces of naval artillery, six hundred muskets, four hundred pistols and sabres; that the purser should sell so much of the stores as would raise the amount of the forty per centum advanced for the outfit, and that when we should have received the said forty per centum we would leave the city of New York and not re-enter it until the 10th of February, 1820; and that the purser should have our consent and authority to return the three ships to their original owners on such terms as he should think just and equitable. The preamble and resolutions passed unanimously. It was eleven o'clock at night when we adjourned to meet at twelve o'clock on board the Eagle, at the foot of Twenty-fifth street, on the East river, going there by twos on different streets.

The first thing done after being on board was to awaken the sailors, some fifteen in number, who, with about the same number of our party skilled in naval affairs, worked the ship from the wharf into the middle of the river, partly by sails and partly by barges with oars, where it was anchored about opposite Eighteenth street, and the cable paid out at different times to scatter the arms and shot so that they could not be recovered. Two cold and anxious hours of my life passed there, when the hold was thrown open and the stevedores descended and began to raise the arms and shot to the deck, and we to cast them overboard. This employed us five hours, until sunrise, when we had thrown everything overboard that was thought likely to confiscate the ship.

The other two ships had no arms of any kind on board, and the uniform clothing for one thousand men of all arms, in a warm climate, was all that could excite suspicion. The arms, ammunition and clothing had all been purchased in England, and no part of it opened since its importation. It had been immediately transferred from the deck of the ship in which it was imported to the decks of the ships of the Columbians, as we denominated ourselves.

Having finished our task, all went into the cabin, and most of them assisted the captain as much as we could in consuming the liquid part of his stores provided for the contemplated but abandoned voyage. They also adjourned to meet again, according to my request, at seven o'clock in the evening at the same place where we had last met, to hear my report of what I should be able to do in the way of raising funds to be distributed. We were then landed in the city by the ship's barges in three parties, and dispersed. A revenue cutter boarded and searched the ship before noon, but discovered nothing, and left her unmolested otherwise.

On landing, I repaired immediately to one of my Masonic brethren for advice and assistance. He said I needed only to employ a commercial brother, and with such a large job to operate on, I could raise twenty-five per cent. on my invoices. He went with me and introduced me to one who was an Englishman and a Mason, and made known my business. The broker advised to move the two ships at once alongside of British ships loading for Liverpool, and to transfer the stores to them, and send them for sale to firms there who had houses in New York, and have the house here advance the funds necessary, as it was a very common way of doing business. I consented to this, as I was too ignorant to attempt anything else, and dared not venture into a public place for other suggestions. I therefore sent written requests to the two captains to move the two ships and transfer the stores to two British ships which were named. The messenger returned with an answer to the effect that the captains were both absent, and the ships could not be removed without their order; but as the freight was under my control, they would deliver it to whomsoever I directed from their decks. The broker then made arrangements with the British to receive the stores from our decks. This manœuvering consumed so much time that it was two o'clock P. M. before the ships were alongside each other. However, late as it was, sufficient stores of rice, peas, beans, flour and pork had been transferred to enable me to obtain an advance of six thousand dollars, with which I was able to pay the forty per centum of the amount furnished by eleven captains and forty-eight lieutenants, who had advanced fifteen thousand one hundred dollars to purchase the arms we had thrown overboard in the morning.

Fearing some accident or miscarriage if I took that money into my own possession, I persuaded the broker to accompany me, with the money in his pocket, to our place of meeting, and had him pay it over. All seemed well satisfied with my action that night as they took their pay, and I thought that I deserved their good will at least, for I had done what they directed by resolution. But it resulted otherwise, and a very trivial act seemed to be the cause of great annoyance to me afterwards. I had a full list of all engaged in the expedition in alphabetical order, and their rank, and paid them in that order, and took their receipts in full from each separately. There being fifty-nine present, it was midnight before we were through.

In the meantime, some of those first paid had returned half drunk or more, and no one having authority to keep order, all was hurry and noise until we came to the last one to be paid, when he saw there yet remained but two twenty dollar notes of the six thousand dollars, he having been out drinking with those first paid. He seemed to think we intended to pay him no more, and although I took forty dollars from my own pocket and gave it to the broker, who paid him (without taking his receipt) the whole eighty dollars due him, yet, instead of leaving the city, as he promised to do, he visited all three of the ships on the next day inquiring for me, and having a stranger with him, who I suspected might be a United States deputy marshal, to arrest me. His presence in the city, his knowledge of all our transactions, his causeless apparent hostility to me, and the evident uselessness of a longer stay in the city, determined me to leave at once and seek a place of greater safety. I took the broker to the three principal creditors and stated as near as I could the condition of all that was left for them; that I was going to take only one hundred and twenty dollars more of the broker, which would leave me exactly as great a sufferer as the rest of the party, and that when I sold the seventy-one Columbian bonds I would pay them what remained due after they should have collected the net proceeds of the sale of the stores and forty thousand pounds of powder concealed in flour barrels in the hold of the Eagle, and seven thousand pounds of lead.

The creditors were all Masons, and each had my receipt for the stores furnished by himself, and it was agreed that each should collect the balance of the proceeds after six thousand one hundred and twenty dollars was deducted from it *pro rata* on the invoices I held, and I gave orders for the bills of lading to be made in the name of those who furnished the stores, and returned to them their own bills to enable them to do it correctly. I also gave the largest creditor an order for my purser's books and papers, and authority to discharge my clerk then on the Eagle and pay him out of funds in the office, and credit me with what remained.

The utmost confidence at that day prevailed among us. There was no such thing as *secession* thought of then among us. My brethren did not even ask me what I had done with the Columbian bonds which they knew were delivered to me when I gave bond and took the oath of office as purser in the navy. It was then the last day of the year, on Saturday. I had done, as I thought, all I could for my friends—I had spent ten weeks uselessly in the city—expended nearly one half of the money I had started with—was bound to leave the city to seek a new home and dared not appear in the public streets of New York. Perplexed as to the road I should take from the city, I spent the remainder of the day in endeavoring to determine on some fixed course of future action. It was winter, the day cold and cloudy, and my spirits and hopes at a low ebb, when I determined to leave the city and State by crossing the ferry into New Jersey, which I did in a barge, it being the usual conveyance of pedestrians at that time, and took lodgings near the ferry landing for the night.

CHAPTER XI.

A YEAR OF WANDERINGS, EXPLORATIONS AND INQUIRIES, WITH NEW SCENES AND UNDERTAKINGS.

On the first day of January, 1820, I was without any employment or fixed plan for the future. It was winter, cold and cloudy. The shipping was lying in the river before the town apparently idle, and my future prospects seemed as dreary and barren as the scenes about me; for it was Sunday, and I kept within doors to avoid meeting any of my late comrades.

In the evening, a gentleman from Patterson came over from New York, where he had spent the day, and left a friend whom he had brought down in a dearborn wagon (as the vehicle was called), and was to return home the next morning. There being two beds in my chamber, he was introduced as a kinsman, and we soon formed an acquaintance as Masons, spent the night like two old friends together, and started for Patterson at daylight toward his home, as he was in a great hurry to return to his business. I was so entirely without occupation that I could start on the shortest notice, my baggage being all contained in a pair of saddlebags and the pockets of my overcoat. When this gentleman found I was so familiar with the Masonic lectures, he flattered himself he could learn them in a very short time; but being a machinist, and having several journeymen at work for him, he had very little time to devote to anything else, the ten hour system of labor being then unrecognized in the world. The consequence was, I had to stay a week of Sundays, or seven weeks, to gratify him and his friends there. He manufactured, among other things, carding machines, and had two ordered to be sent to Elmira, in Chemung county, New York. When the wagons came for them, I was introduced to the owners, who were also brother Masons, and they invited me to go with them and see the country. As the wagons were comfortably provided with painted water-proof covers, I gladly accepted the invitation and accompanied them, and nearly forgot my disappointments on the hilly road and interesting journey, arriving at Elmira in far better spirits than I had left the last three places.

Soon after my arrival, I met with Dr. Tiffin, of Olean, Cateraugus county, New York, who was at Elmira, and on the point of returning home alone in a sleigh. This gentleman invited me to ride home with him, which I did. We reached Olean on the 2d of March, and I waited there until April 15th, assisting him in collecting his debts in lumber, amounting to ten thousand dollars, as money was very scarce and he could obtain his payments in nothing else. This amount of lumber formed two large rafts of one hundred thousand feet each, which he brought into the Ohio river and sold at Marietta and Maysville. I was obliged to stay with him until he sold this last raft, as I had lent him all my money at Olean to enable him to run his rafts to Pittsburgh, and had taken this as security, which he sold on the 3d day of July, at Maysville, Kentucky, and paid me back my money, and as much as I would take for the use of it and four months' time in assisting him in his business. He then took me by my hand and said he wished to testify his gratitude to me by presenting me with a complete suit of clothes, which he immediately purchased at a clothing store near by.

On our way to the store, a tailor named Ephraim Harris, with whom Dr. Tiffin was acquainted, met us, and the doctor took him along with us to assist in selecting the clothes. After being fitted to my satisfaction, and my friend had bid me a final adieu, Mr. Harris accompanied me to my lodgings, and, being aware that I did not intend leaving town that day, he invited me to go to a family boat he was occupying and spend the afternoon, to which I acceded, and was not long in discovering the object he had in view when inviting me there. It was to afford himself a better opportunity of making his situation and wants known to me than he then had or could have anywhere else, and, by presenting all the facts before me, to be able to induce me to render him that assistance which he stood so much in need of, among strangers at that time. He had his wife with him, to whom he had been married about six or seven months. They had both been born and raised in the city of Norwich, Connecticut, had never travelled before, were very religious, had done no other business than tailoring, and knew very little more of the ways of the world when they left their native city to make this journey by themselves, than Adam and Eve did when the serpent made his appearance in the garden. The consequence was they had been cheated, robbed, delayed, imposed upon and swindled out of their money, and finally left penniless among strangers, with their scanty baggage, on a small family boat, in which they had stayed two days, and had each in turn been through the whole town in search of work, but had found none. This was their condition. Yet their confidence in

God was as firm as ever, and it seemed He did not forsake them; for they persuaded me to purchase the family boat they then were in and accompany them to the end of their journey at Belleville, Illinois, and pay all their expenses on the way. I saw they were like two little helpless children left in a wilderness, while I had all the means necessary to relieve them and make them happy; and the providence of their God, in whom they had so much confidence, had caused them both to see it while I was busily measuring plank on the shore near them.

I had intended to purchase a horse and visit Chillicothe, Xenia, Dayton, and Cincinnati; then, taking the road westward, to pass through the States of Indiana and Illinois, and so arrive at St. Louis, Missouri. This had all to be abandoned if I attempted to assist them. I had had no introduction to either of them, but from their appearance I gave credence to their statements and told them I would assist them. This seemed to complete their earthly happiness and more firmly establish their reliance on the providence of God, if it were possible to make it stronger than it was before. I therefore purchased the family boat, took my baggage and a small quantity of provisions on board, and pushed the boat into the current of the Ohio, which moved then at the rate of about two miles per hour.

We had scarcely floated out of sight of the town when Mr. Harris reminded his wife of their especial indebtedness to providence vouchsafed to them by God for their relief, and that now was the proper time to acknowledge it. They then brought forward their old Bible and hymn books, and he read one of David's psalms and selected a hymn, which they both joined in singing in the most devout manner. They then knelt down, and he first and she secondly offered the most humble and sincere thanks to Almighty God for his kindness and protection that I have ever heard uttered in my long life. I have since been present on great occasions when solemn *Te Deum* has been sung, but never when such piety and sincerity were manifested as was exhibited by those two humble christians on that little boat as we floated down the Ohio.

How far the prayers of those two pious people offered up

on that voyage have effected my welfare I have no way of
learning now, but that that meeting with them has affected my
course in life, and those now around me, more than any other
single circumstance, I have no doubt; and that it will continue
to affect not only my own family but others, and even generations of families who will never see or hear of me or either of
them, I am equally sure.

The current of the river was so gentle and its bosom so
smooth that there was not the least danger of an accident,
and we all went to sleep at night and let the boat float, feeling
the same security as if our homely craft had been tied to a
tree on the shore. The boat seldom struck anything, and
if it did it was but lightly, when it at once gently reversed
its ends, and, being forced a little further into the current,
moved forward as usual. In this easy, cheap and lazy way
of traveling we reached Shawneetown, Illinois, on the 1st
day of August, 1820, having stopped to view all the towns on
the river that we came to in the daytime, but not failing to
float every night, as our light boat traveled one-third faster
by night than by day on account of a daily south or head
wind blowing in summer.

Wishing to view the interior of the State of Illinois, we left
the Ohio river at Shawneetown and took passage to Belleville,
St. Clair county, in a four-horse wagon, at about one o'clock
P. M. When putting our baggage into the wagon, the driver
asked me where our provisions were. I looked at him to
learn what he meant, and said, "What do we want with provisions?" He replied, "Well, I don't know, but should suppose
you want them to eat; that is what I expect to do with mine
there," pointing to a large side of bacon and a box of hard
bread. I asked if there were not plenty of taverns along
the road. He said, "No. If you are going to eat anything
for a week, you must get it here, for after to-day we will be
obliged to perform the whole journey by traveling in the
night, to avoid the prairie flies, and can stop at no house, as
there are but three on the road for one hundred miles of the
distance." Mr. Harris and his wife heard this conversation
and looked sad. I asked the wagoner to show me where he
got his goods, which he did, and I also procured a sufficient
supply, together with a tin tea-pot, a loaf of sugar and some

tin cups. On our return we found Mr. Harris and his wife
cheerful as ever; so, putting our supplies in the wagon, we
started on our journey, traveling during the remainder of
that day through a heavily-timbered section of country, and
about dusk encamping for the night.

We rose betimes the next morning, got a hasty breakfast,
and started ahead of the wagon on foot, and, just as the sun
had risen, came, at a short turn in the road, in full view of an
Illinois prairie, about ten miles long and six broad, level, and
surrounded by a fringe of as yet unbroken timber, and
covered with a growth of prairie grass, interspersed with a
luxuriance of wild flowers of every size, shape and hue,
all in full bloom; and, to add to the beauty of the scene,
five deer were feeding near the road, which, on seeing us
approaching, raised their heads, and, after viewing us, showed
their white hairs, then bounded off among the flowers out
of sight. I had read descriptions of the Western prairies
and of the Elysian fields of the ancients, but they had given
only a faint idea of the beautiful and happy fields here
spread out and as yet tenanted only by the untamed inhabitants of the wilderness. I thought it then the most beautiful
scene I had ever viewed, and would think so still if I had
not since seen other prairies in Illinois of vastly greater
extent and beauty.

We traveled one hundred and thirty miles, over a smooth,
unwrought road, without seeing a stone or an acre of land
that was not suitable for a garden, and arrived at Belleville
after a journey of six days, having seen the heart of the
garden State of the Federal Union.

Here at Belleville we met with the brother of Mr. Harris,
who took us to his house and introduced me to his family,
which consisted of a son and five daughters, several of whom
have since become the ornaments of some of the best families
of the State, the youngest being now the president of the
Female Charitable Society of Belleville. Mr. Harris, his
brother, and all his family, have always manifested a great
interest in my welfare, and appeared to take pleasure in my
success, as if they thought me the greatest of benefactors,
and as if they could never do too much for me.

Mrs. Martha Harris, wife of Ephraim Harris, died a few

7

weeks after her arrival at Belleville, with bilious fever, so I
never saw her after I came to St. Louis. Mr. Harris lived
many years after, and bought a half acre lot near the court-
house in Belleville, improved it, and finally left it to his
niece, Mrs. Hill, who kept house for him latterly.

Having recuperated a little at Belleville, I came over to St.
Louis on the 10th of August, 1820, and took lodgings at the
boarding-house of Mr. Pitzer, on Third street, a little south of
Market street, and began to explore the village, as it then
was, until near sundown, when we took tea and had an
opportunity of seeing the guests of the house.

Three distinguished personages were at the table, who were
all waiting to enter on the duties of the offices they each
afterwards held, and the admission of Missouri into the
Union was the whole theme of their conversation at table.
The first was Judge David Barton, afterwards United States
Senator from Missouri; the second was Judge Peck, United
States Judge for the District of Missouri; the third was
Judge Alexander Stewart, afterwards Circuit Judge of the St.
Louis district, which included other counties. From the
positions I understood they were to occupy, I had supposed
I should derive much information and pleasure by being in
their company, but in this I was entirely disappointed. I
learned nothing useful or entertaining from either of them,
and they prevented my learning anything from any one else,
by engrossing the whole conversation and consuming the
whole time on egotistic subjects connected with the admission
of Missouri into the Union. I was quite disgusted with their
selfish and supercilious manners, and at the end of the week
I removed my lodging to the house of Mr. Joseph Charless,
Sr., the most fashionable family in town, and whose dining-
room was a high school of etiquette and learning. Here I
became acquainted with three other learned gentlemen, whose
manners and morals were quite unlike those I last mentioned.
They were Judge McGirk, of the Supreme Court of Missouri,
Judge Lawless of the Circuit Court of St. Louis, and Mr.
Farris, District Attorney of the St. Louis Circuit, each respectively filling these offices afterwards. These gentlemen and a
few merchants of the town formed our social family circle,
together with Mr. Charless' two sons and two daughters. As

I had been introduced to Mr. Charless by Mr. Beck, a Mason of high rank, he introduced me to his family and his boarders in such a manner that it put me at once quite on a par with any and all of them, and I was no longer a stranger in the family. The consequence was, that within the next two weeks I had been introduced to almost every prominent American in the town, and several of the French. Among them were Governors Clark and McNair, General Ashley, Colonels Easton, O'Fallon, Farris, and Loper, Majors Guy and Christy, Doctors Farrar, Lane, and Merry, of the Americans; and Judges Lucas and Ledue, the two Colonels Paul, and Messrs. Chénie, Lebarge, Soulard, and Brazeau, among the French. The most remarkable personage, however, that I became acquainted with at this time was the late Colonel Thomas H. Benton. He quite eclipsed all the rest, and left a lasting fame and example to us.

After having spent three weeks in examining the condition of affairs in St. Louis, and seeing how flat and dull business was, I determined to return to Ohio and visit Xenia and other towns; so bidding adieu to my new friends and St. Louis, for the present, I started back, advancing ten dollars to a wagoner to carry me to Shawneetown. He started at eight o'clock in the morning from Illinoistown, and drove twenty-five miles to his own house that night. We stayed over night at his house, and he rose early the next morning and killed a lot of chickens, which his wife cooked for our breakfast. After breakfast we loitered about an hour or two, and I supposed he had been waiting for his wife to bake bread for his journey, as he said I had brought plenty for myself on the trip. At length, about nine o'clock, I began to think he would wait until evening and drive by night, to avoid the flies, as the other wagoner did who brought me out, and asked him if that was his intention. He slowly said, "I have given up the trip." It is easier for any one to imagine my disappointment and vexation at this announcement than for me to describe it. I had no written contract or receipt to show for the ten dollars paid him. Before I had time to complain, however, he offered to refund the money I had paid him, and give me a return passage to St. Louis, or carry me back three miles to the forks of the Shawneetown and Vincennes road, at the place where the town of Mascoutah, in St. Clair county, now stands, or I might stop with him until I got a passage in some other direction that would suit me better. These offers, and the fact that a copious shower of rain had fallen and prepared his twenty acres of wheat land for the seeding, which he wished to do, reconciled me to my fate. After spending another night with him, and receiving back a reasonable portion of my money, he carried me back and left me at the forks of the road, at the house of Mr. John Deaton, where I waited for a passage one week without finding one in any direction.

Mr. Deaton had, in the meantime, seen me reading a Greek and Latin testament, and supposing I could teach a school, solicited me to defer my journey for the present and teach a school for them, promising that he would take all the trouble of collecting the scholars, and guaranteeing the payment of a good salary. Being idle, I accepted the proposition, and he obtained a subscription for a good school that very day, and told me they would build me a house the next Saturday. It was then Thursday evening, and I doubted his ability to build a house in one day suitable for the purpose. But on Friday he and two or three others rode around through that part of the Looking-glass Prairie, giving notice to the settlers that a house was to be built the next day for school and religious purposes, and all the men must come with their wagons, teams and tools, and all their wives must come to cook, and bring all the utensils to do it, and plenty of provisions.

Early on Saturday morning the neighbors began to assemble, and by nine o'clock there were fifty men and about half as many women, and plenty of teams and tools, so that it looked as if there was to be a great camp meeting here. The number continued to increase until nearly sunset, when the house was ready for use, with seats, tables and door, and this house was the nucleus around which the now flourishing town of Mascoutah has grown up with its thousands of inhabitants.

On the Monday following, I opened my schoool with about forty scholars, of all ages from five to twenty years, who had assembled from the surrounding country for the distance of five miles, as there had then never been a school within that distance of the place. Many of the scholars came on horseback, usually two or three on one horse. Several fathers and mothers brought their children to school three and four miles on horses. Often a wagon came that distance filled with scholars, and, waiting through the day, returned at night. I found plenty of employment in my school, for I was under the necessity of teaching the alphabet to fourteen of my pupils, which was a very irksome task to a classic teacher of my rank. But the scene was varied each Saturday by the neighbors joining in a hunting party to shoot deer and grouse, or hunt bee-trees, and I was always furnished by them with a good horse and outfit for the occasion. Horses and company were always ready on Sunday to travel in any direction I chose within ten miles, or as far as we could and return the same day, for horses were plenty, labor cheap, and no one in haste about business of any kind. Corn was plenty at ten cents per bushel, wheat at twenty-five cents, and pork at two dollars per hundred weight on the farms, and would not sell for cash at that price.

I succeeded well in giving my patrons satisfaction in teaching, and invited them to be present at the close of the quarter, and the parents of nearly every scholar were present. As I was closing my school, a man named Gaskill rose, and, addressing me and my scholars, went on to give the most florid account of my success in teaching, and my pupils' improvement, that it was possible for him to do, and ended by declaring that he felt that such a teacher and such scholars should not be separated. This opened the way for other speakers, who all expressed their satisfaction and their desire to support the school. I, however, dismissed my school, not intending to stay in Illinois any longer. Standing near me was a Mr. Land, the poorest man in the house, who, as he saw me disengaged, handed me a handful of silver dollars, the amount of his tuition bill. Colonel Brown, seeing it, said, "Mr. Land, you have acted unwisely. This gentleman does not need money, but we need his assistance. It is now winter, and we can spare our sons and have them taught to some purpose if we can keep him; but if not, we shall lose what has been accomplished." This brought my pupils thick around me, who, seizing my hands and clothes, and prompted by the example of their mothers, clamored until I said I would teach them another quarter; which promise I fulfilled, with equal success and satisfaction to all concerned. My success and long stay at this place gave me a reputation far beyond my circuit of travels in the vicinity, and I had propositions for opening school at Lebanon and Belleville, with very flattering prospects. Similar inducements were held out to me for opening a school at Turkey Hill, a settlement of wealthy farmers, four miles east of Belleville.

The reminiscences of my short sojourn in St. Louis made such an impression on me that I could make no engagement until I had paid another visit to that town, which I did in March, 1821, and again put up at Mr. Pitzer's. I found St. Louis as dull as ever, and all or nearly all the politicians gone to Washington City to secure the admission of Missouri. At this time, Mr. Pitzer urged me to open a school in St. Louis, and said he would board me for the tuition of his two sons, as his wife was dead, and they were being ruined by idleness; and at last put them under my sole care, to take them from town, to board and teach them where I pleased. I at once determined not to take two such promising boys to a village, but to the country. I therefore opened a school in the Methodist meeting-house at Turkey Hill, St. Clair county, Illinois, and procured board for the two boys with the Rev. Samuel Mitchell; while, to accommodate the other scholars, requisition was made on, and hospitably granted, by almost every house in the vicinity, so that I soon had as many unexceptionable pupils as I could advantageously teach. This created a kind of selfish uneasiness in the minds of some, lest I should make too much money, or not give all my attention to their particular children, and led to an incident I will relate.

When my school had been in operation about a month, and nearly every young lady in the vicinity was in attendance, a widow lady by the name of Elizabeth Hill, who had a small farm and six young children, sent her son, ten years of age, to ask me if I would teach his sister, in consideration of having my wardrobe kept in good order, this being her only means of remuneration. To this I cheerfully consented. While I was gone to my dinner, two of my scholars went and brought her to the school and introduced her. I saw at once she was a favorite among them. She was about fourteen years old, and very intelligent. The other young misses soon elicited from her that her sister was not coming, and the cause why she would not. It was that her mother was unable to pay me. I therefore told her to bring her sister and brother the next day, and I would not charge for them. She, however, only brought her sister, who was twelve years old, saying that her brother could not get off without another brother, who was only eight years old, being left in great distress. I told her to bring both the next morning, and they accordingly came. The boys had just been seated, when a wealthy man who had some children there walked in, and after staring a moment, exclaimed, "Oh! Mr. Shepard, you have spoiled our school." I was provoked at his conduct, but determined to act with coolness; so I smilingly said, "Well, if I have spoiled it, I must make another." He replied, "You have scholars enough for two schools." I asked him to take one half of them and teach them this forenoon. He replied, "I am no teacher." I told him I thought he was quite out of his place, then, as this was a private school and not a public arena. He stood a moment as if in search of a suitable answer, and then remarked, "I believe you are right," and walked out of the house without bidding me adieu. This was the only complaint that I ever heard was made against me while I taught nine quarters in Illinois.

During the first part of the time in which I taught in Illinois, the Rev. Dr. John M. Peck taught a private school at Rock Spring, in his residence. Having been introduced to each other as scholars, we compared notes and found ourselves about equal in point of classic studies; he had studied divinity, I law, and neither had a collegiate diploma, and needed none to show our respective attainments. After continuing his school two or three quarters without much success, he abandoned it, and advised his most advanced scholars to finish their education at my school, several of whom followed his advice and became my pupils. The most prominent among these was Miss Mary Thomas, who, about eighteen months afterwards, became my wife, while I was professor of languages in St. Louis College, then studied three years under my instruction, next assisted me in teaching my popular school eleven years, and finally spent the balance of her life in assisting me in acquiring one of the largest estates in Missouri, and died on the 6th of June, 1864, after living with me above forty years, and was buried in the Shepard family-graveyard in the township of Henderson, Jefferson county, State of New York. I shall have occasion to mention her often in the next chapters of this record.

CHAPTER XII.

PREPARATIONS FOR SPENDING A LIFETIME IN MISSOURI, AND MARRIAGE OF THE AUTHOR.

While spending two years in Illinois, I often visited St. Louis, and became acquainted with many of its inhabitants, particularly with the Free Masons. I was anxious to enter upon the practice of law, but my friends advised me to open a classic school. I therefore was induced to open Belleville Academy, under a board of trustees, intending to review my law studies in the meantime with Mr. Blackwell, of St. Clair, Illinois, which I did, and at the end of the quarter to come to St. Louis and engage in one or the other occupation, I had not then determined which. I had, however, engaged to go into partnership with my pupil Miss Mary Thomas, and we were to have been married on my return from St. Louis, after securing there a suitable house for our residence. With this intent, and for the purpose of forming acquaintances with persons of station and influence, I came over to St. Louis, and took lodgings at the Missouri Hotel.

While at this house, Colonel Joshua B. Brant, a Free Mason and United States quartermaster, arrived from Sackett's Harbor, where he had been stationed, and where we knew each other well, both as Masons and soldiers. We had been with Generals Winder and Chandler when they were surprised and made prisoners, and narrowly escaped sharing the same fate; and both of us served through the war of 1812. He

Mary T. Shepard

introduced me to his wife, who was the sister-in-law of General Leavenworth, and afterwards the mother of Mr. Henry Brant, of St. Louis. Our wives became intimate with each other, and remained so until the death of Mrs. Brant. Subsequently, her son Henry became one of the promising pupils who gave such great éclat to our school on Fourth street. Colonel Brant and myself were always good friends. It will not, therefore, be thought flattery for me to state, so long after his death, how he attained such distinction in the United States army.

In 1814, the American army was closely besieged in Fort Erie, and at a council of war it was determined to make a sortie early the next morning, and each officer had a particular duty assigned him. One colonel was directed to select the bravest lieutenant and twenty of the most determined men of his regiment as a forlorn hope, and to assault and take a block-house, two-stories high, that stood just at and outside the angle of the British intrenchments at the head of a ravine, and which contained four pieces of cannon and forty men and officers. Colonel Brant was then a quartermaster's sergeant, writing in the council room at the time, and, hearing the order given to the colonel, whispered in his ear that he wished to have the leading of the party, and could furnish the lads who would delight in the task. The colonel, having obtained the general's consent for the change, gave the sergeant the command, and he immediately repaired to his company, saying he wanted twenty of the swiftest and stoutest of them for a desperate expedition which he would lead. The whole company at once offered themselves, from which he made the selection of his party and led them to the sallyport, where they all heard their final orders and had leave to retire if they chose; but all were anxious to participate. The whole garrison being under arms, the sallyport was opened and the party marched out, followed by the army.

It was about two o'clock in the morning when the party passed the last of their own intrenchments and moved silently and swiftly to the foot of the ravine about half a mile distant, thence up the ravine some forty rods to within one hundred yards of the block-house, when a British sentinel discovered

them, fired his musket, and ran for the block-house; but
Brant overtook him, knocked him down, and got to the block-
house door just in time to thrust his musket between the door
and doorpost as it was being closed by those within. A
great struggle then ensued, those within striving to close the
door, those without to open it. At length the door was forced
open, and Brant, thrusting his loaded musket into a box of
cannon cartridges, called on the British to surrender instantly,
or he would blow them all up at once, They immediately
surrendered.

Sergeant Brant was made an officer on the battle-field for
his conduct on the occasion, and continued in the United States
service until he attained the rank of colonel. I should
state, perhaps, that after the surrender it was found that
seventeen of his men had been killed or wounded in the
assault on the block-house, and before its capture.

After renting a house and advertising that I would open a
school in St. Louis on the 23d of February, 1823, I was offered
a situation as professor of languages in St. Louis College, a
Catholic institution supervised by the bishop of the diocese,
and conducted by the reverend gentlemen who officiated in
the cathedral. The salary offered was low, but I was assured
it should be increased in the ratio of their ability to pay me.
I therefore accepted the proposition, and continued with them
until January, 1826, perfectly satisfied with their treatment,
and, as far as I could ever discover, they were equally well
pleased with my conduct and services. In short, we lived
together as brothers; and now, when they are all dead, I must
say I never saw a better company of gentlemen. I spent with
them three of the happiest years of my life, and laid the
foundation of my subsequent prosperity.

Having completed my arrangements for housekeeping, I
returned to Belleville, Illinois, and obtained of the clerk of
the St. Clair County Court a license to marry Miss Mary
Thomas, and went to her the next day to consummate our
marriage and make arrangements for removing to St. Louis.
When she was informed that I was to become professor of
languages in the St. Louis College, she said we ought to
postpone our marriage until I should become well established
in my new situation and have my arrangements made to

correspond with it. This seemed so reasonable that I acquiesced in her wish, and we postponed our marriage to the 10th of August following, which was the first Sabbath in the summer vacation, when we were married by the Rev. Edward Mitchell, a Methodist preacher, at the house of her father, John Thomas, Sr., in presence of both parents, seven brothers, and three sisters.

During the interval of the postponement and final consummation of our marriage, Miss Thomas taught a private school, and then, after her arrival in St. Louis, commenced the study of the classics under my instruction, and continued it about three years with good success, when she reluctantly and gradually relinquished it in order to assist me in teaching my private school, which had become quite large and required another competent teacher. Having once commenced assisting me, it seemed I could never after dispense with her labors in our school-rooms.

The 23d of February, 1823, is an epoch in my life, and will be distinctly recollected for many years hereafter by many of the best business men, jurists and scholars that ever adorned the society of St. Louis, as the day when I commenced teaching them, and others now dead, in the old St. Louis College, situated on Second street, between Market and Walnut streets, near where the old cathedral then stood.

The Rev. Mr. Niel was president of the college and curate of the parish; the Rev. Mr. Day, the Rev. Mr. Saulnier, and the Rev. Mr. Odigio, were professors in the college, and also officiated in the clerical duties in the cathedral; Colonel René Paul, as a volunteer professor, instructed the class in mathematics, and I had charge of the English department. The whole institution, however, was under the supervision and control of the bishop of the diocese.

The students were all young, none being over seventeen years of age, and very few younger than twelve years. They were all present, thirty-seven in number, when I was introduced, and were just through the recitation of their lessons in the French language for that morning, and appeared to be waiting for me.

Having some knowledge of physiognomy, I took a scrutinizing view of their faces and heads, and thought I had never

before seen such a fine collection of intellectual youthful
countenances, and that if I did not succeed in improving them
rapidly I should be greatly disappointed.

As I continued to teach all of them until they left that
institution, and have watched with much care and solicitude
their progress in after life, and seen with the greatest pleasure
and satisfaction their success and usefulness in society, I
should do injustice both to them and myself if I neglected to
name those of them who now stand as ornaments, pillars,
and guides in the business transactions of St. Louis. I will
first mention three who married ladies who had been pupils
in our private school, and for whom we had the same solicitude
for their prosperity that I had for their husbands. They have
each fine, promising families, and I feel much the same
interest in their parents.

The first of the three was that well-known, reliable business
man Theodore Labeaume, who married Miss Hammond, and
who needs no eulogium to place him among the very first
citizens in integrity and usefulness. The next was Judge
Wilson Primm, of the Criminal Court, who married Miss
Guion, and resides in Carondelet. The third was Captain
Edmund·Paul, who married Miss Amelia St. Vrain, and
commanded Company E of the Missouri batallion of infantry
volunteers in the Mexican war, in the years 1847 and '48, and
was with me in New Mexico and Chihuahua.

Another who was present that morning, and has had the
most busy and tranquil life of us all, is Sograin A. Robinson,
at present cashier of the Bank of the State of Missouri, and I
think he has never done any business outside of a bank, and
not excelled in purity of character by any man living.

I wish to mention also the following named gentlemen as
then among my pupils: The Hon. William Ferguson, Judge
of the Probate Court of St. Louis county; Mr. Edward Tesson,
the well-known banker; Mr. William L. Ewing, the wholesale merchant; the two Messrs. Berthold; General Réné Paul,
a distinguished officer of the United States army; Hon. French
Strother, late Speaker of the House of Delegates of the State
of Virginia, and a member of Congress from that State before
the civil war; the late Joseph Walsh, long the clerk of the
St. Louis Circuit Court; Hon. Jesse Benton, who was a

member of the Texan Congress while a republic; James O'Toole, a good classic scholar, who became a successful merchant at Weston, Platte county, Missouri; Lewis M. Clark, late Surveyor-General of the United States at St. Louis.

Besides these, there were the four sons of Governor McNair, then the chief Executive of the State, who would at that time attract the attention of the most casual observer by their manly bearing and conduct, and each afterwards took honorable positions in active life. Dunning, the eldest, entered the United States service in the Indian department, and was killed by lightning on a western prairie while in the line of his duty, at the age of about twenty-one. Frederick died at New Orleans with yellow fever, at about the same age, and Alexander died at the close of the Mexican war from disease he had contracted while performing his duty in the United States army. Mr. Raigh McNair is now the only survivor of Governor McNair's five sons, and resides in the city of New York, where I have no doubt he maintains the same high character for probity and honor that he and the whole McNair family have always sustained in St. Louis.

There are still living, I hope, other very deserving men of the thirty-seven present on the occasion referred to, but more than forty years have since elapsed, and I have heard of the deaths of more than one half of the whole number, and all the professors except myself are also dead.

The next week after I commenced teaching in the college, five of my former pupils, from Illinois, came and made application for admission. They were Edward Mitchell, now a merchant of Philadelphia; William Mitchell, a well-known Methodist clergyman of Illinois; Oscar Rapier, of the same place, and the two sons of Mr. Pitzer, who had come (as they informed the president) to be as much as possible under my control and tuition. This was regarded as a good omen of my scholarship by the other students; and it went further than that when they heard them recite a lesson, and found the youngest of them more advanced in English than any of the oldest of the former students of the college.

Nicholas Bolvin, one of the most agreeable persons that I ever had the pleasure of instructing, as soon as he heard the judgment of the class, hastened to the president and informed

him of what had transpired, and I was not long kept in igno-
rance of the pleasure it gave him to learn that the whole body
of students were satisfied with his selection of me for their
instructor; and if they ever changed their minds, I was not
informed of it.

My first engagement was to teach four hours only in each
of the recitation days in the week, and to be confined to
English branches alone; but I was applied to so often to hear
the Greek and Latin classes, that the students soon discovered that the other professors considered me quite as good a
linguist as any among themselves.

Shortly afterwards, Governor Edwards, then United States
Senator from Illinois, sent his son Ninian (since attorney-
general of that State) to me with letters, in which he offered
me a greater salary to teach his three sons in Edwards-
ville than I was then receiving, and to furnish me with a
house and allow me to take as many other scholars as I
might think proper; but if I could not consent to accept his
proposition, to place his son in the St. Louis College for
instruction in the classics.

I accordingly placed Ninian in the college, and as he had
learned the contents of his father's letter to me he communicated the same to other students, so that the president heard
of the proposition, and early the next morning asked me if I
had received such a letter. I told him I had, and gave it to
him to read, which he did; then casting an anxious eye on
me, said, "Well, it is a very liberal offer. What will you do
with regard to it?" I replied, "I have, as you know, by my
placing Governor Edwards' son in your college, declined to
accept the offer, as I am engaged here for twelve months." He
said, "That pleases me. It is just what I have said I was sure
you would do. You shall lose nothing by it. I will add a
hundred dollars to your salary, and give you five per cent. of
all we collect this year besides." With this addition to my
income, I had a very comfortable salary, and, with but light
duties to perform, passed the time very pleasantly, as the
bishop had a very fine library for our use.

Soon, however, the number of students increased so rapidly,
and the duties of the other professors were so much inter-
rupted by their more important duties in the cathedral

during Lent, that I was asked to teach the Greek class until after the Easter holidays, which I did; and when Easter was passed, I could not get the students to return to their former teacher, for they also brought their Latin books and insisted on being taught both the languages by me, so that, in order to retain their friendship ever after, and to gratify them, I was obliged to teach them.

I must now begin to mingle the history of St. Louis with my own.

The Legislature of Missouri had authorized the inhabitants of St. Louis to make it an incorporated city if a majority of them should so decide at an election to be held on the first Monday in April, 1823. Accordingly, preparations were made to test the question fairly on that day. There were then about five thousand inhabitants in the town, one half of whom spoke the French language, and were opposed to its becoming a city, and voted against it, while all others (Jews and Gentiles) voted for it; and the majority in favor of its becoming a city was, I think, but seventeen votes. There was then not a yard of side-walk or pavement in the whole town, or a macadamized road or turnpike leading to it. There was no steamboat owned here, and but one steam engine. Wood was the only fuel used by the inhabitants, and there was no public school or court-house at that time. The first pavement in St. Louis was laid on Main street, between Market and Walnut streets, in October, 1823.

It was in the spring of this year that the late General Ashley fitted out his well-appointed boat expedition to the Rocky Mountains, which met with a bloody disaster on the Missouri river, by the A'Rickaree Indians, for which they were afterwards severely punished by the United States. As one of my former military comrades was going, I went to see the boats start. He was sadly wounded in the battle with the Indians, and returned to New York in the fall after; yet he fared better than a near neighbor who was employed for the same expedition. The latter was directed by General Ashley to take a two-horse cart load of the best rifle powder from a store in town and bring it to St. Charles. He hired a Mr. Lebarge, who lived near the college, to go with him, and another

man accompanied him on foot.   This party were observed by
Mr. Saulnier and myself as we were walking leisurely near
where the court-house now stands.   After they had got a little
ahead of us, they stopped and took up the man who was
walking, and went on.   Mr. Saulnier remarked, in bad English,
"They are careless men; one is smoking."   We kept on about
three blocks further, at which time they were probably five
hundred yards from us, on what was then called St. Charles
street, when we were suddenly startled by a terrific explosion.
The powder had by some means been ignited and killed all
three.   We ran to them, but they never moved after we arrived
there.   Mr. Saulnier was much distressed by the accident,
and predicted disaster to the expedition, as the party had
mostly neglected their religious duties, and started with too
much ardent spirits and too little piety and prudence; and it
turned out as Mr. Saulnier had said it would, but without
establishing his character as a prophet.

After the Easter holidays, the college had as many students as could possibly be accommodated; and as the government of them fell chiefly on me, I was kept very busily
employed until the vacation in August following.

About three weeks before the vacation, all the other professors began to prepare their classes for an examination and
exhibition of their acquirements, and suggested to me the
advantage it might be to me to be putting my classes in preparation.   I at once answered in Latin, " Semper paratus," and
continued my usual course of recitation to the day of the
exhibition without any change.   There being then no hall
in the city suitable for such an occasion, a platform and seats
were erected in the college yard to accommodate a large
audience, and, it being as fine a day as could be desired, a
very large number of the inhabitants attended.

It was arranged to have each class examined by its own
instructor, but I prefered to have my classes examined by
some one else, as I had confidence in their ability to acquit
themselves well, and asked the president to excuse me, which
he did, and at the request of the president, Mr. Neil, my
classes were examined by Mr. Horatio Cozens, then the most
profound and accomplished scholar in Missouri.   He gave all
my classes a most careful and thorough examination, and

closed with the Latin and Greek classes. Having finished, and closed the books, he rose and said he wished to address a few words to the classes he had just examined, and hoped the scholars would give attention to what he would say to them. He was a fine orator, and a man of most pleasing countenance and address; but it is not possible for me at this late day to repeat his words, nor, if I could, to give them that beauty and strength he did. The substance of his remarks was that they had distinguished themselves by the accuracy and readiness of their answers, and had demonstrated their perfect knowledge of the meaning of the authors they were studying, and had reason to congratulate themselves on having been placed under such a competent instructor as they were favored with, as was evident from their performance without his presence. He then stated that he had never seen me to his knowledge, but he had seen my scholarship in them, and that had given him full proof that I was a first-class scholar, and ended by a most flattering eulogium on the performances of all my classes.

A cart load of diplomas from all the colleges of the United States could have added nothing to my reputation as a teacher in St. Louis after that, as Mr. Cuzens' scholarship and judgment were known to the whole community to be of the very first order, and he had assigned me my rank among scholars.

CHAPTER XIII.

ASSUMPTION OF TEACHING AS AN OCCUPATION, AND ITS ENTIRE SUCCESS.

My arrangements having been made for teaching in the college an indefinite length of time, and as my duties then required me to take my meals there, I procured rooms and boarding in the house on Second street, next north of the

8

college, in which Mrs. Elliot kept a female boarding-school, the only one then in St. Louis, and removed my wife from Illinois to it, where she commenced the study of the classics under my instructions, and intended to stay there while I remained at the college.

She had been there but two or three days when Governor McNair and his wife called on her and invited her to come to their house and stay as one of their children, while I taught their sons. They could not prevail on her to accept their kind proposal, but she consented to take a suite of rooms in the west wing of their residence on Spruce street, between Main and Second streets, and there we commenced housekeeping October 16, 1823.

As Mrs. Shepard was an entire stranger in St. Louis, Mrs. McNair introduced her to her lady friends as she would have done had she been her daughter, and thus she became acquainted with almost all Mrs. McNair's friends in the city, who were very numerous, as she was the first in the rank of female society in St. Louis at that time, and maintained that position during her long residence here.

Mrs. Shepard has often said in my presence that Mrs. McNair was the most accomplished lady and most exemplary mother she had ever met with in St. Louis or elsewhere. She assisted in forming the first female charitable society in St. Louis, and was one of its first officers, and other acts of her benevolence are still remembered by her old neighbors, while she is doubtless gone to reap the harvest of her labors. Among those whom we often met at the McNair residence were Mrs. Auguste Chouteau, Mrs. Thomas H. Benton, Mrs. Wm. Carr Lane, Mrs. George F. Strother, Mrs. Daniel D. Page, Mrs. Henry Von Phul, Mrs. Chenie, Sr., Mrs. Joseph Roubideau, Mrs. Brazeau, Mrs. Bernard Pratte, Mrs. Soulard, Mrs. Dr. B. G. Farrar, Mrs. Dr. Walker, Mrs. Billon, the two Mrs. Papin, Mrs. Hunt, Mrs. Dr. Simpson, Mrs. Christy and daughters, Mrs. Benoist, Mrs. Cozens, Mrs. Garnier, Mrs. Bosseron, Mrs. Gratiot, Mrs. Lebarge, Mrs. Berthold, Mrs. Sarpy, Mrs. Danjen, Mrs. Tesson, Mrs. Dumaine, the two Mrs. Paul, Mrs. Forsythe, Mrs. St. Vrain, Mrs. Peter Ferguson, Mrs. Labeaume, Mrs. English, Mrs. Ortis, Mrs. J. Charless, Mrs. Robinson, Mrs. E. Tracy, and Mrs. Massie, a constellation of ladies who have done so much for St. Louis that their names should be preserved in memory as long as the city retains its name.

Having spent one of the pleasantest years of our lives, we removed, as Governor McNair had sold his house and was about to vacate it. I then rented the most northern house on Fourth street, which stood between Green and Morgan streets, removed to it and put it in fine order, paid the rent and improved the garden; but before the time had half expired for which I had rented it the landlord contrived to oust me from the premises, and I had taken him through a lawsuit and recovered back my money and costs, besides learning to appreciate real estate more than I ever had before. This lesson was useful to me in after-life, as I then determined to invest my spare means in real estate as soon as I had sufficient to purchase a lot and built a small house. In pursuance of that resolution, in the summer of 1825, I purchased a lot of forty-five feet front on St. Charles street, between Fifth and Sixth streets, and built a small house on it that fall. We removed to our new home in November, 1825. Being entirely out of debt, and both in fine health, our hopes and expectations were very buoyant, as we knew almost every person of any distinction in the city, and were regarded as permanent residents.

Several of the original professors having left the college, and their places being filled by strangers who manifested less interest in the institution than their predecessors, I determined to withdraw at the end of the year, and notified the president of my intention, that he might have due time to engage another teacher to supply my place. He at once offered to increase my salary to as much as they could pay and lessen my duties. I then informed him I thought I could make more money alone than we all could together, and the result verified the prediction.

I advertised that I would open a private school on the first Monday in 1826, at the southwest corner of Market and Third streets, and solicited public patronage.

On the day appointed, I opened my private school with about thirty-five scholars, many of whom were from the college, three of Governor McNair's sons, three of Judge

Bent's sons, George Knapp, William Ewing, and the two youngest brothers of F. L. Billon, among the number.

With such a promising lot of youths it needed no prophet to foretell the fate of the school. It was full at once. The Rev. Salmon Giddings then had a private school in his own house, which stood on the south side of Market street, opposite the court-house, and being about to marry Miss Collins, and wishing to do a favor to his Masonic brother and friend, he offered to transfer his school and furniture and rent me his school-room, as I desired it.

I accepted his proposal, and, without any unpleasant occurrence, united the two schools. This sudden enlargement of my school rendered it necessary to have an assistant, and then it was that my wife began to assist me in my school, and continued to teach more than twelve years, being one or two years after I left the school to engage in other business.

I had no ladies in my school when Mrs. Shepard began to teach, but as soon as she made her appearance there our school was overflowing with applications by young ladies to be admitted, and Mrs. Shepard took a few from mothers with whom she was at that time acquainted.

The first she received was Miss Garnier, the wife of Hon. John Hogan, member elect to Congress; the second, Miss Caroline Bobb, her intimate associate, now wife of Mr. Alex. Lyle; third, Miss Martha Farrar, daughter of Dr. B. G. Farrar and wife of Mr. Sweringen; soon afterwards, Miss Ann Simpson, daughter of Dr. Simpson and wife of Major-General Smith, United States army, and Miss Julia Page, daughter of D. Page and wife of H. D. Bacon. Others were soon added to the number, until our house was quite too small for our school, and I rented a house near the southwest corner of Second and Walnut streets, and removed my school to it on the 1st of October, 1826.

Having, as I supposed, a suitable house for my school, I employed my brother-in-law, William Thomas, to assist me, and all went on well until the Circuit Court of St. Louis county commenced its session in the next house south, with Judge Stuart (a great lover of whisky and tobacco smoke) on the bench, a grog-shop in front, and vacant ground all around for teams, talk, noise, and play—which put an end to all pleasure, order or progress while it lasted, which was about five weeks. This quite disgusted me with my new location, and I sought in vain for another, for there were no other private rooms as large in the city at that time.

The year 1827 had now commenced, when a memorable event occurred in our family—it was the day of the birth of our only child,

MARY MELINDA.

She was born on Sunday, January 21st, 1827. There were three neighbors present at the time, but none of them now survive. They were Dr. Bernard G. Farrar; Mrs. Metta, a French lady, and Mrs. William H. Pococke, an English lady.

Our residence being remote from our school, we leased our house and boarded with Mr. Phineas Bartlett, on the opposite side of the street from our school-house. Here we were well and comfortably situated, and had as fine a school as could be desired, but the noise, bustle and proximity to the court-room incommoded us. To obviate that inconvenience, I purchased a lot on Fourth street, immediately in front of the court-house, thirty-six feet front by one hundred and fifty-five feet in depth to an alley, for four hundred dollars, on which I built a brick school-house during the summer of that year. At that time, Mr. Horatio Cozens lived in a house on the east side of Second street, a little south but nearly oppo-site our school-room; consequently, the crowd about the court-house endangered his little children, as well as those in my charge, and thinking his son William (now the well-know civil engineer) would be more safe with me, he placed him, when about five years old, in my school, where we taught him to read. Kept in this state of anxiety, we were at all times on the alert for the safety of our small pupils, and particularly for him, as he seemed the most exposed, when, not long afterward, a black boy ran to my door and said in great alarm, "A man is killing Mr. Cozens!" Supposing it must be at his own house, I ran in that direction; but seeing no one about the door, I turned my eyes towards Elm street and saw people running eastwardly in the direction of Judge Penrose's office, and hastened there, where I saw the lifeless body of Mr. Cozens still bleeding, and his murderer, French Strother, a young lawyer, standing near the middle of Elm street, between Main and Second streets, but a few feet from where he had murdered Mr. Cozens, and appearing the only unconcerned person present, although he was surrounded by a dozen persons watching him to prevent his escape, and one holding the dirk with which he had committed the murder. After viewing this horrid scene, I returned to dismiss my school and get my hat, and then saw a crowd going with the murderer to Justice Peter Ferguson's office, and followed it there to hear the examination of the case.

On the examination, no cause of irritation or of previous unkind feeling was elicited, nor has any cause since been disclosed; and as both parties are now dead, the true cause will probably never be fully known. It appeared in the examination that a trial before Justice Penrose, by a jury, was in progress, in which Mr. Cozens was engaged on the part of the defendant, and while addressing the jury, Mr. French Strother walked alone into the office and stood nearly behind Mr. Cozens until he was through with his defence, when, either by low words or signs, he indicated to him that he wished to have a private interview with him outside of the office, and walked out, Mr. Cozens following him to the side-walk. A moment afterwards, Mr. Sutton, a juror, who sat in a window near the door, heard Mr. Cozens say, "You are acting like a savage," and looking out of the window he saw Strother striking at Mr. Cozens with a dirk, which the latter was trying to ward off with his hands and arms. All the people in the office immediately rushed to the door, but before any one got out Mr. Cozens had fallen on the side-walk and was dying, while his murderer was slowly stepping backwards to the centre of the street, where he was arrested by the constable then present. Thus fell by a base assassin one of the best scholars and brightest ornaments that ever adorned the St. Louis bar and the society of the State, leaving a widow and several little children and a great circle of admiring friends to mourn his irreparable loss, being taken from them in the very meridian of usefulness and life. The murderer was committed to jail to await his trial, but found means to escape and fled to the Mexican States, where he has lived until within a few years, when he died at Matamoros, in the State of Tamaulipas, with *mania potu.*

This was an eventful and prosperous year with us, and our

patrons seemed to participate in it as well as ourselves, for we had built a good, permanent school-house in a fine location, out of noise and danger, and removed to it in October, 1827.

I cannot let this opportunity pass without mentioning with gratitude several persons who patronized us during this year and enabled us to build a house suitable for our business and their children's education. The most prominent among them were Dr. Simpson, Dr. Farrar, Dr. Carr Lane, Messrs. Antoine Chénie, D. D. Page, J. P. Spencer, John Cowie, David Massie, Mr. Mullikin, Elkanah English, David Shepperd, Mr. Lebarge, Lucien Dumaine, Mr. Mills, P. Bartlett, D. B. Hill, James J. Purdy, George Morton, Joseph C. Laveille, S. Mount, Judge Bent, Thornton Grimsley, William Grimsley, Beriah Cleland, Mr. Walker, John Goodfellow, Major E. Dobyns, Colonel J. B. Brant, Edward Charless, Peter Primm, Mr. Philipson, Mr. Guion, Samuel Hawkins, Ephraim Town, William Renshaw, Joseph Roubideau, A. E. Orme, Mr. Wetzel, Colonel Easton, Joseph Montaigue, Mr. McDonough, St. A. Michau, Jabez Warner, Jacob Cooper, Mrs. Verdin, B. Mount, Joseph Walton, John Bobb, Mr. Papin, William Mull, Mr. Maddox, Mr. Collet, Thomas Andrews, Mr. Mountrup, Mr. Galletin, R. Hall, P. Dejardin, and Wm. Piggott, to which I must add the name of the late Judge Mary P. Leduc, for he sold the lot to me on a credit, and by his influence among the Papin connections, which is the largest of any in St. Louis, kept most of them in our school while we continued to teach.

At the time we removed our school to our house on Fourth street, there was no court-house in front, nor was Fourth street graded or passable to Olive street, for a deep gully ran down Fourth street to Pine, then turning south-eastwardly it crossed the block in front of the Planters' House nearly diagonally, and intersected Chesnut street between Third and Fourth, making Chesnut street impassable at that point; therefore we had no dangers to fear from travelers, nor noise or disturbance from any cause. Our scholars were well pleased, and their parents seemed satisfied and paid me promptly, as my school was full, and the scholars saw I was unable to accommodate one half of those who made application for instruction. Our pupils were industrious, and gave us but little trouble, for they were often informed they could leave the school when they had as much knowledge as they desired, and we would take some of the many applicants they daily saw refused to fill their vacant places. Thus the time passed pleasantly and profitably to all concerned, and it is very satisfactory to recall those hours and scenes to my memory at this distant day, as I know so many of the pupils have made good use of the knowledge imparted to them.

At that time banks and banking-houses were but little known in St. Louis; United States bank notes and coin were the circulating medium, and all or nearly all the business transacted for cash in hand. Lead and peltries were the chief exports. The money in circulation was mainly brought into the country by immigrants, and, as there was no homestead act then, much of it was paid at once into the land offices for government land, which left but little in circulation among the people, and kept prices low and business dull. These causes greatly retarded the growth and improvement of the city; but far the greatest obstruction was the fact that nearly all the ground lying west of Seventh street (the old western city limits), bounded by Franklin avenue, Grand avenue and Lafayette avenue, belonged to four old gentlemen, who had long used the same as farms, and were unwilling to break them up into town lots, and then spend the evening of their days in disposing of them, collecting the money, and watching it. The example of Henry Shaw had not then taught the people of St. Louis how to expend money for refined, rational pleasure; nor had Benton said, "There is the East—there is India!" Neither had Chouteau's Pond been filled, over which is now built a railroad leading to the Pacific Ocean; or Morse taught the world to telegraph. But St. Louis has had a John Mullanphy, an Ann Biddle, and Anne L. Hunt, to donate and endow hospitals, asylums and schools for the poor, and a Bryant Mullanphy to provide a home for immigrants to the West. Their names are now immortal.

I must snatch the name of the venerable Elijah Hayden from oblivion for what he has done for the St. Louis Public Schools. When a boy, he acted as guide to General Marion in the war of the Revolution, and when he was older he was one of the earliest advocates for the levying of a tax to build school-houses and support schools. He was long one of the directors of the Board of Public Schools. I hope a public school-house in St. Louis may yet be embellished with his name, since he has been long removed to the great city of the dead, and has left no more worthy or lasting record of his life than may be found on the records of the St. Louis Public School Board.

Besides teaching a day school, I also taught an evening school for the instruction of such as could not attend the former, and among the evening pupils were several who have since distinguished themselves as our most industrious and enterprising citizens. The most remarkable and successful among these was Colonel George Knapp, one of the youngest and smallest of the school, but by his industry in a day school in the two preceding years had become well qualified to make good use of an evening school. He had nothing about him very encouraging more than other scholars, except the affection and good-will of all who knew him for his kind and friendly disposition, and his frank and open countenance. His mother was a widow, with seven young children entirely dependent on their own exertions for their support, and on which they always entirely relied. He had been under my instruction in the St. Louis College about one year, and about the same time in my private school, during which time he had made reputable progress, when his mother requested me to select for him some suitable trade, and procure for him a good situation. It was the first and only task of the kind I have ever undertaken; but as he seemed much attached to me, I was very anxious to obtain the most suitable place. I did not much fancy the occupation of printing for *him* because it required a large capital to begin business; but I was well acquainted with all the Charless family, and I knew there were no better people. I was also intimate with the family of Dr. Stoddard, the father of Mrs. Charless (now widow of the late Senator Geyer), and that they were all honorable people, and would be kind to a dutiful and well-behaved apprentice boy, and teach him the manners of a polished gentleman. I therefore applied to Mr. Edward Charless to teach him the art of printing, which he said he would do if the boy should suit him and the occupation suited the boy. Accordingly, George was sent to the office.

After a few days, Mr. Charless met me and told me the boy was less than he supposed, not being tall enough to reach the types for setting. I suggested a temporary platform being provided until he grew taller, as he was so young. A few days elapsed, when he met me again and said, "The boy is quite too young for my business; he cannot carry a full bucket of water, and we use a large quantity in washing the types." I replied, "I suppose your bucket is a heavy oaken one, holding five gallons. Why not get a light tin one suited to his strength?" He said he would try it, as his wife was pleased with him and his workmen also. After this I heard no want of capacity complained of, nor dereliction of duty.

When George had been two or three years with Mr. Charless without any indenture or special contract whatever, and had become very expert and useful, Mr. Charless called on me, and with a very serious countenance informed me that the boy was progressing very well in acquiring a knowledge of his trade, but as he was not indentured, there was great danger that he would be misled and ruined by outsiders, and it would be better to have him bound by indentures. I did not seem to manifest so much interest in the binding part as Mr. Charless, and suggested that the boy was young and might yet prefer some other trade. Mr. Charless replied, "He will never wish to learn any other trade, for he knows that he is worth as much to me as any other person in the office, and all that is wanting is to keep him from roving; and you can do it, for he will do whatever you say is right." As I found it impossible to persuade him otherwise, I promised to consult with George and his mother and do as as they should desire, but that I would do nothing that either objected to or were not consulted on, or which I thought objectionable. On viewing the subject in all its phases, it was agreed I should become George's guardian, with his and his mother's approbation, Mr. Charless to be my security on the guardian's bond and pay all the fees, and I, after the appointment, to apprentice George to Mr. Charless until he should become twenty years of age.

All this was accordingly done, and George returned to the

Missouri Republican printing office, where that veteran prin-
ter and editor, Mr. Nathaniel Paschall, was foreman, and
really conducted the whole business of the office, and, with
him as his instructor, and guide, completed his apprenticeship
and formed his character. In all the vicissitudes of the last
forty years, these two gentlemen have remained generally
engaged in printing the same paper, and, although in different
positions, still together so far that the history of that great
paper is their history.

The *Missouri Republican,* under their direction and skill,
has grown from a weekly sheet of medium size, worked off by
hand, to the mammoth-sized daily issued *Missouri Republican* of the present day, worked off by steam on one of Hoe's
largest rotary presses.

Soon after Mr. Knapp had arrived at his majority, he married Miss Eleanor McCartan, who had been one of our
scholars, and now has ten as fine children as adorn any gentleman's family. Seven are sons and three daughters. Mr.
Knapp's industry and economy have enabled him to acquire
an ample estate and do much for his friends and the public.
His brother, Colonel John Knapp, another of our scholars,
appears to have fallen but little behind his brother in enterprise and energy, and nearly with equal success. He also
married one of our scholars, Miss Wright, and is one of the
present proprietors of the *Missouri Republican.* They both
volunteered and served under General Taylor in Mexico, and
are now in the full tide of usefulness and enterprise in this
city, where no men are better known.

While I mention those who have so remarkably distinguished themselves, I must not overlook others whose sterling
worth, industry and perseverance have carried them into the
first rank of useful, enterprising and eminent citizens. I will
first mention four who have passed away at mid-day of life in
the full tide of hope, success and usefulness, and all left
among us wives and young children to mourn their irreparable
loss and bereavement. They were Chauvin Lebeau, Charles
Sanguinette, John Spence, and Edward Tracy, who were all
so well-known, and have left us so recently, that their names
will recall their virtuous actions without my recounting them.

To these I should add the name of the late William Simpson, son of Dr. Robert Simpson, an artist, who, although he died young, has left specimens of his skill in the portraits of several of our well-known citizens that will compare favorably with those of our most celebrated artists.

Among the living who have often of late attracted my attention by their prominent position in the business and society of St. Louis, and have often been mentioned with pleasure by Mrs. Shepard as having been our scholars, are a large number whom I occasionally meet with in the streets and greet with great pleasure, for it recalls the days of my activity and many pleasing reminiscences of the scenes through which I have passed in preparing them for that theatre of usefulness and honor in which they all seem so actively engaged. It will not, I hope, be expected of me that I can record the names of all the deserving or successful ones, but I will mention a few of the prominent scholars in both the male and female schools who seem at present to have been successful in life beyond their fellows, and leave it for others to point out the causes of the difference between the most successful and those who appear less so now, but are still active and hopeful.

While engaged in my professional duties, I endeavored to teach and treat all my scholars alike, and I think all the causes of the difference in their success has arisen from circumstances outside of my school-room or my acts. I will here state the remarkable fact that I taught above fourteen years in St. Louis, and always with a full school, yet of all the great number I taught in the St. Louis College, or in my private schools, not one has been indicted and convicted of a crime, nor has one of my female scholars so far misconducted herself as to exclude her from the society of honorable ladies; so that to be recognized as one of the pupils of Shepard's school has long been a sufficient passport to place any one in the best society of St. Louis. And now, that more than twenty-five years have passed since we closed our schools, it is not probable that there will be any great changes in the character of our scholars hereafter.

One of my most successful and enterprising scholars, Louis Primeau, a fur trader, is now little known among his old associates; but in the mountains, and also among all the red men of the west, no one is better or more favorably known; and his schoolmates, the Labarges and Brazeaus, are equally as well-known by those who navigate the Missouri river. Messrs. Turner Maddox and James Verdin have gained their positions in society by their own exertions alone. Captain Ezra English has shown what can be done by persevering industry and economy.

Mrs. Shepard, who was a close observer of boys, used to remark that John Platt and George Knapp resembled each other more in disposition and industry than any of our pupils, and that they would be successful in business because they relied on nothing else. They have both shown that her judgment was correct, and she lived to see it verified.

It was a pleasure to teach such scholars, and we had whole families like them, which greatly relieved the toil of teaching. Such families as Messrs. Tracy, Wetzel, Mills, Simpson, Papin, White, Letcher, and Dumaine, I never was tired of teaching, and they seemed never wearied by learning.

To these I should add a great number of others, who, although they did not complete their education with us, remained sufficiently long for us to observe their capacity and traits of character. Among the prominent of those who distinguished themselves in their several avocations by their assiduity, are Messrs. Frederick Colburne, the railroad agent; Honorable Barton Bates, Judge of the Supreme Court; Robert Hall, and the Glasgow Brothers, wholesale grocers; Jotham Bigelow, the builder; Samuel Mills, the portrait painter; Mr. Speck, importer of fancy German goods; Jerome and Napoleon Mulliken, steamboat officers; Z. Wetzell, the wholesale druggist; August Pococke, the tin and copper manufacturer; John Middleton, the iron dealer and clerk; Dr. Spence; Dr. Horine, the dentist; John Yates, the plasterer; Charles Klunk, the United States mail agent; Mr. Ortise, the writing master; Mr. Hawkins, the gunsmith; Mr. Floyd, merchant of Potosi; and I might add pages of names of others who deserve my long and grateful remembrance for their dutiful conduct in school, and the kind and affectionate attention they have always paid to Mrs. Shepard and myself since we ceased to be their instructors.

By the year 1829, the giant strides of St. Louis towards

becoming a great city had been noted by even the casual observer. The pillory and whipping-post, which had stood on the public square in front of my school-house, had been removed, and a new court-house erected on its site; a new market-house was being built, and a branch of the United States Bank established. Encouraged by so many signs of prosperity, I built the two-story brick house now standing on Fourth street opposite the east front of the court-house, in which we taught our large schools many years with uniform and unparalleled success.

In the meantime, the city grew apace, and the old land-marks were broken up and removed to give place to the new improvements and new order of things. Several of the great landholders died, and their estates were divided and sold. Others, being more liberal and far-seeing, divided their lands, sold a part and improved a part, and thus the opening was made for the wide-spread improvement that followed. Having been impressed with the conviction, even long before I had seen it, that the site of St. Louis was the best adapted of any on this continent for a large inland city, I have, to the extent of my ability, tried to act in unison with that impression, and to identify myself with its best interests and welfare.

As I am writing my own biography, and not the history of St. Louis, I intend only to touch upon so much of its history as will show the part I have acted in it; and I will take this opportunity to say, I have never taken an active part in politics, or been present at a caucus or political convention of any kind, in my long and eventful life. Yet I took interest enough in the welfare of my country to go forward and vote, and act decisively in any emergency; and as a volunteer fireman and soldier, very few are better known in the city. At the formation of the Central Fire Company, I was appointed on the committee to draft its constitution, which I did, and acted as its secretary as long as that office was without emolument, and no longer.

In the erection of the Planters' House, I took an early and lively interest, and paid the first money advanced toward its completion, and had twenty-five shares of one hundred dollars each in it. I therefore watched its progress with care and anxiety, and having discovered that the directors first elected had mismanaged what funds had been advanced, and would render the company insolvent, and thus be unable to finish the house with the one hundred thousand dollars subscribed, I endeavored at the second election to have a more efficient board elected; but having failed in the effort, I was beginning to expose the acts of the board, when one of their warm friends desired me to be silent, and accept ten building lots on Easton, Victor and Anna streets for my twenty-five shares in the new hotel, on which I had paid two thousand five hundred dollars. I therefore desisted, and accepted the ten lots as proposed. Soon after, the whole interest of the stockholders was sold to pay the debts of the company, and the building was finished by the purchasers without the stockholders realizing one dollar for what had been paid on their shares.

In the autumn of 1832, the Asiatic cholera made its appearance in St. Louis, and many of the citizens left town. One writer of the history of St. Louis states that all the citizens left who were able to do so, which was not the fact, for many remained and did their duty by assisting their own families and their neighbors as usual. It was a gloomy season indeed, but Mrs. Shepard was a philosopher who could not be panic-stricken or alarmed at unavoidable dangers; and although we had it in our power to leave as much as any other family, we remained at home and continued our schools as usual, except when called away to assist our neighbors. We, in turn, spent alternate nights with our sick neighbors while the disease prevailed, which was about four weeks. The disease returned the next year, but with less virulence, and its treatment was better understood, so that although it prevailed much longer than in the previous year, it did not create a panic as before, nor much alarm. One of the latest subjects of the epidemic at this second visitation was Mrs. Shepard, who was attacked while I was absent from the city, and had passed the crisis of the disease before my return. Dr. Call, her attending physician, informed me that although her attack was very sudden and severe, she met it with the same coolness and intrepidity she had always exhibited when attending her neighbors suffering under the same frightful malady, and which seemed quite as important as medicine to carry patients successfully through the trying ordeal.

My school was very full notwithstanding this awful scourge was in our house, and to show the condition and good order of our school at that time, as well as the affection of our pupils, I must relate what transpired in it immediately after the announcement of Mrs. Shepard's sickness, which was on Saturday morning. On the Monday morning following, all her eldest pupils came to visit her, and, seeing her prostrate condition, knew she would not be able to resume her labors in school for several weeks. Regretting the necessity of the suspension of the school, they undertook to obviate it, and, selecting one of their number as best qualified to instruct, urged Mrs. Shepard to let Miss Priscilla Spence (now Mrs. John T. Martin, of Brooklyn, New York) take charge of her department of the school, and all would assist her. She consented. The school then proceeded as usual until the health of Mrs. Shepard permitted her to resume her labors, when Miss Spence took her place in class, and all rejoiced together at their teacher's return. This kind and accomplished scholar, after leaving school, was married to Mr. John T. Martin, then a well-known clothing merchant of St. Louis, who soon removed to New York, where he acquired a princely estate and raised a fine family of most industrious and enterprising children, and has since retired to a splendid mansion he has purchased in the city of Brooklyn, opposite New York.

In 1834, the estate of Mr. Aug. Chouteau having been divided, and a considerable portion having found its way into the hands of speculators, sales of real estate became of more frequent occurrence, so that in a comparatively short period the area of the city's improvements was greatly enlarged. Being offered the whole block on which the Turners' Hall now stands for the sum of seven hundred dollars, I purchased it. It is bounded north by Market street, east by Ninth street, south by Walnut street, and west by Tenth street, and is now, at the end of thirty years, worth one hundred thousand dollars. This block of ground was conveyed to our only child by Mrs. Shepard and myself by a deed dated July 1, 1845. She owns it still, and by that deed it will descend to her heirs after her death. Our object in conveying such a piece of real estate at that early age was to give our daughter something that would be as lasting as possible, and most likely to attach her to St. Louis. To people who had resided a long time in St. Louis, my purchase of a block of ground, with water upon it deep enough to drown a man, seemed to indicate a willingness to invest in that kind of property, and in 1835 several persons offered to sell me lots of that description at low prices. Having the same confidence in the growth of the city which I had long entertained, I purchased a half block on the west side of Sixth street, near the Central Market, between Spruce and Myrtle streets, for the sum of eight hundred and seventy-five dollars, which I still own, and receive an annual ground rent of twenty-four hundred dollars for it, and all the taxes paid by the lessee. The half block has now fourteen three-story houses on it, and is worth fifty thousand dollars exclusive of the buildings.

The safety of money invested in lands that can be leased to yield an income of six per centum has induced me to prefer it to any other investment, and I have done well in all my operations tending in that direction. It constitutes the whole secret or science by which I have acquired a large and productive real estate. My practice has been to purchase low-priced unimproved lands, but not with the hope or expectation of selling them; and I never have sold any unless I obtained a sum of money which, if put at interest at six per centum, would produce a sum greater than the rent of the land. Thus I purchased block No. 157, on which the O'Fallon Mill stands, at the junction of Fourth and Fifth streets, for three hundred and five dollars, and sold it for fifteen thousand dollars.

The foregoing property was all purchased at private sale. I have very seldom been able to purchase at a public sale, as some one would outbid me if there was a good bargain in land pending.

Sixteen years had elapsed since I left the State of New York, and I had suffered great annoyance on account of my participation in fitting out the Columbian expedition, as I expected to be called on for the seventy-one bonds, or to pay the remaining debt as soon as my present situation should be known to the creditors. I had watched the progress of Columbia with great solicitude during that long period. I

9

had seen its independence acknowledged by nearly all the world, but I also saw that it was distracted by internal dissensions until its bonds were quite valueless in the money market, and the republic was divided into two republics, Venezuela and New Grenada, and its name omitted on the map of the world. Notwithstanding all this, I had followed the prudent rule of retaining possession of all documents that on their face appeared to be valuable, and thereby, at that late day, was relieved of all anxiety on account of my participation in the affairs of the Columbians.

My last acts in an affair that has had great influence on the course and actions of my life, and affected many others besides myself, are the most agreeable transactions to recall to my recollection now, in the last years of a long life, after the lapse of nearly thirty years, and I will here relate them.

In April, 1836, having suspended my school for that purpose, I returned to the city of New York, determined to relieve myself from the anxiety under which I had long labored, let the result be what it might. Having carefully preserved my bank certificate of special deposit, on the day of my arrival in the city I employed a man to guide me to the Bank of America, where I had deposited the bonds, and showing the certificate I asked if I could see them. The teller looked carefully over the paper, and then at me, and said, "I must see before I can answer. This is an old document, and drawn before my time." He then sent for the cashier, to whom he showed the certificate. The cashier said he had no doubt the bonds were in the bank, and could be found, but not immediately; that he would get them in the morning. Accordingly, the next morning, after describing their appearance and exhibiting the one I held, they were shown to me. This made me quite easy, and I went in search of my old friends, but found the city so very much changed that I could scarcely find a place I recognized. All seemed new except the burnt district, for the great fire had lately marked that place. I therefore employed another guide, and soon found one of my old friends and informed him who I was. He said I had changed very much, if, indeed, I could be the same person. I showed him the Columbian bond, at which his sight seemed brightened, and he appeared willing to acknowledge me when he found I had not forgotten the Masonic lectures or lost sight of the principles and landmarks of the Order. He said he had never been able to hear from me after the day I left, although he had seen nearly or quite all the rest concerned in the Columbian affair; that they were always in want of something, and inquiring for me, and that he was in the habit of saying I was undoubtedly dead. On inquiry, I found the purser's account books had been obtained on my order and held by one of the creditors until his death, which had been thirteen years before that time. By them it appeared that about thirty thousand dollars had been due the deceased at the abandonment of the expedition, and that the books and papers were still preserved by his family. I also learned that the creditors had honorably and amicably settled with the commercial broker, and divided *pro rata* the proceeds of what he had been able to collect for them; otherwise, everything remained as I had left it so long ago.

We waited but a short time before we went to visit our surviving brother, who resided a considerable distance up town. In conversation on the street, I told my friend I had that day seen all those old bonds, when he at once seized me by the hand, shook it, and embraced me, until the passers-by stopped to view him with wonder. When we arrived at our destination, I was announced by our friend by name, and the gentleman we sought came and spoke to us as though we had met the day before. After a few commonplace remarks, my friend who accompanied me asked the other if he recognized me as an old acquaintance. He replied, "No; the name is familiar, but I do not recollect ever having seen him before." He was then informed who I was, and said, "I have not thought of him in ten years but as one who was dead, and have often wished to know the time and place of his decease." I then informed them I had not done a single act in relation to the Columbian enterprise since I left the city on the last evening of 1819, and would never leave the city until that affair was so far settled that I should be entirely relieved from all responsibility, either real or imaginary, as it had given me more uneasiness than all the other acts of my life; that I still had control of all the means I ever had, and thought I would be able to arrange matters satisfactorily. My friends assured me nothing should be wanting on their part to help me, and recommended having an attorney to assist and advise me, saying they would pay all expenses to have the settlement made in a legal and proper manner. We spent the remainder of the day in speaking of the past and digesting our own plans for a full and final settlement.

On the following day we visited the widow of the deceased creditor to obtain the books, but could only learn from her that the whole of the account books found in possession of the deceased at his death had passed into the hands of the administrator; and there they were all found, carefully boxed, and the estate settled. As soon as the administrator discovered that search was being made for those books, he got out new letters of administration, and seemed more interested than any of us. This, however, did not operate against me, for they all manifested a disposition to act honorably; and after spending two days in arranging and adjusting the accounts, it was determined what amount each party ought to be paid.

On my part, I had shown frankly that I had possession of seventy-one Columbian bonds of one thousand dollars each, dated at Maracaybo, in Venezuela, July 1, 1819; that the bonds were worth sixty-eight cents on the dollar; and that I had come from Missouri to New York especially for the purpose of settling a demand which was valid in honor, but not in law, as soon as the Venezuelians had determined to pay all the Columbian bonds issued at Maracaybo to carry on the war of independence while they were united to New Grenada as the Columbian Republic. In this position of the accounts, it appeared that about thirty-one thousand dollars was due to the estate, eight thousand to one individual, and nine thousand to the other; that the bonds were worth forty-eight thousand two hundred and eighty dollars, besides the interest, and that the bonds had but little over three years to run. Matters remained in this condition until Monday, when we met by appointment at the house of the administrator, on account of the books and papers being there, and prepared the documents for the final settlement of this long-standing account.

On the settlement, it was found I had but one hundred and sixty-three dollars left for all my expenses and time spent, as well as for my share of the money furnished to purchase the armament. Yet I was so anxious to be relieved from all responsibility that I would not bring that subject up for consideration, and as soon as all the receipts for payment in full were signed, we went to the bank, where I received the seventy bonds and distributed them, saying, "It is safer for you to sell these and get the money, than for me to do it, although I have had a bid for all of them at one house;" and then, putting the bond I had kept about my person so long into the hands of the administrator, I said, "This is my last act as a Columbian officer." He replied, "Sir, this is the greatest act of your life. There are but few who would have done it." He then gave me my vouchers, with the proper receipts, and a check for the balance due me. The other gentlemen also gave me like receipts and vouchers. Thus, after more than sixteen years of anxiety, I was entirely relieved from all responsibility undertaken in behalf of the Columbians.

When we had our business completed, one of my friends said to me, "We had nearly forgotten you, but shall never be so near it again. You have lost money in this transaction, while I think we have not, and it has been saved by you; we must not let you sustain a loss." He then drew a roll of bank notes out of his pocket and handed it to me, saying, "This is from all of us." We then shook hands and separated. When I examined the roll of notes I found it to contain one thousand dollars, a large sum at that time, and highly appreciated from having been received at a period when I could use it to great advantage in improving our vacant lots.

I then spent about three months in visiting the place of my nativity in the State of Vermont, and also where I had spent my happy schoolboy days in Massachusetts. I walked about those places alone where thirty years before I had played and gamboled with my classmates, all of whom seemed to return fresh into my memory, with their histories as far as I had known them. I also visited my kindred and old neighbors in that vicinity, and enjoyed the pleasing melancholy which arises in sensitive minds on visiting the place of their nativity, or places once much frequented and then again visited, and in conversing with the old inhabitants and learning the history and fate of old associates, neighbors, and friends.

On my way homewards, I visited my aged mother, and brother and sisters, near my father's old mansion on Lake Ontario, none of whom I had seen during the last sixteen years. Three of my youngest brothers had died in the meantime. The face of the country had been greatly improved, and the canals appeared nearly as perfect and extensive as they do at this day. I made but a short stay there, as I intended to spend the next summer in visiting the most interesting places in the United States with my family, and this vicinity in particular.

Passing through Buffalo and Chicago on my way home by the Lakes, I viewed those places and considered their locations and their advantages, hearing the laudations of those interested in their growth and prosperity, and the comparisons made between the sites of those places and St. Louis. In answer to them, I said then, as I would now, "If you could have my eyes to look through, you would see that neither of those places has advantages half equal to St. Louis, and art can never change their positions permanently." All three of these places have advanced with most astonishing strides since that time.

I returned to St. Louis and resumed my labors in school and continued to teach until May, 1837, when I was elected to the office of justice of the peace for St. Louis township, to fill the office made vacant by the resignation of Daniel Hough, Esq. I was then entirely out of debt, and had acquired by teaching an estate that I then estimated to be worth fifty thousand dollars, and I therefore considered my vocation a success.

CHAPTER XIV.

FOUR YEARS IN THE OFFICE OF JUSTICE OF THE PEACE.

As soon as my patrons learned that I had been elected to an office that would compel me to leave my school, they began to call on me, the French people in particular, who had been longest acquainted with me, and those who had female scholars in Mrs. Shepard's department, and all objected to the breaking up or even the partial discontinuance of the school. It was in vain that I recommended other private schools, for there were no public schools then in St. Louis. They would not listen to a change, and I perceived they would be greatly disappointed if I discontinued our school. I therefore hired Mr. Josiah Brown to assist Mrs. Shepard, and she continued our school nearly two years longer, with good success, when we discontinued it on our account, and allowed our employee to continue it on his own in our school-rooms.

Mrs. Shepard had been a teacher more than twelve years, and I had taught eighteen years. We had taught together in our private schools eleven years, and had one hundred and eighty-one scholars present the last day we taught together.

I have always been more fond of teaching than any other kind of business, and have been attached to my scholars, and felt, and still feel, an affection for them, and a great desire for their welfare and happiness. While they were under my charge, I urged them forward as fast as possible, and I meet them now with pleasure, as all seem to be acting an honorable part in the world, and some in almost every position have distinguished themselves.

During the first year of my term in office, there were but four justices and one constable in St. Louis city and township; therefore those officers had as much business as they could attend to, and, as I had a very extensive acquaintance, I had a large share of the business, and was compelled to employ a swift penman to assist me as clerk. There had been much business done on credit, and consequently there were many suits which put a large quantity of money in the aggregate into the hands of the constable, who was very popular at the time, and very liberal withal.

After being in office a few months, I discovered that all the small executions were returned, but the large ones were not, and cautioned the constable that he had become liable for the amount of them. He replied, "You have as much business of your own as you will get safely through with these times." I was vexed at his remark, but was silent. On the next day he handed me an execution which I had issued sixty days before for over one hundred dollars, in favor of Henry Von Phul, and said he wished me to renew it by order of the plaintiff. I informed him I was not authorized to do it; but when he should make his written return on the writ, I would at once act as the plaintiff directed, either by issuing an alias execution or otherwise, but I would do nothing that could involve me in trouble. He took the execution and left me, and the plaintiff lost this debt.

I had become a member of Wildey Lodge No. 2, I. O. O. F., of which I am still a member; and as our lodge met on Olive street each Tuesday night, I had occasion to pass the constable's office on my way home after each meeting of the lodge, frequently at a late hour. On one of these evenings I had a friend with me, and he, observing a light through the transom, said, "Let us stop; Dan Busby is in. He has collected some money for me, and will not pay me only at his office, and he is never in while there is daylight." We therefore drew near the door, when we heard a quarrel in progress concerning the rules of a game at cards called "brag." It soon subsided, however, and the parties seemed to settle the matter by taking a drink and beginning the game anew. Having satisfied himself that all was peaceful within, my friend knocked for admittance. Not succeeding, we passed on towards our own homes, a few yards distant.

While walking home, my friend asked me to go and demand his money of the constable the next morning for him. I declined doing so, but accompanied him in the morning, and he got a check for his money. Being offended at not obtaining the money, he remarked, "We heard the rattling of ten times as much money here last night as would have paid me." This imprudent remark induced the constable to follow me immediately to my office and charge me with meddling with his affairs. Knowing his enmity was now unavoidable, I de-

termined to begin the defence before there was an onslaught.
He had in his hands about twelve hundred dollars collected
for me as administrator of the estate of James P. Spencer,
deceased. ' I therefore asked him to pay over eleven hundred
dollars of that money, and tendered the receipt for it. He
said I yet had six months to report in, and he would pay it
before that time. I then made a formal demand for the
money, but he still refused to pay it over. I therefore called
immediately on Mr. Charles D. Drake, and, showing him the
papers, asked him to bring suit for me. He replied, "I am
Mr. Daniel Busby's legal adviser, and cannot assist you now."
At this moment the constable entered his office, and I passed
out. I then employed Mr. Thomas B. Hudson to commence
the suit; but before he had time to examine the papers, the
constable came into my office and said, "There is your
money," at the same time laying down a roll of bills on my
table. I immediately gave him the receipt tendered him
before. I had no doubt Mr. Drake advised him to pay the
money over, in order to avoid the cost and trouble of a lawsuit. On the roll of bills being examined by my daughter, it
was found to contain twelve hundred dollars, so I returned
one hundred dollars to him the next morning, which was on
Thursday, and saw him no more for several weeks, for he
dashed about the city with a large hickory cane, collecting
every dollar he could, and, to avoid paying any one, kept
away from his office, uttering complaints and threats against
me as his only enemy on earth. On the Saturday following,
he took his family on board a steamboat and left for New
Orleans.

The next day being Sunday, and the day on which William
Mull, his deputy, posted the constable's books, I called at
the office. At a glance, on entering, I saw Mull had on the
table all the executions in the constable's office, and I asked
him what he was doing with them. He said he was going to
return all that had been paid to the justices who issued them
for Busby. I then asked him for those I had issued, and, on
receiving them, said, "Now what are you going to do with
those uncollected, since Mr. Busby has left without leaving a
dime to pay any of all these plaintiffs." He made no answer,
and I walked off with the executions, which, on examination,

I found amounted to more than three thousand dollars that I was confident he had not paid over, and, as there were three other justices, I was sure he held over ten thousand dollars belonging to different plaintiffs, with which he had absconded.

Feeling bound by duty as well as interest to notify his official bondsmen, I called on Mr. John H. Gray early the next morning and informed him of what had transpired, requesting him to avoid mentioning my name in connection with the affair. On hearing this, Mr. Gray's face seemed to change its configuration miraculously, and, after looking a moment at the large bundle of executions, hastened down the street to inform Colonel Thornton Grimsley, the other bondsman on the constable's official bond, of some thousands of dollars.

It being the day of the municipal election, the news of the defalcation was circulated throughout the city, but scarcely credited by those who had most assisted Mr. Busby, and who were still his warm friends and advocates; and most prominent among them was Mr. Charles D. Drake, the attorney. On the morning after the election, Mr. Drake met me in the street, and, with an air peculiar to himself, informed me that I had circulated a report that Daniel Busby was a defaulter, and that he would return in a few days and demand that satisfaction of me which any gentleman had a right to demand of one who had circulated a calumnious report against him, and I would be bound by honor to satisfy him. I quickly informed Mr. Drake that if Mr. Busby would come back and pay his debts I would give him that satisfaction which one gentleman had a right to demand of another, and, moreover, I would waive the return of Mr. Busby if Mr. Drake, or any of his friends who ranked as high, would ask satisfaction on his behalf; that I would give it to him, and not ask a longer time for preparation than was necessary to procure a twelve-foot square room and two double-barreled shot-guns. At this, friend Charles walked on, and in the afternoon of the same day I saw him completing the papers in the office of justice Joseph Walsh for a suit in attachment against D. Busby.

Colonel Grimsley started in pursuit of Mr. Busby on the next steamboat that left St. Louis, and overtook him at Galveston, in the republic of Texas, and brought him back to St.

Louis, full of wrath and threatenings against me. I was soon informed of his return by several persons who seemed anxious to know what course I would pursue. I was silent, however, and at my usual hour of dinner returned home and found his sister-in-law at our house, crying, wringing her hands, and imploring my wife and daughter to dissuade me from going out again, as her brother-in-law would surely kill me, for he was armed with a double-barreled shot-gun, and had been watching to shoot me in my yard from the windows of a house near by, and if he could not see me there he would shoot me in the street or in my office. I informed her I did not thank her for her pretended manifestations of solicitude for my safety; that I was able at all times to defend myself; that I had no doubt Busby had sent her there to disturb the quiet of my family, and that I wished her to hasten home and inform him that my family was less troubled for my safety than for his, and that there was more probability he would avoid me or his creditors than that either of us would avoid him. She soon drew down her veil and left, and I went about my business as usual, without being molested by any further belligerent demonstrations.

Messrs. Gray and Grimsley paid the amount of his official bond, and other parties lost about forty thousand dollars by his defalcation.

About that time, great efforts were being made to get our present public school system into operation; and if there is any one act of my life that I look back on with more pleasure than another, it is the part I took in favor of it. By legislative act, there was a vote of the citizens to be taken to decide whether we would tax ourselves to build houses and put the system into full operation. As soon as the day was appointed for the election, I began to exert myself in favor of the tax. I had a good number of tenants, and went to them all individually and asked them to vote for the law, and also to bring their friends to the polls. I visited my old patrons, who were very numerous, and urged them to assist by their votes and influence; and on the day of the election exerted all my ability, up to the last moment, to secure votes for the measure, notwithstanding my landholding neighbors were cautioning me against increasing my own taxes thereby.

I assisted Dr. Cornelius Campbell and the late Judge B. Mullanphy in examining the first teachers for the St. Louis public schools, and gave to the Board of Directors the lot on which School House No. 1 is situated. The first gentleman selected from the applicants as a teacher in the public schools was Mr. David H. Armstrong, and the first lady was Miss Salisbury, each of whom gave good satisfaction, and did much to give the St. Louis public schools that high character which they have now attained.

The public schools having opened, our patrons at length seemed willing for us to close our private schools, which we had continued for more than thirteen years, and had assisted in educating more of the most prominent and enterprising persons that compose the society of St. Louis than any other two individuals will probably ever be able to do. It is my intention to append at the end of this record a list of as many of them as I can recollect.

After we had closed our school in 1839, we spent the summer traveling with our daughter, visiting the great cities of the United States east of us, and the Canadas as far as the city of Quebec and the Falls of Montmorency, and returned to St. Louis by way of the Lakes and Mackinaw, spending many days viewing the grand scenery that such a trip afforded.

The Canadian rebellion of 1838 had been suppressed but a few months before our arrival, and a guard was sent with each boat on which we traveled in Canada to insure its safety. All the cities seemed well secured by guards of British soldiers. A brigade of infantry and a squadron of horse were then quartered in Montreal, and we had the pleasure of seeing them, on a fine afternoon, exhibit their military skill and tactics on the Champ de Mars in grand review and sham fight. I had before seen the British manœuvre, but not so accurately, nor with quite the same safety or pleasure to the persons engaged, and it afforded me a fine opportunity to contrast their display here, in time of peace, with the one I had seen about the same number of them make at Sackett's Harbor in time of war, in May, 1813.

After our return, I was very busily engaged in the office of justice of the peace for two years, when the time for which I had been elected expired.

CHAPTER XV.

SHORT EXPERIENCE IN STEAMBOATING.

I saw the first steamboat that ever navigated American waters, when it arrived at Albany from New York, in 1807, and had made observations on the great changes that from time to time had taken place in their construction, management, and success. I had also noticed the operations and success of their owners and navigators for more than thirty years, and had come to the conclusion that steamboat stock was the most dangerous property a man could own, and that steamboating was the most uncertain and precarious business a man could engage in, and had therefore resolved to have no stock in a steamboat. I often so expressed myself to my friends, and among them to Louis Dubreuil, who had been my pupil, and done business for me as constable a long time, and knew my aversion to that kind of property. About the first day of the year 1842, I went to Dubreuil's office to see him on business, but found he had gone to sell a steamboat at the wharf; so I went to him and found him engaged in reading the advertisement of sale of the steamboat we were on. When he finished, he asked for bidders, and called on me to start the bidding. I did so at five hundred dollars, and immediately six hundred, seven hundred, and then eight hundred dollars, were bid successively by three different persons, when Dubreuil looked at me, and I nodded; then he called for other bids, but, as no one bid for a second of time, he struck the boat down to me at nine hundred dollars, amid roars of laughter, as Dubreuil said we would all have "one grand frolic" on the boat at the expense of the owner.

Expecting a lawsuit about the title, or that the sale would be set aside, I only removed the boat to the upper end of the steamboat-landing, where it laid until spring, when, at very little expense, I fitted it up for running in the Illinois river. After placing John Pointer in the office, and other competent officers on the boat, she made twenty trips from St. Louis to Peru without accident, and, besides paying high wages and all expenses, I saved four thousand dollars out of her earnings.

I then sold the boat to the officers for two thousand dollars, which they earned while on the same.

While this was transpiring, my prejudice against steam-boating had so far subsided that I loaned two thousand dollars, and took a mortgage on another boat to secure the payment, but allowed her to leave port, as the officers assured me that the two thousand dollars liquidated all debts due the boat's crew or any one else. On the return of the boat, I found I had been deceived by the misrepresentations of the whole crew ; that they had claims amounting to one thousand four hundred dollars, and that the boat was to be sold under an old deed of trust. Had I patiently submitted to the loss of the two thousand dollars, I would have avoided great vexation and many dangers, but I would have remained ignorant of the adroitness, claptraps, and legerdemain of dishonest steam-boatmen, which is so essential to be known to all who desire to escape their grasp. Being unwilling to lose my money, I called on the owner of the boat to whom I had loaned the money, and insisted on his confessing a judgment for the amount, that it might take precedence of other claims ; which he did, and an execution was issued for two thousand and seventy-five dollars, and levied on the boat. As soon as he had left the court-room after confessing the judgment, he proceeded to the boat and induced all the crew to bring suit against the same, when judgments for nearly nine hundred dollars were obtained, and executions issued therefor, and the boat sold under them, as they took precedence to my execu-tion of two thousand and seventy-five dollars.

To save my debt, I procured a person to purchase for me at the sale in his own name, but when the property was bid off to him he would convey but half of it to me, and when I discovered his want of principle I was surprised that he did even that. He immediately transferred the other half to Mr. Ringrose Watson. On the same day, this same steamboat was sold under a deed of trust, and brought the trifling sum of about twelve dollars. Small as the sum was, it afforded the pretext of a cause of legal action against me, and a theme for a vast array of words from Edward Bates and F. F. Risk, which, by the way, they were never paid for, unless they considered it payment to be allowed to abuse me an hour or two before a court and jury that paid no respect to such claims, as the plaintiff would not pay the costs when judgment was rendered against him, because he had been wheedled into the suit.

While this vexatious suit was going through all the by-paths that pettifoggers could follow out, the boat had about as brilliant a career in the Lower Mississippi as Bates and Risk had in the Circuit Court; that is to say, none of them made anything. On a close examination of the books of the boat after the second trip, I found that it was eleven hundred dollars in debt in consequence of an alleged accident, but, as I believed that it was an act of sheer carelessness, I determined to go on the boat one trip and see how the business was transacted, taking no part whatever in the business of the boat. It made a very slow trip, being delayed by running aground, yet it was a profitable one, as I had seen the folly of hiring a cheap pilot through favor, and corrected it. I still thought there was something wrong, and I tried to get Mr. Watson to send one of his three sons as clerk, but he declined, and I let the office be filled as before. The boat was about leaving, when the clerk brought his wife on board, who was a very genteel and good woman, and was staying at my house. As soon as the captain saw her and her trunk on board, he came to me and said, "I must quit your boat." I saw no reason for this action, and asked the clerk the cause. He said he knew of no cause, but would take the captain's place, and, stepping into the office, he took the boat's papers and went to the custom-house where he had his name inserted as master of the boat, which was done with my consent. The boat immediately left for New Orleans, and made a speedy trip. On our return, the former master advised me never to have an officer's wife on the boat while he had a duty to perform, for in case of real danger he would be worse than nobody. I thought this good advice, and followed it. Of necessity I had taken charge of the office on the last trip, and slept in it, being assisted on shore by the barkeeper, a fine clerk. As I had a full cargo engaged below, I spent but a short time at St. Louis, and left on the 15th of March, 1843.

Soon after leaving St. Louis, the master of the boat asked me to let him occupy the bed in the office. I told him I had

my own money, as well as the boat's, locked up there, and I
chose to watch it myself. This seemed to give him offence, and
led me to suspect he had some other object in view than sleeping in the office; and being at leisure, I determined to examine
the books and see if it was not to find some error in my mode
of book-keeping. He had taken charge of the books one trip
to New Orleans and back, and I had done the same, so I
compared the two accounts, article by article, and found them
very similar until I came to the last item, wood. Here I
found a great variation, amounting to forty per cent. We had
a printed receipt-book, and here was the explanation of the
mystery. He had filled up false receipts for cash paid for
wood, made marks for the signatures of fictitious names and
amounts, and pocketed the money. It was gone, and I knew
where, and I determined to dismiss the master in St. Louis on
our return, and not to take any valuable freight from New
Orleans with me. I therefore purchased a load of salt, as
that could not be easily stolen, and left for St. Louis, arriving
at Memphis at a time when freight to New Orleans was plenty.

Here I contracted to take a thousand bales of cotton to New
Orleans immediately, much against the wish of Simons, the
master, who was very reluctant to go back, and would not
assist in the least. However, the mate discharged the freight
on a wharf-boat and reloaded the boat with cotton the
same day, and we left that evening, the captain coming on
board at the last moment. I saw him very seldom on the
way down, and when we arrived, and before the boat was
in its berth at the wharf, he went on shore, unseen by
any of our people, and was absent two days. Before we
had a bale of cotton on the wharf, a gentleman came 'on
board in a rage, asking for the captain, and was answered
he was not on board. He then asked for the clerk, and I
was pointed out to him. He asked me what we had done
with his money, and why we were back in New Orleans
so soon. Supposing he was insane or mistaken, I said,
" I have spent all the money and came back to get more,
but I think you are mistaken." He replied, " No, I am not
mistaken, nor have you had time to spend the money," and
opening his pocket-book he showed me a bill of lading,
showing that he shipped on the steamer Minerva one sack

containing eight hundred and seventy-five dollars in silver coin, to be delivered to John Zeigler at St. Genevieve. At sight of that I was satisfied the intention of Simons, the captain, was to appropriate that money to his own use, and that it was still on the boat, or he had already disposed of it and left me to refund the amount to the shipper. On investigation, I found that he had hid the money in the ice-box in the bar as soon as it was brought on board, and, while I was busy counting the bales of cotton as they were delivered to us at Memphis, he took it from the boat and deposited it in the bank at that place to his own credit. This I learned from the barkeeper, who assisted him in carrying the money, which weighed about fifty pounds, to the bank, and had been pointed out to me as being present when the money was received.

Being satisfied of the captain's unworthiness, I took the boat's papers to the custom-house and had my name substituted for his, and advertised the boat for a trip up the Wabash river to Lafayette, in Indiana, and soon had a full freight and a fine lot of passengers at good prices. When I had steam up and was on the point of leaving the wharf, Mr. Simons, the late master, came on board and said he was aware he had been discharged, and wished to settle with me. I answered, "I am ready; write your receipt," which he did, and handed it to me. I said, "Now write an order on the Memphis bank for the eight hundred and seventy-five dollars, and I will discharge you." He said he would not do it. I then threatened to send for a police officer, when he said he hoped I would not do that, as his wife was at my house, living as a daughter or a sister, and it would distress the whole family. He consented to be confined in one of the state-rooms until we came opposite Memphis, where I called on him again for the order, after having the boat ready to anchor in the stream until I could procure his arrest if he refused. Seeing my preparations to arrest and punish him, he wrote an order for the sack. The boat was landed on Sunday, and I took Stanard, the barkeeper, with me to the bank to bring back the sack. When we arrived at the bank, we found the cashier was at a church near by, where I waited until he came out, and then informed him of the transaction. He said he would immediately deliver the money to me if I would identify myself by a citizen

10

known to him. A merchant named Shaw, owner then of a wharf-boat, introduced me and offered to give a bond that the bank would lose nothing by delivering the sack to me. I then received it, and engaged Mr. Shaw to ship it to its place of destination, and, as I never heard of it after, I presume the owner received it. On my return to the boat, I learned that Simons had left it, with his baggage, as soon as I was out of sight, and I never saw him afterwards when he could avoid it, which he generally managed to do.

Having relieved myself of this perplexity, we continued our voyage to Lafayette, and on returning into the Ohio made a very profitable trip from Clover Port to New Orleans and back to St. Louis, where I found we had made money enough to pay all the expenses of the boat, and the damages we had brought upon the owners, which I held in my own hands. I therefore paid off all demands against the boat and owners, and removed it from the wharf to a place of safety, where I sold my share in it for less than I had paid, besides losing my judgment against the boat for two thousand and seventy-five dollars with costs, to say nothing of the trouble and vexation I had undergone.

CHAPTER XVI.

REMINISCENCES OF THREE CAMPAIGNS IN THE WAR OF 1846 WITH MEXICO.

On the 16th day of May, 1846, I volunteered in the service of the United States for a six months' campaign in Company A of the St. Louis Greys, commanded by Captain Stephen Coleman, of the St. Louis legion of infantry, under command of Colonel Alton R. Easton, which was mustered into service on the 18th of May, 1846, by Colonel Davenport, of the United States army, at Camp Lucas, outside of the city, as it then was, in a field near where the Lucas Market now stands.

When the legion was formed into line to be mustered, Colonel Davenport walked from the left to the right of the line, about two yards from it, and viewed every countenance as he passed along; then going to our officers, who were standing grouped in front of us, he turned around and pointed me out, asking Colonel Kennett who I was. On being informed, he walked to within about ten yards of the line, and, calling me by name to come to the front, commended me for the example I had set, after having served in the army so long, to offer my services again at my advanced age, and told me he considered it more than my share of the military burden, and I might retire with the thanks of my officers for my example. I immediately touched my hat, and thanked him for the compliment he had paid me, and the kind offer he had made, but informed him I was fully aware of the duties I was expected to perform; that I had come prepared to undergo them, and that if I should be thought disqualified from age, I must not abandon my neighbors, but would take passage and go with them on my own account. He replied, "I have no doubt of your ability to perform the duties of a soldier, and that you will be prompt to do them; I will, therefore, at your own option, muster you with the companions of your choice." I was accordingly mustered with the legion, being then in the fifty-first year of my age.

On the following day, Mrs. Kennett presented a splendid stand of colors to the legion, which was received with the usual ceremonies, speeches, &c., and the same evening we received orders to be in readiness to march on Saturday, the 23d. Clothing, camp equipage, and arms, were issued on the 21st, and an order was given for a dress parade and review on the 22d of May, 1846. On the morning of that day, a paragraph appeared in the *Missouri Republican* concerning me, stating something of the part I had taken in the war of 1812, and in the present crisis, and my present position in society and condition in life. When the legion was formed for review, I was placed on the color guard and posted at the main entrance of the camp, where I was seen and recognized by a large number of my acquaintances, who expressed their astonishment at my volunteering at so advanced an age to go on such a distant expedition into such a warm and unhealthy climate, and seemed to manifest great anxiety for my personal safety and welfare on that account.

On the morning of the 23d of May, I took leave of my family
and repaired to camp, where we soon after struck our tents
and marched on board the steamer Convoy, making a fine
martial appearance, and a crowd of citizens, who accompanied us to the boat, expressing their good wishes for our safe
and speedy return. Every preparation had been made to
depart as soon as we were on board, when, just at that
moment, a boat arrived from New Orleans with the news of
General Taylor's victory at Palo Alto, and our boat backed
out from the wharf amid the cheers and rejoicings on that
occasion. Passing up stream in front of the city, we saw all
the steamboats covered with people, who were cheering and
waving their hats and white handkerchiefs, and then, turning
down stream, the boatmen commenced firing a small cannon
by way of salute, and at the second discharge, which was
premature, one man was killed and another mortally wounded,
which was the first bloody effects I saw of the war, and was a
caution to the careless. Another steamboat accompanied us to
Jefferson Barracks, filled to its utmost capacity with warm-
hearted friends, who took back to St. Louis the wounded and
dead man, while our boat received on board three companies
of the legion who had been waiting for transportation at that
place. The boat then proceeded to Memphis, where we heard
the cheering news that the Mexicans had been entirely defeated at Resaca de la Palma, and had fled from Texas, which
they had invaded because it had been annexed to the United
States by an act of Congress passed March 2, 1845, and that
the Americans had advanced to the Rio Grande.

Very few persons went on shore at Memphis, and the boat
proceeded to New Orleans, where we arrived on the 28th, having made the trip in five days. On its arrival, the legion was
saluted with artillery and repeated cheers from crowds of
people on the levee and shipping. About sunset the boat
crossed the river to Algiers, and we were disembarked and
encamped in a field, where we were carefully drilled until the
3d of June.

While we were encamped here, I received a very kind and
pressing invitation, as Grand Master of the Independent Order
of Odd Fellows of the State of Missouri, to visit one of the
lodges of the city on a certain evening named, and to bring

with me all our brethren who were in the legion. With permission of the colonel, I accepted the invitation, and, taking about twenty of our brethren, we went over to New Orleans in the afternoon, and spent one of the most pleasant evenings of our lives with our brethren.

Until the 3d of June, there had been some expectation that we would be discharged at New Orleans without seeing Mexico, but on that day, at about four o'clock P. M., the steamship Galveston raised steam at New Orleans and came to Algiers, on which the legion embarked and passed down the river, thus giving us a good view of the vicinity of the city before dark. Early on the 4th, we passed the Balize, soon losing sight of the turbid waters of the Mississippi, and shortly after the increased motion of the ship gave me a genuine fit of that well-known disease, sea sickness.

At daylight on the morning of the 7th, we came in sight of the shipping off the port of St. Isabel, or Brazos Santiago, and were landed the same day on the west bank of the Brazos or arm of the sea that forms the inlet to the harbor of Point Isabel. This land appears to be a bank of sand washed by the violence of the waves from the bottom of the sea and formed into a kind of ridge or barrier to protect a shallow bay in its rear, which is in danger of being filled up and the bank united with the main land, owing to the prevailing powerful winds from the gulf. We spent the remainder of the month encamped at this place, improving our skill in manœuvres, observing the novelties that surrounded us, and amusing ourselves in bathing, swimming, and fishing.

I had my writing apparatus with me, and wrote each day the news of the camp, in the form of letters, to my family; and when a vessel touched at the wharf, I closed my letter, put it on board, and began another. I thus kept my family informed of all that passed in our camp day by day. Extracts from some of my letters were printed and brought back to our camp, which afforded some amusement and some astonishment among those interested. One was an account of the battle of the Sand Hills; the other the sickness of Lieutenant-Colonel Kennett, which brought his wife to his bedside, two thousand miles from home, before his friends found time or inclination to write or communicate with her, until they saw her in sight of his quarters, on a visit to him, to their no little chagrin for their neglect of her who had presented them with a most beautiful stand of colors. Our adjutant, one of the youngest of our officers, essayed, as an apology to escape the dilemma in which they found themselves placed, that they should say it was my duty to inform her of the indisposition of her husband; for although I was only a private, I was the eldest member of the legion, and the only experienced soldier in it. The last clause of the preceding sentence was literally true at that time, strange as it may appear at this day that seven hundred citizens should compose one entire regiment and yet include but one man whe had ever been in a battle.

On the 1st of July, we removed our camp to the mouth of the Rio Grande, distant about nine miles, marching along the sea shore, which formed a pleasant road, except in one spot, the Boca Chica, a place about three hundred yards broad and three feet deep at low tide, formed by the flux and reflux of the tide-water in its passage to and from the long shallow bay in its rear, and which is quite impassible by fording except at the lowest tides. This place we all passed by fording, the water being about waist deep, but we had prepared ourselves for that purpose. On our arrival at the river, we waited until the 4th, when we were taken on board two steamboats and landed at the upper end of a ridge of hills called the Hights of Barita, in the State of Tamaulipas. We remained here until the 6th day of August, and spent the first three weeks in preparing ourselves for active service; but then, finding the country free from enemies, and that we were soon to be discharged, we relaxed our discipline and passed the last ten days of our time in making sundry explorations in the vicinity and in visiting the camps of other regiments.

During this time, I visited General Taylor at his headquarters at Matamoros. I had gone up the Rio Grande with his brother, who bid me come to the general's tent in the morning after our arrival, and he would introduce me to him. I went as directed, but the press of business in the quartermaster's department had taken the colonel off before my arrival, yet he had left such a full description of me that the general called me by name at once, and spoke and acted as if he had known me during my life, inquiring after many persons with whom we were both acquainted, and in turn informed me of the fate of our mutual friends, so that I enjoyed a pleasant visit with him.

I did not explore the country to any great distance from the river, but saw enough to satisfy me that it is bound to be one of the richest countries in the world, and that at no very distant day.

On the 6th of August we embarked on two steamboats, and left the battles to be fought by other troops, because our term of service was too short, and started for home. We returned by the same route on which we went out, with similar means of transportation, and arrived at St. Louis on the 21st of August, amid the cheers and rejoicings of the whole population, as it appeared when viewed from the deck of the boat.

During our absence from the city, all kinds of business and improvements appeared to have gone on as if there had been no war progressing abroad. The Odd Fellows, in particular, had exerted themselves most commendably, and had their beautiful edifice at the corner of Fourth and Locust streets in an advanced state of completion, so that, being Grand Master of the Order in Missouri, on the 4th of November, 1846, I assisted in the ceremonies of the dedication of the hall, which is still the place of our weekly meetings.

Scarcely had we deposited our arms in the armory, when many of the men who had served with me in the legion began to solicit and urge me to take command of a company of volunteers, which they said they were able to raise themselves, and return to Mexico to serve during the war. I promised to do so the next spring, and accordingly, on the 10th of May, 1847, I was mustered in with a maximum company, which was designated as "Company A, Missouri battalion of infantry volunteers," to serve during the war. My three lieutenants were most efficient and excellent officers, and well suited to the positions they occupied. The first was Samuel A. Holmes, now commanding the fortieth regiment Missouri volunteers, who has greatly distinguished himself on the battle-field, and was a fine classic scholar and attorney before he entered the service; Major Thomas Levant, a farmer, and at present manager of the first railroad station at Carondelet, was the second lieutenant, an excellent disciplinarian, of gigantic strength and resolution, and of undoubted probity and honor; the third was William Prichett, a youth of twenty years, who quit the bench of a saddler, with the consent of his father and employer, to join my company. With these officers, and ninety of as good men as an experienced surgeon could select from one hundred and twenty, who had offered themselves and been mustered into the United States service, we commenced the next day to prepare ourselves for usefulness, and during the two campaigns that followed no officers or men could have more faithfully served their country than they.

A few days were first spent at Camp Lucus in drilling and issuing quartermaster's stores preparatory to a march across the Western plains. On the 15th, I received orders from Colonel Wharton to remove my company from Camp Lucas on board the steamer Mandan, then at the wharf, commanded by Captain Cheever, and proceed to Fort Leavenworth and report to Lieutenant-Colonel Scott, in command of that post. Accordingly, I notified my company to prepare to march at 9 o'clock A. M., and taking leave of my family, at their residence in front of the court-house on Fourth street, at the time appointed we marched from camp through the city, amid the throng of friends and neighbors, who lined the sidewalks the whole distance, expressing their good wishes for our welfare.

My company being all on board, I placed a sentinel at the boat's gangway to prevent the men from going on shore while I went to a drug store for medicine. On my return I found one of my largest men attempting to pass the sentinel, which he effected, but got slightly wounded in the leg, which so enraged him, that, on reaching the shore, he picked up a stone in each hand, and, running up again on the stage-plank, cast one at the head of the sentinel, who dodged it with great dexterity, and then, advancing on his assailant, who turned and attempted to run, he thrust his bayonet quite through the body of the soldier, so that I saw three inches of the weapon protruding through his jacket at the pit of his stomach. I sent him immediately to the city hospital, where he was carefully attended by Dr. Thomas McMartin, surgeon of the institution; but owing to the severity of the wound, and eating and drinking immoderately, he brought on an inflammation of the stomach, which occasioned his death seventeen days afterwards, as was ascertained by a *post mortem* examination by the surgeons. Such an occurrence at our first outset drew forth many remarks from the by-standers at the dispatch of business of this kind, and the editor of the *Republican*, in his issue of the next morning, commented to the effect that it was demonstrated what the discipline of the company might be expected to be from its first essay.

As soon as the boat could be cleared of the crowd, we left the wharf and reached the middle of the river at the upper end of the city, when it was discovered that the boat was on fire in the hold. I knew there was a large quantity of gun-powder on board, and that our only chance for safety was in subduing the fire; that it must be done by the boat's own crew, and that our company must be kept aloof from them. With the assistance of my officers, we kept entirely away from them until the fire was out, and in the meantime had a good opportunity of watching the countenances of each indi-vidual as he saw death apparently staring him in the face. Captain Cheever exhibited as much coolness and promptitude as I have witnessed in any individual, and the occasion was a good one to try the metal of men, and will probably be recollected as long as they live. There was no clergyman, physician, woman, or child, among us. This day, and the events as they transpired, as well as the different persons present and acting under my notice, are more indelibly fixed in my memory than any other of my eventful life.

Our trip to Fort Leavenworth occupied six days and was attended with no remarkable occurrence, and we were received at the fort by Major Scott, Captain Steen, and my former pupil, Captain L. C. Easton, United States quartermaster at the post, in the most cordial manner and treated with the greatest attention. The reception was so different from what most of the company expected would be given to volunteers by officers of the regular army that they were most pleasantly disappointed by it. We spent the first night in the quarters assigned to us in the fort, but, as we were to escort the first government train going to Santa Fé, it was thought best to encamp in an open field and inure ourselves to camp life before we began so long a march. Accordingly, we were furnished with tents, and took the field, where we drilled until the 17th of June, at which time we were ordered by Colonel Wharton to escort a very large train of ox wagons, loaded with commissary stores, to Santa Fé, which we did in such a manner that every article was delivered safely and in good order. To obviate the necessity of my soldiers being obliged to carry their knapsacks such a long distance, I purchased a wagon, chains, and three yoke of oxen, in which their knapsacks were carefully packed, with no other trouble to themselves than to act the part of teamsters to them. I took a fine pony with me, which I rode, or lent (as seeming exigencies required) to the lame and weary soldiers who were liable to be left behind a place of safety or relief.

Our march with an ox-team train was of necessity slow and tedious, and made more so by the unfavorable circumstances that surrounded us, as at that time there were no white settlements in the State of Kansas, and roving bands of Indians infested the road for the greater part of the distance. I will not attempt to describe the lands through which we passed on our march, but will state some of the most interesting incidents connected with it.

A short time before we commenced our march, Lieutenant Love, of the United States army, had left Fort Leavenworth with a company of dragoons to go to Santa Fé, and having a fine-looking company of men, and more confidence than experience, advanced rapidly into the prairies until he came to a train in the road owned by a citizen whose teams a band of Indians had just driven off, when, instead of immediately pursuing them with his whole force, in person, he divided his company and sent a sergeant with a detachment in pursuit, while he remained at camp. The Indians, observing the strength of the party in pursuit, retreated to a convenient position for their purpose, then turned upon it and nearly annihilated it. Not wishing to try any further West Point tactics with such fellows, he went on without notifying me of their whereabouts, thinking probably I would find that out myself the next day. I, however, saw nothing of them, perhaps from the fact that I could not readily discover them unless they were so disposed. Having passed the place of this disaster, which is about three miles west of Pawnee Fork,

I found that Colonel Easton, with four companies of infantry and one company of cavalry, had taken the north branch of the road to Fort Man, forty miles distant, and that a recent rain had made the road bad; I therefore took the south fork, or river road, which is several miles longer. Buffaloes were plenty, and my men were very desirous to be allowed to kill them, but I refused, and kept them to their duty. Several murmured at this, and complained that the discipline was too strict for them. We started early the next morning, July 21st, and had traveled about five miles, when one of the front guard came running back to say that they had found a battle-ground. I laughed at him, but the guard and train halted, and I went forward to see what had excited them so much, and found traces that Colonel Easton had left the north road and come to the river here, and had several of his men killed and buried in the road, where his corral had been formed for the night, that, by tramping down the freshly dug earth, the place of their sepulture might not be discovered and their bodies exhumed by the Indians. Near that spot, in a conspicuous place, was found a stave of a butter firkin, on which was written in pencil a brief account of the slaughter. As soon as my men ascertained the extent of the mischief, each man promptly took the post assigned him without waiting for my order, and from that time I heard no murmurs against my strict discipline.

Two days after, we overtook Colonel Easton's command, learned the particulars of his disaster, and saw the wounded. This afforded my company an excellent opportunity to indulge in their propensity to boast, and they were careful to avail themselves of it to an extent that could hardly be justified, as we were then but half way through our perilous journey. However, we performed the march without seeing an enemy in arms, but another and most unlooked for enemy destroyed one of my most robust men. This was a tarantula, a large species of spider, seldom seen in as high a latitude, but quite common further south. At our first camp on the Arkansas above Fort Man, John Foos, with others, spread his blanket on the grass and slept until the dawn of day, when he was awakened, and saw, as he supposed, a large spider crushed on his blanket near where his head had lain, and soon began to feel pain in his cheek, where were plainly visible the marks of a bite which had made four punctures of the skin, as if in two pairs opposite each other, at about a line apart, and the cheek commenced to swell rapidly. The weather being warm, we started early, and had traveled some three miles before I was informed of the circumstance, when I immediately ordered the man to be put in a wagon and carefully attended by a hospital nurse named William Harrison, who administered alcohol to him, which he said was the best antidote for that poison. I think his theory was correct; for when he commenced to drink it, in table-spoonfuls, he was swelling rapidly in all his limbs, his eyes were quite closed, and his features out of all due proportion; yet, after he had taken about a half dozen potions, at intervals of ten minutes, the pain and swelling began to subside, and had nearly ceased, when the alcohol failed, as I had but one bottle, and no more could be procured. He was then much prostrated, and so remained five days, subsisting on cold coffee and bread, at the end of which time he seemed in a fair way of recovery, when, contrary to the advice of his messmates and nurse, he ate a breakfast of hot fried cakes and hot coffee, when all the first symptoms returned with greater virulence than ever, under which he suffered most indescribable pains and swellings for about four hours, and then died the most painful death I ever witnessed. He was buried on the same day with the honors of war, near where he died.

After this sad occurrence, we continued our march to Santa Fé without further molestation or excitement, and arrived at that city on the 25th of August, having occupied seventy days in the trip. We were received with gladness, as we had brought full supplies, and had safely escorted Mr. Frank Coons' train of merchant wagons, which supplied the town with goods.

CHAPTER XVII.

INCIDENTS AT SANTA FÉ AND ON THE MARCH DOWN THE RIO GRANDE.

On our arrival at Santa Fé, there were but few troops there, and our presence was much needed to keep the Mexicans in awe. They had lately rebelled and murdered Governor Bent. We were therefore stationed in the town, and performed garrison duty until a larger force could be concentrated; in the meantime our battalion was being well drilled. At length Colonel Newby, in command of the sixth regiment of Illinois infantry, arrived, and assumed command of the entire force. As he outranked our colonel, his officers seemed as if they might show a kind of superiority and give us examples in performing military duties. Not many days had passed when I was detailed as officer of the day, and took my station to inspect and receive the guard, and the adjutant of the Illinois regiment, a splendid young officer, formed the guard, and, saluting me in military style, informed me the guard was ready for inspection. I cast my eyes on them, and replied, "Several of them are without coats and cannot be received." He hastened to their camp and brought forward others to fill the complement, when I inspected and received the guard· This trivial affair made every soldier in the command learn my name, and to treat me as a father and friend of soldiers; and the same young officer having met my daughter at Belleville, Illinois, long afterwards, mentioned the circumstance to her.

On the 23d of October, 1847, I received orders to escort a train, loaded with commissary stores, down the Rio Grande, and on the following day left Santa Fé and marched to the little stream called Gallisteo, and encamped on the south bank, the train on the opposite side not being able to cross in the night. The waters of the Gallisteo are slightly alkaline, and very disagreeable and sickening at best, but doubly so when low. Our wagon-master, being ignorant of this, allowed his oxen to drink of it, which killed twenty-nine of them. This compelled him to remove the train in detachments to the

Rio Grande, and while doing so a team broke from one of the drivers and ten more oxen were drowned. These disasters caused the quartermaster to detain us until he could go to Santa Fé to reinforce his teams with other oxen before we could proceed further. On his return, we proceeded to Albuquerque, where we waited for further orders.

On the 11th of November we received orders to resume our march down the Rio Grande, and to keep within protecting distance of the assistant quartermaster and commissary's train, and then, crossing to the right bank, we moved very slowly down the river until we came within five miles of the town of Socorro, where we halted, and were soon joined by four more companies of our battalion, with orders for me to take command of them and put them and my company into winter quarters at the most suitable place in the vicinity. I therefore fell back and put them in quarters in the village of Limitar, nine miles above Socorro, as ordered, and awaited the arrival ef Colonel Easton and staff.

Soon after his arrival, he was detailed, with myself and the second lieutenant, to serve on a court martial. While I was absent, two of my best men were taken sick with typhoid fever, and I lost them both a few days after my return. I was very sorry to lose two such men; but what pained me most was, that when I returned to camp and went to visit them, they wept like two little children with joy at seeing me, and told me that they now hoped to recover, as they knew I would see they were attended to and made comfortable; that they had been neglected, lain cold, and passed whole nights without fire, on the bare floor, without even straw to lie upon. I did all I could to cherish and save them, but failed, and buried them at this town.

Not long afterwards Colonel Easton was ordered to Santa Fé, when the battalion again came under my command, and I determined to put it in a high state of discipline in the least possible time, and was well aided by every officer of the command. We succeeded beyond our most sanguine expectations, and acquired an expertness that was astonishing, so that any officer of the battalion could manœuvre it with ease.

It was now the 3d of February, 1848, the mountains around being covered with snow, when a messenger arrived from

Colonel Ralls, stationed at El Paso, requiring reinforcements. I had no doubt it was my duty to respond at once, but believing it would be gratifying to my brother officers to at least be consulted on so important an action as breaking up our winter quarters and marching one hundred and thirty miles, ninety of which were through the *Gran Jornada del Muerto*, or Journey of Death, without water or wood, in midwinter, to reinforce an army already outnumbered by the enemy six to one, according to the best information that could be obtained. I therefore assembled them all at my quarters, laid the whole matter before them, and asked what advice they would give, as I thought we should respond at once by marching immediately to El Paso. Captain Cunningham, the senior officer, said that he felt it his duty and his privilege to thank me for my deference and respect shown them in a matter of so much importance and interest •to each one of them, as it showed as well my willingness to share the honors as the dangers and labors of the movement; that he coincided with my views of duty, and would do all in his power to aid me. Each officer then in turn expressed his concurrence and his confidence in his superior officers, and his willingness to obey them, and do all in his power to promote the reputation and welfare of the battalion; and we separated amidst great enthusiasm and warm feelings.

The whole night and next day were spent in baking bread and cooking rations, washing, and in preparations for battle. At evening I reviewed the battalion with the surgeon, and, leaving at the post all who were unwell or feeble, marched on the following day to Socorro, where I halted and assumed command of the Santa Fé battalion, whose commanding officer refused to accompany us unless I would assume the command and then he would obey me; which I was constrained to do, and he faithfully kept his word and obeyed orders.

Early the next morning, being the 6th of February, 1848, we commenced a forced march. My command then consisted of one company of light artillery with a battery of six pieces; three companies of cavalry, which formed the Santa Fé battalion, and five companies of infantry, which formed the Missouri battalion of infantry volunteers—all troops enlisted to serve during the war, and mostly men who had served two

152 AUTOBIOGRAPHY OF

campaigns in Mexico, the whole numbering about five hundred men, and all about as self-reliant as Julius Cæsar's tenth legion.

We continued our march to within seven miles of the ford of the Rio Grande, two miles above Fra Cristobal, and prepared for fording the river when the teams should be warm and not much exhausted. The infantry arrived first, and, to their dismay, found the stream five hundred yards wide, covered with ice in broken pieces of all sizes from fifty feet square and under, and four inches in thickness, which had been shattered among the rocks a little above. The prospect was so gloomy that those who first arrived began to make fires, until Lieutenant Levant came up in command of my company and asked me where he should ford the river. I told him that as he would be expected to lead—as I must see all pass—he had better select the place for crossing himself and pass the company over, and take a good position to cover the ford, and not leave it until he saw the last wagon of the train safely over.

Lieutenant Levant was a gentleman as old as myself (both had served in the war of 1812), and was over fifty years of age. Having formed the company in line as skirmishers, he ordered them to observe where and how he would ford the river; and as soon as they saw him on the opposite bank, to follow one by one in the same place and manner. He then stripped himself, and, taking his clothes in his left hand and his arms in his right, he walked in among the ice, while a breathless silence prevailed in the company, although half the men had stripped themselves and stood ready with tent poles in their hands to assist him, in case of necessity, by pushing away the ice. The anxiety was of short duration, for he passed the stream in less than fifteen minutes, and as soon as the men saw him fairly out of water they cheered, and the shout was taken up by the other companies who had arrived, then succesively by the others until it reached the extreme rear, when all shouted from front to rear, and the hills reverberated with echoes the like of which were never probably heard there before.

Captain Hassendeubel of the artillery, in command of the Santa Fé battalion, soon came up from the rear, when I placed his battalion in front, and, knowing he was one of the most

competent officers, I requested him to move forward to Fra
Cristobal and put both battalions in readiness to enter the
Jornada—which order he promptly executed—while I remained
with the guard to protect our trains, a vital necessity at this
time.

I waited on the right bank of the river alone until I
saw all the wagons pass over, although the last wagon
detained the whole train more than all the rest, and by the
want of vigilance of its driver subjected the whole command
to more delay than all other impediments we met with on the
march. It was a fair specimen of the connected evils of negli-
gence, laziness and fraud, and may as well be noted as a
beacon to others in all the long marches to be made hereafter
across these plains with teams.

A wagoner whose duty it was to groom his own team,
engaged a soldier to do it, and rewarded him by allowing him
to ride concealed in his covered wagon, contrary to rules and
orders, and was the last of the train to enter the river; and
being somewhat impeded by the ice and extra load, the team
balked and halted in the middle of the river, where it remained
immovable as a rock. There was no time for delay, so the
wagon-master instantly unloaded two wagons and taking them
and six men passed over to me, expressed his regret that he
had detained me so long alone, and ordered the two wagons
to be placed on either side the stalled one and all its load to
be put into the empty ones. They then passed into the river
and were placed as he had directed, and when the wagoners
began to unfasten the wagon cover in order to reach the
freight they discovered the concealed soldier, who at once
attempted to escape. Immediately the shout was raised,
"Catch him! catch him!" but he slipped out behind, ran
down the stream into deeper water and got safely to the shore,
and followed the command. Thinking him sufficiently
punished I paid no further attention to him that evening,
and crossed the river as soon as the wagons were over, when
the whole freight was arranged and the train at once moved
to Fra Cristobal, where we partook of a "hasty plate of
soup" and prepared for a night's march.

From here I sent forward sergeant William Smith and two
men to El Paso with a letter to Colonel Ralls informing him

11

that I had safely passed the Rio Grande and was on my way
to join him with two battalions and a battery of six pieces of
artillery, and would make a forced march to El Paso. As
there was neither wood nor water on the route for ninety
miles, both of the named aqueous and ligneous articles were
put in small quantities in the wagons, and all unnecessary
ones thrown out, and each soldier required to carry his own
baggage up the mountain and assist in urging forward the
train or artillery, by pushing with his hands or musket, until
we had attained the summit.

It was a clear, cold evening, with the sun about one hour
high, when, all being ready, our little army commenced the
ascent—Captain Hassendeubel, of the Santa Fé battalion,
commanding it as the right of line in front of the train, and
Captain Cunningham, commanding the Missouri infantry battalion, in the rear or left of line, all prepared for battle and
momentarily expecting it. We were all, however, happily
disappointed as no enemy appeared, but we suffered the most
intense cold that mortals could endure. I led my horse a
short distance, and then turned it over to the officer of the
rear guard to assist in bringing up any footsore soldier that
might be left in the rear.

At about ten o'clock at night we attained the plain, or Jornada, a most beautiful elevation, about two thousand feet
above the waters of the Rio Grande, which river washes its
base on the west. This plain is covered with a fair growth of
grass interspersed with the soap plant, a very luxuriant
perennial (I think), growing from three to twelve feet in hight,
with broad leaves on all sides, which, being killed by the
frost, furnish an inflammable article of uncommon brilliancy
when set on fire. The soldiers soon perceived this and ran
furtively from the line to set them on fire, which made the
front and rear of my command appear as clear in view as at
mid-day.

In this wise—in line of battle and no one to fight but the
terrible frost, and which suffered us not to go by without a
victim—we passed one of the clearest and coldest nights I
ever experienced, and in this manner we marched thirty miles
in twelve hours, when we halted for refreshments. The wagoners began to take their sacks of corn from the wagons to

feed, when one seeing a soldier's cap and blanket partly covered with straw, and knowing that allowing soldiers to ride
without orders was strictly forbidden, hastened to the officer
of the guard and informed him that a soldier was sleeping in
his wagon. A file of men was dispatched to arrest him, in
which duty they met with no opposition, as on unrolling the
blanket they found the corpse of the soldier who had the day
before attempted to cross the Rio Grande in a loaded wagon,
frozen as thoroughly as an iceberg. Thus perished a stout,
well-formed young man, twenty-five years of age, purely
through disobedience of a reasonable · order, which all his
comrades had, with safety to themselves, obeyed with alacrity
and apparent willingness. He was buried with the honors of
war by the roadside, and in digging the grave the earth was
found frozen to the depth of two feet, from which some idea
of the intensity of the cold on that elevated plain may be
formed.

As soon as this sad duty was performed we continued our
march through the plain, halting to rest and eat but four
times, and arrived at the southwest end of the Jornada on the
9th at about the same hour we left the river on the 7th, having
marched ninety miles in forty-eight hours.

At an early hour, after a night's rest, we moved forward
through the village of Doña Ana, the stores and public houses
of which I had ordered to be closed, and the sale and distri-
bution of liquors stopped for the day, to avoid straggling,
disorder, and drunkenness. In this I succeeded well, but,
unfortunately, one of the best soldiers of my own company
purchased of a Mexican, in the street, one dime's worth of
dried pears and grapes, and ate them as he marched along,
which, swelling in his stomach, produced an inflammation
that killed him the same night; and we buried him with
appropriate honors the next morning, near the Rio Grande,
covering the place with a large pile of willow-brush to prevent
its being disturbed. I was more distressed by this occurrence
than any other that happened during the war, for his mother
was a poor widow, who allowed her only son to enlist with me
to enable him to obtain a farm and a little money to improve
it, which he seemed in a fair way to do until this unhappy
day, when all his fond hopes were blasted by death, and

buried forever. His name was Gannon; he was born in the city of St. Louis, well instructed in the Roman Catholic religion, and as fine a soldier as ever shouldered a musket. When he perceived that his life was in danger, he began to prepare for death, and showed at once his faith and his thorough Catholic education by continuing to pray and exhort his companions as long as he could speak, and seemed to die confident of passing immediately into a state of eternal felicity, which was all he desired. After his death, several half eagles were found sewed in the waistband of his pantaloons, which I brought to St. Louis and delivered to his mother.

As we were about to leave this camp, I received a most flattering and complimentary letter from Colonel Ralls, thanking me for my promptitude in hastening to his assistance, and informing me that the danger was past, and I might suspend a forced march and advance *ad libitum*. I showed the letter to Captain Hassendeubel, and informed him he might march at will, as his battalion could out-travel mine, and report to Colonel Ralls at El Paso, and I would march as I found most convenient. Accordingly, the Santa Fé battalion left us, and we leisurely pursued our march, and crossed the Rio Grande above El Paso, near where Fort Bliss now stands, on the 15th of March, and halted about two miles above town to form in proper order, to show to best advantage on entering the place.

CHAPTER XVIII.

ENTRY INTO EL PASO, AND INCIDENTS DURING OUR STAY IN THAT TOWN.

The battalion present consisted, all told, of three hundred men, in five companies, all well-dressed and clean, with not a sickly man or boy among them. Being all formed into companies of equal size, and the officers properly distributed, the battalion was wheeled from line into column by sections in open order, on a good smooth road, when I placed myself on foot at its head, and with common time music I marched it into the plaza or public square of the town, and, moving to within half the length of the column to its centre, I wheeled the column into line, halted, dressed the line, ordered arms, rested, and went and reported to Colonel Ralls.

I received from him the most flattering testimonials of respect for me and the officers of our battalion, and he expressed his regret that he was unable to go out and meet them and congratulate them on their safe arrival, in consequence of his long indisposition; but that he had directed the post quartermaster to have suitable quarters prepared for all of us, which he had no doubt were in readiness, and would be pointed out to us when we were ready to receive them.

He then informed me that Lieutenant-Colonel Lane was under arrest, and that I was now the ranking officer fit for duty at the post, and would be expected to direct and command in any emergency, and desired me to come and stay with him until he was able to go on duty himself. I replied that I would do so until he could procure another officer to fill the place, which was satisfactory to him. I then returned to the battalion and informed them their quarters would be ready and assigned to them in half an hour, when all must be present to receive them. The battalion was then ordered to stack their arms and break ranks for that period, and the time was spent in shaking hands and congratulating each other at their meeting so far from home in the enemy's country.

At the expiration of the half hour, I called the battalion into line, when they took arms, and each captain led off his individual company to the quarters assigned it by the quartermaster. As my company was being led off by Lieutenant Levant, some one asked him why I did not command my own company. "Because," said the old man, "the colonel has given him the command of this place, with the three battalions in it, as Lieutenant-Colonel Lane is under arrest for allowing Mexicans to sell liquor to the soldiers; and I will venture to say the Mexicans will not sell liquor after to-day until our captain leaves town or is relieved."

I knew nothing of this at that time; but having had my

private quarters assigned me at a distance from my company,
I walked to the company quarters to see how they were
situated for the night, and found my men in a large house and
about half drunk with wine. I asked where they got it. They
said at the first door back. I took an interpreter and informed
the man who kept the house that he must close and lock his
door and keep it locked until my company left the town, or I
would have him punished. He promised to do so, and I left
him. Early the next morning, the same man, and another
who represented himself as the proprietor of the wine cellar,
came to me with an interpreter, and, with woefully elongated
visages, complained that my soldiers had broken down the
door of their cellar and were drinking their wine. Believing
the report, I took my sword and hastened to the place, the
three Mexicans following slowly behind me; but I found
the cellar deserted, with no sign of a door or any violence,
except about half a cart load of broken wine jugs on the
floor and wine mingled with the fragments about three
inches deep. The affair needed no explanation, and I asked
none, so immediately returned to my quarters, having no
doubt I should hear the whole history of the affair during the
day. In this I was not disappointed. When my company
had breakfasted, knowing the day was to be devoted to rest
after the forced march, several of the men came to my quarters
as to their father's house, as was their custom, and, supposing
I had had no hint of what had transpired the evening before,
began a history of it.

They said that although the Mexican had promised me he
would not open his cellar while I remained in town, yet he
had followed me to my quarters, and, when he had seen me
out of sight, he came back to the cellar with another man,
opened the door, and began to sell wine to the soldiers. A
shrewd, far-seeing soldier of my company, named Edward
Taylor, although he had but one eye, perceived this would
lead to mischief, and advised to take the cellar door from its
hinges and cast it into the river, so that, should their captain
return, he could not close the door on them and transfer them
to the guard-house. It was but a small job, and was soon
accomplished. When the party returned, a few more assistant bar-keepers, with their tin cups, were added to those

already engaged. Business was brisk, the cellar crowded, and more arriving. Some paid, others did not, according to taste or convenience. At length the Mexicans discovered the current of business was too rapid for profit, and determined to close the cellar, and went to the entrance, when they perceived the door had been removed, so they placed themselves in the doorway. This displeasing the boys in blue, they discharged them, and conducted the business on their own account until its close, which was speedily done by breaking every *tinaja* or jug in the cellar, after which the soldiers returned to their quarters.

The Mexicans soon circulated an account of this affair which corroborated their own connivance, and led to the promulgation of stringent orders which effectually stopped their selling liquor to the infantry while in El Paso.

Three days later, General Price arrived with his staff and several other officers, Colonel Easton among the rest, which relieved me of any command except my own company, which I drilled carefully. Preparations were immediately made for an advance on Chihuahua and Durango, and I was ordered to garrison El Paso with my company, thirty dragoons, and the invalids, fifty in number, for thirty days, and then, if I received no counter order, to escort the two trains of quarter-master and commissary stores to Chihuahua. When my company learned such an order had been given, they murmured, saying, "We are left behind because we have old officers." I thereupon went to General Price and informed him that I was willing to undertake the performance of the duty assigned me without my company, if he would take it with him, and I would supply its strength from among the wagoners. He inquired how I expected to be able to do that. I told him that, as soon as the army was gone, my orders would be the law, and I would make soldiers of the wagoners, and there were one hundred and twenty of them. He suggested they might object to serving as soldiers. I replied, "I can change their notions, with the assistance of the dragoons and the veteran invalids." He said, "You may try;" and I hastened to inform my company, who were greatly elated at the tidings, but appeared pained that I must stay behind in so dangerous a position.

On the 5th of March, 1848, General Price marched south from El Paso, and I began my preparations for holding the town by posting a guard of ten men on the roof of the church, which was flat and overlooked the plaza, on which all the wagons were corraled, and removing all the ammunition from the wagons into the house lately occupied by General Armijo (late governor of New Mexico), and known as Armijo's palace, where I had my quarters alone, as I would trust no one in the house with me except Frank Hinch, my German servant, as I had a hundred thousand dollars in gold left with me by the army paymaster, which I kept hidden in ammunition boxes, privately marked, so that Hinch and myself only knew where it was. We then placed twenty loaded muskets in convenient position for use in case of an attack, and I informed Hinch that it was my intention to fire one of those muskets into a box of ammunition if the Mexicans should get into the house, and that, in such an emergency, he had better run out of reach of the explosion that would follow. He replied that he would not move an inch, as we would have plenty of money for us both to spend all our lives. Having thus disposed of the money and ammunition, I turned my attention to the wagoners, and sent for the two wagonmasters and told them J wished to see if the wagoners had all their arms, equipments and ammunition in good order which the United States had furnished them with, and for that purpose they might assemble their men, and, when ready, notify me with lists of all their names. I then prepared for re-arming them, as I expected to find they had lost most of what they had received in their outfit, and charge them for what was missing. On assembling, they made a very grave appearance, and began to reproach the soldiers with having taken the missing articles, to which I paid no attention, but furnished everything that was lacking, and had it charged on their pay-roll. I then formed them in line, and explained to them the reason why they were armed, and the necessity of their being drilled and taught to act together. They were then dismissed and ordered to assemble again at five o'clock for drill. As soon as they had broken ranks, they began to discuss the propriety of my order, and threaten to disobey it. I therefore ordered the lieutenant of dragoons to parade all his men not on post, at five o'clock, in the plaza, and also ordered a sergeant to bring forward all invalids who were able to bear arms. All were punctually there, and all the wagoners also, and I drilled them one hour without a sign of disobedience, although half had said they would not do it.

The next day was to be observed as a great holiday among the Mexicans, who are all devout Catholics, and on such occasions manifest their piety by a very prompt attendance at church in the morning. In pursuance of this custom, at a very early hour in the morning they began to assemble in large numbers in the plaza in front of the church. The wagoners observing such a crowd rushing while it was yet dark into the plaza, filling every vacant place, became alarmed, and, seizing their arms, ran to my quarters and called most vociferously for me to rise and see what was going on. I had heard the movement and gone into the upper story of the house, from whence I could see in daylight every wagon, beast and person on the plaza; but it was yet too dark to perceive any signs of danger, except that I could hear the rumbling of the wheels of a twelve-pounder which had been left with me, and which the wagoners had taken and loaded and shotted with a shirt-sleeve full of musket balls, and were bringing it to the front of my quarters, where they placed it and covered it by a line of their own forming, and all called loudly for me.

I went out on the piazza and asked the cause of their calling for me. They answered that there were more Mexicans already in the plaza than would be required to carry off every pound of provisions in both the trains at once. I told them I was afraid of that yesterday, when some of them were unwilling to drill, but I did not think there was any danger now of that. They said they would feel more safe if I were down among them. I therefore took my sword and revolver and went out to them. As soon as I was on the pavement, they cheered and drove the Mexicans from that side of the plaza, and would not let them pass between themselves and the trains. Soon the doors of the church were opened and gave admission to the crowd, estimated at three thousand. We remained under arms until sunrise, when, at their own suggestion, I formed them into two companies, appointing the two wagonmasters captains, each over his own men, and others as officers and non-commissioned officers. While this was being done, they assured me that I would never need the dragoons and invalids to drill them. We immediately organized an additional guard, called the "Wagon Guard," and that day nailed our much prized banner to a long flagstaff, and raised it on the top of Armijo's palace, where it floated until I left the town, when I took it with me to Chihuahua, and have it now in my own possession, with the nail prints visible to this day.

The wagoners, during my stay at El Paso, had manifested the strongest desire to qualify themselves for defending the trains and themselves, and I spared no pains in instructing them, so that when I left for Chihuahua I had the same confidence in them that I reposed in my own company, for several of them had come from Fort Leavenworth with me the year before, and knew me well.

CHAPTER XIX.

MARCH FROM EL PASO TO CHIHUAHUA.

Elated by my success in training the wagoners and gaining their confidence, and the time appointed for our stay here having fully expired, without any trouble or disaster, and having a force I considered equal to two hundred good men for any short skirmish or battle, I left El Paso with the two assistant quartermasters and their trains, and all the sick, lame and lazy who had been left behind the army.

On account of the freshness and stubbornness of the cattle we moved but seven miles the first day, and, camping where there was no grass, started early the next morning in order to reach pasture. We halted opposite the town of San Elizario, and as many Apache Indians were said to be in the vicinity, we posted a line of our best men as sentinels on the ridge of hills that lie about a mile from the right or west bank of the Rio Grande and put out the cattle to feed between the river and the hills, as no Indians dare be seen near the river, and we therefore considered them safe there. After they appeared to have fed and rested sufficiently, they were collected and arranged for moving, when it was discovered that seventeen pairs of the oxen were missing, and that the trains could not be moved without them. I therefore detached all the mule teams and sent them forward with one quarter-master and the lieutenant of dragoons and twenty men as an escort to the train of forty wagons, while I sent the remaining ten with a sergeant and interpreter into San Elizario to bring their chief magistrate and padre to my quarters, where they arrived a little before sundown, and, after dismounting, were introduced by the interpreter. They endeavored to be ceremonious, but I cut the matter short by telling them the people of Elizario had stolen our oxen, and if they were not brought back the next day I would punish them. The alcalde said they had strayed. I told him it was false, and ordered them to leave my camp instantly. They both mounted and left, the priest riding a very fine gelding, which the sequel will show attracted the particular attention of a dismounted dragoon named Jackson, whose horse had been stolen the night before his company left for Chihuahua and himself left to recover it.

When I perceived that I must stay in this camp an indefinite length of time, I placed sentinels along the river, and turned out the cattle to graze, while I waited for the return of those that were missing. As I had but little hope of recovering them, I directed my thoughts to the best plan of obtaining a supply from the Mexicans, as the wagoners had found the tracks of their horses where they had hid under the bank, and, unseen, drove off our cattle as they came to the river to drink. Learning this, I sent some scouts across the river to discover by the trail in which direction they had been driven, and was kept during the day in momentary expectation of hearing from them.

About three o'clock in the afternoon, two Mexicans brought back five of our cattle, which they said they found near the town, but they had the appearance of being worried down by travel, and their yokes were gone. I paid them two dollars for their trouble, hoping to recover the remainder, but in this failed entirely, as no other Mexican came to us that day.

About dark, the scouts returned and informed me that they had traced the tracks of our oxen, and the ponies that followed them, around the mountain, which is ten miles east of San Elizario, and down another valley to within five miles of the town, where they saw some of our oxen in a herd of not less than six hundred cattle of all sizes feeding together, and, it being late, they passed without disturbing them. When I heard that, I was confident the Mexicans would make but a moderate profit out of me in this transaction, and ordered two days' rations to be immediately issued and cooked preparatory for a march, and every man and horse about the camp ready to go on duty at sunrise with a complete supply of arms and ammunition.

The next day was Sunday, and I informed the wagonmaster that he must guard his wagons and teams against the Indians, and I would watch the Mexicans. I then put all the dragoons under the quartermaster, with an order to furnish himself from the Elizario herds beyond the town with the cattle necessary to move his train. He was soon in the saddle, when the dragoon Jackson asked me to let him cross the river and try to purchase a horse. I consented with the condition that he would return with the dragoons, which he promised to do. He mounted behind another dragoon to cross the river and soon was out of sight. In about an hour he returned with a fine black bob-tailed and roach-maned gelding, bare-backed, and, riding up to a certain wagon, dismounted, then, pulling out his own saddle, placed it properly upon the horse, and, leading him up to me, said, " Captain, I am a man once more, ready to fight ten Mexicans anywhere you may direct me." I replied, " Very well; I may find a job of that kind for you this afternoon." He seemed well pleased, and left me.

At ten o'clock, I ordered the oxen to be chained at the corral and all the sentinels to be withdrawn and stationed around it, and sent Jackson with his new horse to watch the ford where the Mexicans stole our oxen, which was one mile above us in the rear. He had gone but a short distance on the way to his post when the padre or priest of San Elizario, accompanied by the prefect, alcalde, an interpreter, and the priest's peon carrying a large quantity of very long black horse hair in his hand, came to me and complained that one of my men had come to their town in the morning while the priest was saying prayers in the church for the salvation of souls, and, seeing the priest's servant leading his fine black horse to water, took off the bridle and put on another, mounted and rode off to a secluded place, cut short the long hair of his tail and mane, and had come to my camp; that they had followed him, found the hair and brought it along to prove the horse, and, showing it, asked me to restore the horse. I told them if they would restore our oxen and yokes, I would do it, but not otherwise; and if I was compelled to stay here another day, I would spend most of it in burning their town. When the interpreter had translated what I said, the padre shook his head and exclaimed, "¡Ay, qué malvados!" and left me, apparently satisfied that I would not be likely to dismount a brave, well-armed soldier, in the presence of enemies, to give his horse to a priest whose parishioners had stolen seventeen pairs of our oxen, worth one hundred dollars a pair, and their yokes, which could not be replaced in that country.

When they had been gone about half an hour, several reports of muskets or carbines were heard from the opposite side of the river, which at once alarmed the invalids, and they got under arms and came to my tent, offering to do anything I would direct to save the train. The wagoners seized their arms, formed a line and sent for me to command them, as they said the train must be held as long as there was a man of the command alive. It was an exciting scene, calculated to rouse the most stupid energies of the human mind, when shouts of the dragoons and quartermaster began to be heard, and soon a great drove of cattle appeared, driven by the dragoons, and plunging into the Rio Grande swam across, followed by them to our camp, where a lunette of men was formed that forced the whole herd into the wagon-formed corral, which was immediately closed by running a heavy wagon across the entrance. The dragoons, being hungry and weary, went immediately to their quarters to eat a little of their cold cooked rations; but before they had half finished their meal, Jackson, on his bob-tailed horse, rode furiously by into camp, saying, "All the Mexicans are crossing at the upper ford and will soon be here." This announcement ended the meal and brought every invalid and wagoner armed to the corral for its defence.

About forty Mexicans, unarmed, soon followed, and, as no danger was apprehended, we allowed them to enter our camp with freedom, when they went directly to the corral and began to point out the oxen and bulls they claimed. I concluded to indulge them with a good view of them, for I thought it probably might be the last they would ever have. Jackson in the meantime kept riding back and forth in front of the corral entrance on his bob-tailed horse, which the Mexicans all recognized as an old acquaintance, although somewhat shortened in his caudal appendage, which annoyed them exceedingly. Being in good humor with them, I heard their different claims to the cattle, and pointed out six of our speckled oxen marked "U. S." and asked who claimed them. They said "No one. Mexican cattle are all black, and branded." I remarked that I did not think I had time to look them all over that evening, but I would take their names and the number of cattle each one had furnished, and began to write out a list and affix the number stated by each. When I had finished, and found the aggregate to be one hundred and eighty-three, I called the quartermaster to see if the number was correct. He said that it was not; that he had driven in sixty-four Mexican cattle and six of our own that had been stolen, and he supposed each Mexican claimed them, and thus the aggregate became so great. I then informed them they must leave my camp and not visit it again. The interpreter, however, took the liberty to add to the order, that I said I would shoot every Mexican that did not get over the river in five minutes. This false report alarmed them at once, and mounting their horses they plunged into the river and swam to the other shore, to the great amusement of our men, who shouted and huzzaed.

We had then plenty of fine cattle, but they were nearly as wild as the buffaloes, and among them were several bulls that could not be excelled in size and ferocity, and the process of yoking began by taking the largest bulls and yoking them together by pairs. The animals made all the resistance they could, but, surrounded with sixty wagoners armed with whips and ropes, the poor animals were soon confined, yoked, and their eyes, noses and mouths filled with sand, so that, blinded and half-suffocated, they were easily attached to the wagons and willingly walked off to avoid any new process of torture, in which these wagoners were very proficient. The yoking process completed, the train was soon again in motion, having been detained two days by the felonious occurrence narrated.

We traveled about twelve miles, when we halted for the night where there was water, and turned out our cattle to graze on the dry grass, setting a guard over them and our camp. At about nine o'clock, fires in the distance began to appear on all sides, which created great alarm among those not used to seeing prairies on fire, thinking it was the work of Mexicans—although it might have been occasioned by Indians on a hunting excursion, when they often fire the prairies to drive the game in a certain direction where they lie in wait for it. Being unwilling to risk a stampede of our stock, we corraled it, and lay on our arms during the night prepared for battle, and at early dawn put our train in line for moving, when it was found that two pairs of our oxen were missing. We had plenty of cattle, but no more yokes, and so drove on with what we had remaining. The dragoons were in front, while I guarded the rear with the invalids, who rode in wagons. When we were about a mile on the road, I saw Jackson standing by the roadside holding his horse, and asked him what was wrong. He said he was informed two pairs of oxen were left behind and he wished permission to go back and recover them. I remarked, "I think it is too hazardous for a man to go back alone; but if another of your comrades will accompany you, I consent. He mounted, galloped forward, and soon returned with another as daring as himself, and both at full gallop were soon out of sight.

About four o'clock, after traveling fifteen miles, we halted, put out a cordon of sentinels, and turned in the oxen to feed, when we heard a great shout from the sentinels, and looking saw their hats raised on the points of their arms, and, looking still further back, saw Jackson and his comrade driving our

lost oxen into camp and each leading a saddled horse besides
his own. The whole camp seemed at once intoxicated with
admiration and joy. I told them I thought as soon as they
had made sufficient noise they had better be examining their
arms and ammunition to see if all were in order for immediate
use. They assured me they would do it, or anything else I
thought best. Soon after, Jackson led up a good Mexican
horse, and said, "Here, captain, is one of the horses we have
taken to-day from the two thieves who stole our oxen last
night. What shall I do with him?" I replied, "Keep him
until the thieves call for him." The wagoners rejoined, "Jackson, the horse is yours," and enjoyed a good time in hearing
him describe the race they had after the thieves, whom they
found, by their tracks on the burnt prairie, driving the cattle
about five miles from our old camp. He said, "We passed
rapidly up the road three miles above our old camp, where
the road and river are near together, without signs or tracks,
then went directly from the road about one mile, when we
struck the trail of the four yoked oxen and two horses,
and followed it about two miles, when we saw them a mile
ahead, and gave chase. The Mexicans abandoned the oxen
and fled, in opposite directions, towards large chapparals, in
which they hid, leaving the horses for us, which we have
brought along with the oxen into camp.

After this exploit, we pursued our march to Chihuahua
without further molestation. When within about two or three
miles of the city, I met all my company not on duty, who had
come out to meet me, having heard that I encamped the night
before but five miles from the city. Our meeting was most
cordial; I have never seen another more so. Forty of my
company were present, and each acted as if he had met his
father.

We arrived at Chihuahua about eleven o'clock, when I sent
for Major Spalding, the paymaster, and transferred the one
hundred thousand dollars in gold to him; then delivered the
provisions to the commissary, sent the invalids to the hospital,
and turned over all the wagons and stock to the quartermaster, who at once assigned me a fine house for my quarters and
sent my baggage to it.

Having fully obeyed my orders, I went to General Price's

headquarters and reported myself to him. He expressed himself well pleased with my performance and complete success in training wagoners and teaching them to become soldiers.

CHAPTER XX.

INCIDENTS, OBSERVATIONS, AND DUTIES OF THE AUTHOR DURING A STAY OF THREE MONTHS IN THE CITY OF CHIHUAHUA.

On my arrival at Chihuahua, I took command of my company, which was in a high state of discipline, well clad, neat, cleanly, and healthy, and consisted of seventy-five men and three officers. I was proud of them, and I have cause to think they were equally so of me. On the following morning I led them, in all their martial perfection, to the dress parade, and, having formed them on the right of line, took my proper place, and waited the formation of the residue of the line by the adjutant, my first lieutenant, now Colonel Samuel Holmes, commanding the fortieth Missouri regiment of infantry volunteers at Mobile, Alabama. After the ceremonies of the parade were through, and we were ready to retire, the adjutant produced and read a general order, the purport of which was: "Captain Shepard, commanding Company A, Missouri battalion of infantry volunteers, will turn over the command of his company to his lieutenant, and report himself to-morrow morning at the headquarters of the general of the department, to enter upon the performance of the duties of the office of provost marshal, and all persons will thereafter respect and obey him as such." The parade was then dismissed, and I marched my company back to their quarters, and after addressing a few words to them, turned over the command of the company to my veteran lieutenant, Thomas Levant, and retired to my quarters.

I was informed that, after I left, the lieutenant addressed the company, and remarked that he was not surprised that

12

the general had taken their captain from them and made him absolutely the master of the police of the city, when there were nineteen other captains present, since all knew my reliability of character, and that there would be no mistakes, and he hoped I would not be pained by being obliged to arrest any of them; that I would not lose sight of them, but would visit them in their quarters each day, he had no doubt, and would attend to all their wants. I did not disappoint them, but was there once each day thereafter.

Having arranged my quarters and dined, I began to perambulate the city and ascertain the locality of the offices and quarters of the different officers. I soon found I had chosen the worst period of the day for my purpose, as the whole army had in this short time acquired the universal habit of the Mexicans, of taking a *siesta* after dinner until three o'clock. I therefore could see none of the officers at. that time of day. However, after three o'clock all their doors were opened, and I made several visits, among them one to General Price. On being shown into his parlor, I observed three Mexicans seated, and no one else, and, while waiting for the return of the general, scrutinized them more closely, when I came to the conclusion I had seen them all before. Soon the general returned, and, after the usual salutations among friends had passed between us, he turned to the Mexicans and said, " This is the officer you say took your oxen; we will hear what he has to say about it." I related the whole history of the affair, which was translated to them, and the general added, "Lieutenant Paul has made the same statement. This officer has nothing to do with it now. Go to the quartermaster." By this time the countenances of the Mexicans had become much chop-fallen, and bidding the general a gracious adieu, they retired, followed by Mr. Skinner, the interpreter, who, when in the street, informed them I had been appointed provost marshal and would be on duty the next day, and possibly the thought might come into my head to arrest and punish them for my detention at Elizario two days, with a hundred men and a large train, and he thought their best move now would be to leave the city by the shortest route, for I had been greatly vexed with the people of Elizario for stealing my oxen, and if I once got hold of any of them I would surely do them some harm or mischief. This was a sufficient hint, and they left the city immediately.

On the following morning, I repaired to the general's headquarters and reported myself ready to receive and execute orders. He replied he had no particular orders to give; that I was an older gentleman than he, and that I had been twice as long in the army; that I was well acquainted with the regulations necessary for the enforcement of good order and law, and he wished them maintained in as much perfection as was now in our power, and I might take such course and use such means as I thought proper to accomplish it. I thereupon ordered every Mexican gambling-house, and all houses of Mexicans where liquor was sold, to be closed at nine o'clock P. M. each evening, and to be kept closed till four o'clock in the morning, and sent a person to notify each of the owners. Through the densely populated parts of the city the order was obeyed, and but two in the whole place failed to obey, and I arrested them both after ten o'clock at night and put them in the Mexican prison, and the alcalde punished them at my request by setting them to cleaning the public stables for ten days. This frightened the whole fraternity so much that there was no similar occurrence, and the streets were quiet during the remainder of my sojourn in the city.

The next subject that seemed to require attention was disorder about the plaza Tauri, a fine pleasure ground of about four acres, well shaded with beautiful trees, and comfortably furnished with permanent, well-dressed, fine stone seats, where the Mexicans with their families spend a large portion of their time in conversation. On the south are ladies' baths, inclosed by a row of buildings surrounding the great bathing and swimming basin, and forming the ladies' dressing rooms. On the west is the Great Circus, or Theatre Taurorum, where the bull fights are exhibited on Sunday afternoons. About this plaza there are no drinking saloons or stores. Every sight is suggestive of pleasure, not business. Yet this place and its vicinity had been the scene of no less than seven assassinations in as many weeks—two of the victims were United States soldiers, and five were Mexican citizens—and no one arrested for it. I therefore took an interpreter and began to investigate the cause of all this violence, and discovered it at once.

The victims had all been murdered in retaliation for some act done by them on this pleasure ground, and never would have happened with one good police officer in charge of the place. A young, ignorant and cowardly Mexican, of a wealthy family, was then keeper of the keys of the baths and circus, and had charge of the pleasure grounds; but, if any difficulty occurred, he had not courage enough to interfere, consequently every one made his own laws and executed them himself, and then followed the murders in retaliation.

It was Saturday, and I had not time to do anything to improve the state of affairs that night, but as there was to be a great bull fight on the next afternoon (Sunday) in the circus, I determined to improve that opportunity for making a trial, and, taking a guard of sixteen men with me, went to the bull fight at an early hour. Soon the seats began to be filled with all the gay people of the place, and our soldiers mixed thick amongst them. A lively chit-chat was going on everywhere, but no bickering or disorder, as they all saw me occupying a front seat and the guard seated behind me ready to appre-hend the first person who should disturb the general enjoy-ment. At length the hour of commencement arrived, and a Mexican, well mounted, with a peculiar pike fourteen feet long in his hand, entered the arena from a side gate, accompanied by another man on foot, dressed like himself in white pants and red shirt, bearing in one hand a dart and in the other a small red flag, and both commenced running in all directions about the arena, when a gate was opened on the opposite side, and a large black bull was driven in and the gate closed.

The bull stopped short at sight of the crowd, and raising his head, his eyes big and red with rage, he uttered a horrid roar, snuffed, snorted, and then rushed furiously at the foot-man with the red flag, who dodged, and wounded him as he passed, as did also the horseman, who was then attacked and compelled to fly several times around the arena, the bull, with tail up, in hot pursuit, until the footman blinded him with his flag and ran him butt against the fence, amid loud cheering. This was considered a great feat and called forth loud applause, and still louder when he withdrew the flag and (being directly in front of the beast) dropped a dart into his back, which, being barbed, stuck fast. The infuriated animal stood a moment as if at a loss which to attack, and again rushed on the horseman, who received him by a thrust of his pike in his nose, turning aside the horn which menaced the horse's breast, and would have killed him but for this dexterous and judicious thrust. This about closed the strife, and the poor beast was soon slain.

Two other animals were afterwards brought in and treated in the same cruel manner by fresh sets of tormentors, and all their carcases given to the poor, which is the disposition always made of them.

The performances being over, the spectators withdrew quietly to the plaza, and when all were out I marched my guard to the centre of the plaza and halted them, and mounting a long stone seat, with an interpreter by my side, called on the Mexicans to give attention. There were at least one thousand present. I told them seven persons had lately been murdered about the plaza by unknown persons, and I had come to prevent any more killing, which had always been done after nine o'clock at night. Therefore I forbade any Mexican, male or female, being on or about the plaza between nine o'clock at night and sunrise, and if I caught any of them there, I would put them to cleaning stables with the two grog-sellers I now had performing that task for disobeying me. This had the desired effect; the plaza was as silent as a graveyard after nine o'clock while we remained in Chihuahua, which was from April 23d to August 15th, 1848, and there was no homicide within a mile of the place.

On the morning following, a man named Holland told me he had found a printing press and types in a house where they had lain idle twenty-six years, having been confiscated to the State, and asked me to permit him to use them to print a Spanish and English paper. To this I readily consented, and he spent the day vainly trying to get some one to edit the paper, when Colonel Easton told him to ask me, which he did, and I wrote all that appeared in the editorial columns of the *Chihuahua Union*, the first number of which was printed on the 29th of April, 1848, and a copy of which I still have.

On the 1st of May, there being several persons under arrest, a court martial was ordered for their trial. I was appointed president, and directed to try all then under arrest, and adjourn from time to time as I should think proper—but not dissolve the court—and try the delinquents as soon as possible after their arrest, until further orders. The court thus operating continued until the 12th of August, 1848, when it was dissolved, preparatory to leaving Chihuahua and returning to our own country to be discharged from the army.

CHAPTER XXI.

DEPARTURE FROM CHIHUAHUA, AND INCIDENTS ON THE MARCH TO INDEPENDENCE.

On the morning of the 13th of August, 1848, I called as usual at General Price's headquarters, when he told me he wished me to take my company and march to the ford and' pass of Sacramento and arrest all Americans and detain them until further orders, as several Mexicans had complained to him that their horses had been stolen, and he hoped I would be able to recover and restore some of them.

I called on the quartermaster for wagons and the commissary for rations, and at one o'clock left the city with all my men, every one of them being able to march, which I attributed to the watchful care of Lieutenant Levant and myself over their cleanliness and culinary arrangements from the beginning. We marched eighteen miles in six hours, and encamped in a line across the road in front of the ford, and set our sentinels in the form of the letter V, spreading the opening towards Chihuahua, so that when passers-by were hailed they could not retreat or escape. The company all knew their business, and were proud of being selected for this duty, and appeared anxious to perform it well.

All was silent until about one o'clock in the morning, when five horsemen were stopped at the ford with six animals and brought to my tent by the guard. I ordered them all under guard, and directed the animals to be stripped of their saddles and bridles, tied to the wagons, and strictly guarded there. Soon others arrived, and still others, so that at sunrise we had twenty-one prisoners and twenty-three horses and mules; and at ten o'clock, thirty prisoners and thirty-four horses and mules, and a fine yearling jack. The appearance of these prisoners was sad indeed. Some had been clerks, some merchants, some gamblers, some soldiers, some wagoners, but now all were considered thieves and robbers.

About three o'clock P. M., two Americans and five Mexicans came into camp, and, jumping from their horses, ran to the tied animals and applied some strangely-shaped irons to the marks on them, saying, "These are ours; they were stolen a week or more ago, and General Price sent us here to-day to get them." I thereupon delivered to them twelve animals which had evidently been marked with those strange branding irons. Through the remainder of the day and following night the trap was well patronized, and we had fifty-six prisoners when General Price sent Captain Clarkson with a company to relieve me, and inform me I might pursue my march *ad libitum* toward home. Just then four other companies of our battalion came up and placed themselves under my command, and I advised them to ford the river before they encamped. This induced Captain Clarkson to pass the river to encamp and left the prisoners still with me. In the meantime a crowd of Mexicans arrived claiming stolen horses, and having their palpable proof, I returned thirty-two more to them, making forty-four out of sixty in all. The remaining sixteen animals I turned over to the other company with the prisoners, and as the company had left Chihuahua that morning with their canteens full of whisky, they neglected their duties and allowed all the prisoners to escape with the animals during the night following.

It being now the 16th of August, and the weather very warm, we started early, and had marched about five miles, when most of Captain Clarkson's company passed us at full gallop without officers, and in about an hour the captain and other officers passed, having quit the post without leave when they saw the country full of thieves and robbers, and were sent to arrest them.

Two days after, General Price and all his staff passed us, having left the city on the 17th of August, 1848, and as the weather was very dry and warm and water very bad and scarce, no time was allowed to be spent in salutations and ceremonies, but all urged to press on to water as fast as possible, which we continued to do. The infantry and animals were suffering fearfully. One of my sergeants, William Seward, had been left exhausted on the road and was picked up by General Price and carried forward in his wagon to El Paso. This act was characteristic of him. I consider him one of the kindest and most accomplished generals I ever saw. I served under Generals Taylor, Scott, and Brown, and was well acquainted with all of them in the days of their greatest glory and activity, as well as with General Price. It is most astonishing to me that any hallucination has since misled him.

Soon after General Price had left us, Colonel Easton overtook us and relieved me from the care of any but my own company, which needed all my attention to alleviate their distress and keep them together.

At length, on the same day, we arrived at St. Mary's Spring, one of the curiosities of the country, mostly natural, but evidently greatly changed by human hands. The spring gushes from near the bottom of a precipice, two hundred feet in hight, formed of strata of grey granite, which here composes the base of a mountain several thousand feet high. The water escapes from between two strata about one inch asunder in the middle and twelve feet long, closing gradually toward each extremity, suggesting the idea of its being a mouth. The velocity with which the water issues indicates that the fountain is very high and abundant. The channel by which the water is conducted to the plain seems to have been the work of men, as it is straight and formed by removing several strata of the rocks through which it runs to the fertile plain below. About the spring are many mortars dug in the rocks, being all about the same size and shape—that is, eighteen inches deep and ten inches broad—in which the Indians, or former inhabitants, crushed or ground their corn. In all these indications of labor there was not a mark or sign of their having used an iron tool, and they had removed quite out of sight all the stones that had been quarried about the spring.

Our stock had become so much exhausted that it was

deemed most prudent to rest one day at this fine spring and good pasturage. This afforded me a good opportunity to view the country from the top of the lofty mountain eastward, which overlooks a vast fertile region round about, without an inhabitant within twenty miles of the spring. When it was known that I was preparing to ascend the mountain, about a dozen officers asked to accompany me, as I had a fine field glass, which would enable them to view everything within the range of vision, and I permitted them to do so, and each one procured a good musket and plenty of ammunition. This I was sorry to see, as it would tire and incommode them in their ascent, and be of no possible utility to any one. My advice to leave half the muskets was useless, and we started on a journey of three miles as we supposed, but found it to be seven. When we had reached the highest point we could see from the plain, we found ourselves at the base of another of equal altitude. Here three officers turned back. We rested a little while, and then proceeded. The sun shone bright, but our altitude was such that no inconvenience was felt from it; yet those heavy, useless muskets drove five more men to abandon the trip and return to camp before we reached the top. When we had reached the summit of this ridge, my four friends seemed quite discouraged at seeing another ridge of almost equal hight of those we had ascended still before and east of us. The muskets had become doubly heavy and useless, for the game was scarce and shy, and always saw us before we did them. We sat and rested ourselves for half an hour, when I rose and walked slowly forward, lingering until I was quite out of sight of them, and sat down to await their coming up, remaining until I was satisfied they did not intend to follow me any further, when I again started forward. I had climbed but a few yards up the mountain when I heard a great rustling of stones and gravel rolling down the mountain at my left, and turning my eyes in that direction I saw two large elk running up the mountain within fifty yards of me, and as they passed they observed me, and, turning, ran in front of me, stopped and gazed at me two or three minutes, showing their enormous horns then in the velvet or soft state, and then hurried on out of sight unalarmed.

In the meantime, I had lost all hope of being overtaken by any of those I had left behind, and pressed up the mountain as fast as possible. Having no guide, my progress was slow, for I was compelled to make many detours to avoid those lofty precipices that present themselves in broken sections on all sides of this highest peak. On attaining the summit, I was surprised to find it broad, nearly level, and covered with oak and pine timber, grass and flowers. I walked about one mile north to the highest part, for the table land was higher at the north of where I ascended the mountain. From that point I viewed the surrounding country through my glass, and found all the mountain-tops covered with a fair growth of pine and oak timber, but not a habitation, improvement, or a domestic animal, within the range of vision.

Having viewed and duly considered the immense solitude that here surrounded me, I began to make my way back to the plain by taking the channel of one of those vast ravines that lead from the apex of the mountain to the plain. The channel was perfectly dry, but obstructed by huge rocks and precipices, so that I was often compelled to retrace my steps and make detours. In making one of these of large circuit, I passed near an overhanging precipice, and was proceeding along its base, when I began to hear a noise above me resembling the noise of a man snoring in sleep. I stepped off a few yards from the precipice and looking up saw a large grizzly bear, followed by two cubs, walking in an opposite direction along the edge of the precipice, and about thirty yards from me. I lost no time in putting a greater distance between us, often looking back as well as forward during the afternoon. The ravine conducted me to the plain about three miles south of the spring. This is probably the best route to the apex of St. Mary's Mountain, although the distance will be ten miles, while the air line is not more than seven, or eight at most. On my arrival at the plain, I took the road which runs along the base of the mountain to the spring, not knowing the distance, or supposing it to be half as great as I found it. I was much fatigued and hungry, while the heated air of the plain assisted to make me still more uncomfortable. Under such exhaustion, those miles seemed the longest I ever traveled over.

When I arrived within about half a mile of our camp I met

my faithful man, Francis Hinch, going in quest of me, with his musket and haversack full of cooked rations. As soon as he saw me he threw down his musket and ran to me, weeping for joy, and, clasping me in his arms, declared he would never let me leave him behind again; that I was an old man, and he had thought I was lost in the mountains, and would now starve to death and be eaten by wolves. He said all those who started with me had been back six hours, and they told him if I ever came back it would be by this route, by which they had all returned. We sat down on the grass, and I ate from his haversack until I was well satisfied, and rested, when we returned to our camp to prepare for marching the next morning.

We struck our tents early, and that evening encamped at the Ojo Caliénte, or hot spring. This is pure, well-tasted water, and where it rises is about as warm as one can well bear his hand in; but the inhabitants have formed a long kind of basin below, by enclosing the stream within a good stone wall, to allow the water to cool for general use and stock, as it is near Carisal, seventy miles west of El Paso.

Hot springs are very numerous in all parts of Mexico, but good water is generally very scarce. All crops are raised by irrigation, and provisions are cheap and abundant. Having filled all our water casks and canteens with pure water, we moved forward, knowing that we must march thirty-six miles without water suitable for men to use. This required a steady march of two days to what is called the Miry Spring, a very appropriate name for that place. The spring is large, and as it rises in a marsh of about two acres, is easily disturbed, made muddy, and apparently stopped up by allowing stock to walk into it at will and otherwise to defile it. We arrived weary and thirsty at this place when the sun was about two hours high, and found that General Price had been encamped here a day or two and had just resumed his march, leaving the marsh and spring a quagmire. Our colonel was disgusted and angry, and, instead of encamping and trying to cleanse and settle the spring, he ordered the stock to be watered and the march resumed. Our thirsty soldiers rushed at once into the marsh with their tin cups and canteens to secure a little water to slake their raging thirst, and enable them to obey what they thought an unnecessary order. The teamsters also with their mules splashed in, amid the remonstrating and execrating soldiers, to obtain a share of the beverage. The offended officers and soldiers said to me, "This order would not have been given to-night had you been in command of us." It was indeed true; yet none of us had any conception of the alarms, dangers and sufferings we had to pass through before the next day ended.

About four miles from this place, the road to El Paso forks. The east fork goes near San Elisario and Rio Grande, and is well supplied most of the way with water, but is twelve miles longer than the west fork, which passes through a plain of fine sand ten miles broad, with water on the road but in one place. The men and mules having drank a little, were put in motion just before sundown, in order to enable them that night to reach water four miles ahead, as I supposed, on the east fork of the road; but when we had marched two miles to the forks of the road, I saw the head of the column rising the hill on the west road, and knew the die was cast. There was not a drop of water on this road for twelve miles, and it was nearly dark, and the men had already marched twenty miles. It was clear in the east, but a long, low, black cloud lay near the western horizon and began to threaten us with a great tempest.

We had proceeded about three miles into the sandy plain, when, with lightning and thunder the most terrific, but without rain, the storm burst upon us. At the first blast the wind and sand so completely filled the eyes and nostrils of men and animals that they seemed unable either to see or act. The horses and mules all turned their heads from the storm, and the men took shelter behind the covered wagons and mules. The sand was blown about and drifted like snow. Eyes, ears and nostrils were filled and refilled. The mules were obliged to be detached from the wagons to prevent their breaking the poles; many got loose and ran away, and some teams ran off before the gale with their drivers on them. At length, when the storm had exhausted its fury, the clouds passed away, and the weather became clear and still, the last half of the night exhibiting a wonderful contrast with the former part of it. The wagons were scattered widely over the plain, with half the mules missing, the soldiers wandering from wagon to wagon to ascertain what was doing. When the storm abated, our colonel forsook his scattered and distressed command, and I saw him no more until our arrival at El Paso.

In the morning, as soon as we could see the timber on the farther side of the plain, I sent forward a number of wagoners to bring back the escaped mules that had run to the nearest water (which that animal always does, and can smell it ten miles or more), and then forwarded as many wagons as we had mules to haul through the deep sand, accompanied by a strong escort, for the vicinity of large springs is the haunt of roving bands of Indians. I remained with a few soldiers to protect the immovable wagons, one of which contained all our unissued ammunition.

At the rising of the sun, other distress than thirst fell upon us. The silver-colored sand glistened in our unwashed eyes, producing a blinding painfulness that is indescribable; and as the sun rose, the heat became greater and our thirst more distressing. We had sheltered ourselves in the shade of the wagons to avoid the burning sun, having no hope of relief before the return of the wagoners, when Samuel Parks, a private soldier of my company, rode up with six canteens of water. He had found his way to the Ojo Grande, or Great Spring, and, having slaked his own thirst, he called to mind the suffering condition of his comrades, borrowed some canteens, filled them with water, and started back seven miles to relieve his friends. He had proceeded on his errand of mercy about a half a mile, when he was met by a mounted soldier going to the spring, who asked him where he was going, and, on learning his object, told him to come back to the spring until he could water his horse, and he might ride him on the trip. He turned back, accepted the horse, and performed the journey. It is unnecessary to state the standing of such men in their companies, or on a battle-field—they would be found in place. The expressions of gratitude to Parks by those he had relieved must have been a good reward to him at that time, and I think he must feel it renewed as often as he recalls the kind action. The wagoners returned about noon with plenty of teams and soon took the wagons to the spring, where we spent the following night.

Near this spring, about three weeks before our arrival, two discharged soldiers, one formerly belonging to my company, had been murdered by a treacherous Mexican, whom they had hired to attend their horses from Chihuahua to El Paso. They had not been buried, nor was their death known to any of the Americans. When the infantry had selected a place to encamp upon, they went in search of fuel, and soon found parts of infantry uniforms, human bones, and finally two skulls which were recognized as those of our men, and it was evident they had been murdered and eaten by the wolves. Our men found most of the bones of the two men, but not all, and buried them. On our arrival in El Paso we found the murderer in jail, being confined there for the double murder by the Mexican authorities. General Price did what he could to have justice done, but I have not heard the result.

On General Price's arrival at El Paso, a lot of Mexicans from Elizario renewed the claim for my taking their cattle by presenting him with a large roll of their affidavits concerning the affair. The general took papers, affidavits and all, and handed the whole of them to Colonel Easton, saying to him, "This belongs to your battalion." Colonel Easton then brought them to me, and said, "Here, captain, are some papers that belong to these men," pointing to five Mexicans; "I wish you would attend to them, as I know nothing about them." I took the papers and waited until the colonel was out of hearing, and then informed my Mexican visitors, through their own interpreter, that they could take their papers and depart in peace; but if I should ever find them again in or about my camp, I would bind them to a wagon and whip them like slaves. When the interpreter had finished, I gave him the papers, and they all left, and I never heard of them afterwards.

They had just gone, when I received an order to cross the Rio Grande with my company and post them in a position to cover the ford, protect a merchant train near there, and stop all persons suspected of having stolen horses, saddles, or mules, and dispose of them as I had done at the pass of Sacramento. I immediately left El Paso, and took post where Fort Bliss now stands. The thieves in El Paso soon learned my location and kept out of my trap, so that I was not able to arrest any of them there. The action of the general and the slow and cautious movements of the thieves showed how both parties appreciated the duties I had performed at the pass of Sacramento and other places.

The general and quartermasters having disposed of all useless United States property at El Paso, on the 1st of September, 1848, evacuated the State of Chihuahua and marched up the left bank of the Rio Grande to Santa Fé, arriving there on the 18th, where I remained two days, and discharged twenty of my men who wished to stay in that territory.

I was then again ordered forward as usual, and for the same purpose, and had caught one thief with a stolen mule, when some travelers reported my location and my success in Santa Fé, which ruined my further usefulness and turned the rogues by another route. I had sent the thief to Santa Fé by two of my soldiers, and, having placed him in the guard-house, they engaged with the quartermaster to drive teams to Independence for a dollar a day, and came back with their discharges for me to sign. I asked them if they were not afraid to show me such papers now on a march. They said no; they knew I would be glad to see them get a dollar a day extra all the way home. I signed their discharges and they returned to Santa Fé.

The next morning, General Price, with all the volunteers remaining of his army, passed me on their march homeward, our battalion among the rest. My company, now reduced to fifty men, but all well and fit for duty, took the rear and watched the ammunition and train until our arrival at Independence on the 1st of November, 1848, without any loss of men or animals, and all still in the most perfect health, which I attributed to their cleanliness and diet; for both Lieutenant Levant and myself had given them the example and compelled all to follow it for their own comfort and safety.

The battalion's greatest feat during this year was eating five thousand sheep, which our quartermaster purchased at Limitar and drove four hundred and seventy miles to Chihuahua, and from Chihuahua fourteen hundred miles to Independence, those most easily caught being the first butchered and eaten each day until all were consumed, the last of which were slaughtered at Blue River, a short distance from Independence, after the poor sheep had swam all the rivers on that road.

CHAPTER XXII.

ARRIVAL AT INDEPENDENCE—MUSTERING OUT OF MY COMPANY, AND OUR RETURN TO ST. LOUIS.

On our arrival at Independence, we found Colonel Hitchcock waiting to muster us out of the U. S. service, he being the mustering officer, and we the last troops to be discharged. I had been so much on detached service, and had so much public property to account for, that I was kept very busy day and night; and added to this, a crowd of clothing merchants beset me on all sides to aid in having my men get a new citizen's dress, each, out of their three months' extra pay to be given them. I, however, got my muster and pay rolls ready before any of the captains present, and the mustering officer being furnished with the rolls properly made out, and the paymaster also, they informed me I would be waited on first, and appointed an early hour the next day to discharge and pay us.

In the meantime, a captain of a steamboat called on me and asked my assistance in procuring passengers, promising to take my men in the cabin to St. Louis at ten dollars each and to start the moment I came on board. I told the captain I thought I could send him twenty or twenty-five passengers. Having all the discharges duly prepared, I paraded my men for the last time, and in presence of the mustering officer delivered to each one his discharge, and told them their money was ready, and I would go and see them paid. The paymaster had each man's money counted, wrapped in a paper, marked and numbered, and calling them forward in their order, he paid them as fast as they signed their names, which was soon done, and each man going to St. Louis repaired to the boat. I then bid adieu to all who remained, very few of whom I have ever seen since, as they nearly all went to California from there the next spring.

I then went on board the steamer and found thirty-two of my late company in the cabin, all neatly dressed in new citizen's clothing, sitting and waiting my arrival. As soon as I was on board, the boat got under way, and a short time afterwards we had tea. At table were four United States regular officers, my late soldiers, the steamboat master, Lieutenant Levant, and myself.

After supper, as we sat in the cabin, the captain said to me, "How did it happen that none of your company came to go home with you?" I replied, "These gentlemen have all belonged to my company, except Major Scott and those United States officers with him." I have seldom seen a person manifest such perfect astonishment; and he said, "I have compelled them to pay twelve dollars; I will refund two dollars to each one, and fulfil my promise to you;" and he ordered the clerk to do it then.

Major Scott rose and said, "Gentlemen, you all know me. I did not recognize any of you. I know you now. I predicted something extra of your company when I sent it to escort the first train to Santa Fé and saw it commanded by two officers who had served in the United States regular army in Canada in the war of 1812, and under General Taylor in Mexico in 1846, and the first to bring provisions and a reinforcement after the rebellion at Taos." He then introduced his brother officers to them, and all came forward and were announced by name by Lieutenant Levant, and after a very cordial shaking of hands we all settled down to a most perfect equality during the voyage.

It was a very quiet trip, made entirely in daylight, the water being low, and no deep drinking, noise, or gambling, was attempted. The result was we had ample opportunity for seeing the snags, logs and sandbars in the Missouri river, and to view the farms and villages along its banks to its mouth. After a most pleasant and agreeable voyage, we arrived on the evening of the sixth day at sundown, and all took leave of each other, and since that day I have not met with more than about ten of them, as all the men were unmarried except one, and mostly left for California the next spring, and none have since returned to St. Louis.

13

CHAPTER XXIII.

A YEAR OF TRAVELING AND WANDERINGS WITH ALL MY FAMILY
DURING THE CHOLERA SEASON OF 1849, LEADING TO NEW
OCCUPATIONS.

Having been absent from St. Louis about seventeen months,
I returned to my family, whom I found all in good health, but
boarding abroad. My daughter had become the mother of a
promising son named Shepard, born on the evening of November 7th, 1847, the same evening that St. Louis was first lighted
with gas, and was then about one year old, and could already
walk.

I remained at home but a very few days with my family, as
I held claims against the government on vouchers for supplies
in the medical, commissary and quartermaster's departments,
and as they soon were to be withdrawn, I hastened to have
mine adjusted here; but after a fruitless effort I was compelled
to go to Washington and stay five weeks, while the clerks and
petty officers in the departments used every art to get a bribe
out of me; they failed however, and I was paid.

On my return from Washington, I took my family on one
of the Mississippi palatial steamboats and visited New
Orleans, spending several days there in the St. Charles Hotel.
In the meantime, General Taylor, then President elect, came
to the city and stopped, took rooms at the same house, and
held levees there in the forenoon. As our rooms were near
together, I attended his first levee with my wife and daughter.
When I entered the parlor, he approached, calling me by
name, and saying he had watched my movements during the
war, and knew where I had been and what I had done. I
then introduced him to my wife and daughter, with whom he
became well acquainted, as we four, at his own request, took
our meals at a separate table in the ladies' ordinary, while he
remained in New Orleans. During his administration, we
spent most of our time in the city of Washington, where we
saw him almost daily, and received from him great attention
and consideration. He was a most agreeable man in familiar
conversation, and always made everybody in his company at

ease. We spent many hours with him during our summer's stay in Washington.

Soon after our return to St. Louis, the Asiatic cholera began to make its appearance in the city, and several had already died with it when I again left town with my family, and was absent six months, during which period ten thousand persons died in the city with that disease. This appalling mortality, and the great fire of May 17, 1849, occurring in the meantime, make that year an epoch in the history of St. Louis.

On my trip to Washington in 1848, I fell in company with Mr. Frederick Woolford, of Washington county, Missouri, who had learned my situation in life, and that I had several land warrants to enter; and offered, for a proper remuneration, to point out to me some very valuable lands in Washington county. We agreed upon terms, and I employed him to enter what is known as the Kaolin Estate, on which is a queens-ware factory and the little village of Kaolin, in Iron county, at a point where the road from St. Louis to Pocahontas, in the State of Arkansas, is crossed by the State road from Iron Mountain to Springfield.

On the 5th of July, 1850, the improvements at Kaolin were commenced, and in the next year a large building for a factory was erected and filled with machinery, a store built and stocked with goods, and several other buildings put up for the accommodation of workmen, teams, &c. About the first of January, 1852, a full set of hands arrived to put the new factory into operation. The workmen were shown through the whole establishment, and were pleased with the prospect before them. I was absent at the time; but those present, not satisfied with what they had seen, undertook to test the drying and warming apparatus, and put it in full operation, remaining in the factory until bedtime, then locked the doors and retired. The result was as might have been expected. Before twelve o'clock the main building, eighty feet front, was so completely wrapped in flames that not a door was opened. The slip house on the north and the glaze mill on the south both escaped damage, the wind being from the westward.

This involved me in a loss of three thousand dollars; and losses did not end here, as there were now twenty-one persons just arrived left idle and unable to leave as it was winter, and

Mr. Woolford, easy soul, was persuaded by them to pay them the high wages of mechanics three months, while he built a temporary edifice at great expense in winter and procured machinery and tools of poor quality, so that I lost two thousand dollars at least by that mismanagement and on account of my nephew crediting them. In April I returned to examine the state of affairs at Kaolin and at once stopped any further losses through the manager's want of capacity, by discharging him and putting a competent English potter in his place; after which, all went on well while he retained his health. He, however, after about six months, fell sick, and as I could find no other person capable of managing the English potters and working them harmoniously, I quit manufacturing on my own account and leased the factory the two following years, while I gave my attention to opening and improving a farm about Kaolin and planting an extensive orchard.

After having expended about ten thousand dollars in and about Kaolin in the space of six years, I determined to abandon all attempts at manufacturing and to make Kaolin a summer residence, as I think there is no healthier place on this continent, it being also well watered by springs running from the hills that surround it, which are covered with lofty pines and oaks. I enlarged the orchard and farm, improved the gardens and buildings, opened good roads through my lands, and removed such objects as were offensive to the sight, such as dead trees, &c., and gave the whole place as fine a rural appearance as the nature of the ground would permit.

While I was engaged in these operations, my wife and daughter had spent about a year in Washington City; they also made a trip to Virginia and visited the place of my wife's nativity and her relations residing there, and looked over the places where she had spent her childhood and youth. My wife had also visited all her relations of whose residence she was cognizant. Although many of them resided in Ohio, and more in Illinois, she visited them all, and gave them an account of each other's welfare. It must have been very gratifying to her at that advanced period of her life to renew acquaintance with the playmates of her childhood, after a separation of above forty years, and to see their grandchildren standing thick around them, looking on with astonishment at the affectionate meeting of such old people as they then mostly were.

After her return, we spent much of our time at Kaolin for several years, raising stock and improving the farm and garden, as we had been relieved of a great part of the care and burden of our estate in St. Louis by the marriage of our daughter, in 1854, to Mr. D. Robert Barclay, who assisted us in its management there.

In the spring of 1857, I returned to the State of New York, and built a permanent stone wall around the Shepard grave-yard, where my parents are buried. It is the best executed work of the kind that I have seen. It was laid on a flat lime-stone foundation, three feet below the surface of the earth and raised six feet above it, two feet thick, and capped with stones thirteen feet long, thirty-two inches wide, and ten inches thick.

After my return, I continued to improve our garden, and introduced other good varieties of small fruits; planted a vineyard, and made cedar-post fences; and purchased several kinds of improved stock, so that my place attracted the notice of travelers. Moreover, I had been appointed postmaster; we had regular mails, and all the conveniences to make a country life pleasant and attractive. In short, we felt ourselves safely and comfortably situated at a place remote from noise, tumult, envy or danger, and were happy and contented.

CHAPTER XXIV.

INCIDENTS, ROBBERIES, AND LOSSES, RESULTING FROM THE GREAT REBELLION OF 1861.

At the commencement of the rebellion, my wife and I were more comfortably situated than we ever were during the forty years we had lived together. We either had all we desired, or abundant means to procure it. While in this happy and contented condition I received a very kind letter, from an officer of the first regiment Missouri State militia, inviting me to come to St. Louis and go with my old comrades, the St. Louis Greys, as I had the year before, into a camp of instruction, and spend a few days as pastime. As I was not very busy, and had a good foreman to conduct my business, I left Kaolin on the 4th of May, 1861, and came to St. Louis, and the next morning paraded at the armory with the company preparatory to marching to the celebrated ground called "Camp Jackson." When the roll had been called, Captain Stephen Coleman, who had been my captain in Mexico fifteen years before, informed me that a seat had been provided for me in an ambulance to ride to the camp, as I was the oldest person in the regiment, being then nearly sixty-six years of age, and requested me to accept of it, which I did, and entered the camp immediately after the regiment and stacked arms with them.

Soon after, the baggage wagons arrived with the tents, and I assisted to pitch them in proper order, which was the only duty I was permitted to assist in performing. All seemed to regard me as the patriarch of the brigade, and I was treated accordingly.

I walked leisurely about the camp and seemed in a fair way of becoming acquainted with all of them, when, on the 10th of May, 1861, General Lyon and his columns appeared in view and put a period to my enjoyments by taking us all prisoners of war, while under the protecting folds of the United States colors, and confined us in the arsenal for the night without our suppers. This outrage was not perpetrated without other atrocious acts of violence committed within a few yards of me, by which about thirty innocent persons lost their lives, under that false plea, "military necessity," by order of a malicious, dogmatical officer, who delighted in carnage and blood, and could find no other way but this of gratifying his evil propensity. We were closely guarded, and I occupied a position in the line of prisoners most favorable to observe and hear the whole transaction.

After being confined in the arsenal, I was treated with more consideration by General Lyon than any other prisoner. He sent the surgeon (Dr. Franklin) and another officer, to bring me to his quarters as soon as he found I was there, and at once set me at liberty without oath. I however, the next day, put my name on the roll of paroled officers and exerted all the ability I possessed to induce all the old officers of the regiment who had served with me in the war with Mexico to do the same. I succeeded with them, and indeed with all I had occasion to address on the subject, until I came to Captain Emmett McDonald, who said to me, " Old men for counsel, Captain Shepard, but young men for war; " and then declared he would never sign the parole, though every other prisoner did, and he pugnaciously kept his promise.

After all had been paroled except the captain, we were escorted on board a steamboat and landed at St. Louis about dark on the evening of the 11th, having been robbed of all our private property in Camp Jackson by the Home Guards of St. Louis, for none of General Lyon's soldiers were permitted to leave their ranks during the 10th of May, and could not have done it, and all should be exonerated, except Colonel Sigel's regiment of Home Guards.

After I had been set at liberty in the arsenal, General Lyon sent David Watson to me to request me to come to his room. I went immediately, when the general informed me he was forming other regiments, and if I wished to enter the United States service he would appoint me to any office I would accept in the next regiment. I replied that I highly appreciated his magnanimous offer, and were I ten years younger I would accept it; but now I had entered far into my sixty-sixth year, and it would appear childish in me to attempt or even desire to fill a military office in active service at my advanced age. He said he thought my views were correct, and he hoped I would yet have many years added to my long life, shook hands with me, and bade me good morning, and I never saw him afterwards. He was killed three months after at the battle of Wilson's Creek, near Springfield, Green county, Missouri.

I waited but a few days in St. Louis, and then returned to Kaolin, our summer residence, a retired place, deep in the pine forests. Here I supposed we might repose in quietude; but in this I was much mistaken, for about the first murder and robberies were perpetrated on my premises, and these outrages were practiced by both parties on me to the end of the war, when I had not a hog, horse or sheep remaining on my farm of five thousand acres. Half of the fences, three dwelling-houses, and two other large buildings, had been burned. In the meantime, of the twelve laborers engaged in 1861, eight had joined the rebel army, five of whom died with sickness, two had been killed, and one deserted and came back, but dared not stay at my farm. Of the other four, one had been murdered, and three had been driven off for feeding bushwhackers, and the guerrillas became such a terror that there was not a man on the farm and only one woman at the close of the four years civil war.

In July, 1861, Governor Claiborne Jackson sent a commission to me as a paymaster, which I returned by the same person without a written acknowledgment of its receipt, and supposed that I should hear no more about commissions from him ; but I was mistaken as well as himself, yet not in the same way. He thought I wished a command in the field, and sent me a colonel's commission, which I returned as before, and then stated the objection I had to receiving either of them, which I have no doubt was correctly reported to him, as I heard nothing from him afterwards.

On the Saturday after I had declined the acceptance of a colonel's commission, Captain Benjamin Talbot came to me with about twenty of his men, and offered me the command of his company to go and join General Price at Springfield, saying he would resign in my favor and serve under me in the ranks. He had been under my command in Mexico, where he was a lieutenant and knew me well. He seemed greatly disappointed at not being able to induce me to accept the command, as his company consisted of over one hundred young men enlisted in my neighborhood. The next morning (Sunday) he took post in front of a small Baptist church, on the south end of my farm, and as the congregation generally rode their best animals there, he seized them as fast as they arrived and in that manner got possession of all the best horses and mules in the vicinity of my farm and factory. Some objected to the proceeding, but he made the usual plea of tyrants, "military necessity," which was the only satisfaction he offered. This was the beginning of a series of robberies which were continued by both parties for the four following years in that vicinity. The following day he took the horses he had seized to my blacksmith shop in my absence, and compelled my blacksmith to shoe them all with my shoes and nails, and at evening threatened to hang the smith for saying this was "an act of bold robbery." He also took from my store all my ammunition, together with my shot-gun and apparatus.

Having noticed the lawless conduct of such a large portion of my neighbors, I determined to remove my grandson, then about thirteen years of age, from their bad examples, which I did, and kept him from them during the four years' war, in which time more than half of the men he knew before the war had lost their lives. In short, my flourishing neighborhood had become a desolation. Where, at the commencement of the war nineteen families resided near to me, only four remained at the close of it. I had been obliged to absent myself from my house about half the time during this reign of terror to avoid being murdered for the acts I had performed against rebels, robbers, and guerrillas, who infested that neighborhood from the commencement to the end of the war.

I was postmaster the two first years of the war, but in 1863 the guerrillas robbed the mail, and the carrier of his horse and clothes, thus effectually breaking up the route; so I resigned the office and removed my family to St. Louis in 1863.

CHAPTER XXV.

SICKNESS, DEATH, AND BURIAL OF MRS. SHEPARD, WITH REMARKS ON HER CHARACTER AND EXEMPLARY LIFE.

In the autumn of 1862, Mrs. Shepard was severely attacked by that disease which terminated her useful life on the 6th of June, 1864. She bore her long and painful illness with the same patience and fortitude which had distinguished her through life, retaining her mental faculties to the last. On her demise, intelligence was conveyed to me at our country residence with difficulty and danger, as our whole region was infested with rebels and guerrillas, who were robbing, burning and murdering in all directions, and ours was the most exposed and prominent point, being on the direct road from St. Louis to Pocahontas, where the road from Pilot Knob to Rolla crosses it at right angles. On receipt of the melancholy news, I returned to St. Louis to prepare for her obsequies.

When we were both in good health, we had selected a most beautiful and conspicuous site for a family graveyard on the hights of Kaolin, where we intended to be buried, and had a red cedar fence framed ready to set, but the dangers that surrounded the place precluded the possibility of its being used at that time. I therefore did that which I conceived to be nearest to our original plan yet in my power, and changed our burying place to the shore of Lake Ontario, in the Shepard graveyard, where many of that family are interred. There a marble slab, inscribed with the names of the places and the dates of her birth and death, now marks the spot where repose the remains of her who had been my companion more than forty years, and beside whom I desire my remains to be placed when, like her, I have finished my course.

Mrs. Shepard passed a very active, successful and useful life, and its effect must be felt in St. Louis for generations. Her example is worthy of all imitation by those who would succeed in any great enterprise. On her arrival in St. Louis, in 1823, although married, she immured herself for three years, and studied all those branches which she knew would qualify her to take the highest position in St. Louis as a female teacher. She was not disappointed. During the following twelve years, she was the morning and the evening star in St. Louis among female teachers, and during that time she qualified more ladies for the higher circles of female society in her own city than any five other ladies have ever done.

But the half and the best is yet untold. Of all the ladies she educated, not one has ever misconducted herself so as to exclude her from the best female society, so that to be able to show that a lady had been one of Mrs. Shepard's pupils, was a passport to the best society, without further investigation. It was not alone in a school-room that the abilities of Mrs. Shepard were conspicuous; they were equally brilliant in the bed-chambers of her sick and dying neighbors; for where duty or charity called her, she was sure to go, let the labors and dangers be what they might. In the appalling season of the cholera in 1832, when the disease was a stranger among us, she confronted it with me, and continued her school as in ordinary times, although, in the universal gloom and dismay that overwhelmed the public mind, all our scholars but four absented themselves. Yet she seemed unmoved by the general terror, and visited her sick and dying neighbors as she would had they been ill with an ordinary disease, instead of a fatal contagious malady. Her example was a tower of strength that might be leaned upon. She watched each alternate night during this distressing period with some one of her afflicted neighbors, and I did the same the other alternate nights, while the disease prevailed, and we both escaped unscathed that season. But during the prevalence of the epidemic the next year, 1833, Mrs. Shepard was suddenly and severely attacked, superinduced as she thought by fatigue and exhaustion in setting a neighbor's house in order while the family were absent burying the father, who had died with the cholera. She met the attack with the same firmness and courage in her own case that she had so often inspired in others; the result was that she was out of danger in a few hours, and soon recovered.

Mrs. Shepard was never a member of any church, but took the Holy Scriptures as her guide in faith and practice, and required no priest to expound them. Consequently there was no mystery or contradiction in them as she interpreted them, and she would enter into no controversy on any point contained therein, as it was unprofitable at best, and had a tendency to grieve away the Spirit of truth and to leave the mind in darkness and at a distance from God, as she believed. She was one of the most prayerful persons I ever met with, yet I never heard her utter one word of prayer. She "entered into her closet," and I have no doubt obeyed the injunction of her Divine Master, from her appearing to be "rewarded openly." She believed the Spirit of God was at all times present with us to teach us our duty, if we wished to be guided by its dictates. In short, she was a Friend, or Quakeress, but was tolerant to all Christians. During the twelve years she taught, her school-room was used as a meeting-house on Sundays, and was kept in order, warmed and lighted by her, without any charge to the occupants. Thus the Baptists, Episcopalians, Unitarians, Presbyterians, Campbell Baptists, and the Cumberland Presbyterians, shared in her benefactions until they were able to build houses for themselves in the city.

Industry, frugality and economy were striking traits in the character of Mrs. Shepard, but her financial abilities far outshone all her other extraordinary qualifications. My absence from home in our armies in Mexico during the three campaigns, afforded a test of her ability to manage a large estate adroitly. Her far-seeing eyes early foresaw the future glories of St. Louis, and foregoing the tinsel of the day she urged the investment of all that could be saved in cheap lots, so that at her death she left her family the owners of at least a million of dollars' worth of real estate that was rapidly enhancing in value. The history of St. Louis will be always incomplete without the prominent mention of her name and useful instructions in the infancy of the city, and on the threshhold of its prosperity and rising greatness.

CHAPTER XXVI.

BURNING OF OUR QUEENSWARE FACTORY BY A FEDERAL SOLDIER, AND ROBBERY OF MY PERSON AND COUNTRY RESIDENCE BY GUERRILLAS.

Immediately after my return from the burial of my companion, I left the city and hastened back to our country seat, and arrived on our own lands, when I found the woodlands filled with smoke, the wind blowing from the west. I hastened forward, as it betokened mischief; and when I came within sight of the village, I saw the largest factory building on fire and nearly consumed, having been fired by one of a party of fourteen Federal soldiers, who had lagged behind to commit that arson while his comrades pressed forward on their march. He was met a short distance from the fire by my hired man,

when, spurring his horse, he passed him at full speed, and was
out of sight before it was discovered what he had done. On
learning the facts, I proposed to follow the party and make
complaint, but reflecting that officers and men were here lost
to all sense of shame or justice, and burned, robbed and
murdered *ad libitum*, without remorse or fear of punishment
in this world or the next, I abandoned all thought of pursuit,
and let it pass, as it was a circumstance of very common
occurrence at that time in that neighborhood.

I remained at and about my farm eight weeks, seeing thieves
and robbers prowling about my premises almost every day,
and missing hogs, corn, fruit and garden vegetables constantly,
while my few remaining industrious neighbors were losing
all their valuable horses and other stock. I therefore sold
most of mine at low prices, and, so far, saved them ; I also
sold twenty-seven beef cattle, which led to my having the
honor of a visit from a band of eleven guerrillas, and of being
robbed in my own house, in open day, in the following scientific manner. I had been informed the preceding day that
eleven guerrillas had been seen going up the east or Pine
Grove road toward Caledonia, and that they had probably
gone there after having first started up the road toward Kaolin,
and then turned back, crossed Black river, and, taking a bridle-
path at a distance from the main road to avoid immediate
pursuit, after traveling about one mile, entered the Iron
Mountain road and pushed forward to within three miles of
the mountain to the residence of a Mr. Prow, whom they
robbed of six hundred dollars in gold and greenbacks and his
fine team of four good horses, then burned one house, and
returned to my neighborhhood, and got breakfast at Mr.
Northdurf's, three miles from Kaolin. Being well mounted,
and dressed in United States uniforms, they started through
the woods to visit me about nine o'clock in the morning, and
came into the road about one mile east of me. On entering
the road, they proceeded westwardly in the direction of my
residence, and soon met Mr. Levi Gipson, whom they robbed
of eighteen dollars and his fine mare, worth one hundred
and fifty dollars, and then mounted him, trembling, on one
of their stolen horses, brought him a prisoner with them to
my village, and released him. Seeing them coming leisurely

down the long hill toward me in good military order, with the ten foremost dressed in United States uniforms and two in summer clothing, I supposed they were the sheriff with an escort coming among us to collect taxes, and, instead of escaping into the vineyard or cornfields, as usual, I walked out into the street to meet them, and was in their immediate presence before I observed anything which excited suspicion or distrust. I then saw they were clad in the uniforms of cavalry, artillery, rifles and infantry, and one wore the badge of a hospital steward, and I thought it an uncommon escort for a sheriff. But the chief, dressed in a summer suit, plied me so rapidly with questions that I had very little time for observation or reflection. He propounded such questions as these: "What is the news? Have you a horse you would swap? Have the rebels been about here lately? Have you sold your beef cattle? Are you prepared to pay your taxes?" I could not get half through one answer before he asked another question; then turning his horse suddenly round from the left of his party, he passed in rear of it and came round to me on its right, and, dismounting from his horse, he placed himself by my side, when, addressing me by name, he informed me that I was mistaken as to who they were, and said to me, "We are Southern men, and want your money or your life." I informed him that of the two alternatives, it would be most agreeable to furnish what little money I had about the premises. He said he would allow no witticisms and would kill me if I attempted any, and ordered me to hasten to my house and show my money and my plate. On the way to the house I informed him that Mrs. Shepard had been dead about two months, and that all our plate had been removed to St. Louis, which, after entering the house and seeing no woman or child, he seemed to believe, and said no more about plate. I took him immediately into the second story and handed him a small tin box containing one dollar and seventy-five cents, and while he counted it I took out a full black suit of new clothes from a trunk to find my pocket-book which laid at the bottom. On seeing my clothes laid out, he lifted them up with his revolver and said, "You are no bigger than a rat; your new clothes will fit none of us," and left them. I then handed him my pocket-book containing five dollars in greenbacks, which he examined and put in his pocket. He then asked me if I had any boots, and on my replying in the affirmative, he asked their number. I replied, "Eights." He said, "We can wear them. Get them." I walked down into the lower room, and as I took the boots from under the bed-curtain he chanced to see a new pair of saddlebags, which he said he had need of, and took them and one box of matches, and left. I attempted to follow him to take another and better view of the party, but he prevented my going to the street by threatening to shoot me if I followed them a single yard.

I was very angry and desirous of revenge, and obtained it in the following extraordinary manner. As soon as I was driven back into my house, I ran up into the upper story and looking out of the west window I saw the whole party pass up the road between my vineyards, the chief riding in the rear on a fine mouse-colored horse worth three hundred dollars, a good saddle worth fifty, and a bridle worth fifteen dollars or more. As soon as they were out of sight, I called my hired man from his hiding-place in the buckwheat patch and ordered him to catch and saddle my horse, being determined to prevent their robbing any more of my neighbors at that time. My horse was soon ready, but my man was so much frightened after I was mounted and had learned I was about to follow them, that I could not get him to go to the street and open the gate to let me out, lest they should see him and return and murder him. I therefore dismounted and opened the gate myself, and hastened forward in pursuit, notwithstanding the remonstrances of Mr. Gipson and two other neighbors who had arrived from the eastward and were frightened back by what had passed. I followed their trail to the apex of the hill on the road toward Rolla, where the party left the main road at right angles, six going southwardly and five northwardly. After following each trail a short distance, I took the main road westwardly and notified my two nearest neighbors to hide their valuable horses and keep out of their sight and power, or the guerrillas would compel them to produce their fine horses, and perhaps murder them for attempting to conceal them from view. At the last place I visited, I met two well mounted United States soldiers and engaged them to go and inform Mr. Samuel Tullack that the guerrillas had robbed me that morning and would probably visit him that day or night, and to be prepared to give them a suitable reception. The soldiers found Mr. Tullack at a thrashing machine, with six other men and their horses, and delivered their message. They at once quit their work, went for their arms, and took post at the ford of James creek; here they awaited with great anxiety the approach of the marauders until nine o'clock, by which time they despaired of their coming that night, and were on the point of going home, when they heard them coming rapidly into the ford, and ordered them to halt. The guerrillas instantly turned back and fled, the citizens firing on them, by which their chief, Willim Carty (or "Devil Bill," as he was called) was dismounted, being wounded in the ankle. His fine mouse-colored horse, as soon as he felt himself riderless, left his master in the woods on foot and alone, while he escaped to my farm, where I caught him early the next morning with his saddle and bridle on, and delivered them to Captain Lonergan, the provost marshal at Pilot Knob, taking his receipt for the same. These were afterwards delivered to me, and I intend to keep them as heirlooms in our family for all time to come. The provost marshal also gave me a written permit to carry arms at all times where I pleased; to which Mayor Thomas added his permission to the same extent in the city of St. Louis, during the civil war, for my protection.

Early the next morning, after I had delivered Carty's horse to the provost marshal, I received a note from the brigand chief, stating he had seen his horse about my premises, and requesting me to put it in my stable, promising to call for it in a short time. I immediately burned the note and left my farm, removing all my property that the guerrillas could drive off. Soon after my departure, the enrolled militia drove off my hired man and his father and family because they had fed the guerrillas and had not notified me that they were on the farm while my life was in danger from them.

Being unable to find a loyal man who dared attempt a residence then at my farm, I left all my property in custody of the widow of one of my former foremen, who did all she could to preserve it, but to very little effect, as almost every man, woman and child within five miles, who was able to carry off anything, rushed forward, and, forcing open the doors of the store, dwellings, and factory, they carried away what suited them best, books, beds, furniture, clothing, cooking utensils, farming tools, crockery, and even the glass windows and sash, in presence of the person in charge, paying no more attention to her remonstrances than to the chirping of a sparrow, so that the doors stood open nine months afterwards, to the end of the civil war.

CHAPTER XXVI.

NINE MONTHS AT HOME—VOLUNTEERS IN THE UNITED STATES ARMY—ENLISTS IN THE "OLD GUARD"—SEES THREE OF HIS FORMER PUPILS, ON THE SAME DAY, OCCUPYING THE SEATS OF JUDGES IN ST. LOUIS.

After retreating from the guerrillas about Kaolin, I reported Samuel Trollinger to the provost marshal at Pilot Knob as the most dangerous bushwhacker in Iron county, he having assisted in the murdering of my foreman, Josiah Morgan, and was then prowling about the neighborhood of my farm, with only one man with him, named James Barton. After this I came home to St. Louis and reported myself to the proper officer as ready to serve the United States in any capacity for which I was qualified. I was informed that a position in Captain Clark's company, the "Old Guard," would be most suitable for me. I therefore enlisted and served in it. I was the eldest man in the company except Mr. Samuel Hawkin, who was two years older; but I had seen more of military service than any of them, as I had served in the United States army six campaigns against the British and the Mexicans, and had been in ten battles. We were drilled very regularly while General Price was making his raid through the State, but it was gradually discontinued as the dangers disappeared,

14

and was finally suspended after the fall of Richmond and
Sherman's "march to the sea." There has been no death
among the members of the company, although numbering
over one hundred men, the past year, or since I became a
member.

I spent nine months at home in St. Louis, writing slowly at
this work, and walking leisurely about the city and contemplating the mighty changes that have been made in the last
forty years in the appearance of the city and its environs. In
1826, there were but three houses between St. Charles and
Market streets and Seventh street and the Wedge House, and
only the same number between Market street and Chouteau
avenue and Seventh street and the Wedge House. Now, in
1866, that space, which was then almost entirely in the sole
possession of two individuals, is now owned by thousands,
and many of the most superb buildings of the city occupy the
space that was then a hazel thicket or pasture lands.

In one of my rambles through the central portion of the
city a year or two ago, I passed through the court-house, and
saw three judges, who had all been my pupils in former days
in St. Louis, presiding over courts there, all being elevated to
those high positions by the votes of the people. They were
the Hon. Barton Bates, of the Supreme Court; the Hon. Wilson Primm, of the Criminal Court, and the Hon. William
Ferguson, of the Probate Court. It is entirely out of my
power to describe the pleasure I felt at such an agreeable
and unlooked for event; this pleasure was intensified soon
after by Judge Primm remarking to me, that of all the vast
number of pupils I had taught in the city of St. Louis, not one
had ever been convicted of a crime in any court.

My long expulsion from our farm was not spent in gloom
and despondency. The reminiscences of acts of other and
former days were revived, and may be related here in
connection with other acts of mine which my descendants
may wish to know long after I have left them.

I had some years ago donated a lot extending from Capitol
avenue to Marine avenue, one hundred feet wide, to the
Board of Directors of the St. Louis Public Schools, on which
they had erected a splendid edifice and named the school
taught there the "Shepard School, No. 1." At the close of

the academic year, there was an examination of the pupils by the superintendent, before the committee of the board, the parents of the scholars, and invited spectators. Feeling some curiosity to know the progress the school that bore my name was making, I went in to hear the examination, and was much gratified by what I saw and heard. When the exercises were finished, the superintendent asked me to address the school, which I declined doing, and he did it most satisfactorily himself. He commenced by commending the pupils for the progress they had made during the year, and the decorum they had exhibited on the occasion, and then, turning to me, introduced me to them as their benefactor, who had raised a lasting monument to his memory by donating this lot, which was growing more valuable every day, and had brought this school to their very doors ; and closed by expressing the hope that I would live long to see the fruit of my labors ripen. I was quite embarrassed by this episode, although I knew it was indeed all true, and all about me knew it. I had not been in that neighborhood for a long time before, and when I came out on the avenue several persons stood waiting to accompany me to the Shepard Market, then being erected on a lot which I had donated to the city for that purpose. It was difficult to determine which the people in the vicinity were about to appreciate most, the school-house or the market-house, both being so much needed.

There is no church of any kind in that part of the city, and the people there seem to manifest no taste for any at present, their devotions being now mostly paid to Terpsichore in the Concordia Park, located in that vicinity. This state of things, however, I think is destined soon to undergo a great change, mostly through my management during the last twenty years. About the beginning of the year 1846, several ladies of the Second Baptist church, most of whom are now dead, applied to me to purchase for them a suitable lot for a cemetery, and said they would soon refund the money. I purchased a ten acre lot, cornering southwesterly on the Concordia Park, for the sum of one thousand and ten dollars, which I paid and had the deed made to nine trustees named by the ladies. It was laid out in lots, and a few sold and used while I was absent in the army in Mexico, and two hundred dollars were refunded to me. In 1849, the cholera prevailed, and as the people seemed to bury there *ad libitum*, no more sales could be made or money raised; the ladies, therefore, offered me the great central lot in payment in full for my advancement, which I accepted, and took a deed for it. As soon as I had recorded it, a law of the city forbade its use as a cemetery, and it so remained until it was stripped of all the fencing and trees, and it became a waste, and was nearly forgotten by the church members. Four of the trustees were dead, and most of the ladies who were prominent in its purchase were also dead, when it was found to have risen in value to at least twenty times its original price, notwithstanding its dilapidated condition, and yet was useless to its owners or the public. I therefore drew up a petition to the Legislature praying them to vacate the lot as a cemetery, and to authorize the trustees to dispose of the ground and refund to the lot-holders what was equitable and just, and turn over the residue to trustees for the benefit of the Second Baptist church. This petition I presented to the members of the church, who all signed it, and the Legislature passed an act in accordance with the request of the petitioners and authorized the proposed sale. On receipt of a copy of the act, a church meeting was held, to which I was invited, and attended; and being requested to do so, gave a full history of the affair to those present, several of whom had never heard of the purchase, as it had happened eighteen years previously, and was quite before the birth of some of the members present on the occasion. After hearing my statement, Mr. Camden and Mr. Samuel Davis stated that I had to their knowledge paid more than four-fifths of the purchase money eighteen years before, and was now willing to accept one-fourth of the land in full satisfaction of my claim, which would leave the remaining three-fourths to the church for the two hundred dollars, and worth now not less than twenty thousand dollars; and they thought the offer a liberal one, and should be accepted by the church with gratitude. The church acquiesced in it, and unanimously passed a most flattering vote of thanks to me for my many benefactions to the Baptist church. The majority of the trustees soon after divided the lot by streets and alleys according to law, and then by proper deeds assigned to each party its proper portion. I then paid special tax bills and costs against the lot for macadamizing the street on the south, amounting to about three hundred dollars, as a donation to the church funds, to leave it free of debt. It is now proposed by the Baptists to set apart one hundred and twenty-five square feet at the south end of one of the blocks for the erection of a church, as it is a fine location, in a growing neighborhood, and at a good distance from the Concordia Park, or a noisy street. It is also proposed to sell the remainder in lots for the benefit of the Second Baptist church. Should this be done, I shall have been a real benefactor to that church, as I had subscribed liberally to the sum paid the Episcopalians for the house at the corner of Chesnut and Third streets, and took a lot donated to them by old Mr. William Christy, at a thousand dollars above its estimated value, in payment of a loan of three thousand five hundred dollars used in a payment to the Episcopalians, and then divided the last debt of the church of eighteen hundred and thirty dollars with Samuel C. Davis, and each paid nine hundred and fifteen dollars of it, and thus relieved the church of its indebtedness. Subsequently, I purchased a new carpet for the church, which was the first ever laid down in a Baptist house of worship in St. Louis.

CHAPTER XXVIII.

LAST DAYS OF THE GREAT REBELLION—DEATH OF TWO DANGEROUS ENEMIES, AND THEIR BURIAL NEAR KAOLIN.

During the raid of General Price into Missouri in 1864, he was deserted by a large number of his most desperate and lawless men, who, secreting themselves among their relations and friends in all parts of the State, rendered life and property as insecure as at any period of the war, particularly such property as horses and mules. No part of the State probably suffered so much, according to what it had, as our neighborborhood, whether men, horses or other personal property are considered. We lost more than half our able-bodied men by death, and more than half our movable property by rapine and plunder.

A large number of my neighbors had been taken at the court-house in the town of Potosi, and all our militia called to Webster, so that the whole country south of Kaolin could be traveled over without opposition by robbers and guerrillas, except now and then when a small party of militia were allowed to visit their families and see what depredations were being committed.

In February, while this state of affairs continued, two noto riously bad men, Samuel Trollinger and James Barton—whom I had reported to the provost marshal, as mentioned in the last chapter—rode about the country, guiding parties to steal, rob and murder with impunity, until they were both checked in the following manner:

A loyal man, named Strickland, living about four miles from the residence of Trollinger, was serving in the militia at Webster, twelve miles distant from his home. His wife being out of wood and flour, sent for him to come home. His captain consented, but, fearing that Trollinger might kill him if alone, sent five other soldiers along with him, and directed them to arrest Trollinger, if possible, and bring him with them to camp. Srickland arrived at home before night, and began to chop wood at his door, when a woman, a neighbor of Trollinger, passed by, and, seeing Strickland at home, informed Trollinger's wife, as he was not at home. On his return, he was informed Strickland was at home again, when he immediately went back for his friend Barton to help him kill his neighbor Strickland the next morning. Both prepared themselves accordingly, and at dawn of day started for Strickland's residence. Strickland, however, in pursuance of his captain's orders, had got his comrades ready at an earlier hour, and started to arrest his neighbor Trollinger, and had traveled about three miles in the direction of his residence when he saw him and Barton, his friend, coming swiftly towards him on horseback, both well armed. Strickland had but one of his men in sight with him, the other four being a little behind, when Trollinger espied them approaching, and, instantly dismounting, both parties posted themselves behind trees and opened fire on each other. The four soldiers, on hearing the firing on their friends in front, separated and ran far round, two on each flank, to prevent a retreat, and, commencing firing, killed Trollinger at the first shot. Barton, seeing him fall, and the present inequality of the combat, attempted flight, but soon fell in between the two soldiers posted on the line of his retreat, and was likewise instantly killed. Thus I was relieved of two of my most dangerous and inveterate enemies, from whom I had often fled during the war, and one of whom had waylaid and beaten me, assisted by another person, until they both supposed me dead, and had assisted in murdering my foreman at the commencement of the war. When the soldiers saw that their orders had been efficiently and summarily executed, they took the arms and horses of the dead men preparatory to returning to their camp; but reflecting that wolves or hogs might devour or disfigure the bodies, and render the spot more bloody and frightful, as there was then several inches of snow on the ground, they removed the bodies to where a tree had been partially blown down and placing them beneath its roots, chopped off the trunk of the tree and let the roots fall back and bury them. After accomplishing this rude sepulture, the soldiers returned with their trophies to their camp, receiving the plaudits of their comrades in arms, and the hearty thanks of all persons who had anything that could be stolen in that vicinity.

The son-in-law and family of Trollinger still remained at his late residence, but, being strongly suspected of harboring robbers, were soon driven off and their houses burned. The brother of Trollinger removed his remains to a graveyard on his farm, adjoining mine, and placed his family, now ruined, in the vicinity. The visitation of this just retribution seemed to check and intimidate the small bands which roved about the country up to this time, and their depredations ceased. Only one party of four men has since been seen robbing in that neighborhood; that was headed by William Carty, the same man who had robbed me the August before, and whose horse I had delivered to the provost marshal at Pilot Knob. He came to the house of the woman I had left to watch the farm and inquired for me, threatening vengeance on me for giving up the horse; but said if I would pay him two hundred dollars in gold, I might at once return and stay in peace at my farm, but if I did not, he would come and kill me or drive me entirely off the place. He then searched her house and person for money, but found none, although she had two hundred and fifty dollars on her person which was quilted in a garment which she constantly wore. On his being unable to find any money, he robbed her of a very fine bed-quilt that cost her seventeen dollars for the materials alone.

Soon after, General Sherman completed his masterly march through Georgia to the sea, and the rebel armies surrendered and retured home.

In May, 1865, I ventured back to my farm, and on my arrival found two of my so-called loyal neighbors watching their stock feeding on my garden and vineyard. They expressed great surprise at seeing me there, as they supposed I would not be able to stay in that neighborhood for fear of guerrillas. I replied, that the war was ended, and that I had nothing to fear but from such cowardly thieves as they, who had not ventured to serve in either army, but prowled about the country and plundered both parties, while they fought the battles. They said very little in reply, but hurried off the stock, and I have not seen them since. They were not out of sight, when another neighbor arrived and informed us that one of these men had just returned from Ironton, where he had been to answer to an indictment found against him for robbing old Mr. Asher of part of a sack of corn meal at Asher's mill, assisted by another of his fraternity, and had given bail to appear and answer at the next term of the court. Such acts show to what a low state the morals of men were reduced.

CHAPTER XXIX.

RETURN TO KAOLIN AFTER THE CIVIL WAR—DESOLATION AND
APPEARANCE OF THE PLACE—RESUMPTION OF THE CULTIVA-
TION OF THE FARMS, ETC.

The total absence of all inhabitants at Kaolin; the recollection of the deaths of so many of my friends and neighbors
during the war; the devastated state of the remaining buildings, with the doors all open and the glass broken out; the
lonely appearance of the standing chimneys of the buildings
that had been burned; the fallen and absent fences; the
unpruned state of the vineyards and orchards, and the dead
standing stalks of the weeds that had grown the year before,
filled my mind with gloom, and seemed to forbid my attempting to repair the waste at my advanced period of life. I
walked about the farm during the day, and observed the
astonishing growth of the brush and brambles that had
remained unchecked and undisturbed for three years, and
then seemed almost to defy control.

We had then ten farms in Iron county, eight of which
were without tenants, and all in the same condition except
one, which had the house and fences burned off it. In this
state of affairs, I offered any of the farms free of rent for
one year, or at a nominal rent and the taxes for five years,
but could only dispose of two of them on these liberal terms,
as most persons feared the guerrillas would renew their
depredations as soon as the Federal armies were disbanded
and returned home. We were, however, kept but a short
time in doubt as to the intentions of the guerrillas that
infested our neighborhood; for, as a party of paroled Confederate soldiers passed their rendezvous on Spring river, near
the Arkansas line, they sent word to several who had lost
horses to come to their rendezvous and receive their horses,
as the war on their part was now ended and they would
restore them. Five young men, in accordance with this
invitation, went to the place appointed and were kindly entertained by the guerrillas, who restored them nine horses, which
they brought back and returned to their proper owners in our

neighborhood. They stated that any person who had lost property recently might come among them and search for it, and if found it should be immediately restored to its owner without fee or reward. This course of conduct on their part, and the return of several of our neighbors to their homes, quieted much of our fear, and enabled us to enjoy what little we had left with better zest and apparent security. We have had no robberies or murders in our vicinity since the withdrawal of the troops from Pilot Knob, and the roads begin to be traveled again by unarmed men, as in former times, unmolested.

Having completed my arrangements for the preservation and partial cultivation of our farm at Kaolin, I returned to St. Louis, and spent the summer watching the movements of the two great disbanded armies returning to their homes, and writing slowly on this work at intervals.

On the 15th of October, 1865, I attained the full age of seventy years, being then in good health, active, and sound in body and mind, so far as I could perceive, as I had been during the last fifty years. I had never had rheumatism, gout, or any of those distressing pains that impair the intellect and destroy the pleasures of life, nor had I ever had any long or serious illness. I had generally been temperate, studious, industrious, frugal, enterprising, and successful in all my business where I directed it myself. I spent the day mostly in reflection on the interesting scenes through which I had passed, and in calling to remembrance a vast multitude of friends and acquaintances who have fallen on the right hand and on the left through the long journey of my life.

On the following day I visited several of my old friends, among them Mr. Henry Von Phul, he being the eldest and only merchant now in business who was in the mercantile trade when I came to St. Louis. I spent more time with him than any other, comparing ages and prospects. He remarked that he knew me and my mode of life, and all the old inhabitants of the city, and thought I was now more likely to live through the nineteenth century than any other man of all his acquaintance.

I soon after returned to the farm, intending to prune the vineyards and orchards, but found too few laborers there to gather the corn crops and sow wheat in season, and therefore abandoned the pruning and returned to St. Louis, where I have since employed myself in preparing this autobiography, which is as full and complete a history of Mrs. Mary T. Shepard and myself as I am able to write from memory alone up to this evening, January 10th, 1866.

Early in March, I returned to Kaolin, intending to spend the summer there and repair the damages of the war, cultivate my vineyards, and prune my orchards. On my arrival, I learned that two horses and a mule had disappeared from the farm a short time before, and no trace of them could be found. The circumstance created no alarm, nor was suspicion fixed on any person as having stolen them for several days, when one of my neighbors informed me that Wm. Carty, the guerrilla who robbed me in 1864, had been prowling about the vicinity with two other men, inquiring for me and when I was expected to return, and dined at a near neighbor's two days before my arrival at Kaolin. This satisfied us that any further search for the animals would be useless, and no intelligence has ever been received of them since. I therefore began to keep at a distance from his accustomed routes of travel and depredations, and at length retired to St. Louis for safety.

On the 21st of May, 1866, I was walking on Main street in Ironton with my neighbor Levi Gipson, when I was accosted by Granville Carty, who asked me if my name was Shepard, and on my answering in the affirmative, he said, "I am sent to you by another man to get pay for a horse belonging to him which you sold to the government." I at once recognized him as one of the guerrillas that robbed me in 1864, and asked him to give me his name. This he refused to do, and left me. I then procured a warrant and had him arrested, and subsequently indicted for robbery. He was arraigned and gave bail for his appearance for trial at the November term of the Circuit Court of Iron county for 1866, but returned to the bushes again, while I withdrew to St. Louis to avoid being murdered by his associates, as my foreman had been in 1861.

Several of my Masonic brethren have urged me to take an active part in pressing forward the building of their hall at the corner of Market and Seventh streets, as I had the Odd

Fellows' Hall at the corner of Locust and Fourth streets, in 1846, while I was Grand Master of the Grand Lodge of the State of Missouri. This I have engaged to do, and have thus far seemed to be progressing satisfactorily.

On the 24th of June, I accompanied my brethren, the Sir Knights of the St. Louis Commandery of Knight Templars, on an excursion to Salem, Marion county, Illinois, to attend a Masonic celebration of the anniversary of St. John, by invitation of Masonic brethren of that vicinity. A very large number of Freemasons attended the celebration, which was a very imposing and novel affair, as the different orders, in full regalia of their distinctive ranks, were marshaled in the most perfect order and marched to a beautiful grove in the vicinity, where an appropriate address was delivered by one of the brethren, and listened to by a vast and attentive audience ; after which, a bounteous collation was spread on the lawn by the lady friends of the Order, and the whole multitude invited to partake of it. It is beyond the descriptive powers I possess to give a proper idea of the scene, and the rational pleasures that followed. Suffice it to say, that beauty, hilarity, cultivated intellect, and kind feeling, united to make the grove truly the Elysian field that will long be remembered. Ten Sir Knights and eight lady friends formed our party from St. Louis, and we were met at Salem by several other St. Louis ladies who were spending the summer in the country with their friends, and thus our party was considerably augmented. This addition · to our number brought with it some advantages we had not anticipated, as they were acquainted with most of the people in the vicinity, and introduced us to many of them, by which our circle of acquaintances was greatly enlarged, and more zest added to the entertainment. Among my new-formed friends were some in whom I soon took a lively interest from the peculiar condition in which I found them placed, and will mention them again hereafter.

On my return home, I began to make efforts to form a Historical Society in St. Louis that shall continue for ages, and, by personal application, collected the signatures of two hundred and seventy of the longest residents of the city, who were favorable to extending an invitation to the citizens generally to assemble at the court-house on the 11th day of August, 1866—that being the centenary anniversary of the day on which the first grant of land was made in St. Louis— to assist in forming such a society. This invitation, with the signatures annexed, I caused to be published in all the city journals. Accordingly, on the day designated, a most interesting meeting was held in the Circuit Court room, and the preliminary steps taken to effect an organization. In the course of the proceedings and speeches, I received a due share of flattering commendations from my learned and modest friends for the active part I had taken in promoting this enterprise.

At a subsequent meeting, the society was fully organized and officers elected by ballot. I was chosen recording secretary, and entered at once on the discharge of the duties of the office. I was kindly assisted in this by Mr. James L. Butler, the Missouri State Commissioner appointed by the Governor to present the products of Missouri at the great fair of the world to be held at Paris, France, in 1867. To him the society is greatly indebted for much labor, valuable information, and many collections. Through him the suggestion came of collecting the photographs of the remaining patriarchs and builders of the fame of the city of St. Louis. In this Mr. George P. Hall has rendered the society a service that should place his name among its great benefactors, he having gratuitously furnished the greater part of the photographs.

CHAPTER XXX.

SECOND MARRIAGE OF THE AUTHOR—HIS TRAVELS, WITH NOTES AND OBSERVATIONS.

Most men who have passed an active, eventful, and successful life, until they have attained the age of three score and ten years, are unwilling to embark in new and important enterprises, and retire quietly to the still scenes of life, without manifesting any desire to continue the struggle longer. But having enjoyed good health generally, and being of a cheerful and contented disposition, time had made less impression on me than most men of my age, and permitted me to retain my strength and activity in about the same degree I did at the age of fifty. Moreover, my ancestry had for many generations mostly attained a great age, which, reasoning from analogy, induced me to conclude that I might probably, like them, survive still many years if engaged in active life. I had an estate of such magnitude and variety that I could indulge myself in almost any mode of active life if I could procure a companion qualified and willing to engage in such an enterprise at my advanced period in life.

I therefore determined on selecting one whose habits of life were formed and resembled as nearly as possible those of the lady with whom I had spent more than forty happy years, because usefully and profitably employed, and to conform my actions to her circumstances and wishes as far as possible. In this I succeeded beyond my most sanguine expectations, and was married on the 18th day of December, 1866 (being then in my seventy-second year), to a lady who possessed those qualities in a high degree and had managed an estate of her own for several years in the most economical manner, and was prepared at once to join me in new enterprises. Her family was well suited to my tastes and circumstances, and hailed my advent among them with as much apparent pleasure as if I had come by a preconcerted invitation from each individual for their own particular benefit. Nor did her neighbors and friends manifest less pleasure on receiving me into their society than her own children. In short, I could not have been given a more cordial welcome by all her acquaintances and friends.

Being both in good health, and our family comfortably situated in their own mansion, we planned an extensive excursion, and after making the necessary preparations, left the city on a steamer bound to New Orleans, taking with us my wife's eldest daughter, then about eighteen years of age. The water being very low, the trip was unusually protracted, but this afforded us a fine opportunity for viewing the country and towns along our course, which we did very satisfactorily.

On arriving at New Orleans, we took lodgings at a most

convenient house to view the city, and spent one week there, during which it rained or snowed every day, so that what we saw of the city or its business was under the most unfavorable circumstances, and we left it and its mud (without wishing to see it again), after securing passage and embarking on the steamer Cuba, bound for Havana, where we arrived after a pleasant passage of five days.

It being one of the most pleasant winters ever experienced on that island, the contrast of weather and pleasure was very great and agreeable, and we enjoyed its full fruition. We visited several of its towns and remarkable places on the different railroads, the most noted of which was the extensive grotto of Villa Mar, near Matanzas, and the tomb of Columbus, in the rear of the altar in the cathedral of Havana.

It may be instructive for me here to remark that the remains of Columbus were first entombed in the cathedral of Valladolid, in Spain; but after the lapse of many years they were removed to St. Domingo, and from thence to Havana, lest the negroes of Hayti, in their frenzy to destroy all that was Spanish, should cast his ashes into the sea or otherwise scatter them forever. Many travelers visit his tomb and lay their hands upon it through respect and veneration; and scarcely one does it without emotion and awe, as if in the presence of a deity.

We remained sixteen days on the island, and enjoyed every opportunity we desired of observing the manners, customs and peculiarities of the inhabitants. We had established ourselves at the Hotel de Inglaterra, which is immediately in front of the public promenade, one of the gayest and most orderly places I ever visited, where all the fashionble people assemble each evening and converse, or pass like a panorama before you. From the lofty balconies and more lofty flat roof of this remarkable hotel, we could view at a glance the vast multitude and all their movements, while they seemed to have come thither to exhibit themselves to the best advantage, and for the public enjoyment.

During our stay on this island we formed the acquaintance of several gentlemen whose attentions, kindness and hospitality have fixed their names indelibly in our memories. The first of these was Mr. D. A. Carr, a merchant of Matanzas, who spared no pains to make us acquainted with all that was interesting or novel to us. He introduced us into his family, and made us feel as though he was our brother, and finally accompanied us on board the steamer Liberty, when we left the island, and commended us to all our fellow-passengers. In his endeavors to accommodate us, he was greatly assisted by Professor Dryfoos, a most accomplished gentleman, who spoke several languages, and wrote the most varied and prettiest hand of any person I ever met with. This gentleman had also traveled in many countries, and, possessing a cultivated mind, he made himself a most interesting and companionable person.

Another most amiable and kind gentleman was Captain T. W. Brown, who commanded a large British merchant ship then lying in the bay of Matanzas, who, having learned that my wife and daughter had never been on board a merchant ship, sent his barge on shore and took us all on board, and showed us all that was novel and curious, and paid us other attentions that have embalmed him and his kindness in our memories through life.

Our consul at Havana, Mr. Minor, also did all in his power to make our stay agreeable and interesting, visiting us at the "Inglaterra," and exhibiting that urbanity for which he is so deservedly distinguished.

I have thus far only spoken of men of peaceful professions who strove to entertain us. I now come to mention those of a martial nature, whom we found equally assiduous and successful in their endeavors to please, amuse and instruct us, although their opportunity seemed at first quite limited and unexpected. On our arrival, several armed ships lay in the harbor of Havana, but among them none from the United States. About eight days after, however, the U. S. war steamer Winoosky, commanded by Captain Cooper, entered the harbor, and, as is customary, several of the officers came on shore and visited at the "Inglaterra." Prominent among them was the commander himself, the second officer, Lieutenant G. Patchke, and the purser, Mr. Parker, with whom we spent many pleasant hours during our stay on the island, visiting with them the most noteworthy places in the vicinity, and, by special invitation, the man-of-war itself, where we saw the whole drill of the ship's complement, and were shown the novelties peculiar to naval affairs on board. When the day for the ship's departure at length arrived, we went to the shore opposite the Moro Castle and saw her go out to sea, her officers exchanging salutations with us as she passed.

The following day we also took our departure. We embarked on the steamer Liberty for Baltimore, and on the passage touched at Key West. We enjoyed a pleasant run until we reached Chesapeake bay; here we met with ice, and were landed at Annapolis, where we found the ground covered with snow. We had for traveling companions several distinguished gentlemen, the most prominent of whom was General Gonzalez, who had been second in command in Lopez's expedition to revolutionize Cuba, and was pardoned by the Spanish sovereign; he afterwards served through our civil war as major-general and chief of artillery in the Confederate army, and is now a resident of the State of South Carolina.

After landing at Annapolis and viewing that venerable city, we continued our journey to New York by railroad. The weather was very cold, and as we were so recently from the tropics we felt the change very sensibly.

We spent two days in the city without much opportunity for sight-seeing, on account of cold winds, and then left by the usual railroad route for St. Louis, where we arrived, after an absence of about two months, without any accident, or any occurrence to mar the pleasure of the journey on our way homeward.

CHAPTER XXXI.

INCIDENTS AND OBSERVATIONS CONNECTED WITH AN EUROPEAN TOUR.

Having long contemplated visiting the eastern continent and viewing there as many of the wonders of the world as I could, I made the necessary arrangements for the journey, and taking with me my wife and her two eldest daughters,

15

Miss Emma Card and Miss Ida Card (both of the most suitable age to make a tour of that kind pleasant and instructive
to them), we visited Washington City and several other large
towns on our way to the seaboard. I had procured a passport
of Mr. Seward, the United States Secretary of State, for myself
and family, and as I had been appointed by the Governor an
honorary commissioner for the State of Missouri to the Paris
Exposition, the Secretary had inserted that statement in my ·
passport, which never failed to attract the attention of officials
and gain their kind offices wherever we had occasion to
exhibit it in Europe.

While waiting several days in New York for the sailing of
the steamer on which we took passage, we visited many of the
most remarkable places of that city, which gave me a fine
opportunity of contrasting its present condition with what it
was in 1819, when I resided there and assisted in fitting out a
fruitless Columbian expedition. At that time the city was
estimated to contain one hundred and thirty thousand inhabitants. Less than half a century has since elapsed, and now,
in 1867, the city contains ten times that number. The Croton
water-works, gas-works, railroads and telegraphs, have all
been introduced within that period, and such other improvements made, that it was with difficulty I could recognize any
place or thing with which I had been familiar, except the
Battery and a neighboring church and graveyard, and even
they had been modernized to some extent, and all changed
about them. I was unable to find a single individual with
whom I had been acquainted in 1819, or a house in which I
had been, so completely had time obliterated everything then
so familiar to me.

It is impossible for me to describe the effect on my feelings
on observing the contrast, and casting an inquiring thought
on the future to know what new things more may come into use
while I may be able to see them, as there never has been a
period since the invention of letters when the human mind
was so intensely engaged on inventions and improvements as
the present, or with such remarkable success.

On the 27th of April, we went on board the British packet
steamship Cella, and sailed for Brest, France, where we
arrived on the 13th of May, after a very pleasant passage.

There we spent two days viewing that ancient city, some of whose walls are older than the Christian religion, having been built in the days of Julius Cæsar. The city, having been so long built and of such durable materials, had a very antiquated appearance, and was in strong contrast with New York, yet fresh in our recollection. We gazed about, and saw other things equally strange: women with shovels and hoes, cleaning the streets and gutters, loading carts with every kind of street sweepings and rubbish, while plenty of idle men stood round smoking or lounging on stone seats, under the shade of enormous trees, planted by former generations, and appearing to enjoy the scene as if it was so arranged by nature for their exclusive pleasure. In the meantime, well-dressed *gendarmes*, happy fellows, with nothing to do, in good humor, wait around, ready to answer politely any question a stranger may ask, or guide him to any place he may desire to go without fee or reward. The city seemed to be finished—no one was in a hurry—everything plentiful and cheap—and no signs of discontent manifested.

Anticipating much pleasure in traveling by railroad from Brest to Paris, we entered the cars about midday and proceeded, but had accomplished only a few miles of our journey when the appearance of the country and its inhabitants convinced us that our route lay through the least interesting part of France. The towns and villages through which we passed appeared ancient, sombre, and lifeless; the farms, cattle, and horses, small; the houses, low and dimunitive; the out-buildings scattered and inconvenient, and the lands tilled with primitive shaped tools, and animals harnessed in rudely constructed gear. The roads are all good, but the vehicles were clumsy, ill-shapen, and heavy. The route is uneven, crooked, and uninviting; yet the country must be healthy and favorable to longevity, as no part of the world shows a greater proportion of old people than this part of France. After passing Rennes, the scene is changed; buildings appear of more recent date, and changes are being made corresponding with the improvements of the age. Yet it must be a long time before this part of the country will be altered much, as every structure seems built of the most durable materials and in the best manner for preservation. It is only where railroads have altered the channel of business near the great cities that changes are extensively made.

The distance between Brest and Paris is three hundred and thirty-six miles. More artificial beauty is displayed in the last thirty-six miles than on all the rest of the route.

On our arrival at Paris and locating ourselves, we soon learned that the object of the Grand Exposition was to fill France with money, and we prepared for it; but it was soon evident that the course many had adopted would defeat that mercenary purpose. As soon as the improvements were commenced on the Champ de Mars, the Parisians seemed at once turned into sharpers, extortioners or speculators, as they laid their plans to extort and obtain as much as possible from the strangers who should visit them, and give as little as possible in return. As a natural result, an alarm was soon raised, and thousands stayed away, others remained but a limited time, and economized so that Paris had not a franc more money on the last day of 1867 than she had on the first.

Other cities and countries profited greatly by the Exposition. The English and Bremen ships carried most of the passengers that traveled to the Exposition by sea, while other countries received the benefits of the railway intercommunication. Visitors at Paris, from all parts of Europe, were constantly pointing out other places in the vicinity, or within easy reach, as more pleasant and fascinating than Paris, crowded as it was with strangers, where prudent people could enjoy more at less expense ; and in this way they soon made it fashionable to spend but a short time in Paris and more in the neighboring cities.

The result was ruinous to such companies as had gone into expensive arrangements in fitting up places for public amusement and pleasure, and came on so suddenly, and was so unlooked for, that, in its effects upon everything connected with the Exposition, it can be likened to nothing else than the complete destruction that marks the path of a resistless tornado. Socially and intellectually, France was a gainer by the Exposition, but financially and morally she was a loser.

When we had spent a few days here, and become somewhat familiar with the many pleasing and interesting objects of this most polished city of the world, we visited Méhun, Dijon,

Lyons, and Marseilles; and, as the weather was very fine and pleasant for many days together in the growing month of May, we saw France in her most fascinating condition, and were quite willing she should rejoice in the name of "La Belle France," and by which Napoleon I. was so fond of calling her. It would be difficult to point out a route on the face of the earth, of the same length, where so much may be seen and enjoyed in the same time and at such moderate expense. Beautiful cities, villages, farms, vineyards, gardens, palaces, and dwellings, line the road the whole distance. The people appeared cleanly, happy, industrious and contented, and welcomed every one. All kinds of domestic animals appeared plentiful and well fed. No lands laid waste in morasses and unsightly thickets to mar the landscape, but flocks and herds covered the hills and uneven places too rugged for cultivation, always attended by careful keepers. The orchards and groves were in blossom, and innumerable birds filled the air with the music of their notes. All nature seemed to hold holiday on this route, and to welcome the advent of new-comers and cheer them on their way.

Marseilles, the southern terminus of the route, is one of the most important and remarkable cities in France, having less than one-fourth of the population of Paris, yet it has a greater commercial importance. It was built by the Phœnicians six hundred years before the birth of Christ, and no scholar can visit it without calling to mind the names of Pytheas the astronomer, Mascaron the preacher, Paget the sculptor, and M. Thiers the historian, son of a blacksmith, all born here. Standing on the hights near the cemetery, and viewing the landscape round about, we thought this city one of the most remarkable places in the world, and very naturally attracted the far-seeing eyes of such men as the Phœnicians and brought them to improve it at an early age. It was no part of our business to write a description of the cities we visited, so, when we had gratified ourselves by viewing this interesting place with its innumerable collections from all parts of the world, we left for new scenes.

Leaving Marseilles for Toulon, we soon had experience of the difference of the climate on the banks of the Seine and shores of the Mediterranean, and observed other changes quite as remarkable. Olive groves and idleness, squalid and ragged children and beggars, became more frequent, and increased as we traveled eastward, showing a wide difference between the northern and southern French people. We spent but little time at Toulon, where naval affairs seemed to engross the attention of a great part of the population. We however saw enough to convince us that any other people must be busy building ships if they wish to excel the French in it.

Journeying eastwardly, at various distances from the coast of the Mediterranean, we enjoyed great variety of scenery, and witnessed with how much less labor the people of this part of France live than those of the northern part, on account of the mildness of the climate in this region. So many idle and half-clad people appear on this route that one is led to conclude most of the inhabitants of this vicinity live entirely on the products of the olive groves, which are here very numerous and extend in all directions.

The railroad passes through many short tunnels, and over many short bridges spanning the little streams falling into the Mediterranean, on which are villages, trees, houses, and gardens, surrounded with walls so time-marked that we may safely date their building before the age of letters. The railroad is the only thing which indicates improvement on this route. The windmill, sickle, and ass, are as much in use here as ever, and seem to fill the measure of all that is left vacant by nature to supply the people of this productive region with food. Probably no people on earth spend so much of their time in ease, leisure, and quietude, free from the extremes of heat or cold, as those dwelling on the line of the road from Toulon to Nice. Picking mulberry leaves to feed silkworms engaged half the people we saw employed.

Nice is a city of fifty thousand inhabitants, whose position is favorable to health and pleasure, and has many attractions in and about it well calculated to delay the archæologist or man of classic tastes. Its name, which in Greek signifies victory, would seem to indicate that the founders may have been Grecians, and the remains of ruins of great antiquity go far to strengthen this belief. It has been the scene of many important events mentioned in the history of former centuries.

Massena was born there May 6th, 1758, and the Italian patriot Garibaldi on July 4th, 1807. It is the most suitable place for invalids that I have ever visited in my long and roving life, and I think it my duty to note it as such.

From Nice to Genoa we traveled by steamboat on a fair still day, and spent our time on deck viewing the coast towns, villas, gardens, groves, and the Alps mountains in the distance, some of whose tops were covered with snow this late in the spring. It was one of the most pleasant trips we made by water, and most instructive. The whole of this part of the coast was covered with vineyards, olive groves, and *morus multicaulis* trees (for feeding silkworms), which constitute the riches of Italy. Asses and goats were very numerous, but animals of any other kind seemed very scarce, except fine horses for war or pleasure.

Being at the Hotel Feder, near the custom-house, in the commercial part of Genoa, which was making great preparations to celebrate Garibaldi's victory of May 26th, by a general illumination, we took a coach early in the morning, before the multitude thronged the streets, in order to visit the elevated portions of this grand and imposing city of palaces, the birth-place of Columbus, and rival of Venice in former times.

No two cities in Europe are built on sites so unlike each other. Each is on a gulf to which it has given name. One is nearly on a level with the Mediterranean and the other five hundred feet above it. The surroundings of Venice are a dead level, those of Genoa are of the most beautiful and diversified character, including the lofty snow-clad peaks of the Appenines and the broad Gulf of Genoa, whitened by the canvas of all nations, without an island to obstruct the vision.

Genoa has a population of a hundred and twenty thousand, and is a city of great antiquity, as some traces of old Roman walls still remain visible and add interest to its history. The monument of Christopher Columbus, the discoverer of America, stands here surmounted by his statue. An inscription on it relates that he was born in this city in the year 1442, and recounts some of the acts of his remarkable life. This city is celebrated for its admirable police. It enjoys a freedom from thieves, robbers, and beggars, nowhere else experienced in

Europe. The city was most brilliantly illuminated at night, and we walked about its streets and saw it in all its grandeur without the least danger of harm, disorder, or thieves, disturbing us.

The next morning we steamed out of its harbor between those two gigantic moles, *vecchio* and *nuovo*, which rise nearly four hundred feet above the sea and form its chief defence; and looking back upon the city and surrounding country, we enjoyed one of the grandest views that nature and art, combined in about equal parts, have ever presented to the eyes of men.

On the following day we landed at Livorno, or Leghorn, a great commercial city of eighty thousand inhabitants, among which are more Mohammedans than in any other Christian city of Europe, and here we first saw a mosque for their accommodation. This city is well watered from a stream thirty-two miles distant, and has a cleanly and commercial appearance, as well as a somewhat political one.

On the same public square stand two statues, one of a sovereign dethroned by his people for refusing them a constitution; the other, of one enthroned by his people for giving them a constitution. They stand at opposite sides of the square, with the head of the former somewhat bowing, as if in submission, and that of the latter in an erect position, as if enjoying their approbation and love.

Twenty miles north of this flourishing city, on the right or north bank of the river Arno, stands the renowned city of Pisa, or, more properly speaking, the remains of it. One thousand years ago it contained one hundred and fifty thousand inhabitants and was the most commercial city in Italy; now it contains but twenty thousand inhabitants, one-tenth of whom are beggars. It is surrounded by a fruitful country, and has a mild climate, but wealth and want seem to be very unequally distributed among the people, who all appear desirous to make their condition known. In the days of this city's greatest prosperity, its magnificence was displayed in numberless marble edifices, most of which remain to this day and require no description. The very gradual decline of the city (for it was never sacked) has afforded enticing shelter for the lazy, beggarly crowd that at present inhabit it, and are its greatest and most intolerable nuisances. The objects most interesting to visitors are situated near each other, and can soon be viewed and left behind, unless one should desire to look over the works of former ages, now going rapidly to ruin and out of view, and contrast them with the mighty works of the present age. In Pisa's day of prosperity and glory, no railroad, telegraph, gas or steam facilities had come to aid in its building or its magnificence. Now all these seem to combine to build up her more youthful sisters, and to despoil her of all that nature and art had so profusely lavished upon her; yet her decaying magnificence is the most interesting and attractive feature. The Leaning Tower, the Museum of Tombs, the Cathedral, ancient Baptistry, and the University in which Galileo taught, are the most noteworthy objects.

On the banks of the same river Arno, thirty-five miles above, stands Florence, the new capital of the kingdom of Italy, containing one hundred and fifty thousand inhabitants, to which has been awarded the title of "Fairest city of the Earth." It is revered as the birth-place of Galileo, Boccacio, Petrarch, Dante, and Michael Angelo, whose labors have filled such conspicuous niches in the temple of fame that the appreciative mind delights to linger about a place that has given birth to such noble contributors to poetry and art. We do not propose to mention but a few of the many interesting objects presented in this busy, pious, and fascinating city, yet some are so remarkable that to omit mentioning them in this place would indicate inattention or want of appreciation of worthy and sublime objects.

The *duomo* or cathedral of Santa Maria del Fiore is a structure of vast size and magnificence, being five hundred feet long, its transept three hundred and five feet, and three hundred and eighty feet to the summit of the cross. The cupola is one hundred and thirty-eight feet in diameter, being the widest in the world, and the edifice exceeds in size that of St. Peter at Rome. The *campanile*, or bell tower, adjoining it, rises to the hight of two hundred and seventy-five feet. The staircase consists of four hundred and thirteen steps. From this edifice we saw the celebrated patriot Garibaldi and about two thousand of his surviving soldiers marching to the cathedral to say mass for the repose of the souls of those who had perished in the wars under his command.

In this city may be found such a vast number of interesting objects that no one need fear a want of pleasant employment during leisure hours while here. Among the chief places
of interest is the studio of Hiram Powers, a native of the
State of Vermont. He has spent twenty-five years of his life
here, and immortalized his name by his statues of American
statesmen.

The morality and taste of the people of this city seemed to
be better than any other we have as yet visited; still the
intolerable nuisance of beggary is permitted to annoy strangers here, as in every city of Italy, and detracts much from the
pleasure of traveling in that country.

The railroad from Florence to Rome is new, and has the
appearance of having been built by engineers of most profound skill, who perfectly knew the topography of the
country, as it is located in the only place that nature had
left practicable without herculean labor to accomplish it. It
passes through a spur of mountains of such formation that
nature seems to have exerted herself more than usual to
impede travel through this part of Italy, and which remained
almost impassable for ages. This circumstance adds much
interest to the journey, and affords great variety of scenery of
the most agreeable character. Half the distance is along the
banks of the river Tiber, which it crosses many times, and
exposes its size so much that Missourians, from its diminutive
amount of water in motion, lose all respect for its name as a
river. It has, however, figured so long on the pages of history
—to which our eyes have been so very familiar on paper,
believing it to have been at one time an important river—
everything on its banks engaged our attention and led us
back to our childhood days and studies, now nearly forgotten.
From its source to its mouth, the ruins of ancient edifices,
fortifications, monuments, towers, and walls, are more or less
in view—and no new ones—which produce many gloomy
reflections.

Stock-raising seems to employ a great number of the inhabitants along this rugged route. Their flocks are not generally
large, but numerous and of fine quality. The cattle are
remarkable for the magnificence of their horns, and their
being almost uniformly of a dark brown color. Mills and
milk are plentiful along the Tiber; consequently beggars are

less numerous in this part of Italy than any other. It may be proper for me here to remark, that I have never in all my travels seen the wife or children of herdsmen or farmers begging.

As you approach the city of Rome, the size and grandeur of the ruins, as well as the edifices of later ages, seem to expand and prepare you for the Exposition of the fallen "mistress of the world;" for such she will seem to be, before you arrive within her gates, by the scattered fragments of her former pride and greatness, going daily more to decay and becoming a more complete ruin. At some miles' distance from the city, the police officers demand from travelers their passports, and learn the character of their owners, and, although they treat every one civilly, they make a marked difference in their attention to different individuals, and show by their conduct in what light they appreciate them and the country to which they belong.

I will spend no time in giving a description of Rome as it is, or as it was, or the numberless remarkable things to be seen in it. More time and labor have been spent in describing it, and what it contains, than any other city of the earth. The whole now is of no great utility to the world, and her own native-born citizens cannot be classed among the great inventors, discoverers or benefactors, by having contributed anything useful to the general good. Franklin, Fulton, Whitney, Morse, and McCormick, have no equals among the Romans; and omitting Columbus, Galileo, and Faust, few among the thousands of other Europeans have enlightened and benefited the world and made their names immortal.

After spending seven days in viewing what remains in Rome of the collections of more than twenty-six centuries, we left for Naples on the new railroad through the plains of Capua. The land along this road is the best adapted to the growth of wheat of any we saw in Italy, and as we passed through it in the middle of its harvest we saw more of that grain in one day than we had ever before, and all harvested without machinery, by the slow process of the sickle. The ruins of ancient edifices, towers, walls, and fortifications, are scattered over the hills and strategic places along the whole line of the road, continually reminding the traveler of Hannibal and other destroyers.

Capua is on the line of this road, and still retains in great profusion the same allurements which drew the Carthagenian general from his victorious course, to waste his time and strength in her enervating embrace. It is situated about twenty miles north of Naples, in a broad fruitful valley, with a portion of the city overlooking the other, and giving it a most inviting appearance. Its delightful climate, fruitful soil, and its easy facilities for reaching other points, render it one of the most pleasant places for a family residence in all Italy, yet very few travelers of late have noticed its attractions on account of Rome and Naples having engaged their whole attention. These two cities, therefore, may be passed alike as familiar acquaintances, needing no description.

Naples, however, has latterly attracted much attention from its proximity to Mount Vesuvius, lately in such active eruption as greatly to endanger the safety and threaten to overwhelm it in the same manner it buried Herculaneum and Pompeii, one of which was more remote from Vesuvius than Naples by several miles.

I will here state that excavations, explorations, restorations, and works for preservation, are daily in active progress under proper government officers, and a vigilant police to develop and preserve all that is valuable and interesting in these two long buried and ancient cities.

With a passport and competent guide, we were at once recognized as American travelers and escorted by an officer through these once rich and populous but now tenantless and forsaken cities, and shown into the spacious temples, halls, tombs, baths, theatres, cellars, and mansions, which have been restored and now appear in almost as perfect a state as at the day of the great catastrophe in A. D. 79. The ashes, mud and cinders, with which the cities were overwhelmed, are all carefully examined where they have lain so long, and every curious or valuable article taken out, noted and preserved, and the remainder carted to a marshy piece of ground, preparatory to its being converted into a public garden. This marsh is just outside the old city walls, which are now as perfect as ever.

The Harpers have published descriptions of these places, and others about Vesuvius, which relieve me of the onerous task; and as I have seen the places and read *their* description, I know them to be very correct.

I have no doubt the eruptions of Vesuvius within the past few months will call forth a more perfect history of it, and of the cities about it that have been affected by its convulsive throes since the age of letters, than any now extant in the libraries of the world, as no more interesting subject seems to engage the attention of literary men at the present time.

The weather being oppressively warm at Naples, and the season so far advanced, we abandoned our contemplated tour to Egypt, and returned to Rome, where we spent several more days in viewing this celebrated city and its innumerable curiosities, which have been so often and fully described by others that nothing is left untold. But I should, perhaps, notice a custom in Rome which prevails in no other city I have visited. The venders of milk drive the animals that produce it to the doors of their customers and express it in their presence, as if to show them by actual demonstration its perfect purity. This practice might be adopted in America with great satisfaction to customers.

Our next visit was to Ancona on the Adriatic, by railroad, over the chain of the Appenine mountains, a trip of pleasing interest from its varied scenery, in which you may yet see traces of the labors of all the different possessors of that country from its first improvement to the present time. The route is first up the river Tiber to Terni; thence over the Appenine range eastwardly to the Adriatic, nine miles north of Ancona; thence southwardly to the city. This city was formerly a place of great strength, commerce, and importance; but gunpowder, steam and railroads have rendered it a place of no importance, except as a most healthful and pleasant seaside residence, in a picturesque country abounding in all the necessaries and luxuries of life. In the vicinity of this city we saw some of the most desirable country residences that we observed in Europe. The American consul, Carlo Rebighini, Esq., owns one, three miles from the city, where his family resides, that would satisfy the most fastidious. We were entertained here by him in the most agreeable manner.

The population of this part of Italy are mostly engaged in the cultivation and manufacture of silk, a most quiet, peaceful and pleasant occupation, and said to be very profitable to those engaged in it. There is a great sameness in the aspect of the country and the manners and customs of the inhabitants. There have been so many changes of rulers in the present century, that the people seem to view all political affairs with less interest than in any other part of Europe. They however possess everything that can make a country desirable except a stable and satisfactory government, which they appear to long for.

The railroad from Ancona to Venice passes inland through Bologna, one of the oldest and most renowned cities in the world as a seat of learning, and where a scholar will delight to spend a few hours in viewing a city that has borne a most conspicuous part in the field of arts and letters. The most ancient and celebrated university in the world was founded at Bologna in 1119, and in 1216 its pupils amounted to ten thousand. Some of its most famous doctors have been females; Madame Manzolina, Clotilda Tambroni (a Greek), Lauri Bassi, and Novella d'Andréa, were among the number. Joseph Galvani here first discovered galvanism in 1789. The library of the university contains two hundred thousand volumes. This city has been the theatre of many of the most remarkable transactions in Europe, and, like very many other cities, needs no particular description from a casual visitor to make its attractions known.

A campanile, or bell tower, of great altitude and most solid structure, situated near one of its large churches, leans three feet from the true perpendicular, like that of Pisa, but not so much by ten feet. The leaning tower of Pisa deviates from a plumb line fully thirteen feet. Knowing that the leaning of these two celebrated towers had given rise to much controversy as to their structure, whether erected perpendicularly or not, I spared no time or attention to satisfy my own judgment on this point. After viewing them and considering the object of their erection and magnitude, their surroundings and antiquity, I have no doubt whatever they were built perpendicularly. Two theories are advanced concerning the cause of their leaning, both of which have many advocates. The first, which seems very reasonable and natural, was that water reached the foundation from the leaning side, and, softening it, the tower commenced to lean gradually in that direction, but which was discovered in time for the builders to divert the water, when the tower had come to its present position, and by which its fall was prevented. The second, which seems possible but less probable, was that after the mortar and stone had become completely cemented, a mighty gust of wind had forced it so far, and, passing, had left each in its present condition. That no record was made of the occurrence seems to us somewhat strange, but it is likely that those then present had no apprehension the event would be forgotten, and each left it to his neighbor to write an account of it, and all neglected to do so. There were no printing presses in those days, and the theory that they were built in that leaning position no longer finds supporters except among those fond of the marvelous.

No country is better adapted to agricultural purposes than that in the vicinity of Bologna, and the people of every class seem to delight in beautifying their residences with all that nature, art or labor can effect. We saw fewer idle people in this part of Italy than we had been accustomed to meet, although wages were lower. It was the season of wheat harvest, and we saw a much larger number of females than males engaged in reaping it, the sickle being the only instrument used for that purpose. Stock of all kinds was abundant, and appeared to be carefully attended by those interested in their welfare.

On the route from Bologna to Venice, the lands are well improved, and every scene indicated the abode of plenty and pleasure, as much as I ever beheld.

On entering Venice we located ourselves at Hotel de la Ville, a very convenient place to obtain all that is generally desired by travelers in quest of knowledge. We found plenty here to amuse and instruct as well as to contemplate and investigate. This cluster of little islands—at first the abode of humble fishermen, then of unhappy fugitives, next of traders and merchants, rising to unmeasured opulence, and making this obscure place the centre of the commercial world, the city of palaces and princes, and the arbiter of nations by its maritime power, and enlightening the world with its knowledge, but now gradually sinking and apparently will-

ingly taking a low rank among the cities of Europe—afforded
ample range for the reflecting mind. This slow decay of a
great city brings with it a quietude and stillness ill-suited to
my mind and taste, after having spent the best years of my
life in the young and flourishing city of St. Louis, the heart
of North of America, and destined at no distant day to be
the standpoint from which to view and visit the world.

Having satisfied ourselves with viewing and contemplating
the wonderful collections of ages here, we took passage on a
steamship to Trieste, the great seaport of Austria. On entering the port of Trieste, a visible and agreeable change for the
better presented itself. A magnificent wharf and breakwater
were in an advanced state of construction. Neatness, well-
paved streets, buildings in good order, and well dressed
people, show that an industrious and enterprising population
inhabit this most rock-bound city of Europe. Sloth, idleness,
want and beggary find no advocates or practitioners here. It
was in this city Napoleon II, present emperor of France, was
born, as also Maximilian, late emperor of Mexico, and his
unhappy widow still occupies his former mansion, which
descended to him from his ancestors.

The vicinity of Trieste, on the route to Gratz, is rocky and
sterile, but well cultivated, and almost entirely by the Austrian women. They use cows for their teams, singly, one
leading the cow and the other holding the plough. This
custom of women cultivating the lands with cows does not
prevail in Austria alone; it is practised in several other European countries, and is said to succeed well, as the animals
generally meet with very kind treatment from them. The
profession of arms is more popular in Austria and most other
European countries than in the United States, although the
pay is much less, and this seduces the young men from
agricultural pursuits and imposes a greater burden on the
women, which they seem to bear with great fortitude and
patience in this empire.

From Gratz to Vienna, a distance of a hundred and forty
miles, the railroad runs through a most beautiful and interesting country, diversified with hills, valleys, rivers, bridges
and railroad tunnels, fixing the landscape of this route more
indelibly on the memory than any other in Europe. There are

twenty-eight tunnels on the route, and the little river Semmering is crossed thirteen times. The great battle-ground of Wagram and the immense Austrian ironworks are to be distinctly seen from the road at a short distance from the city of Vienna. The founding of this city, its history, and present condition, and what it contains, are so well known that it is unnecessary for me to remark further on them than to say we spent one week looking over as many of its objects of interest as we could. In doing so, however, my attention was drawn to a few things which I should mention. Vienna is not, like Venice, finished, but, like Paris, improving every day. The present emperor has abolished all his private parks and hunting grounds but one small one, and devoted them to public use, which has made him very popular with his people. The French and Prussians, separately, each defeated his armies and stripped him of part of his possessions, but his people pity rather than blame him for it. The Austrian military men do not strut about the streets as if to exhibit their military badges, but may be found in the cafés and saloons, where they often indulge in blaming their generals and leaders for want of vigilance, sobriety, capacity and courage, and thus bringing upon them the evils they still deplore, and which seem to sting them to the soul.

Cleanliness and good order everwhere prevail; and if want of the necessaries of life exist, they are concealed from public view. The system and accommodations for the permanent military establishments are very complete, and work with ease in that staid empire. But their financial affairs are in a worse condition than in our United States. Their paper currency is not as well executed as ours, and is at a greater discount, yet both are equally potent in forcing specie from circulation among the people.

In passing through an old well-cultivated country on a good railroad from Vienna to Munich, in Bavaria, a stranger will observe nothing to mark the dividing line between the empire and the kingdom; but when one enters a hotel, he will perceive that he has approached France, and its bland manners and people are appreciated here. The city is gradually improving, and there is less of a martial spirit apparent here than in the other European cities we have visited, although a

16

great military institute is in progress of construction on a prominent site overlooking the city proper, at the head of one of its broadest streets, and enclosed within a magnificent oval wall. The Bavarians are chiefly Roman Catholics, fond of pompous religious exhibitions in the streets, one of which we witnessed. It was conducted in the most solemn and orderly manner, by the highest dignitaries of the church, and in presence of the royal family and the great officers of state.

In no other city in Europe can a man of learning and kind feeling find more objects to instruct and amuse him, and meet with fewer to pain and disgust him, than in Munich. The people of this city seem to have for a long period selected and put forward their most able men to build up, fill, and adorn their city with all that is useful, pleasing and instructive, without leaving a blot or stain of inhumanity, avarice, or covetousness. Its libraries, monuments and museums have few equals in the world. The inhabitants of but few cities under a monarchy enjoy so many advantages as the people of Munich.

On quitting the Bavarian territory, we left all her military men at the Switzerland boundary, and traveled on, both by land and water, as in our own country, without let or hindrance by officious dignitaries. We saw no palaces, extravagant equipages, idlers or beggars about the stations and hotels, but a busy, tidy people, relying on their own industry for a subsistence among these mountains, lakes and rivers, and not on favor and charity. Situated in a temperate latitude, at the source of so many rivers, having no marshes or stagnant waters about them, but mountains and hills that give salubrity to the atmosphere, and the most beautiful landscapes on earth, they seem to have seized upon and improved all these advantages and reveled in their fruition, and to have opened wide their gates to all friends to come and enjoy with them; and no people in the world probably rejoice in so many and varied pleasures as the Swiss. So all strangers feel at home in Switzerland, and purchase their jewelry, gewgaws, and toys, with a liberality that would subject them to the charge of insanity if done in any other country ; but done in Switzerland, among the flower-baskets, it all appears perfectly sane and reasonable.

On our way back to Paris, we passed through Neufchatel, a city located on a lake surrounded by the most varied and beautiful landscapes in Europe. The railroad from this city to Dijon in France passes through a very uneven and picturesque country, with fourteen tunnels on the southern or ascending part of the route, and twelve on the northern or descending part, which afforded ample variety of scenery and amusement to the passengers. Dijon is now one of the most staid and quiet cities of France. It seems "finished and fenced in," and has few new edifices to attract attention; but it has the massive works of ages, which give it a most venerable and unchangeable aspect, well suited for people of advanced age and easy circumstances in life, with which the city is well filled.

When we arrived in Paris, we found the city less thronged with strangers than we anticipated, owing, as it was said, to the exorbitant prices fixed by the Parisians on all indispensable articles, by which they had hoped to enrich themselves by supplying their pleasure-loving neighbors, but which the telegraph prevented by turning the throng of visitors into the neighboring towns and cities, or keeping them aloof from the Exposition altogether. However, a vast multitude visited the Exposition daily, and the great fair was a success, but it did not fill the coffers of any one as had been contemplated. As an episode, I may state that just after the close of the exhibition a mighty tempest blew down the edifice erected for the occasion, and so effectually destroyed it that not a vestige of it remains to be seen.

The French Exposition benefited other nations in various ways as much as it did its own. It afforded the best opportunity that distant nations ever had enjoyed of becoming acquainted with each other, and of exhibiting their productions, and they nearly all embraced it, being generally well represented. The Sultan of Turkey came in person, and was entertained by the French Emperor, who, accompanied by him in an open barouche, made several excursions about Paris and its spacious parks, so that we all had a free view of the two sovereigns and their attendants, which seemed to be highly appreciated by the gathered thousands of many nationalities.

CHAPTER XXXII.

TRAVELS IN BELGIUM, GERMANY, PRUSSIA, AND RUSSIA.

Being wearied with sight-seeing, my family passed over to England to visit their relatives, while I lingered at the French capital to show that Missourians, as a State, had a lively interest in the Exposition. Being now alone among two millions of strangers, imagine my pleasure on meeting my old friend and neighbor, ex-mayor James G. Barry, also alone, and just arrived by way of the Mediterranean and Marseilles. With my thorough knowledge of all that was to be seen, and with his company, I spent a most pleasant and interesting day in again viewing the Exposition and pointing out the productions of our own Missouri. It must be seldom that two such neighbors meet alone so far from friends, home and country, and yet in the midst of overwhelming thousands. We could have found plenty to amuse us longer here, but other engagements separated us; he journeyed to Italy, while I departed for Belgium and the countries on the Baltic.

The nearest foreign city to Paris is Brussels, a city without fortifications, yet famous in martial history from its always being made to feel the evils of European wars without any adequate recompense, until after the great battle of Waterloo, since which it has been made the great INN for the inumerable visitors to that immortal field, and has reaped a silent and peaceful harvest, which has made its inhabitants the quietest and happiest people in the world since that event.

No person who attempts to make the tour of Europe should fail to take Brussels and the field of Waterloo in the route. In the former will be seen the inhabitants from almost every nation under heaven, clad in the costume of their country, pursuing their occupations as at home, without attracting attention, so universal is the education of the people of Brussels. Nearly everything that can be found in any country may be seen here, whether divine, sage, novel, ludicrous, or instructive. In the latter class may be seen the buildings, fields, walls, and gardens, nearly in the same condition they were on the 15th of June, 1815, three days before the great battle, except the marks and disfigurements made on the walls and buildings by balls, shot, or shells, during the conflict between the two greatest captains of the age; also a most stupendous monument two hundred feet high, surmounted with a bronze 'figure of the Belgic lion, commemorating the events of that bloody and decisive day. All of these are now, as much as possible, preserved intact by their owners for the gratification of visitors, who flock there daily in pleasant weather from all countries to view this death-place of thousands, and who quietly enrich the vicinity by their expenditures and gifts.

This is by no means the only place in Belgium celebrated by martial feats. This country has been styled " the cockpit of Europe," and often made to bear a very unprofitable part in its neighbors' quarrels, and also suffer great changes in its rulers and government. It was Burgundian under the Dukes of Burgundy, German under Maximilian, Spanish under Charles V, Revolutionist during the troubles of the Netherlands, Austrian under Maria Theresa, Republican in 1794, French under Napoleon I, Semi-Dutch under William, and Belgian now under a king.

Interpreters are numerous and intelligent at Brussels, and very reasonable in their charges—five francs per diem. Hotel and other bills are also quite moderate. Fine promenades, parks, museums, libraries, public edifices, factories, and fountains, are numerous, some of which are unique, far-famed and ludicrous, so that no one need fear *ennui* in Brussels.

It is quite out of my power to make lengthy notes of all the places or things that I saw and which I deemed useful, novel, or entertaining; I shall therefore be a little more concise in my remarks in the following pages, but shall notice those that seemed most interesting.

Antiquarians may find in the city of Cologne more objects of wonder and amazement than its external appearance and present importance indicate. It has been a great city for more than a thousand years, and was the birth-place of Agrippina, daughter of the Roman Emperor Germanicus, and had a colony placed in it by her, whence its name. It contains a most magnificent cathedral, that has been more than six hundred years in building, and will require five millions of dollars to complete it, which is being rapidly done at present. In it are many churches of great magnificence and antiquity, containing the most rare, valuable and unique collections on earth.

The church of St. Ursula contains the most remarkable sights. 1. St. Ursula herself is exhibited in a coffin, surrounded by the skulls of a few of her favorite attendants. 2. The fetters of St. Peter, and a vessel used by the Saviour. 3. What Hood says is the most chaste kind of architecture. 4. On every side marble shelves are built in the walls, and on them are piled in the most ingenious and regular manner the bones of eleven thousand virgins who attended St. Ursula from the city of Basle on a pilgrimage to Rome, and were all met and murdered on their return by the Huns because they refused to break their vows of chastity, and prepared to defend their persons to the last extremity with their table knives and forks. Thus says tradition. Whether it be true or false, the sad spectacle is there; and that the bones are those of females from the age of twelve years to thirty, there can be no doubt whatever. The gloom in this receptacle of the remains of the ancient dead affords a more suitable theme for the imagination than the pen. The city is full of antiquities and objects of great interest to those traveling in quest of knowledge, and the vicinity is rich in everything that mortals covet. Poetry and prose have been exhausted in describing the beauties and enchantments on the banks of the Rhine. It is finished and requires no improvement.

There is great sameness in the aspect of everything seen by travelers passing through Holland, but on entering the Prussian territory a change is at once visible. Strong fortifications cover the approach to all the great cities, and a most tidy soldiery everywhere shows itself and seems to be interested in everything. If a child is tardy in reaching school, a soldier is seen kindly urging it forward; if astray, putting it in place; or an animal or team loose, it is secured. No disorder or waste is allowed, yet all is done quietly. The soldier seems to consider himself a gentleman, and responsible for the good conduct of all about him, and is therefore circumspect in all his actions. He is regarded with greater consideration by the ladies of his country than the soldier of any other nation appears to be by his countrywomen. He is always accepted as an escort by ladies without the least regard to his rank in the army. It is however very observable that they view with pleasure a profusion of badges on an escort, these alone being the reward of meritorious conduct.

The system of education is more perfect in Prussia than in any other part of Europe. Religious toleration is everywhere recognized by law, and the morals of the people good. The marriage of men is prohibited by law until they have served three years in the army and are discharged, or exempted by disability, from military service. It is considered unwise by ladies to listen to propositions of marriage from soldiers in service; consequently there are fewer disappointed lovers to be met with in Prussia than in any other country.

The women of Prussia perform more agricultural labor than any other women in Europe, and appear to do it with greater willingness and zest; but they are seldom seen in quarries, mines, or attending horses. The Prussians are fond of frequenting places of amusement, and, if possible, always take their families with them, and appear as proud of showing them as other nations do fine equipages. We never heard of a real Prussian forsaking his wife or denying he had one if she was living. In short, she constitutes his wealth and happiness, at home or abroad. Nor is it to be wondered at, when one reflects that it is no uncommon spectacle to see a mother quit the plow-handles, feed her weary cow, and on entering her house to engage at once in instructing her children, even in solving the abstruse problems of Euclid. So universally are the Prussian ladies well educated, that they are regarded as the most enlightened in Europe. Their studies are the same as those of the men, except in the military schools. At no distant day the Prussian system of education must prevail wherever public instruction is universal.

It may be asked: How has Prussia attained to such eminence in so short a period? for Prussia was a power of the fifth rank in Europe at the commencement of this century—its first king was crowned and its first Academy of Sciences founded in the last century. We answer: This school for kings and nursery for statesmen has filled Prussia with efficient counselors, philosophers, and scholars, who have kept the whole nation united in endeavoring to reach the acme of national greatness, and has at length quite formed the characteristic of the people to suit such a condition.

The Russians have observed their progress and are making rapid strides in the same direction, but as their devotions have hitherto been paid more to Mars than to Apollo, it will be a persistent task of long duration that can make them equally successful. However, no people are more devoted to their country than the Russians, or more willing to pay for knowledge. Therefore the most liberal salaries are paid to professors from foreign countries, as no prejudices exist against them, and every facility and encouragement afforded them.

Serfdom having been but recently abolished, a greater disparity in the condition of the people appears in Russia than in any other part of Europe. In this the people appear to acquiesce with great patience, and as there never was any difference in their language or color to mark their former condition, a few years will obliterate all remembrance of it. The title of prince or princess is of less consequence in Russia than any other country, for all the children of a prince or princess are allowed the title, although it is often all the patrimony they inherit. In like manner their children take the title and strive to maintain its dignity in all places.

Their public edifices are all erected with a view to their future greatness and the heterogeneous character and taste of coming generations. All styles of architecture may be seen in the same building, as if the different parts had been assigned to architects from different countries and each had followed his own taste. There will be seen gilded domes and cupolas; towers of every form, round, square, septagon and octagon; pointed roofs and steeples of every hight, style and color, ornamented with the most whimsical devices and incomprehensible inventions—the whole forming a laughable yet agreeable picture when viewed at a proper distance. Their costumes are as varied as any of their possessions, and are no index of their wealth, as their country is cold and moist, which causes them generally to wear an over-garment which is common to the prince and the beggar.

This sketch of my observations will be incomplete unless mention is made of a universal sentiment that prevails in

Russia, and is always observable by their friends when they are speaking of the policy of their government. They think that Turkey in Europe justly belongs to the Emperor of Russia, and that he is kept out of it by usurpation. The Russian claim is thus founded:—Ivan III espoused Princess Sophia, niece of Constantine Palæologus, who was conducted to him in Russia by ambassadors sent from Rome. After this mariage, Ivan assumed the title of Czar or Cæsar of Russia, and all nations acquiesced in this as legitimate; and when he saw Constantine and his family dispossessed as well as totally destroyed by the Turks in 1453, as neither himself nor any of his household could ever be found after the battle, he claimed the title to the European section of the empire, and his successors will probably at no distant day obtain it as a legitimate right.

The Russians always consider the Americans as recognizing that right and desirous of their obtaining it; hence that friendship for Americans amounting almost to a passion, which they do not attempt to conceal. At a banquet given to an American citizen at Moscow, a major-general of the Russian army stated in a speech that Russia had sold Alaska to the United States to make them strong and not for the price paid, for it was but nominal when nationally viewed, and would have been donated but for the fear of exciting the jealousy of neighboring nations against both.

Having digressed a little from my original purpose to remark on what struck my mind as important subjects, I must return to what more immediately concerned myself while in Russia. On my arrival at St. Petersburg, I repaired to the residence of our minister, Mr. Clay, but found him gone into the country. It did not, however, derange my purpose of seeing or retard my progress. I was at once treated with all the attention I desired, and was introduced to several officers of distinction, all of whom spoke English and offered their services to me. This was of great advantage to me afterwards in visiting Cronstadt, Peterhoff, and Moscow, as I was on all occasions escorted by an officer, who introduced me to all distinguished personages he met, informing them of the extent of my recent travels and future designs, and pointing out the objects most worthy of my attention.

When I had spent more than one week in viewing the wonders collected in and about this interesting vicinity, I left for Moscow in company with three Russian officers, who were returning to the camp of instruction, six miles from the walls of Moscow. These gentlemen gave me the most pressing invitation to visit their camp, saying no American traveler of any distinction had ever visited it, and it would afford their superior officers great pleasure to have me do so, which I promised to do. Accordingly, after spending several days in viewing this ancient and half Asiatic city and the Empress's villa at Sparrow Hill, and had stood on the same spot in the porch where the First Napoleon stood in 1812—where he saw with astonishment and horror every house and store on fire which contained anything that could comfort a famishing soldier in Moscow—and had viewed all the cannon taken in that campaign, and which are now arranged and displayed as a monument in the Kremlin, I prepared to visit the Russian camp of instruction. Taking a competent interpreter, I presented my card at the entrance of the camp and asked for the officer of the day, who immediately appeared and introduced himself as a colonel of artillery, and, entering my barouche, pointed out the way to the general's headquarters, accompanied me there, and introduced me to all the officers he met, expressing a regret that most of them were absent twelve miles at a race course, at the same time assuring me they were glad to see me and would entertain me as well as possible by showing me through all the workshops, storehouses, arsenals, hospitals, and quarters, when in full operation. This pleased me, and I spent one of the most interesting days of my life viewing what was shown me and hearing their explanations. They further manifested their kindness and attention by furnishing me with perfect drawings of every article I had seen in process of construction, which I brought home and donated to the Missouri Historical Society of St. Louis. After visiting the factories, and dining with them at the officers' mess-house, they took me through the summer and winter quarters, showed me the rations of Russian soldiers in process of cooking, their bakeries and bread, and had me taste of the victuals from many of their cooking vessels and mess trays, and lastly walked with me among the camp tables to see the soldiers eating, and escorted me to my barouche, assuring me I would hear from their superior officers on their return.

On the following day I received a very complimentary invitation to be present at a review of the armed corps under instruction at the Emperor's camp near Moscow, signed by the lieutenant-general in command, and delivered by an aid-de-camp in full dress at Hotel Dusoux. I acknowledged the receipt of the invitation, and promised attendance. Accordingly, on the day appointed, I took with me in a barouche, my interpreter, Frederick Schranz, and Colonel James V. Swan, secretary of the Gas Company of the city of Moscow, an Englishman, who spoke the Russian language fluently, and proceeded to the camp, where we were met by an officer who escorted us to the general's headquarters. Here we were met by several prominent officers, introduced to them, and furnished with refreshments, after which fine caparisoned horses were provided for each of us, and mounted grooms to attend them. The troops by this time were getting in position on all parts of the field, and soon after the signal was given that all was ready. A colonel who spoke English then informed me he had been directed to attend and assist me during the day. I informed him I considered it as a high compliment and a great kindness bestowed on me and my country, and begged him to take the entire direction of my movements during the time I should be with him, which he promised to do. We then all mounted our horses and rode to the point where the review commenced.

There were eighteen thousand men in camp, and it was estimated seventeen thousand men of all arms were on duty under arms and in sight at the same time. I had never seen above half that number of men in motion at one time before, and it is not probable I will ever see so many again. The sight was therefore one of great interest to me, and I had all the advantages I could desire of enjoying it. We were led to near the middle of the camp or ground, which is more than twenty miles in circumference, and was formerly the park or hunting grounds of the imperial family, whose residence, a magnificent palace, stands a little east of the camp and overlooks every part of it. Here we had a fair view of every individual of that vast multitude, with their arms and machines of war, as they passed in review, without being able to detect the least mistake or omission in performing the salutes with so many different kinds of arms, and operating with so many different animals. By the time the last regiment had passed us, the whole were in position for manœuvering in a sham-fight, which commenced by degrees and became more and more animated until all appeared to be engaged, when the line most remote began to be broken and marched off; and the smoke ascending, we soon saw all the regiments removed from the field except the artillerymen, who were distributed into the several fortifications in order to exhibit their skill in gunnery. These [fortifications are said to have been built for the defence of the imperial palace and Moscow while the state departments remained there, and were altered to accommodate the military school after the seat of government was removed to St. Petersburg. In these fortifications are all the different kinds of cannon used in the Russian service, and gunners trained expressly to use them, with all necessary accompaniments convenient for use. The signal being given, we dismounted and took positions for observing the exhibition of their artillery practice, which soon commenced with great celerity and creditable effect, but not with that accuracy I thought they might attain by more deliberate sighting, which they will probably adopt hereafter as an improvement. After the exhibition of the gunnery and their system of telegraphing to the gunner the result of his shots, until all kinds of pieces from three hundred pounds to one had been discharged, the signal was given for dinner, which was obeyed with the same alacrity that had characterized all their movements.

The dinner, or more properly banquet, was served in a large wooden edifice adjoining an uncovered theatre, which has an artificial swimming pond on the other side, all constructed for educating and practicing cadets. The area of the building being of sufficient size for manœuvering a regiment in inclement weather, gave latitude for the display of the most sumptuous repast I had ever seen spread. The tables, thirteen in number, were ingeniously arranged, with a long one in the centre and six on either side placed obliquely, so that all seated at them could by a slight deflection view the person presiding at the head of the center table. Four hundred officers being seated at the tables, a chaplain said grace devoutly—for the Russians are a very pious people—and soon the hungry officers began to lessen the huge pile of rich dainties from every land with which the tables were loaded, until all seemed willing to advance in the programme.

The cloth being removed, beverages and their concomitants followed the viands in quick succession, and hilarity lagged but little behind. Toasts were next in order, in the fashion of our own country. They first toasted their Emperor, who, as they said, presided over a hundred nations united in one, a beloved and popular ruler of all; next, the Empress of all the Russias, a shining example to her sex; lastly, the United States of America, the real friends of the Russians, represented here by the presence of one of its venerable citizens. I thought it incumbent on me to respond to this compliment to my country, humble and unqualified as I felt myself. I therefore arose, and said, "I thank you, Mr. President, for this compliment to my country and myself, and I think I express the sentiments of my countrymen in saying, may the Turks, who are but Arabs and robbers, be driven out of Europe, and the Emperor Alexander of Russia be put in possession of Constantinople, that all the ladies of Russia may bathe their feet in the Bosphorus." The applause that followed this sentiment is quite indescribable. At this point a major-general arose, and advancing towards me, stretched forth his hand and said, "Those are the sentiments of friends; the Americans are *our* friends; we will make campaigns together." The applause was then redoubled, and, to add intensity to their demonstrations, two tall Cossacks from the Don, who sat over against me at table, sprang from their seats and running round the end of the table to me, one seized me and placing me on the shoulder of the other, they each threw an arm around the other's waist, and each holding one of my hands in theirs, galloped round the table, crying out, "We have an American citizen! we have an American citizen!" amid the most vociferous applause and shoutings. The doors leading to the theater were then thrown open and my Cossack friends conducted me to the seats set apart for distinguished visitors.

On the rising of the curtain the plays began with the celebrated scene of *"Orpheus playing to the Nymphs on the lyre
he had received from Apollo,"* the Nymphs being young
soldiers dressed in nymphian costume, for no women are
allowed to enter a Russian camp. Then his conquest over
Eurydice; their nuptials and short happiness; her death and
entry into the infernal regions. Then Orpheus' entry there
with his lyre in pursuit of her; his wonderful performance
before Pluto, by which he gained admittance; the stoppage of
the wheel of Oxion and rolling of the stone of Sisiphus.
Then Orpheus' sight of Eurydice and her sudden vanishment
by his looking back in his eagerness of seeing her. Then his
interview with the Thracian women; his coldness to them, for
which they tore him to pieces while he was still crying "Eurydice! Eurydice!" in his last paroxysm of death and destruction.

The second piece was " *The Russian Lady's Excuse to her
Husband on his return after an absence of twenty years,"* the
term of service in the Russian army. The parties had been
engaged to be married on a certain day. On the day preceding he was conscripted and notified to appear instanter.
Instead of obeying, he went directly to his affianced and was
married at sunrise the next morning, and as he emerged from
the church with his bride he was seized by a file of soldiers
as a deserter and kept twenty years in service without a
furlough, that being the penalty for first fault, but in the
meantime had covered his bosom with badges of distinction
and honor by his services. His wife had by the Russian law
taken possession of his large estate and kept a gentleman
about the house as near his age as she could procure, as she
said, to keep her in memory of how he probably looked, and
to assist in escorting her in her excursions and visits abroad.
The soldier inquired why the gentleman he saw sitting near
her when he entered, had left so suddenly and unceremoni-
ously. She replied she employed no persons in his place but
those who knew better than to be present in such a crisis;
that she kept nothing about her that was superfluous. This
answer appeared to satisfy him, and, embracing her, said she
had done well; to now make ready to entertain their friends
and have them present. Thus ended the first act. On the

rising of the curtain, she brought forth an antiquated dried cake. and informed him she had never despaired of his returning, and was yet enjoying this cake, which she made with her own hands and drinking with him from this flagon which she had found in his cellar. The old friends, male and female, soon assembled, and, after enjoying the viands and libations, are called to order by one representing Terpsichore, who with harp in hand entertained them a moment, then changed the feasting into dancing, which I never saw excelled. Suddenly the music ceased and the curtain fell.

The last piece was "*The Russian Ladies Bathing.*" Female voices in shouts and laughter were heard in the distance, when the audience unconsciously stood erect: the curtain in front disappeared as if by magic, exposing to view the artificial lake before mentioned, surrounded with lights, the water swarming with ladies' forms in bathing habits, performing the most extraordinary feats in swimming, diving, leaping, rolling, dodging, hiding, ducking, mounting and sinking each other, that is possible to describe, yet without the least ill-temper, fear or apparent inconvenience to the actors.

This closed the entertainments of the day and was the signal for a parting adieu, which was given in the usual Russian manner, and is very ceremonious and affectionate, thus: each gentleman takes off his hat with his left hand and throws the arm around the neck of the other person, both at the same time seizing each other by the right hand and reciprocally kissing each other on the cheek. This is the parting ceremony with ladies also. It is improper to uncover the head in the presence of ladies: this is only done in church, or passing a church, or in parting with a lady. There is no other exception.

As it was now late at night, an escort of cavalry was ordered to conduct us within the walls of Moscow, to insure our safety home.

On the following morning, I made a suitable acknowledgment of the honors and kindness which had been shown me at the camp, and spent the remainder of the day in viewing the different parts of the city, and observing the great changes which the grand conflagration of 1812 had made in the streets and style of buildings. The new streets are much broader than the old, nearly all the buildings on them being much larger, and built in modern style. Not one-fourth of Moscow was consumed in 1812. The French fired none of the buildings, and the Russians burned only those containing provisions and clothing.

It had been my intention to visit Nijni Novogrod on the river Volga, and thence, partly by that river and the Don, to visit Sebastopol and Constantinople; but while I waited one week in Moscow, six gentlemen who came in company with me from St. Petersburg went to Nijni to attend a great fair then in progress there, and during their stay lost half their number with cholera in four days, and had returned quite dejected. Their sad account of the prevalence of that disease in all that district of country deterred me from proceeding further in that direction; I therefore returned to St. Petersburg by the same road I came (four hundred and six miles), and leaving Moscow at the same hour of the day I did in coming from St. Petersburg, I saw by daylight the whole country within the range of vision, for that is a very level country, and has the best railroad through it in the world.

This part of Russia is fruitful and easily cultivated. More potatoes, turnips, carrots, beets, oats and grass are grown on the route than I have seen on a like distance in any other country. The soil is well adapted to their growth, and the climate to their preservation. The inhabitants, animals and vegetable productions seemed to compare favorably with those of any other region I have visited; they respectively appeared fully developed, well treated, and generous. In Prussia and Russia, rye flour is used more extensively than any other, both in the armies and families, and the same custom prevails among all the nations dwelling on the waters falling into the Baltic. Indian corn or maize is not cultivated there. Peas are raised in vast quantities in all those countries, and used in fattening stock very extensively. Ireland has become celebrated for its extensive cultivation of potatoes, yet they are even more generally cultivated and used in all northern Europe than in Ireland itself, as wheat does not form one of the certain or profitable crops of those countries as in Ireland and England. Oats and barley are as extensively cultivated there as Indian corn is in the United States, and used for the same purposes in feeding all kinds of stock. The droves of swine from which our bristles used in the manufacture of brushes are obtained, have all been fed on these productions, without seeing corn.

--- --- ------

CHAPTER XXXIII.

INCIDENTS AND OBSERVATIONS ON A SECOND VISIT TO ST. PETERSBURG, AND TRAVELS TO FINLAND, SWEDEN, DENMARK, NORWAY, AND HAMBURG.

On my second visit to this newly built city, I found the object that most engaged the attention of both citizens and strangers was the American squadron lately arrived inside the fortifications of Cronstadt, the officers of which were then visiting and viewing the city. Seeing large numbers going to view the fleet as it lay at anchor, I joined in a trip for that purpose, which proved to be one of as much pleasure and instruction as any I had made in the same length of time about this great city. On this trip down and up the river Neva, we not only saw some of the best American ships of war afloat, but also eleven of the most powerful Russian ships and monitors, all lying spread out and arranged in the most tasteful and friendly manner over the grand naval anchorage between Cronstadt and St. Petersburg, which every vessel passes through in entering or departing from the city. Eight monitors and three other steamships had been out and escorted the American fleet to this anchorage, which none but Russia's best friends are allowed to use. Our naval officers were then being entertained by them with feasts and balls, and all that was novel or wonderful among this enterprising and ambitious people.

Having previously viewed the city and its environs, I took passage on the steamship Somes for Helsingfors in Finland, as it was the first English ship to leave port, and was about half laden with oats and flaxseed, two very important articles of export to England, and would probably make a quick passage home to Hull. In this I was mistaken, but suffered

17

no loss. The captain was on a trip for information as well as business for his new ship, and made a most strenuous effort to obtain it, which afforded me excellent opportunities of visiting several cities, with very little inconvenience, where he sought further business and customers in his line.

On leaving St. Petersburg, we passed within a few yards of the fleet, when all the crews appeared busily engaged at drill, which gave them the appearance of a very busy lot of men and boys. This, however, had few attractions for our captain; for while we were passing, he called the attention of his passengers to the order in which the ships had anchored, and said that this visit was but a manœuvering of the combined fleets to show other nations their friendship and their willingness to unite against any other people.

Continuing our course out of the mouth of the Neva, we passed near the impregnable fortifications of Cronstadt, and observed the ceremonies and signals exchanged by the officers and pilots at every passage of ships by this remarkable natural and artificial stronghold and naval gate to the Russian capital. The morning being very clear and fine, and vision unobstructed except by the innumerable vessels passing in and out of port, we had a most satisfactory view of all the fascinating objects that in a state of nature struck the philosophic mind of Peter the Great, and caused him to change this far-spread waste and rude fishing-ground into beautiful pleasure-grounds and sites for cities and palaces that rival those of the most favored climes and locations. The whole of this scenery appears new. There are no old dilapidated edifices, fences or trees to mar the beauties of the landscape or cast a gloom over the buoyant mind. All appears active, vigorous, and progressive. There being no tides in the Baltic, or room for the gulf of Finland to raise high waves about the mouth of the Neva, the works of art are less liable to change and destruction by water than those of almost any other country, as the Lake Ladoga keeps the waters of the Neva always at about the same elevation. Therefore all improvements are made with a view to permanence and utility, and all in modern style.

Our first landing was made at Helsingfors in Finland, and as we were to spend the day here I lost no time in visiting its splendid park, donated long since by one of its former wealthy citizens, whose name is inscribed on a large rude stone with a statement that he has given this tract of land to the inhabitants of Helsingfors for a place of recreation and pleasure, and to be used for no other purpose; and from the number of persons I saw walking and riding in its beautiful groves, I have no doubt the Finlanders are carrying out in full the wishes of the donor. I was forcibly reminded by what I saw here of my long tried and worthy friend and fellow-townsman, Henry Shaw, who has done a similar act for the people of St. Louis, which will embalm him in the memory of the living, and call forth expressions of gratitude from generations far in the future, and render his name as lasting as the name of the city itself.

At this city I saw miniken steamboats used about the harbor in conveying passengers to and from the ships in and about the harbor and river, and on short trips of pleasure, which I think might be used with good success about many of our own cities, where it has probably never been attempted.

The Finlanders are the most peaceful and handsomest people in Europe, if not in the world. When under the king of Sweden, they were his most loyal subjects; and now, under the emperor of Russia, they sustain the same character. They appear to have no aspirations for office or military fame, but are very fond of literary, domestic and peaceful pursuits, and in all conditions of life are remarkably cleanly in their appearance. Therefore, a stranger will not readily discover such distinctions among them as are at once perceived among the people of some other countries when in company with each other.

From Helsingfors we passed between innumerable small islands and the main land to Abo, the capital of Finland. This was the slowest and most difficult trip I have ever seen a steamship make, and yet there was so much to attract and engage the attention that I spent most of the time on deck looking at the different and varied objects which were constantly presenting themselves on the islets and vessels we successively passed.

On our arrival at Abo, and landing on *terra firma*, we were informed a free concert was to be given in a grove near the city, and many persons were on their way thither. We joined the throng, and as the afternoon was pleasant we enjoyed an excellent opportunity of viewing the Finlanders as they appear in their churches, for they are emphatically a religious and moral people, which accounts for their beauty and happy contentment. Their officers and policemen all wear the same kind of badges as the Russians, and fine dress swords instead of blugdeons as in some other countries. The concourse of auditors was immense, being composed of people of all ages, infants in the arms of fathers as well as mothers, for there are no Africans to be met with in Finland or any of the inland towns north of the Baltic; and the number of males and females seems to be more equal there than in most other countries, and their occupations more equally shared. It is a very common practice in this vicinity for women to bring boat-loads of vegetables to market without the assistance of men, and the quantities brought here for sale are quite astonishing, when the climate of this high latitude is considered; and their quality still more so, as potatoes, turnips, carrots, beets and cabbages are raised here in as great perfection as in Holland, England or Ireland, and in as great abundance. The Finlan ders appear to be as industrious and economical as they are moral and tidy; consequently, strangers are not disgusted and annoyed by beggars and thieves, the greatest nuisance that travelers encounter in Europe.

Leaving Abo at sunset, with fair weather and the moon nearful full, we had good views of the islands scattered along the coast of Finland, and as the sun rose the next morning we found ourselves in sight of several islands off the coast of Sweden, and a great number of vessels of various sizes about us, among them four pilot-boats apparently at nearly the same distance and all striving to board the steamship. The engine was stopped and most of the people on board stood silent and amused to witness the strife. But one could win, and the victor was soon on board. The other boats at once changed their course to find other customers, while the successful pilot took the ship into port.

Stockholm is quite a city, with over a hundred thousand inhabitants. It is built, partly on islands and partly on the main land, at the entrance of Measter Lake, and is one of the most grand and imposing cities to view on approaching it from the east—as we did on a clear morning, with the sun shining on all the windows, towers, roofs and steeples—that I have ever visited. I am not minutely describing cities, or what I saw in them; but I venture the assertion, that this city contains more pleasing and praiseworthy objects, and fewer revolting ones, that any city in Europe. Some writers have said the ladies of Sweden are the handsomest in the world; but this must have been while Finland belonged to Sweden, for that is the real land of beauties. Here Jenny Lind established her musical fame and immortalized her name by founding a school of music for the poor, which no Missourian can visit without calling to mind the names of Mrs. Ann Biddle and Mrs. Anne L. Hunt for their munificence to the poor of St. Louis, which will make their names equally lasting and blessed.

From Stockholm to Malmo, a city in Sweden, three hours' ride from Copenhagen, we traveled on a new railroad through a remarkably broken and diversified section of country, abounding in small lakes or ponds, small streams, and heavy forests, yet made cheerful and attractive by the tidy and tasteful aspect of every habitation along the route. No dilapidated towers, walls or dwellings marred the landscape, although Sweden has a history as ancient as any of her neighbors. The character of the Swedes has never been changed by their wars or intercourse with other nations. No one acquainted with them and their country would hazard a contest with the one for the possession of the other. I should mention a custom among Swedish gentlemen which is the reverse of the Russian custom. A Swede always takes off his hat in company with ladies, and a Russian always wears his until parting, when he takes it off, and, taking her hand, bids a most affectionate adieu.

The distance from Malmo to Copenhagen is sixty miles. On this trip we saw more ships and vessels of different forms and sizes, and more different flags, than we had seen in any part of our journey by sea. We were on a Danish steamship, and being recognized as an American was treated with great respect, although the Danes make sad complaint against the Americans, who, they say, were the first people who refused to pay what is called *Sound dues*—that is, a certain toll for the privilege of passing into the Baltic Sea without being molested by them. They say every other nation had paid without a murmur from time immemorial until the Americans refused to pay, and, entertaining kind feelings towards them, they released them from the payment, and now no one will pay because they are in adversity and unable, as formerly, to compel other nations to fulfil their obligations. They charge the English with taking their armed navy from them under a promise of soon returning it; but more than half a century has elapsed since it was made without being fulfilled—and never will be. Moreover, they say the Prussians have robbed them of two of their finest provinces in the presence of all Europe, and no one dared to attempt to protect them or say a word in their behalf, and so, on account of their misfortunes, they have come to be disregarded among the nations, and are nearly blotted from the map of Europe.

Copenhagen, the capital of Denmark, is a city of great antiquity, and was formerly of great importance in the commercial world, made so by her position on the east side of the island of Zeland, and the policy of its government; for it never contained over one hundred and forty thousand inhabitants. It was bombarded by the British in 1807, and much injured; but its industrious and tidy inhabitants have repaired the damage and filled the city with an immense collection of the most interesting and instructive objects, which will enable people of refined taste to spend time here as profitably and pleasantly as at any other in Europe. I remained here several days, and wrote to several friends, one of whom, the venerable General Nathan E. Ranney, did me the honor to publish my letter, showing thereby the kind feeling he has so long manifested toward me.

On my arrival, I visited our minister plenipotentiary, Mr. Yeoman, as I always do in foreign countries, and advise all travelers to follow the example when abroad, as some useful information is sure to be communicated to some party present and the interest of our country advanced. Should there be no resident minister in Copenhagen, be careful to call on our consul there; he is always more than happy to meet his countrymen and enlighten and aid them. Time is very well spent with any of our foreign consuls, as they are sure to be well educated gentlemen, in possession of the latest news, and gladly impart a knowledge of all the local objects of interest in their immediate vicinity.

The Danes are an ingenious, well informed, industrious and enterprising people, who, from their favored location, have participated and profited in maritime and commercial enterprises for many centuries, but now frankly acknowledge that from circumstances entirely beyond their control it is with difficulty they can keep pace in these with their neighbors. Denmark and the State of Vermont are situated most unlike each other of any two States I have ever visited, yet the inhabitants resemble each other in appearance, morals, taste, ingenuity, industry, and economy, more than any others with which I have become acquainted in my travels.

Copenhagen is the cheapest market for every commodity to be found in Europe, as it is a place of the greatest commercial accessibility, when not obstructed by ice, of any off the coast of the Atlanitc. I feel disposed to sympathize with people who are in distress, but I saw nothing calling for sympathy in Denmark, although she is claiming it from all the world because she can collect no more *Sound dues.*

We sailed for Christiana in Norway early in the morning, and stopping at Elsinore, the *old toll-house* of the Baltic, we viewed this *broken bar* of commerce, and felt proud that our country had done it. It is a remarkable fortress at the south end of the Cattegat, and is fully described in the "Life of Lord Nelson." From thence to Gottenburg our ship's crew were constantly on a sharp look-out to avoid colliding with the numberless sailing vessels which float here and appear to disregard steamers in their course. We reached the ancient city of Christiana, the capital of Norway, at mid-day, and immediately taking a guide commenced a hasty examination of the city, which contains nearly forty thousand inhabitants. They have been a commercial people, as well as renowned in arts and arms, for the last thousand years, being remarkable also for morality, integrity, and sameness of character and appearance.

The ship having landed all her passengers but one, and effecting no new engagements for freight or passage here, left with a fair wind for Hamburg, with no person but the captain and myself in the cabin, and we therefore soon became well acquainted.

The ship entered the Elbe at evening, and we saw but little during the night except the busy seamen and tugs working the shipping up and down the river. At daylight the engine stopped, and we hastened on deck. The scene was changed. The greatest activity was now everywhere visible. Ships from all the maritime nations of Europe were crowded promiscuously together, and their people, as if all of one nation, were urging business forward like well constructed machinery driven by some unseen power, in perfect unison with everything about them. The people on shore, as far as the eye could reach, seemed engaged with like activity and regularity in their several occupations.

After viewing and admiring the operations of this busy crowd until business hours arrived, we took a guide and began to perambulate the city. It was very soon apparent that this was more a city of commerce and less of leisure than any I had yet visited. On arriving at the Exchange, a beautiful building, we took a position where we could view the merchants, who appeared to be from all the mercantile nations of the world, and quite astonished me by their number, being estimated at over four thousand present at one time—all intent on business, as it is not a garden of pleasure, but a field of traffic, which has few equals. The morals of these two cities last visited seemed to be in wonderful contrast with each other, and their covetousness even more so. The gates of vice stand open here night and day, to which the most casual observer will have have his attention called if he is a stranger, although there is a splendid Jewish Temple here and several synagogues, besides a St. Peter's and St. Michael's, and other churches, with towers over four hundred feet high, and a library of more than two hundred thousand volumes to enlighten the people and improve their minds and morals.

Leaving Hamburg on a clear pleasant morning, we had a good opportunity for viewing the shores of the Elbe, every acre of which seemed to be in the highest state of cultivation, the women appearing as numerous in the fields and gardens as the men. Here I must remark that ten times as many women are seen laboring in the fields in Europe as in the

United States, and not half as many boys. The shores of the Elbe appear like crowded villages of old-fashioned houses, nearly alike on both sides, and the river between swarming with every sized vessel, all apparently in a hurry.

From Cuxhaven, we had a gentle north wind across the North Sea to the mouth of the Humber, and saw innumerable vessels traversing in all directions, flying flags of almost every description, the "stars and stripes" among the rest. On this short voyage I saw more persons engaged in fishing than I had before observed in my whole tour. The steamship stopped several times as we came near the mouth of the Humber to avoid doing damage to the fishing apparatus which extended out several miles from the shore, their location being designated by buoys, which were carefully attended by the fishermen.

CHAPTER XXXIV.

INCIDENTS AND OBSERVATIONS ON THE VISIT TO ENGLAND, SCOTLAND AND IRELAND.

On entering the Humber, I contrasted it with the Thames, and considered what a mighty change had been made on the banks of the latter since the Normans first landed on this river and made a settlement here in the year 851. Hull was then the great port of the Britons; now it is of very little notoriety except for its antiquity. But as it was the first place at which I landed, it is reasonable to expect me to state what my first impressions were. On approaching the shore, steam seemed to be up everywhere. Rich and poor were busy and on the alert—if they had money, to increase it; if they had none, to acquire it. Even beggars seemed more expert here than on the continent, where they ask alms for God's sake, but here on their own account, and will make change rather than miss a penny. They seldom sit down to beg, as in other cities. The wealthy are neither idle nor indolent, but busy, active, enterprising, and acquisitive. Therefore the English

are regarded as the best custodians of wealth in the world.
Yet no one expects their national debt ever to be paid. It is
the sure source of income to most of the wealthy people of
the empire, who now, from generation to generation, invest
their surplus means in government bonds, bearing three per
cent. interest, called "consols," which means the consolidated
bonds of the government. All the British debt at present is
in this kind of bonds. The English capitalists have become
the creditors and money lenders to all the world. More than
half the capital that has constructed all the railroads now in
operation has been furnished by them, and untold millions for
other public improvements in almost every nation on the
earth. Hence every piece of gold coin in circulation in any
country seems struggling to make its way to the great money
chest of the world to pay interest to those capitalists. It may
be asked where and how was this capital acquired? England
has no gold mines. True; she has no gold mines and needs
none. She has mines of coal and iron more valuable than the
mines of any other country, being more contiguous to each
other and to the sea. England alone furnishes the coal to
propel half the steam machinery in the world, and to light
the cities with gas. She also furnishes half the steam machinery at present in use. Havana, in Cuba, and Moscow, in
Russia, both import the coal from England to gaslight their
respective cities, and all the machinery and fixtures used in
the operation. English capital has done both, and constructed
all the railroads in Russia and Cuba. The immense income
derived from these loans is the current of gold which is seen
constantly tending towards the great centre of attraction and
safety, the Bank of England. In consequence of this steady
movement of specie to this one point, Bank of England notes
sell above par at all the great money marts of the world. This
constantly accumulating capital is the stimulus perpetually in
action to seek out new places of investment abroad. At home
no flattering prospect of profitable investment seems to have
been left untried. Therefore, in whatever direction the eye is
turned, the vision is obstructed by smoke from some contri-
vance instituted to employ capital, and the inquisitive stranger
is led to inquire how long this state of things can last while
there is such a heavy drain of coal and iron from this single

island to supply so much of the world. The sight of the movement of such vast quantities of these two articles fills the mind with astonishment, and causes it to reflect how this mighty current got into motion, and its wonderful consequences, which the wisest men had never thought of at the commencement of this century, but which, before it shall close, will be proved to be at the present day yet in its infancy.

Pleasure-seekers are less numerous in England than in any other kingdom of Europe, according to the number of inhabitants and those who are really persons of leisure. They are so much accustomed to the society of business men, that when traveling abroad they act as if on some business excursion, being apparently in a hurry. Although there is great diversity of rank among the English they seem to take no pleasure in showing it unnecessarily, as on the continent, where badges of merit and distinction are paraded ostentatiously on all occasions as if they possessed some wonderful charm or power. More naval and military men are seen in the British cities than in any other, and all seem overburdened with duties and cares. The whole nation appears more restless than any other people, and to have less leisure to enjoy the pleasures of life; each individual is striving to improve his estate rather than enjoy it. They have professors and amateurs in all the vocations of life who make it their special business to investigate and improve upon all new inventions and discoveries, and their efforts would seem already to have been carried to the *ne plus ultra* of human ingenuity. But if a person examines a little more closely, it will be found that the English have never been more energetically or more industriously engaged in experiments and improvements of every kind than at the present time. They have been very successfully engaged in stock-raising for ages, and their island is the best supplied with fine domestic animals of any part of the world; their herds of horses, cattle and sheep afford the most gratifying and pleasing sights of any to be met with in Europe.

Should our observations stop here, England might be supposed to be a happy home for all. It is far otherwise. More persons are dissatisfied there with their present condition than in any other country, and constantly desire a change.

The lands, animals and wealth of the country are in the hands of so few, and the number now decreasing so rapidly, that the lower ranks can not reasonably hope ever to possess them in any great abundance while they remain where they are. The emigration of the male part of the nation has become so widely spread throughout the world that the family circles are few where there is not a prominent member absent, and anxiety manifested for their safety by all the rest present. In most of these circles a very great disparity in the number of the sexes is at once apparent, and much of the labor performed by men in other countries is here done by women, who appear to outnumber the men by about one-half. These circumstances seem to detract much from social English life, and render that country a less desirable residence with all its improvements than most European countries.

The great aversion to a permanent residence in England, where everything has been brought to such great perfection, is the dread of the effects of the impending pauperism, which is increasing in a fearful ratio in every county in the kingdom. Every effort appears to be making to suppress its growth and hide its appearance; but its weight is felt and calls heard in every part of the kingdom, and must increase until some plan is devised to divide and cultivate the unimproved lands held by the nobility for pleasure grounds, while the poor starve in idleness, poor-houses and asylums, and some of them in prison. The public eye, however, is not pained by disfigured forms asking alms, as in most other countries; but appeals to charitable and gullible individuals are as frequently and as ingeniously made in the United Kingdom as in any other part of the world, but in other modes, and refusals received with as much contempt by those making them. Philanthropists are quite as numerous there as elsewhere, but thus far it has not been very popular to point out the great evil there and suggest a remedy; but that period is probably not very distant. It would be as unpopular in England at this day to attempt to form societies to abolish entailed estates as it would have been ten years ago here to have attempted to abolish slavery entirely in the United States. Yet we have seen it done and the nation live. The emperor of Austria has abolished his deer parks and hunting grounds and opened them to the public, and with all his misfortunes seems more firmly fixed in his empire than ever before. Should the English abolish entailed estates as they have slavery in their colonies, and allow the present holders to divide the estates and sell them, there is no doubt they may gradually relieve themselves of the intolerable incubus, pauperism, under which they now suffer more taxation to support it than any other people, and thus become richer.

More may be seen and learned in England than in any other European country; for they have brought home specimens of everything they could lay their hands on in all parts of the world, and have preserved them with the greatest care, regardless of trouble or expense. This constant accumulation to one great centre is not confined to property alone. Men seem attracted to the same point, and London, though apparently overcrowded, is being constantly enlarged and filled to greater excess by an enterprising and ambitious crowd from all countries struggling to share in the great scramble for wealth.

Since the introduction of steam as a motive power, which has all been in this century, there has been a constantly increasing disposition in British people to locate themselves in and about large cities, and this is as apparent in Scotland, Ireland and Wales, as in England itself. The suburbs of all their cities are being enlarged and embellished with new edifices, while the rural districts show no such improvement. The buildings in the agricultural districts appear of about the same age as the grounds they occupy. There is less disposition to change manifested in English architecture than any other country. A veneration for the taste and labors of their ancestors has taken deep root in the people of these islands, so that to pull down the house that one's grandfather was born in to build a finer, would be considered but little less than sacrilege. Therefore, in almost every part of these islands may be seen buildings in a good state of preservation which have been constantly in use for centuries, and still promise, by their appearance, to compete in durability with any of their more modern neighbors.

No country has better or cheaper facilities for traveling than England by any of the modes of conveyance of which her people are not slack to avail themselves, while English women are noted for their pedestrian feats. It is but a common occurrence to meet ladies with thick soled shoes walking several miles from home while they have fine equipages idle. This, in part, accounts for their fine complexions and robust constitutions.

Although we have traveled on all their great railroads, and visited most of the great cities and noteworthy objects, we think it unnecessary to describe them, as England and all relating to her is well described by other writers.

Wales, although but a small part of Great Britain, has always managed to maintain her national characteristics, even to the extent that it is a general remark in England, "If there is any unmixed blood of the ancient Britons on the island, it is in Wales." They are individually the most self-reliant people of Europe. Welch ladies require less care and attendance than any others. They act more independently at home and abroad than other people generally, and a Welch woman would scorn to wait for an escort if it would be inferred thereby that she was timorous or feeble, or in the least influenced by affectation or desire of vain show. In sprightliness, affection and domestic duties they have long been distinguished, while assisting in holding their native mountains and fastnesses from invading foes and compelling an English Queen to become a mother among them. Acquisitiveness is not a distinguishing characteristic among the Welch, although they are an industrious an economical people. Their country being small and mountainous, there are but few tracts of sufficient magnitude and importance to attract the cupidity of the avaricious mortals that have contrived to wrest the fairest parts of the neighboring districts from the needy poor and force them to foreign lands; consequently, Wales has been able to retain a sufficient number of the descendants of its primitive inhabitants to preserve in a fair degree the type and character of the original Britons. They, however, have kept pace in improvements, learning and arts, in all that is manly, moral, and wise, with their more favored, wealthy and mighty neighbors.

We have said heretofore, "It is of little consequence to a traveler at what point he enters England, as he will find

everything organized, steam up, and all in motion." The same
state of things will appear at first view on entering Scotland,
but a very short stay in any part of the country will convince
a person that the people of Scotland are much better educated, more happy and contented, in their colder country, than
the English. The Scotch have never thirsted for conquest, nor
reduced their country to beggary for martial fame. They
appear like a family of philosophers, providing for their
domestic wants, and enjoying rationally the fruits of their
labors with contentment. Few are very rich, and wealth is
so generally distributed that there is a generous enjoyment of
all the comforts of life, with little or no pauperism. In character, as a distinct people, they have never been excelled, and
have so remained for twenty centuries, unconquered and
unconquerable either by external or internal causes. Revolu-
tions and earthquakes, which have so often disturbed and
disfigured other countries, have left Scotland unstained and
unchanged as the sun that warms it.

Sojourning or traveling in that country, a stranger need fear
no sudden changes, dangers, or vicissitudes, as in most other
lands. Everything has worked so long and uniformly in
the same way, that one may calculate with certainty what will
be accomplished in a given length of time there. The fashionable world has had but moderate patronage among that
people, yet they have never been behind any other nation in
adopting useful improvements, either in costume or furniture,
for civil or martial life. They have acted like a pendulum in
the British empire, to keep it in proper motion and order
among nations. Economical and prudent in everything, no
unfinished enterprise lies falling into decay there. A work
once commenced is sure of being finished. Labor of all kinds
is performed more by both sexes in Scotland than in any
other country. It is a very common sight to see a boy watching sheep and knitting at the same time, while a girl is near
by watching a herd of cows and reading, and a farmer at a
short distance with his wife and children assisting him in
planting or harvesting his crops.

Fewer foreigners migrate to Scotland than to any other
country in Europe. It has but few charms for Jews or Gip-
sies, consequently none are found wandering there. No nation

is more deservedly celebrated for its production of eminent and useful literary men than this, and they are found in all the known parts of the earth, bearing more uniformly than any other people a sameness of character, morals and manners. Strangers without introduction will find it more difficult in Scotland to gain admittance into society than in any place on the continent; yet, when once recognized, all formality ceases, and they are hailed and treated as familiar friends in whom they place most implicit confidence.

An American passing from thence into Ireland will soon observe that he is among those who regard him as a friend, and that he needs no formal introduction. It is sufficient to show that he is an American to have all the attention he is deserving of, and the comfort and security he desires. Every one will appear glad to see him, and be ready to render him all the assistance in their power. They will make him feel more at home than in any other part of Europe. There will be no necessity for that strict watchfulness while sojourning with them as in other European countries, as they all seem to consider it a kind of religious duty to see that no stranger is robbed or imposed on by tricksters and vagabonds in their midst. They seem to take a pride in showing all the civility in their power to strangers, however unpolished their manners may be to each other at home. Every question will be answered with promptitude and civility, and people will turn aside to guide and direct strangers more readily in Ireland than any other country.

A great diversity in the condition of the people and the officers of the government will soon be apparent, and excite in a stranger an inquiry into the cause of this great disparity, so unlike all other countries in Europe. He will readily be answered that it is the result of misrule and oppression, and be shown the well-paid soldiers posted here to assist in collecting the most exorbitant rents and most oppressive taxes that were ever demanded and paid by any people.

At the commencement of this century, the island contained nine millions of people; twenty years ago it contained eight millions, and now in 1868 it contains but six millions, and the inhabitants remaining seem to consider it only a temporary home for a vast number of those still able to emigrate. There are at this day more Irish people in foreign countries than in their own. The facilities for emigrating have multiplied so rapidly within the last few years, that we may look forward to a day not far distant when the oppressed and despoiled people of that fertile island will mostly have found permanent homes in foreign lands, and the descendants of their oppressors will fill their places. At this day, a very large portion of the most valuable productions of the island are exported and exchanged for gold to pay the exorbitant demands made upon them, while many pine in want, or drag out a miserable existence in squalid wretchedness, sustaining life by the least nourishing and most plain and limited means. Notwithstanding all these evils and disadvantages, the love of country is so deeply seated in every heart that no one leaves the island without a pang and a firm resolution to return whenever Ireland shall resume her place among the nations of the earth. This desire to return seems never to forsake them, for whether in Mexico or Russia, if their country is mentioned, each one is ready to respond and assert that Ireland has more friends abroad than at home, and demonstrate it, if necessary, in the most lucid manner.

Every place on the island has been explored and described, and although a vast number of its inhabitants are among us, yet many people have a very limited knowledge of its beauty, fertility, and productions. Some think potatoes and flax are about all a traveler can see in that country. These, however, form but a small part of the exports, as the soil is well adapted to the growth of every production that England can raise, and is under as high a state of cultivation where the taxes and rents are not intolerable. Of her productions, wheat and cattle are among the most valuable, and are exported in vast quantities to England.

No person from the United States can visit Ireland and travel one day in any direction in it without observing the partiality shown Americans by all classes of society, and the pleasure they seem to take in showing the numberless wonders existing there. The Giant's Causeway is most noteworthy, where you are shown his herculean yet handy works, even the prints of the giant's knee on the top of every stone as he pressed them so nicely into place without any other

18

form. This basaltic promontory is composed of several thousand pillars set together with the exactitude of a honeycomb, smooth on all sides, never adhering to each other, of unknown length, and in many pieces, standing perpendicularly one above another, of different sizes and different forms; some being triangular, having only three sides, others more like nonagons, and yet all so ingeniously arranged that they all exactly fit the places they occupy without deranging the order of the mass or leaving a vacant space between them. Who but the Author of the Universe could have conceived such a wondrous work! and then why place it here? There were also many other great curiosities to attract and amuse; but as everything seemed to be gradually passing into English hands, I was more pained than edified by what I saw. The large cities are improving, but the nation is preparing for emigration.

Dublin is a beautiful city and has all the accommodations to make a people happy, saving its own rulers and soldiers, whose power and skill are constantly exerted to obstruct as much as possible the advancement of the people without their total ruin or annihilation.

On leaving the island by any of the great lines of travel, the heart is pained at the sight of the parting of friends in such numbers, among whom it is evident that no hope is entertained that they will ever meet again in their native isle. Every expression uttered on these occasions goes to show that, with rare exceptions, it is the firm conviction of the emigrant and his weeping friends, that he will see his native land no more; for which reason these parting scenes are indescribably affecting.

On leaving Londonderry a tug steamer brought all the freight and passengers to the mouth of the river Foyle, where we were transferred to an ocean steamer, and as we were being transferred every passenger was examined as to the payment of passage and provisions for the voyage, state of health, age and occupation. In doing this some incidents occurred that were painful, others amusing, but still tending to show the willingness of many to leave the island if they had the means, but for the lack of which they are constrained to remain. One urchin about twelve years old had contrived to get on the tug unperceived, and when a large family was being passed slipped in among the children and had eluded the watchman; but, as the number of little folks on the family ticket was complete without him, he was ordered back and left on the tug, weeping, as the steamer sailed. A young man aged about twenty accompanied his sister, who had a ticket, bringing her baggage, and holding her ticket in one hand and satchel in the other, made an effort to go past the watchman, but when stopped burst into a flood of tears, while others besides myself averted their faces to conceal their emotions. It was then about two o'clock P. M. and we soon parted with the tug. There were evidently many sad hearts on board, as the ship had as many passengers as British laws allow, and, as usual, people mostly of the middle sphere of life. After leaving the deck at evening, and before I had written any notes, I reviewed the events of the last few hours, and came to the conclusion I had seen more manifest sorrow and tears that day than I had ever before witnessed in the same time, and yet there had been no death or any appalling casualty.

As darkness came on Ireland disappeared from our view, a moderate north-west wind blew during the night and next day, which seemed to have dried all tears, as I saw no signs of any more on the voyage. When the cooks retired on the second night they left a kettle of lard in the process of rendering, which took fire and was entirely consumed, igniting the whole inside of the caboose before it was discovered, and killing two highly prized dogs, being the only deaths we had on board during the passage. I think the circumstance will add to the vigilance of the crew, as the marks of the conflagration are indelibly impressed where it raged.

We had taken passage on the Columbia, of the Anchor line of steamers, from Glasgow to New York, touching only at the mouth of the Foyle off Londonderry, where we came on board. She was a good poor-man's ship, that is, she was large, staunch and plain; managed prudently, in Scotch fashion, for safety and profit, not for speed and ostentation. We were eleven days on the passage from Londonderry to New York, with a moderate breeze nearly ahead, without a storm during the passage, with ships in view going in an

opposite direction every hour, seeming to be going down stream
they passed us so rapidly, generally under full canvas, beautifying the great deep and chasing away *ennui*. We passed
within about one mile of a village of six houses on the rock-
bound coast of New Foundland, without a fence, tree or beast
of any kind within the range of vision. I could but consider
how different must be the taste or nature of the villagers there
from mine, if they dwelt there with contentment or satisfaction; for in all my travels about the world I had never seen
the attempt at forming permanent homes in so unpropitious a
situation as this appeared to be.

On approaching the coast of the United States we saw pilot
boats much farther from the ports to which they belonged than
we had been accustomed to see off the ports of Europe. This
adventurous spirit of American pilots is probably the cause
why fewer shipwrecks happen about American ports than
European, as American pilots are commonly on board before
dangers appear and avoid them.

Seven months had now elapsed since we passed out to sea
over this same course, and nothing in view seemed changed
about the harbor of New York. The same activity upon the
water and on the land as when we left, and all well and happy
about me, the weather pleasant and cool in both instances,
my health as good as when I left, and all well and happy
about me, and in anticipation of soon landing among their
friends, all combined to render my return most gratifying and
to fill my heart with gratitude to that Providence which had
so long and so wonderfully preserved me amidst such dangers as it had been my fortune to pass through. It was somewhat of a disappointment to return without having been able
to visit Egypt and Palestine, but that circumstance had
afforded me more time to view the different countries of
Europe, and my family to enjoy the society of their friends
and the more refined society of Europe, which we both did in
the most satisfactory manner.

The Columbia anchored in the river, and a tug took us on
shore after our medical examination, and most of the passengers soon found persons to show them new homes; some
however, apparently in comfortable circumstances, lingered
about the customhouse for sometime, as if to see the last

passenger depart to his new quarters and give a parting adieu. These partings, however, were not accompanied with those heart-burstings we had witnessed beyond the seas.

Having telegraphed my safe arrival, I located myself at a convenient hotel for meeting Missourians, and soon met several St. Louisians and learned the news of the city and the good health and prosperity of my friends; and being at ease and disengaged, I set myself at perambulating the city and contrasting its present appearance with what I recollected it was in 1819, when I spent ten weeks in it fitting out ships for the Columbians and drilling for the expedition. Forty-eight years had since passed; the streets then existing were still there, but so changed by new edifices that it appeared like another city. Even about the Battery, the old church on Broadway at the head of Wall street, and all else, appeared new and strange. The water-works, gas-works, telegraphs, railroads, and street cars, were all new institutions, never dreamed of at that time, and yet apparently indispensable at this day. The city then contained one hundred and thirty thousand inhabitants, now ten times that number. I strolled about the city four days observing and contemplating the mighty changes I had seen therein and in the world in my time, and considering the controlling causes that have led me to see and become an actor in an humble way in so many interesting scenes. I endeavored to find some of my friends who assisted in fitting out the ships for the Columbians in 1819, but was unable to find *one* living. Even the houses owned by two of them in 1836 had been sold, and others of greater magnificence now occupy their sites.

CHAPTER XXXV.

RETURN TO ST. LOUIS—FARMING ESSAY—A FAMILY INCIDENT.

I had now spent nearly eleven months in traveling from city to city and viewing the innumerable objects of interest they contain as much as one anxious to see all and learn all could be expected to do at my advanced age, and was anxious to return to my friends and relate to them some of the most interesting incidents of my peregrinations. I had long since learned that it is not profitable or safe to travel by night on railroads, as none of the beauties of the country are seen or enjoyed, or old landmarks recognized. Moreover, unseen dangers disturb the mind and fatigue it, while the society of friends can scarcely be enjoyed and few or no new ones made on cars in motion. I therefore left New York in the morning and traveled home by daylight, enjoying all the beauties of the landscape and sight of the grand wayside improvements, all of which have been made in my day. The sight of such mighty works made in my lifetime caused me to look back on the labors of Europeans I had just viewed—admirable and wonderful though they were—and which they were thousands of years in effecting, and asked myself what wonders would be found in Europe compared with ours if we progress for another generation in the same way.

I returned to my home in St. Louis in good health and found all my family and friends as I had left them, and the city rising to greatness more rapidly and permanently than ever.

There are natural sites for cities and artificial ones—Havana (in Cuba), New York, and Quebec, are of the former; Amsterdam, Venice, and St. Petersburg, are of the latter—and all have become great and important cities without the apparent natural advantages of St. Louis at the present time. This city, as all the educated know, is situated not only in the center of the most extensive and fruitful valley in the world, but midway of one of the longest and largest navigable rivers, nearly in the very center of the territory of the United States, and nearly equidistant between its two great seaports, New York and

San Francisco, now nearly connected by a continuous railroad, over which must pass the traffic of both Europe and the Indies. It needs no prophet to foretell the future greatness of St. Louis. The inexhaustible coal-fields of Illinois on the one side of the Mississippi and the three inexhaustible masses of iron ore at Iron Mountain, Pilot Knob, and Magnet or Shepard Mountain, in the immediate vicinity of the city, insure its lasting greatness.

Viewing this subject twenty years ago as I do to-day, on my discharge from the army, at the close of the war with Mexico, I entered the land warrants I received for my services on lands in Iron county, twelve miles west of the Iron Mountain, on the most practicable route for a railroad from it to the Pacific railroad between St. Louis and San Francisco, now so nearly finished, or, as it will hereafter appear, only begun to be made. To those tracts I have since added several thousand acres by purchase, which I still hold, believing that a most extraordinary era of growth and improvement is about to dawn on St. Louis and all the vicinity where her future' greatness can be felt. No other place on earth within a circle of ten miles diameter contains such inexhaustible quantities of the richest iron ores of the three best varieties as the region about Iron Mountain, Pilot Knob and Magnet Mountain, on the Iron Mountain railroad, eighty miles south of St. Louis, on the apex of land between the St. François, Meramec and Black rivers, and surrounded by the most healthful, fertile and well timbered district in the State. Its many attractions had the effect to make it a focus about which the contending armies of the civil war congregated, to the no small disadvantage of the agricultural interests of the neighborhood. In this few suffered greater losses than myself, as my farm, residence and store were on the direct road from St. Louis to Pocahontas in Arkansas, where the road from Iron Mountain and Pilot Knob to Rolla crosses it at right angles, and all parties seemed to arrange their movements in such order that they could honor me with a call and help themselves to all they wanted without payment, except in one single instance, when there were thirty-five hundred men present, including six hundred horsemen, and all their teams, which were supplied with food and forage for the whole, except bread, without exhausting my stock. This party, however, were soon followed by what might be termed the gleaners, who took what was left, so that I was obliged to abandon my farm to others for safety, as stated in a former part of this work, and so it remained until the spring of 1868, when I attempted its restoration. It is not easily conceived what devastation and disfigurement four years of civil war and three years' want of cultivation had been made on my newly cultivated farm of two miles in length, an orchard of two thousand trees, and a vineyard and garden of three acres. A person must see the standing chimneys of burned houses, the tall brush and dead stalks of old weeds, the broken and dilapidated fences, to comprehend the wide-spread ruin of my former pleasant country residence. Added to this sad change on my estate, half the men within four miles of my house had been destroyed in the war and their places yet left vacant.

To restore these losses at my advanced age seemed to require herculean labor, yet I essayed it under the disadvantage of being obliged to purchase all my provisions at St. Louis on account of the failure of the crop of 1866 in that vicinity. Taking a proper outfit, I soon commenced operations in the garden and repaired my dwelling-house for the reception of my family, who came thither when the St. Louis schools took their vacation and returned when they were about to be re-opened. The agricultural season of 1868 proved quite unproductive. The late frosts of spring nearly destroyed the fruit crop and the severe drouth of summer rendered other crops light. Our health, however, was good, and we passed a very pleasant summer; but disappointment awaited us in autumn, and we returned to the city at the opening of the schools to accommodate some of the younger members of the family who had not completed their studies. Soon after I was elected secretary of the Missouri Historical Society, and commenced collecting the materials for writing the history of St. Louis from August 10th, 1820, when I became a resident and remain so to the present time, which I design to publish in 1870, embracing a period of fifty years.

I have now related most of the incidents of my life, still it may appear somewhat incomplete if I omit to mention my youngest daughter, Rose Amie, who was born on the 23d of

September, 1868, and was named Amie by me on the day of her birth. Being very sick some days after, her pious sister Ida called the Rev. Mr. McCabe of the Catholic church, and prefixing Rose to her former name had her christened Rose Amie; so this is her christian name. It may afford information to some persons to state that a Peruvian lady of the city of Lima, named Rose, is the only American lady that has ever been canonized, that is, placed in the catalogue of saints. Hence my second daughter's name and her early baptism into the Catholic church.

I recently attended the funeral of the late Captain L. Bissell, and published the memoirs of his life, which he had confided to my care in 1866. I have a very considerable number of a similar character, probably more than any other gentleman in St. Louis, and would gladly receive and preserve the memoirs of ladies and gentlemen for history, or to be used as they may direct. I have the names of some St. Louis ladies which cannot be omitted in writing its history. I hope to receive others with copious memoranda appended.

I have recently had the pleasure of listening to one of the most profound and interesting dissertations I ever heard. It was delivered by Captain Silas Bent, late of the U. S. navy, on the most feasible route to the North pole. This scientific gentleman has formed his theory by observing the ocean currents in all the seas, where his duty as a naval officer called him, for more than a quarter of a century, and has promulgated his theory to the world and demonstrated it, showing the system of ocean currents as clearly as the system of the motion of the blood or heavenly bodies. "Bent's Theory of Ocean Currents," has now obtained a notable place in the scientific world and has immortalized his name.

While beholding this giant in intellect and science, and hearing his demonstrations before his audience with his diagrams before him, I recalled the pleasurable moments I had spent in teaching him to read in 1826, when a child. It was a pleasure to teach such young pupils then, and it is indescribably more pleasant now to see the fruits of it in the closing scenes of my long life. Some of the most pleasurable moments of my life have been spent with my pupils while they were under my instruction or after they had entered on the active duties of life. Few men have spent thirty years surrounded with such a large number of his former pupils as myself after finishing their instruction, and none ever had greater cause to rejoice in their virtuous and successful course of conduct for such a length of time. It has always been pleasant to meet with any of my former pupils, for there were no blots or stains on their characters or unkind reminiscences to mar the meeting. Therefore, on seeing them on the streets, I often waited for them, or hastened forward to overtake them, or even often went out of my way to meet them, for I never found one who did not appear glad to see me. Among so many I observed a very great difference in their taste and capacity, some of which were so remarkable, I will mention one who is perhaps as well known as any individual to nearly all the others, and will point out some of his peculiarities for the benefit of all. Mr. Richard Dowling was one of my eldest pupils, and has treasured up a larger fund of information in relation to St. Louis and its inhabitants than any other person in it. In conversation with him, he seems to have been ubiquitous for the last fifty years in the city; to have been present at all public meetings and acquainted with all the speakers; to have been always present at the nearest cobbler's shop to each individual, as that is the bulletin board and forum for publishing the foibles and anecdotes of all the people in the vicinity, of discussing their conduct and character, and rendering an unsealed verdict on them. Having been engaged a great part of his life in a public office or banker's employment, every man's location and wealth were known to him; and as his memory was very tenacious, his perception acute, and his judgment unbiased, his information and advice were more frequently sought for than any other person of all my numerous acquaintances.

When the first public schools of St. Louis were about to be opened, the directors requested me to assist in the examination of the candidates proposed for teachers, which I did with the aid of the late Judge B. Mullanphy, Dr. Cornelius Campbell, and Dr. B. B. Brown. We recommended two gentlemen and two ladies, who were appointed by the directors and opened the first public schools. Mr. D. H. Armstrong was one of the persons appointed and yet survives; the others with all the examiners, except myself, are now deceased. Two circumstances probably led to my selection as one of the examiners. First, I had been one of the most active advocates for the school tax in the city (with a good taxable estate); secondly, I had been long a prominent and successful teacher in St. Louis and was well known to the whole community. Since then I have viewed the steady and unexampled progress and prosperity of the schools with more pleasure, pride and satisfaction than any other improvement about the city. It is at this day the most striking, important and best managed affair we have to point out to strangers, and most worthy of their attention and admiration. It needs but the same unpaid, able directory to continue it the greatest and most beneficent institution of our city, and most worthy of imitation of all others.

It may appear egotistical in an author to find him often mentioning prominent personages by name as his pupils, but the indulgent reader will bear in mind there is a parental interest implanted in the memory of every affectionate teacher that impels him to connect himself with his pupils through life and make them a part of himself. Can it be expected that a teacher who has assisted in educating such a galaxy of eminent personages as have risen from such families as General Wm. Clark, Governor McNair, Colonel Easton, Dr. Robinson, Dr. Farrar, Colonels R. and G. Paul, Judge Primm, Judge Bates, Judge Bent, Mr. F. Dent, Dr. Simpson, Mr. Platt, Mr. Chouteau, Mr. Verdin, Judge Ferguson, Mr. Dumaine, Mr. Klunk, Mr. Roubidoux, Governor De Lassus, Mr. Page, Mr. Primeau, Mrs. Knapp, General Pratt, Colonel Laveille, and the large Papin fraternity, and many others like them, and Mr. A. Gamble and Mr. Tracy's, yet not mention them and exclaim, *Lo, my reward for all my labors and anxieties!* It is difficult to avoid dwelling on a subject that has afforded me so much pleasure as the unparalleled good conduct of all my pupils and the remarkable success of most of them. It affords a theme for meditation, reflection and rejoicing in the silent watches of sleepless nights, or shades of solitude and loneliness, which no robber can snatch from me, or violence destroy.

FINIS.